MUM ON THE RUN

Fiona is an author and journalist who has written for many UK publications including *The Observer*, *The Guardian*, *Marie Claire* and *Red*. For several years she has written a popular weekly column chronicling her family life in *The Sunday Herald* newspaper.

Fiona lives in Scotland with her husband, their twin sons and daughter. She likes to draw, run 10k races, play her saxophone and lie in the bath with a big glass of wine, although not all at once.

To find out more about Fiona please visit www.fionagibson.com.

FIONA GIBSON

Mum on the Run

AVON

AVON

A division of HarperCollins*Publishers*
1 London Bridge Street
London SE1 9GF

www.harpercollins.co.uk

A Paperback Original 2011
12

First published in Great Britain by
HarperCollins*Publishers* 2011

Copyright © Fiona Gibson 2010

Fiona Gibson asserts the moral right to
be identified as the author of this work

A catalogue record for this book is
available from the British Library

ISBN-13: 978-1-84756-249-4

Set in Minion by Palimpsest Book Production Limited,
Falkirk, Stirlingshire

Printed and bound in Great Britain by
CPI Group (UK) Ltd, Croydon CR0 4YY

MIX
Paper from
responsible sources
FSC   FSC C007454

ACKNOWLEDGEMENTS

Huge thanks to my wonderful agent, Caroline Sheldon, and my editor Kate Bradley at Avon, for making this book happen. Thanks also to Charlotte Allen for publicity wizardry. Thanks to Margery and Keith for all your love and support, and to my dear pals Cathy, Michelle, Marie, Cheryl and Fliss for boosting emails and always being there. Without my brilliant writing group I'd be totally stuck: big thanks to Tania, Vicki, Margaret and Amanda. Without my fabulous running buddy I'd be a complete couch potato: thanks to super-whizzy Carolann. Above all, an enormous hug to my wonderful family: Jimmy, Sam, Dex and Erin. In fact it was my daughter Erin's idea to write a book about running in the first place. Clever cookie!

For dearest Jen and Kath
for all the laughs

CHAPTER ONE

'*Thank you, everyone, for coming along to our Spring into Fitness sports day. Now, to round off our afternoon, it's the race we've all been waiting for . . .*'

No it's not. It's the race that makes me consider feigning illness or death.

'. . . It's the mums' race!' exclaims Miss Marshall, my children's head teacher. She scans the gaggle of parents loitering on the fringes of the football pitch.

'Go on, Mum!' Grace hisses, giving me a shove.

I smile vaguely while trying to formulate a speedy excuse. 'Not today, hon. I, um . . . don't feel too well actually.'

'What's wrong with you?'

'I . . . I think I've done something to my . . . ligament.'

Grace scowls, flicking back a spiral of toffee-coloured hair that's escaped from her ponytail. 'What's a ligament?'

'It's, er . . .' My mind empties of all logical thought. This happens when I'm under stress, like when a client blanches after I've cut in layers – even though she's asked for layers – and insists that what she *really* had in mind for her ginger puffball was 'something, y'know, long and flowing, kinda Cheryl Cole-ish . . .'

'It's in your leg,' I tell Grace firmly.

1

'What happened to it?' Her dark brown eyes narrow with suspicion.

'I . . . I don't know, hon, but it's felt weird all day. I must have pulled it or stretched it or something.'

She sighs deeply. At seven years old, rangy and tall for her age, Grace is sporting a mud-splattered polo shirt festooned with rosettes from winning the relay, the three-legged race *and* the egg-and-spoon. I'm wearing ancient jeans and a loose, previously black top which has faded to a chalky grey. Comfy clothing to conceal the horrors beneath.

'Come on, all you brave ladies!' cries Miss Marshall, clapping her hands together. Here they go: Sally Miggins, casting a rueful grin as she canters lightly towards the starting line. Pippa Fletch, who happens to be wearing – like most of the mums, I now realise – clothes which would certainly pass as everyday attire (T-shirts, trackie bottoms) but are suspiciously easy to run in. No one would show up at *Spring into Fitness* in serious running gear. That would be far too obvious. The aim is to look like you hadn't even *realised* there'd be a mums' race when you've been secretly training for months.

'Come on, Laura,' Beth cajoles, tugging my arm. 'It'll be fun.'

'No it won't,' I reply with a dry laugh. Beth, the first friend I made on the mum circuit around here, is athletic and startlingly pretty, even with hair casually pulled back and without a scrap of make-up. I was presentable too, back in the Iron Age, before I acquired a husband, three children and a worrying habit of hoovering up my children's leftovers. Waste not, want not, I always say.

'Oh, don't be a spoilsport,' Beth teases. 'It's only to the end of the field. It'll all be over in about twenty seconds.'

'Yeah, you *promised*, Mum,' Grace declares.

'I can't, Grace. Even if I was feeling okay, which I'm not with this ligament thing, I'm wearing the wrong shoes for running.'

Beth glances down at my cork-soled wedges. 'Good point,' she sniggers. 'I'll let you off . . . *this* time. But next time you forget your kit I'll be sending a note home.'

'Yes, Miss,' I snigger. Beth grins and strides off towards the starting line.

'Take them off,' Grace growls.

'What? I can't run in bare feet! I might step on something like broken glass or poo or . . .'

'No you won't. It's just grass, Mum. Nice soft grass.'

'Grace, please stop nagging . . .'

'Amy's mum's taken her shoes off. Look.' Grace points towards the cluster of super-fit mums, all laughing and limbering up as if this is something one might do for pleasure. Sure enough, Sophie Clarke has tossed aside her sandals and is performing professional-looking leg stretches on the damp turf.

'Any more mums keen to join in?' Miss Marshall calls out hopefully. A trim thirty-something, she exudes kindness and capability. She manages to look after 270 children, five days a week. I find it an almighty challenge to raise three. I am in awe of her.

'Anyway, I didn't promise,' I add. 'I said I *might* . . .'

'You did! You said at breakfast.'

Hell, she's right. She and Toby were bickering over the last Rice Krispies, despite the fact that our kitchen cupboard contains around thirty-two alternative cereal varieties. 'If you stop arguing,' I'd told her, 'I'll do the mums' race today.' She'd

3

whooped and kissed me noisily on the cheek. *It's okay*, I'd reassured myself on the way to school and nursery. *She'll forget.*

I'd forgotten that children never forget, unless it's connected to teeth cleaning. I know, too, that I'm a constant disappointment to her, making promises I can't keep. Pathetic mother with her colossal bra, non-matching knickers and carrying far too many souvenirs of her last pregnancy (stretch marks, wobbly tum), especially considering the fact that Toby is now four years old.

Across the field, Finn, my eldest, is sitting on a plastic chair between his best friends Calum and James. He, like Grace, is of athletic build: lanky with well-defined arms from drumming, and strong legs from playing football in his dad's junior team every Sunday. Toby too exhibits signs of sporting prowess. Only this morning he bowled my powder compact across the bathroom and into the loo where it landed with a splash. Shame there's no medal for that. *And* he denied responsibility. Told me that Ted, his hygienically-challenged cuddly, had done it.

Finn glances at me, then at the clump of mums all eagerly poised at the starting line. While Grace is desperate for me to do this, I know he's praying I won't. I don't want to aggravate things between us even further. At eleven years old, he has become sullen and distant these past few months, and seems desperate for puberty to kick off big-time. Yesterday, I heard him bragging to James in his room that he'd discovered a solitary hair on his testicles. Other recent acquisitions are a can of Lynx and a tube of supposedly 'miracle' spot cream.

'Mummy,' Grace barks into my ear, '*everyone's* doing it except you.'

'No they're not,' I retort. 'Look at those two ladies over there.' Hovering close to the fence is a woman who's so hugely pregnant she could quite feasibly go into labour at any moment, and a lady of around 107 in a beige coat and transparent plastic rain hat. 'They're quite happy to watch,' I add. 'Not everyone's madly competitive, Grace.'

Her eyes cloud, and her lightly-freckled cheeks flush with annoyance. 'Come on, Laura, shake a leg!' trills latecomer Naomi Carrington. Naomi *is* wearing running gear. Tight, bubblegum-pink racing-back top, plus even tighter black Spandex shorts which hug her taut, shapely bottom like cling film, as if this were the sodding Commonwealth games. Her breasts jut out, firm and pointy like meringues, and she swigs from a bottle of sports drink. 'I'm really unfit too,' she adds. 'Haven't trained since last year's Scarborough 10k. Mind you, I managed forty-nine minutes. That's my PB . . .'

'What's a PB?' I ask.

'Personal best. Fastest-ever time.' She throws me a 'you are a moron' look. 'I know, not exactly a world record,' she chuckles, 'but pretty impressive for me. And I'm hoping to do even better this year.'

'I'm sure you will,' I growl, feeling my lifeblood seep out through the soles of my feet. If I ever attempted a 10k, the only way I'd cross the finishing line would be in a coffin.

She grins, showing large, flat white teeth which remind me of piano keys. Naomi is the proud owner of a perfect body, the whole town knows that – thanks to her stint as a life model for the Riverside Arts Society. Dazzling paintings of her luscious naked form were displayed in the Arts Centre café for what felt like a hundred years.

Perhaps I *should* run the race. I've felt spongy and wobbly for so long, maybe this is my chance to snap into action and do something about it. It could be the start of a new, sleek me, who wears racing-back tops and talks about PBs. I breathe deeply, trying to muster some courage, the way I imagine elite athletes do before world-class events. Across the pitch, Finn is poking the damp ground with the toe of his trainer. I know he's wishing his dad were here. Jed would have entered the dads' race and won it. He, too, would have been sporting a red rosette by now. But Jed isn't here. He's a senior teacher at another primary school – one far rougher than this – whereas I work part-time as a lowly hairdresser and can always take time off for school-related events. Lucky me.

Naomi is stretching from side to side, which causes her top to ride up (not accidentally, I suspect), exposing her tiny, nipped-in waist. Grace is chewing a strand of long, caramel-coloured hair, perhaps wishing she had a different mum – a properly functioning one with meringue breasts, like Naomi.

I swallow hard. 'You really want me to do this, sweetheart?'

She looks up, dark brown eyes wide. 'Yeah.'

'Okay. Promise you won't laugh?'

She nods gravely. Something clicks in me then, propelling me towards the starting line, despite my wrong shoes and bogus sprained ligament and the fact that Finn will be mortified. 'Mum's doing the race!' Grace yelps. 'Go, Mum!' I daren't look at Finn.

'Well done, Mrs Swan,' Miss Marshall says warmly. I bare my teeth at her.

'Good for you,' Beth says, giving my arm a reassuring squeeze.

'You know I can't run,' I whisper. 'This'll be a disaster.'

'It's just for fun,' she insists. 'No one cares about winning.'

I muster a feeble smile, as if a doctor were about to plunge a wide-bore syringe into my bottom.

'Your shoes, Mrs Swan,' Miss Marshall hisses. 'You might like to . . .'

'Oh, God, yes.' I peel off the lovely turquoise suede sandals which I bought in a flurry of excitement when my sister Kate came to stay. She chose snug-fitting skinny jeans; I headed for footwear because trying on shoes doesn't involve changing room mirrors or discovering that you can't do up a zip. As I scan the row of women, all raring to go, I realise I'm the fattest mum in the race. What if my heart gives out and I'm carted off on a stretcher? Beth grins and winks at me. Naomi, who's set her sports drink on the ground behind her, assumes an authentic starting position like Zola-bloody-Budd. I ignore her and focus ahead. The pitch doesn't usually look this big. Now the finishing line seems so distant it might as well be in Sweden. 'On your marks, get set . . . *go!*' Miss Marshall roars.

Christ, don't they give you a warning, like some kind of amber alert? These aren't women but *gazelles*, charging off in a blur of limbs and kicking up mud behind them. I'm running too. At least I'm slapping down each bare foot alternately and trying to propel myself with my arms like I saw Paula Radcliffe doing on TV.

The pack zooms ahead. Are they on steroids or what? They must have taken some kind of drug. If I survive this I'm insisting on tests. Right now, though, a sharp pain is spearing my side, making my breath come in agonising gasps. 'Go for it, Laura!' cries one of the dads, in the way that people cheer on the unfortunate child in the sack race who's staggering behind, swathed in hessian, and finally makes it to the finishing line streaming with tears and snot after everyone else has gone home.

There's cheering, and I glimpse Naomi punching the air in triumph at the finishing line. My bra straps have slipped down, and my boobs are boinging obscenely as I thunder onwards. I glance down to assess their bounceage, and when I look up something's terribly wrong, because Jed is standing there. Jed, who should be at his own school, not witnessing the ritual humiliation of his wife. Worse still, he's standing next to Celeste, that new teacher with whom he's clearly besotted, although he acts all blasé (*overly*-blasé, I'd say) whenever her name pops up. Gorgeous, honey-skinned Celeste who, to top it all, is half-sodding-French.

I keep running, telling myself that they can't be here, laughing and standing all jammed up together. It's just some terrible vision caused by over-exerting myself. And they say exercise is good for you. No one mentions the fact that your chest feels as if it could burst open and you start hallucinating.

I glance back to check. Celeste is gazing up at Jed and fiddling with a strand of her hair. Anyone would think she's his cute, doe-eyed girlfriend in her polka-dot skirt and sweet lemon cardi. She reaches out to pick something – a stray thread, perhaps – off Jed's top. *Grooming* him, like a mating monkey. It's sickeningly intimate. He smiles tenderly at her. Whenever I try to pick something off him, he bats me away as if I'm a wasp.

I charge on like a heifer, boiling with rage, my boobs lolloping agonisingly as I try to recall the last time Jed smiled adoringly at me. I can't remember. It's so horrifying to see him looking at her that way that for an instant I forget where I am. I lose my footing, skid on the muddied pitch and lurch forwards with arms outstretched, belly-flopping onto the ground with a splatter.

Dear God, kill me now.

I lie still, waiting for my life to flash before me. A lump of dirt, or possibly a live bug, has worked its way up my nose. With my eyes squeezed tightly shut, I'm poised to transcend to some heavenly Celeste-free zone, where no one is ever forced to take part in a mums' race.

CHAPTER TWO

For several moments, nothing happens. There are no angels, softly strumming harps; just a dull thudding sensation in my ears. Gradually, I become aware of faint drizzle on my face, and a ripple of concerned voices around me. My eyes are still squeezed shut. 'Laura?' comes Jed's voice. 'Are you all right? Can you hear me? Jesus Christ . . .'

'I think she's knocked herself out,' someone gasps.

'Laura!' Jed exclaims close to my ear.

'We should call an ambulance,' comes an urgent whisper. *Don't move. If I lie here without flinching maybe they'll cart me away and cremate me. Jed and the children will manage fine, as long as Grace reminds him that she has gym on Tuesdays and Fridays and he doesn't give Finn brown bread sandwiches in his packed lunch.*

'Try to stand up,' Jed urges. 'You'll be okay, we'll get you inside . . .'

'Is Mummy all right?' Grace cries. My eyes ping open instantly and I stagger to my feet, aware that my nostril is still packed with mud.

'Yes, I'm okay, love. Just slipped . . .'

'Poor Mummy!' Grace's eyes are glossy with concern as she grips my hand.

'God, Laura, that was pretty spectacular,' Jed says, shaking his head despairingly.

'You poor, poor thing,' Celeste witters, craning forward as if eager to witness what kind of stunt I'll pull off next.

'I'm fine, thank you,' I snap. 'I just slipped, that's all.'

'Does it feel as if you've broken anything?' Beth asks gently, easing her way between Jed and Celeste. As they appear to be almost surgically attached, this is a major feat.

'I . . . don't think so,' I reply, wishing everyone would melt away, apart from Beth. Then I'd spill it all out – about Celeste picking something off Jed's top and how the sight of them together made me feel sick and disorientated.

'Are you sure?' cuts in Miss Marshall. 'That was a pretty serious fall.'

'You might have sprained something,' Beth suggests.

'Yes,' I blurt out, figuring that this is my only way to save face: to turn it into a *medical situation*. 'My left ankle really hurts,' I groan.

'Let's get her to the doctor's,' someone mutters.

'No, I don't need a doctor, I'll be perfectly okay . . .'

'Miss Curwin will take you to the office,' says Miss Marshall firmly.

'It's fine, I'll look after her,' Jed says quickly.

Damn. I might have been able to feign a sprained ankle in front of the school secretary, but not with Jed. 'What are you doing here anyway?' I hiss as he helps me to my feet and leads me towards the school building.

'We're due for a meeting about this inter-schools art competition,' he says.

'Oh,' I say hollowly. *We.* How fantastically cosy. Flanked

by Jed, Celeste, Grace *and* Miss Curwin, I hobble towards the main entrance. Over by the goalposts, Finn and James are locked in conversation with Beth's daughter Kira, the golden girl of his class. I pause, waiting for Finn to charge towards me, desperately concerned about my wellbeing. Nothing happens. Anyone would assume I'm some random crazy who's blundered onto school property. Not the woman who carried him in her womb and has tended to his every need for the past eleven years.

In the office, I lower myself onto a chair. Miss Curwin produces the first aid box, extracts a bandage and starts to bind my left ankle. It's quite a crush with everyone packed into the tiny room. So many eyes are fixed upon me that I begin to feel like something that's been dug up from a field and put on display in a museum. 'You'd better go back to the playing field now, Grace,' Miss Curwin says. 'Your mum's going to be fine.'

'Okay.' She smiles unsteadily.

'See you at home time,' I say. 'Don't worry – I feel much better already.'

'Sorry I nagged you and made you break your foot,' she murmurs.

'Oh, darling, it's not your fault. It's mine for being such a clumsy idiot.'

'Yeah,' Grace brightens, turning to leave. 'No other mums fell over, did they, Dad?'

'Er, no, love.' Jed clears his throat, and I catch him throwing a quick look at Celeste.

'Are you in a hurry?' I ask sharply. 'Because I don't want to keep you from your meeting.'

'Well,' he says, 'we are supposed to be meeting Miss Marshall . . .'

'Oh, I can deal with that, Jed,' Celeste insists, widening her pale blue eyes. 'You should take Laura home. Poor thing, she must be in agony.'

'I'm *fine*,' I say quickly, horrified now at the prospect of keeping up the bust-ankle pretence all the way home. 'I'll have to wait for school to finish anyway. That's only an hour. Then I'll pick up Toby and walk home, no problem.' I pull myself up, gripping the edge of the desk for support.

'Don't be ridiculous,' Jed says. 'I'll drive you home and come back to collect the kids.'

'That's crazy! You don't need to do that—'

'Where are your shoes?' he asks.

'I don't know. It doesn't matter, they were just *old* things . . .'

'Do call the surgery,' Miss Curwin adds as we leave. 'I'm sure they'll give you an emergency appointment, get you checked out.'

'Yes, I'll do that.'

'And get plenty of rest,' Miss Curwin calls after us.

I nod gravely, wondering how I might possibly rest in our house, until I remember that there is nothing physically wrong with me.

Our car is parked in the next street. Jed and I don't speak as I hobble barefoot towards it, having been unable to face prowling around the playing field to look for my sandals. As I lower myself onto the passenger seat, wincing with 'pain', Naomi saunters towards us, dangling my turquoise beauties by their straps. 'I rescued these for you,' she announces. They are smeared with mud, plus a curious slug-like substance.

'Thanks, Naomi,' I murmur, tossing them onto the back seat.

'No problem.' She touches her red winner's rosette which she's wearing as a jaunty hair accessory behind her left ear.

I shut the passenger door firmly. 'Better luck next year!' she mouths through the window before guffawing and cantering off down the street.

'Spectacular,' Jed grumbles, starting the engine. 'Honestly, Laura, that really was one spectacular stunt you pulled off there.'

CHAPTER THREE

'Mum broke her foot today,' Grace announces over dinner.

'Aww,' Toby says. 'Poor Mummy.'

'You mean she *pretended* to break it,' Finn cuts in, carving grooves in his mashed potato with his fork. 'Dad, didn't she take the bandage off as soon as she got home and start walking normally? She was totally putting it on.' He takes a noisy slurp of his orange juice and bangs his glass on the table.

'Well, yes,' chuckles Jed.

I glance down, checking that I still exist. Yep, all evidence suggests that I am a functioning human being with a beating heart and everything.

'Why?' Toby asks, wide-eyed, twirling a fork through his still-blond curls.

'To make people feel sorry for her,' Finn replies, 'because she's . . .'

'Excuse me,' I butt in. 'I am here, you know. You don't need to talk about me as if I'm somewhere else.'

'Like hospital,' Finn mutters.

I shoot him a look and push my shepherd's pie aside, unable to face another mouthful. 'I know it sounds stupid,' I start, 'but I didn't mean for that to happen. You see, I was dizzy and confused – concussed maybe . . .' I refrain from adding: and you know what? If it hadn't been for the shock of seeing your darling father and that teacher woman, prodding each other on the sports field, I would *never have fallen in the first place.*

'Were you really concussed?' Jed sniggers.

'It's not funny, Jed. It's one of the most embarrassing things that's ever happened to me.' I eye the pea which Toby has flicked off his plate, and which is now rolling steadily towards the table's edge. It drops off, lands on the floor and trundles towards the cooker.

'*And* me,' Finn adds. 'It was embarrassing for me as well. Everyone was pointing and laughing . . .' He tosses his head so his dark, heavy fringe falls over his eyes.

'Were they?' I ask, appalled.

'Oh, come on, honey.' Jed smiles and reaches for my hand across the table. 'Maybe you're just not built for speed.'

'What are you saying, Jed?' I blink at him furiously. It's okay for him; he's still in excellent shape. Taut tummy, toned legs, infuriatingly firm butt. He even has his own hair and teeth.

'Just that . . . your talents lie in other areas.' He grins cheekily, trying to lighten the mood.

'And what areas might they be?'

He pauses. I can virtually hear his brain whirring as he tries to dredge up evidence of my brilliance. 'All the, er, *stuff* you do,' he says, glancing in desperation at the children. 'Doesn't Mum do lots for you?'

Grace nods eagerly. 'She packs our lunchboxes.'

'She wipes my bum,' Toby says approvingly, flicking another pea off his plate.

'You should be doing that for yourself by now,' Jed mutters.

16

'He can't wipe his bum!' Grace titters. 'Dirty boy with a dirty bum . . .'

'I'm not dirty,' Toby roars, and furious tears spring into his eyes.

'Can I stop having cheese sandwiches in my lunchbox?' Finn cuts in.

'Okay,' I say lightly, 'but what would you like instead? You said you didn't want ham, tuna, salami, chicken or beef . . . and didn't you complain that the egg ones were smelly? It's tricky to think of stuff you *do* like, Finn. Maybe you should start having school dinners?'

'I just don't like cheese, okay?' He shudders dramatically, as if I've just tried to force-feed him a pilchard. 'Ham is fine, I *suppose*,' he adds, 'but not the cheap stuff you usually buy.'

'What on earth's wrong with our ham?'

'It's kinda . . . *wet*. And see when you cut my sandwiches? Instead of two fat rectangles could you cut them in triangles like the ones in shops? That's what James's mum does.'

I hold his gaze. This is what my life has become. Not only am I not built for speed, I can't even make an acceptable sandwich. Not like James's mum does anyway. James's mum who has a nanny even though she doesn't work. 'Would that be an isosceles triangle?' I enquire. 'Or would you prefer an equilateral or, um . . . that other kind I can't remember the name of?'

Finn scowls. 'Scalene. It's called scalene, I learned that when I was eight, Mum. Didn't you get that at school?'

'No, I only got taught how to pick things up off the floor and wipe arses,' I growl.

'Uh?' Finn barks.

'I only asked because I might need to borrow your

17

protractor to cut them really accurately.' I smile brightly, aware of Jed's caustic gaze.

'For God's sake,' he snaps. 'It's time you all stopped being so fussy. Mum has enough on her plate without these ridiculous demands.'

'Yes, she does,' I shout, even though I feel physically ill when people refer to themselves in the third person.

'*I'm* not fussy,' Grace protests. 'I think you make nice lunches, Mummy.'

'Thank you, darling. I'm glad someone appreciates them.'

'Wanna Penguin biscuit,' announces Toby, whose dinner has congealed in unappetising brown heaps on his plate.

'I don't know why we do this,' I mutter under my breath.

'Do what, love?' Jed asks.

'This! These family mealtimes. I always thought, you know, that sitting down to eat together means we're doing something right, that we're good parents and are functioning as a family, getting on and enjoying each other's company . . .' I laugh hollowly.

Finn snorts through his nose.

'But it doesn't, does it?' I rant. 'It always seems to descend into bickering and shouting like this. Give me one reason, Jed, why family mealtimes are a good thing.' He opens his mouth and decides to shut it again. 'The whole concept's overrated,' I add, grabbing a dishcloth to mop up a small pool of juice from the table. 'Sometimes I think we'd all be happier if everyone just foraged in cupboards or picked up scraps from the floor.'

'Yeah!' Toby exclaims, banging the table with his fist.

'What's *foraged*?' Grace asks.

'It's when you go out and find food in the wild,' Jed says quietly, casting me a frown as he gathers up the cutlery.

18

'What wild food is there around here?'

'None,' Finn says with a smirk. 'Mum's just saying it 'cause she's sick of cooking for us.'

'No, I'm not.' I pause, looking around at my children. 'I'm sorry,' I add. 'I don't mind cooking at all. It's just sometimes, when everyone's so picky and critical . . .' My voice catches in my throat. 'It's just been a bit of a day,' I add quickly.

'Hey,' Jed says, squeezing my waist as the children stomp out of the kitchen. 'Why don't you chill out for a while? I'll clear up in here.' I look at his handsome face: the deep brown eyes, which our three children have inherited, and the full, generous mouth which I loved to kiss, before kissing no longer seemed like the thing to do.

'It's okay,' I say, glancing up at the ceiling. Finn has started drumming upstairs, causing the whole house to reverberate. I'm glad he drums, in that he clearly has musical talent, but occasionally I wish he'd chosen something gentler, like the oboe or flute. I glance at the tragic remains of Toby's dinner which now looks like a small, collapsed volcano. For some reason, the sight of the unwanted meal – its ingredients shopped for and lovingly cooked – brings a lump to my throat. Ted is lying beside the plate with a daub of gravy on his matted ear.

'Oh, love,' Jed says gently. 'Not still upset about that stupid mums' race, are you?'

'No, of course not.'

'Yes you are. I know you.' He takes a plate from my hands and sets it on the worktop. I nod, because it's easier than admitting how crushing it was to see him and Celeste, watching the races, as if *she* were the mother of our children.

I know I'm being paranoid. They work together; they'd come for a *meeting,* that's all. 'Know what you need, darling?' Jed says gently.

'A diet,' I mutter. 'Did you see all the other mums? How lean and skinny they were? Especially Naomi . . .'

'Well, she's obsessed,' Jed scoffs. 'She's a freak of nature.'

'No she's not. She's just fit. And what about Beth? Why did I have to choose someone so athletic and sporty to be my best friend around here?'

'It's just the way she is,' Jed insists. 'She's just made that way, love, while you're, er . . .'

'I feel so fat and useless,' I cut in. 'I don't know what's happened to me, why I don't have any willpower. I try to start diets but on the first day, at the first twinge of hunger, I'm scrabbling about for a snack, a biscuit or something . . .'

'Then have a biscuit!' he exclaims. 'Who cares if you're not built like a stick? You've had three children, haven't you? You're normal. You're *fine* . . .'

'Well, I'm sorry but I don't feel fine.'

He grabs both of my hands and squeezes them tightly. 'You just need some time to yourself, all right? A day doing, well . . . whatever you want to do. What do you really love doing?'

'Can't remember.' I glare at the floor, sounding like Finn at his most petulant.

'What about shopping?'

'I don't need anything,' I say, silently mourning my wrecked turquoise sandals.

'I'm not talking about needing things,' Jed insists. 'I mean you could just go out and buy yourself something nice.'

'Don't you think I look nice, Jed?' *God, woman, get a grip on yourself. Stop being so damned needy.*

He inhales deeply, and I detect a flicker of impatience in his deep brown eyes. 'All I mean is, if you buy yourself something new, it might make you feel better about yourself. *And* you'd have a bit of time away from us lot.'

I nod, shamefaced. Jed is instructing me to cast off the shackles of motherhood and spend money on frivolities. If the playgroup mums could hear this, they'd faint with lust. 'Maybe I'll go into town on Saturday,' I mutter.

'Great.' He smiles. 'Celeste was talking about some new shop – some little boutiquey place by the station . . .'

My heart does a mini-thud. 'I'd rather go into York,' I say quickly. 'There's a lot more choice.'

'It's just, Celeste said . . .'

'I know all the local shops inside out, Jed,' I bark. 'The clothes are either for teenagers or people over 150. There's nothing in between. I'd like to go to York if that's okay with you.'

'Of course it is,' he snaps back. 'You can go wherever you like.'

I can sense him glowering as I gather up Toby's Lego bricks from the kitchen floor and fling them into their red plastic bucket. I'm trying not to obsess over this new friendship of his. I haven't interrogated Jed when he's come home two hours later than expected, having stayed on to help The Celestial One with her wall display. I have even resisted reading all the texts she pings at him, perhaps scared of what I'll find.

I march through to the living room to sort out a fracas over whose turn it is to use the remote control. Upstairs, Finn is bashing the life out of his drum kit. A day out on my own, away from all of this: I should be ecstatic. Yet I fear that my patience is stretched dangerously taut, and is about to twang like frayed knicker elastic.

CHAPTER FOUR

What the jiggins is wrong with you, Laura Swan? I ask myself this question as I drive to York on Saturday morning. Usually, I'd jump at an opportunity like this. A few hours in town without Finn complaining bitterly if I dare to venture into the wrong kind of shop – i.e., one with clothes hanging neatly on rails. Grace is tolerant, as long as we schedule a visit to the fancy dress shop. As for Toby – he loves the bustling streets, for about eight seconds, after which I have to placate him with a visit to Jorvik to hang out with the Vikings.

Not today, though. This is what the glossy magazines call 'me-time'. It's supposed to be soothing and restorative. As I stand in a changing room cubicle, with some girl chirping, 'D'you think this makes me look too *thin*?', I suspect I might be having a jollier time sniffing the authentic Viking cesspit with Toby.

'No, you look gorgeous,' her companion enthuses. 'God, I wish I had legs like yours. They go on forever.'

All right, all right. No need to over-egg it, lady. I peer down at mine, which absolutely do not go on forever. They are the colour of raw pastry and urgently require a shave. Disconcertingly, the changing room mirrors are angled in such a way that you can view yourself from every conceivable angle. They should have a warning sign outside, saying it's unsuitable for those of a nervous disposition.

The thin girl is now in the communal changing area. She probably looks like Penelope Cruz and has a Lancôme advertising contract. Standing in my bra and knickers – once dazzling white, now a lardy pale grey – I scrutinise the garment I grabbed randomly from a rail, simply because it's in my favourite shade of blue. Actually, I'd assumed it was a top with little pearly buttons down the front. Nothing too controversial. Nothing to make the children shriek in horror and refuse to be seen in public with me. Now, though, it's clear that this isn't a top – at least not for a woman with a normal-shaped body. It has some kind of bottom-scenario attached. It's a romper suit for a grown-up. My mind fills with a picture I once saw in a Sunday supplement, showing adults who dress up as babies for kicks. Grown men in knitted matinee jackets. Has the world gone insane? This is a respectable department store. They do wedding lists and Nigella Lawson tableware. Surely they haven't started catering for sexual freaks.

I step into the 'thing' and try to pull it up over my body. Jesus. I look like an unconvincing transvestite. In a sweat, I yank it off, shutting my ears to the sound of a seam ripping and a button popping off. After hastily pulling on my jeans and top, I hurry out of the changing room where the Penelope look-alike is twirling in front of the mirror. She is skinny and angular, like a foal – and is wearing the *thing*. The romper. It's several sizes smaller than mine – it would fit a Bratz doll, actually – but is clearly the same style. 'Hi,' she says, catching me staring. 'It's so hard to decide, isn't it?'

'Um, yes,' I say, conscious of a faint throbbing in my

temples. God, it's hot in here. Penelope doesn't look hot, though. At least not in a flushed, sweaty way. Her abundant dark hair cascades around her bronzed shoulders. It's not natural to be tanned in April in Yorkshire. She must have been sprayed like a car.

'Doesn't she look amazing?' says her equally dainty, red-headed friend, emerging from a cubicle.

'Yes, she does.' My back teeth clamp together.

'You've got to buy it,' the redhead urges. 'It's *so* you.'

'Oh, I'm not sure . . .' Penelope leans forward, studying her cleavage in the mirror. She has perky, young-person's breasts. It's a fair bet that they haven't been gnawed by three ravenous infants or leaked milk in the supermarket checkout queue.

'I, er, hope you don't mind me asking,' I say, fuelled by sudden curiosity, 'but what would you call that thing you're wearing?'

'It's a playsuit,' Penelope says, twisting round to admire her minuscule derrière. *Isn't it obvious, Granny?* she adds silently.

'A playsuit?' I repeat. 'Like little children wear?'

She laughs. 'Yes, I suppose so. They're back again. Meant to be the big thing for summer.' The redhead throws me a curt look as if to say: 'No, *she's* the big thing for summer.'

'Oh, you've got one too!' Penelope exclaims, registering the garment scrunched up in my clammy hand. 'Are you treating yourself?'

'Um, I don't think so. It's not really my thing.'

She flares her nostrils. 'Hmmm. Guess you've got to go with what suits you.'

'Yes, of course.' I force a grin, which I hope suggests that I'm on the hunt for some foxy little cocktail dress, and not support hose or a girdle.

25

Back in the sanctuary of the mall, I wonder where to go next. I *must* buy something sexy and completely impractical. I can't face going home empty-handed after being awarded a day off from domestic duties by my beloved. Ignoring a burning desire to check out drum accessories for Finn, or toys for Grace and Toby, I fish out my mobile, deciding to cheer myself up by telling Jed about the playsuit incident. Our answerphone clicks on, and when I try his mobile it goes straight to voicemail. 'Hi, love,' I say. 'Just thought I'd let you know I've bought a playsuit. It looks great, really foxy – thought I'd wear it to your next work do. Hope you're all having a fun day. Missing you. Bye, honey.'

I glare at my phone, as if it's responsible for my husband's unavailability. It's not that I'm worried that Jed is incapable of looking after our children. He works with kids, after all, in the toughest primary school in the area. He's even had a feature in the local newspaper about him. *Jed Swan,* it said, *has scooped a well-deserved Local Hero award for his unfailing commitment to children's artistic and sporting endeavours in the borough.* He's not the kind of dad who needs a map of the kitchen to indicate where milk is kept. Beth told me that, on the rare occasions when she's going away overnight, she still feels compelled to leave Pete, her husband, a list of child-related instructions which can run to five pages. What guidance could a father possibly need in order to care for his two children, I wondered? *'Take kids to park . . . you'll do this by first ensuring that they are adequately clothed according to climatic conditions . . . Leave house via front door remembering to take key . . . In the park you will find a large circular object. This is called a roundabout. No, not the traffic kind. The other kind. Let Jack go on it, and Kira if she wants to, then*

26

proceed to spin them as fast as humanly possible for several weeks . . .'

As I head for Starbucks, I figure that at least Jed does his fair share. In fact, he could probably survive perfectly well without me. He certainly doesn't seem to *need* me. Sometimes I suspect he wouldn't notice if, instead of sleeping beside him, I replaced myself with a cushion. I have come up with possible reasons for this:

1. Severe exhaustion (although toning down his sporting activities might help).
2. He is suffering from some kind of sexual dysfunction and is too embarrassed to talk about it, even though we have been together for fourteen years. Regarding this option, I have delved about on our computer for evidence of him trying to buy Viagra or some kind of pumper-upper penis device. So far, nothing.
3. He no longer fancies me due to my ample fleshage.
4. He is shagging Celeste, a possibility which is too horrific to contemplate seriously and makes me barge into Starbucks in a rather aggressive manner, nearly sending a man flying in the doorway.

'Whoa, after you!' he says, staggering back dramatically.

'God, I'm so sorry,' I bluster. 'I wasn't looking where I was going.'

'That's okay. You're obviously more desperate for a caffeine fix than I am.' He grins, and his cheeks dimple in a distinctly fetching way.

'Guess I am. It's just been one of those mornings.' I smile back, pushing dishevelled hair out of my eyes, and realise I'm still clutching the playsuit. 'Oh, hell . . .' I shake it out and gawp at it.

'Not your colour?' the man asks with a smirk.

'It's not . . . I mean . . . it's not even mine.' Blushing furiously, I meet the stranger's blue-eyed gaze.

'So whose is it?'

'It's the shop's,' I murmur. 'I . . . I *stole* it.'

CHAPTER FIVE

'Really?' He makes his way towards the small queue at the counter. 'You mean you *shoplifted* it? That was very bold of you.'

'I mean accidentally,' I say quickly. 'I tried it on in a shop and it was awful, some kind of playsuit thing that came up to here' – I indicate thigh-length – 'and it was so hot and stifling in there, and I was so desperate to get out I just walked off with it . . .' My entire body tenses in preparation for a hand landing heavily on my shoulder and being named and shamed in the *Collinton Gazette. Mother of Three, Wife of Local Hero, steals playsuit from city centre store* . . . I glance around nervously.

'What did you say it was?' the man asks.

'A playsuit. They're the big thing for summer, apparently. I'll have to take it straight back.'

'Why not have a coffee first?' He narrows his eyes and glances through the window. 'Can't hear any sirens out there. You should be safe for a few minutes.'

'Think so?' There's a faint throbbing in my neck. Not even the sight of all the muffins and pastries can soothe me.

'I'd say you could risk it. I'll keep an eye out if you like.' His blue eyes crinkle appealingly, and I notice how long and luscious his dark eyelashes are. Clients have theirs tinted at

29

the salon to achieve a similar effect. 'After you,' he adds, beckoning me to join the queue.

'Thanks,' I say, relaxing slightly. I order my coffee, choosing a shortbread biscuit for nerve-calming purposes, and buy three giant chocolate coins for the kids. The stranger joins me at a vacant table. 'I'm Danny,' he says. 'Okay if I sit with you?'

'Laura.' I smile. 'Sure, no problem, as long as you don't mind associating with a master criminal.'

He grins. 'Think I can handle it. So, what's the plan with the playsuit?'

'I don't know. How would you go about un-shoplifting something?'

Danny shrugs. 'I might run past and throw it in through the door . . .'

I laugh. 'I'm not running anywhere. You know the parents' races they have at school sports days?'

'Well, I can imagine,' he says with a shudder.

'Didn't even make it to the finishing line,' I tell him. 'It's a wonder my family hasn't disowned me.'

He chuckles. 'Well, don't they say it's not the winning . . .'

'. . . but the taking part that counts. Not at my kids' school. It's a deadly serious business.'

He sips from his mug and wipes a little coffee froth from his upper lip. 'So, how many mini-athletes do you have?'

'Just the three.'

'Whoa. Quite a handful.'

'You could say that,' I laugh, appraising this cute, friendly man with a cheeky smile who has lifted me from changing room despair to a far more agreeable state of mind. Danny has dark brown, slightly unkempt wavy hair, and a hint of stubble. He is chunky, like me, but it lends him an endearing quality and rather suits him. Anyway, men can get away with it. A little extra weight makes them look cuddly and cute. As they don't have the babies, they're not subjected to a barrage of pressure to lose their pregnancy weight in ten minutes. I nearly vomited when Naomi bragged that her body had 'snapped back' to pre-pregnancy tautness within ten days of giving birth to Phoebe. There was a distinct lack of snapping with mine. On particularly fat days I still wear my vast preggie knickers, and fear that they'll still be surgically attached to my rear when Toby leaves for college.

'Laura,' Danny says thoughtfully, 'I've got an idea.'

'Uh-huh?' I lick a spoonful of cappuccino froth. I should have ordered a skinny latte – or, better still, a bottle of joyless calorie-free water. What the hell.

'You could post it back anonymously . . .'

'Great idea. I could include a note telling them that it didn't have a security tag on, so they'd realise there's a fault in their system . . .'

'. . . Which means you'd be doing them a favour,' Danny says triumphantly. 'Or I could take it back for you and tell them I've decided I don't have the legs for it.'

We are giggling like children as we finish our coffees and step out into the bustling street. The grey April sky has brightened to a clear baby blue, and York looks sparkly and alive. 'Think I'll just take it back and explain what happened,' I say, smiling.

'Very sensible.' We pause, then he adds, 'Well, it was nice meeting you, Laura. You really brightened up my day.'

'You too. And I'm sorry I barged into you like that. I'm not usually so rude.'

He grins. 'I'm sure you're not.'

'Bye, then.'

'Bye, Laura.' As we head in opposite directions I turn, briefly, to see if he's merged with the crowd. Danny turns too, catching my eye and giving me a little wave and a cheek-dimpling grin before disappearing around the corner. I stand for a moment, thinking, *what a sweet man*, and tasting sugary shortbread on my lips. I feel giddily alert, as if every cell in my body has just woken from a long hibernation and sizzled back into life.

It's been so long, I realise with a jolt to my heart, since anyone has made me feel like that.

CHAPTER SIX

I return the playsuit, for which I am thanked profusely (although I omit to point out the ripped seam and missing button) and saunter into my next port of call with renewed optimism. Result: they do not cater solely for shaved Twiglets, and actually stock size 16s. Grabbing a handful of dresses, I pull on the first one in the changing room. I don't know if they have trick mirrors or lighting but I look kind of . . . *radiant*. As if I might have been whisked off to a spa, given a thorough all-over scrubbing and hourly shots of wheatgrass. My long, wavy dark hair looks shinier and somehow more nourished, and my normally pale cheeks have acquired a healthy glow. I no longer look like a woman who breakfasted on her children's fried egg whites as all three decided that, from now on, they will only tolerate yolks.

The dress is a gorgeous emerald green and has obviously been designed by someone who recognises that real women have bums and hips and boobs, and knows how to make them look rather yummy. 'Oh, yes, that's perfect,' the salesgirl exclaims when I step out of the cubicle. 'It really brings out your lovely green eyes.'

'Think so?' I ask. 'It's quite bright for me. It's not my usual shade at all . . .'

'Oh, it's definitely the one for you. Are you tempted?' She smiles encouragingly.

I nod. 'Sorely tempted.'

'Well, I hope you're going somewhere special to wear it.'

'Yes,' I fib, 'I am.' Back in the cubicle, I change back into my own clothes at top speed, filled with a renewed sense of purpose. Jed was right: today has done me a world of good. I no longer feel all chewed up about Celeste and all that pathetic picking-at-my-husband's-clothes at sports day. All I'd needed was a little time on my own to put things in perspective (oh, and to have coffee with a cute, friendly man; maybe I've just been starved of male company lately). Trying to tame a rogue grin, I decide not to mention the coffee part to Jed. Or the accidental shoplifting, him being Local Hero, pillar of the community and all that.

As I head for the till, a small thrill ripples through me as I wonder what the kids have been up to today. I know I'm supposed to be grateful to be let off the leash, but I'm not used to being without at least Toby, when I'm not working. God knows how I'll feel when he starts school after the summer holidays. Naomi keeps asking what I 'have planned', which suggests that I should have everything sorted – a PhD to get started, maybe – in readiness for this forthcoming development.

A display of stockings and tights catches my eye in a display cabinet by the till. As I'm not up to flashing my sun-starved legs, I pause to choose a pair. 'Slender Deluxe', one packet reads. 'Impregnated with skin-smoothing extracts. Counters cellulite and offers a silken tone.' Hmm. The word 'impregnated' is a little off-putting, but I'm intrigued by the promise of 'visibly slimmer legs, thighs and bottom after just one wearing'. Can tights really do this? If so, why does anyone bother going to the gym?

Next to the tights are things called Body Reducers which promise to 'squeeze away inches'. I grab one of those too. In the picture on the packet, the model is wearing a curious undergarment which goes all the way from her knees right up to her boobs. It's the colour of a digestive biscuit and quite hideous, like a sort of gigantic support bandage. Surely, though, being all bound up like that is a small price to pay to have inches squeezed away, and less hassle than being lipo-sucked. I pay up and head out, breathing in the fresh, blue-skied morning.

Even without my new fat-melting underwear on, I feel unusually carefree and light. Maybe that Body Reducer starts working in the packet. As I walk, I glimpse a woman's reflection in a shop window, and it's a moment before I realise it's me. I'm striding along like someone who knows where she's going and feels good to be alive. A besuited man heading towards me flashes a wide grin. I smile back. It's as if a switch has been flicked and I am visible again. As I pass Starbucks, where I banged into Danny, I feel a flurry of pleasure.

After a leisurely lunch, and perusing posh make-up which I can't afford (and which Toby would probably destroy anyway), I drive home with the windows open and music blaring. The posh paper carrier bag containing my new dress, tights and corset thingie sits perkily on the passenger seat.

Back home, Toby hurtles towards our front door to greet me. 'Mummy's back!' he cries, wrapping himself tightly around me.

'Hi, darling. Had a fun day with Dad?' I crouch down and bury my face in his messy fair curls.

35

'Yuh. Where you been?' he asks, swinging Ted by a leg.

'Just to York, shopping.' He pulls away and bites his full bottom lip, as if fearing that I might desert him again very soon (unlikely). Even when he's older, lying on the sofa in a fizzle of hormones like Finn, I can't imagine him trying to disown me.

Jed is standing a little behind him, looking rather aimless with hands thrust into his jeans pockets. 'Had a good day?' he asks.

'Yes, great, thanks. Just what I needed.' I meet his gaze. He is sexily unshaven and horribly, irresistibly handsome. I love a grazing of dark, swarthy stubble, until it becomes needle-prickly by which point I usually ask him to shave. Correction: *used* to ask. Jed hasn't bristle-grazed me in a long time. We don't seem to kiss these days. I'm not sure at what point we stopped.

'What did you buy, Mummy?' Grace asks, clattering downstairs. Her caramel hair is loose and wild, and she's wearing a huge black T-shirt with a shark on the front, baring its teeth.

'Just a dress, love, and some tights and, er, an underwear thingie.' I try for a hug, but she wriggles from my grasp.

'Aw, that's boring.'

'Oh, and these.' I tease her by fishing about in my bag for ages. With a flourish, I pull out the giant chocolate coins.

'Yummy!' she squeals. 'Can I have one?'

'Of course you can. They're not for me.' *Perish the thought* . . .

'Thanks, Mummy.'

'Fanks,' Toby barks, ripping the foil from his gift and stuffing it into his mouth. Grace takes a huge chomp out of hers.

'I got this for you,' I say, brandishing the remaining coin as Finn strolls downstairs in a fug of recently-applied Lynx and hair gel.

'Oh. Right. Cool,' he mumbles, which causes my insides to twist a little.

'Guess what,' Grace announces through a full mouth.

'What, love?'

'Celeste was here.'

'Was she? Why?' Frowning, I glance at Jed.

'She was just passing and popped in for coffee,' he says quickly, sweeping back his hair.

'Did she?' I study his face, trying to read his expression and ignoring the fact that Toby is repeatedly whacking my leg with Ted.

'Yeah, well, uh . . .' Jed murmurs.

'I didn't know she knew where we lived,' I add.

'It's just, she still doesn't know many people around here,' Jed explains, looking a little more relaxed now. 'I just said, if she was at a loose end at the weekend she was welcome to pop round, have a bite to eat with us . . .'

'While I was shopping,' I add.

'Yeah, but, uh, I didn't realise . . .'

'Look what I made!' Toby interrupts, dropping Ted and burrowing into the pocket of his rumpled trousers. He extracts a clump of custard-yellow felt which has been glued to form a sort of pouch. 'S'a present for you,' he adds.

'You made this all by yourself? That's fantastic, Toby.'

He nods proudly. 'He didn't,' scoffs Grace. 'Celeste made it.'

My heart thuds to my boots. 'She didn't!' Toby thunders with an ineffectual attempt to punch his sister in the chest. 'I made it!'

'Celeste did it all,' Grace crows, deliberately winding him up. 'She did the cutting and sticking. You couldn't make a purse all by yourself, you're only a *baby* . . .'

'I'm not a baby!' he rages. 'I'm *four* . . .'

'Only just,' she snaps back.

'Hey, don't fight, you two,' I protest, turning to Jed. 'So you had a sort of, um . . . craft session?' I'm trying to keep my voice light, but am aware that it sounds taut and ugly.

'Er, yeah. Celeste had some fabric with her so the kids started making things . . .' He shrugs. He really is overdoing the casual look.

'Oh. That's . . . great.' I grin inanely, aware of three pairs of children's eyes, dark as coffee beans, boring into me. *Celeste was here.* How fantastically cosy. Not only does she show up precisely when I'm grappling with an oversized romper suit, but also happens to have a wealth of child-pleasing craft materials about her person. As you do. On your way to your yoga class or to Mother Earth for your goddamn sprouting seeds or whatever it is she allows to come into contact with her precious insides.

The first time I met her, at a leaving do for Jed's deputy head, she was eyeing the buffet with distaste. We were in the dingy downstairs room of a bar in town, and everyone else was troughing pizza and sausage rolls. I'd tried to make an effort, since Jed was obviously so taken with the newest staff member and had gone on about how much fun she was, and how the children loved her. 'Hi, I'm Laura, Jed's wife,' I'd said, sensing that she looked a little lonely.

'Oh, are you?' she'd said with a quizzical smile, as if surprised that tall, swarthy, handsome Jed should have such a dumpy wife. There'd been a small silence, and I'd babbled something nonsensical about the hassle of booking a babysitter that night.

'Bet it's lovely for you to be out,' she'd said, flicking a gaze towards Jed who was deep in conversation with Carol, his head teacher.

The way she'd said it, and looked at my husband like that – she'd made it sound as if I'd just been released from an institution. 'It's great,' I'd replied, a little tiddly on cheap white wine by that point. 'I'm only allowed out until ten, though. Otherwise they come in a van to take me back.'

'Haha,' she'd managed, grabbing her handbag from the greasy table and scooting towards the ladies'. I'd spotted Mickey and Duncan, Jed's teacher mates, and been awash with relief when they'd beckoned me over and been friendly and chatty and normal.

And now, I'm clutching the felt purse she helped Toby to make, and having to pretend I love it. 'This is great, Toby, thank you,' I say, trying to regard it with fondness.

'Looks more like a codpiece,' Jed hisses into my ear. His arm snakes around my waist, and I muster a smile. Of course I'm being ridiculous. Why shouldn't Celeste *happen to be passing*, and drop in? This proves that nothing's going on between them. No one who was shagging, or even planning to shag their father, would have the gall to make codpieces with our children.

'We had a picnic in the park,' Grace adds.

'That's lovely. It's been a gorgeous afternoon.'

'Celeste came with us.' She grins.

My throat tightens. Jesus, was she here the whole day? Is she planning to move in with us? Shall we build an annexe for her in the garden? Actually, you could probably fit three in our bed if I positioned myself with my arse hanging right off the edge. 'Did she?' I say. 'That's lovely. Sounds like you've all had a great day. Anyway, I'm just going to take my shopping upstairs.' I glower at Jed, who looks relieved to finish this conversation.

In our bedroom, I pull out the emerald dress and hold it up against myself. It's a little skimpy and low at the front, I realise now; my boobs are ample, to put it mildly, and I'm not used to so much creamy flesh being on display. I wonder if my powers of selection had somehow become distorted after I'd met Danny. I'd felt emboldened then, and a little flirtatious, like my old, carefree self before all this weight began to creep on. It had given me a confidence surge, just chatting to him in the café. A smile tweaks my lips as I picture his cheeky, boyish smile, the pale blue eyes fringed with long, black lashes, the slightly dishevelled, needing-a-trim dark hair. How he'd made me laugh, and feel like Laura again, not the twerp who humiliates herself at sports day.

Just a coffee with a friendly stranger. That's all it was – nothing compared to cosy craft sessions and picnics, and therefore not worth mentioning to Jed. I didn't even fancy him, not really. I was just flattered, that's all. Is Jed attracted to Celeste? Of course he is. Any straight man would be. She's beautiful, slim and creative. I am merely okay-looking if you squint at me in a dim light, *and* it took me two whole terms at school to make a rabbit pincushion.

The door creaks open and Grace strolls in, licking melted chocolate from her fingers. 'Hi, bunny,' I say.

She tilts her head, and I notice a grubby smear on her pointy little chin. She looks tired in an outdoorsy way, worn out by a day of fun. 'Love you, Mummy,' she says suddenly, causing my Celeste-vexation to melt away.

'Love you too.' I open my arms and pull her in for a hug. This time, she doesn't wriggle.

'Celeste can rollerblade,' she adds.

CHAPTER SEVEN

There's no chance to bring up the subject of Celeste in the morning as Jed and I aren't alone for a minute. I didn't mention it last night either, being a little unsure of what I would actually object to. The picnic? The rollerblading? The making of purses? When you look at it that way, it's all pretty innocent, child-pleasing stuff. Even so, I feel unsettled all through breakfast, and I notice that Jed is particularly keen to dart off to work.

I must be mature about this. Mustn't seethe as I take the children to school and nursery, or Naomi will spot me and make some spiky remark about me looking wired and suggest, 'I always find the mornings run more smoothly if I get the children's lunchboxes and uniforms ready the night before, don't you?' I'm seized by an urge to supply them with packets of Monster Munch to consume in public. *That* would get her neck vein pulsating.

Finn is marching ahead, all unkempt dark hair and long, gangly limbs, giving the impression that I'm some irksome stranger lurking behind him. Spotting James and Calum swaggering ahead, he hurries to catch up. I've tried to work out why I'm so embarrassing – so much so, in fact, that he no longer allows me to cut his hair and insists on going to some scabby place under the railway arch where they also do piercing. Surely I can't be *that* mortifying. It's not as if I walk to school in a pink bikini, singing opera songs. In fact I try to tone myself down in my extremely plain black trenchcoat and flat boots. I don't think I look freakish. Sometimes, though, I worry that I'm not quite normal. A sensible person would take this Celeste business – the showing up at sports day, the jolly craft sessions and picnics – in her stride. Maybe I should be glad my family has a perfectly nice time without me?

Spotting her friend India across the street, Grace waves and whirls round to face me. 'Can India come for tea?'

'We'll see. I'll need to ask her mum, okay?' For a seven-year-old Grace has an enviable social life, which I'm pleased about – but this also means our house often has the feel of an impromptu after-school club, with mass-catering expected. By the time we arrive at school, Grace has accumulated a bunch of excitable friends. 'Bye, Mummy,' she says sweetly, planting a speedy kiss on my cheek.

'Bye, darling. Have a lovely day.' I glance around for Finn, hoping to say goodbye, but he's already sauntered into the playground with his friends.

'Come on, love,' I say, clutching Toby's hand. 'Let's take you to nursery.' Scamps is just around the corner from school. He charges in, flings his coat in the vague direction of his named hook and throws his backpack onto the floor. I grab him for a quick hug goodbye before he tears off into the main room, and put his coat and bag in their rightful places. 'Hi, Laura.' Cara, the manageress, pops her head around the cloakroom door.

'Hi, Cara. Just tidying up after Toby as usual.' I force a grin.

'Hmm. Did he tell you about his little adventure last week?'

'No,' I say hesitantly.

She crooks her eyebrow, making me sweat. 'Took the plug out of the water tray. Flooded the main room. The children had to sit in the library corner until we'd mopped it all up.'

'Oh, I'd no idea. He didn't mention that. I'm really sorry.'

'That's okay.' She chuckles in a *kids, eh?* kind of way and flutters her eyelashes at me.

'Bet that happens all the time,' I add.

'No,' she says levelly. 'In the fifteen years I've worked here, no child has ever done that.'

Good for Toby, I think, gushing further apologies as I make my escape. At least he thought of something new and different to amuse himself. Although he enjoys nursery, he will only tolerate cutting and sticking for so long (unless Celeste is involved, obviously – in which case he could probably be persuaded to fashion an entire spring/summer collection in yellow felt). As I'm not due at work until ten, I decide to have a coffee and mull over whether I should let the plug incident go, or apply the thumb screws and water torture.

Café Roma is virtually empty. It smells good in here, of delicious things baking, which is especially welcome after the breakfasty fug of our kitchen. When we moved here from London, when I was pregnant with Toby, the small North Yorkshire market town had a time-warp feel about it, and you couldn't get a decent coffee anywhere. Jed had been offered a senior teaching position at Rosebank Primary and I'd welcomed the move. With our third child on the way, I'd looked forward to being a mere half-hour drive from my parents. Now, four years on, there's a clutch of new cafés offering respectable bursts of caffeine to get the nerves jangling nicely.

Dad's no longer here, though. I hadn't imagined having to face that.

Selecting one of the trashier newspapers from the rack, I take a seat at the steamed-up window. A supplement falls out; it's called *Your Complete Summer Grooming Guide*. We've only just staggered through the Easter holidays, yet already I'm supposed to be fretting about the pallidness of my legs. I flip through it. *You might adhere to the old '70s thing of leaving your pubic hair* au naturelle, is where my eyes land.

What '70s thing? What do they mean?

A little light grooming is common courtesy, it thrills on. Are they implying that it's rude not to? I glance around the café. A group of four women of around my age has drifted in, chatting and laughing and smelling of light, floral perfumes. They are all smartly dressed with their hair freshly blow-dried, and I vaguely recognise them from the few times I ventured into the gym. An awful thought hits me: I'm probably the only woman in here who doesn't have her bikini line waxed. Heck, even the chef, who I can see bobbing about in the kitchen through the circular window, probably keeps himself nice and tidy down there.

I glower down at it. Not at my own pubic hair – that wouldn't be fitting in Café Roma – but at the damn magazine. Is this why Jed has un-synchronised our bedtimes? He isn't really staying up marking jotters, planning lessons or even indulging in lurid fantasies starring Celeste. He's simply appalled by my lack of personal grooming. I've been so wrapped up in looking after the children that I've missed a significant cultural shift. Closing the grooming guide, I sip my coffee morosely. That's it: my '*au naturelle*' do is as outmoded as a poodle perm or culottes. Jed has to fight the urge to retch every time he glimpses it. He's just been too polite to tell me.

The café door opens, and Naomi flounces in, flushed with rude health. 'Hi, Laura,' she says. 'Day off today?'

'No, I'm working at ten.' I check my watch. 'Thanks for rescuing my sandals, by the way. And well done with the mums' race.'

'Oh, it was nothing. No one cares about these things, do they?'

'Of course not,' I say with a chuckle.

'Ankle okay now?'

'Couldn't be better, thanks.' I glance at her. Of course, she's *naturally* neat down there – or so it appeared in those paintings of her at the Riverside Arts Centre. It was quite off-putting, trying to eat an apple Danish with all those naked Naomis gawping at me. I'd made a speedy exit, and avoided the place until they took her paintings down and replaced them with landscapes.

Her gaze drops to the table. 'Cute purse. Very homespun.'

'Oh, thanks. Toby made it actually.'

'Really? You're good, doing that sort of thing. Our au pair does all the artsy-crafty stuff . . . Hi, could I just have a dandelion tea?' she calls out to the girl at the counter, who nods.

'It was nothing really,' I witter.

Naomi smirks. 'Who was that girl at sports day? The one standing with Jed?'

'Oh, just a colleague of his from school,' I say lightly. 'They'd come over for a meeting.'

'Pretty, wasn't she?' she chirps, almost as if she *knows*, and is hell-bent on torturing me. 'All the dads were checking her out, did you see? James Boland's dad virtually had his tongue out!'

'Yes, haha,' I croak, scrambling up from my seat and stuffing Toby's purse into my bag. Naomi picks up the grooming guide.

'Mind if I read this?'

'Go ahead. I'm running late actually.'

She flips it open at the *au naturelle* page as the waitress brings her a steaming mug of dandelion witch-brew. It looks like puddle water. 'Oh, Laura?' she calls after me as I head for the door. 'Miss Marshall's looking for parent volunteers to set up a junior athletics club.'

I blink at her. 'That sounds good.'

'She asked me to help to run it. You know, coaching the kids, motivating them, that sort of thing . . .'

'Great.' I try to look excited.

'Thought you might be interested,' she adds, 'in the fund-raising side. Maybe you could do some home baking or something.'

I force a wide smile, hoping it's the smile of a woman who is dynamic, perky and firmly at the helm of family life. 'Love to,' I say. 'Count me in.'

*

'I'd like something like that,' my first client says, thrusting me a snipped-out photo from a magazine. The woman has over-bleached hair which peters out to fine wisps at her shoulders. The photo is of Angelina Jolie.

I take time to study her hair, feeling its coarseness and trying to figure out a diplomatic approach. 'Are you sure you wouldn't prefer something that works with your hair's natural colour and texture?' I suggest, slipping easily into hairdresser-speak. It's not that I loathe my job. Far from it: I enjoy the steady routines, the companionship, and knowing that most clients walk out feeling far happier than when they came in. I especially enjoy the dramatic transformations, when the right cut heightens a woman's bone structure, and she emerges a real beauty. I still preferred it, though, before our grand relaunch as Shine Hair Design, when we were plain old Snipperz. More realistic expectations. Install a bubbly water feature and butter-soft leather sofas and people think you can transform them into Hollywood actresses. It's like the time I joined Bodyworks, the fancy gym over the road, in the hope that I'd somehow be magically transformed by simply wafting around the building.

As I show my client sample hair shades, the magazine photo appears to have been forgotten. She leaves, not as Angelina, but thoroughly de-frizzed and happy.

'Lovely colour you did there,' remarks Simone, my boss, as I check my appointments.

'Thanks. She was pleased, I think.'

'Fancy a quick coffee? I'll make one.'

'That'd be great. I've got a fifteen-minute gap, then I'm booked up pretty much all day.'

In the kitchen, Simone hands me a mug. 'So, good weekend?' she asks.

'Yes, I actually managed to get out on my own and do some shopping.'

'Sounds great . . .'

'Celeste popped in,' I add, 'while I was out.'

'Oh.' She frowns. 'Were the kids there?'

I nod. 'I know – nothing was going to happen while they were around, and I'm probably being ridiculous and reading far too much into it. But still. I felt kind of . . . uncomfortable.'

Simone regards me with striking blue eyes. Everything about her – the flawless skin, perfect nails, the fact that she looks around 500 years younger than I do – screams 'child-free'. 'You know what I think?' she says, raising an eyebrow. 'I reckon they're just friends and that's all there is to it. Maybe he's just enjoying hanging out with a woman. You know – having a female friend instead of just the guys from football and school. Good for the ego and all that.'

'Yes but—' I stop myself. Simone's probably right, and what's wrong with having a close friend of the opposite sex? I used to, at school and college and in suburban hair salons on the fringes of North London. But they all drifted into relationships, as I did, and since we left London four years ago, we seem to have lost touch. I've never made any new male friends to replace them.

'Know what you and Jed need?' Simone adds, swilling her cup in the sink. 'A weekend away, just the two of you. Something to put the spark back.'

'Impossible,' I say. 'Mum's brilliant with the kids, but having all three for the whole weekend would be too much for her.'

'What about Jed's parents? Or your sister?'

I laugh darkly. Pauline and Brian live a five-hour drive away in South London and are, more to the point, beyond clueless. Kate would be willing to come down, but since she's just set up her B&B in Scotland it seems far too much to ask. 'I really don't think—' I start.

'Why not?' she cuts in. 'A weekend in, I don't know – Paris or somewhere would do you the world of good. It might even perk up your . . .' She tails off and grins.

'Simone,' I say, sniggering, 'anyone's sex life would perk up if their children were in another country.' She laughs her throaty laugh, and tosses her gleaming chestnut curls, as we go through to attend to our next appointments.

Although I barely come up for air between clients, our conversation niggles at me all morning. *A weekend away*, I keep thinking as I cut, colour, blow dry and create an up-do for a party. It's obvious that Jed and I desperately need time together but, even if I could arrange it, would he want to go away with me?

Grace has three friends for tea after school, involving an impromptu cookie-making enterprise. One young visitor decides to liven up the proceedings by taking my dressing gown off the radiator in order to wipe her sticky hands on it, then places it on the hob and inadvertently turns on a gas ring. A sleeve is singed black, the gown is extinguished under the cold tap and the kitchen fills with bitter fumes, cancelling out the delicious biscuit aroma which has been teasing my nostrils. By the time Jed shows up, I'm scraping dough off the kitchen floor, a husk of my former self.

'Don't *want* to put pyjamas on,' Toby screams, as if they were made not from the softest brushed cotton but laced with barbed wire. His cheeks are flushed, his dark eyes wet with furious tears.

'You look exhausted,' Jed points out, taking over with Toby. 'Here, I'll sort out the kids.'

'Thanks,' I mutter, sinking onto the sofa with a large glass of wine. As a parent, my husband is far more effective than I am. With Jed, the kids snap into action, whereas my voice drifts ineffectually around the house, no more significant than a light breeze.

As I sip my wine, a mobile starts ringing on the coffee table. I pick it up, realising too late that it's not mine but Jed's. 'Hello?' I say.

'Oh! Um, is that Laura?' Celeste asks.

'Yes, it is,' I say lightly. Why is she calling him now? Hasn't she heard of kids' bedtime?

'Is Jed there? Don't worry if he's busy, it's nothing urgent . . .'

'He's just reading Toby a story upstairs. I'll ask him to call you back when he's finished—'

'No, it's okay,' Jed cries, bounding downstairs all bright-eyed and smiley. 'I'll take it . . .' With a ridiculous guffaw, he snatches his mobile from my grasp and marches through to the kitchen. I stare after him. I have never seen Jed move so fast, not even on the football pitch. Anyone would think Nicole Kidman was on the line.

'Daddy!' Toby roars from upstairs. 'What are you doing? Come and finish my story. Come *back*!'

CHAPTER EIGHT

I stand dead still, still clutching my wine glass, fury fizzing through my veins as I try to make out what Jed's saying. *Ooh, yes, ma petite French angel, you can slather me all over in chocolate sauce as soon as I can get away from the dumpy old wife . . . zut alors, I'm sure the old trout's listening . . .* Okay, he doesn't say that exactly, but he's chuckling, yacking about God knows what. 'Yeah, yeah,' he murmurs, adoration spilling from his lips. 'That sounds fantastic.' *Perhaps we could extend the chocolate-sauce slathering a little lower, Angelcakes . . . ooh yes, just there . . . perfect . . .*

'Daaaad!' Toby screams. 'I want my story!' I scamper upstairs to find him sitting up in bed, gripping his battered copy of *Dirty Bertie* and glaring at me. 'Daddy was reading it,' he says, jutting out his bottom lip.

'I know, sweetheart, but Dad's busy with a *terribly* important phonecall right now. I'll read the rest, okay?' I squeeze onto the bed beside him and pop Ted on my knee.

'Don't want you to do it.' He shuts the book and tosses it onto the floor.

'Tobes, don't be like that. Don't be so sulky. I told you Dad's—'

'I want DAD!' he snaps, exhausted tears springing from his eyes.

'Okay, okay.' With a sigh, I climb out of bed and tuck in Ted next to Toby. 'I'm going to say goodnight and put your light off now, okay? And if you're still awake when Daddy gets off the phone, maybe then he'll come up and finish your story . . .'

'Why are you cross, Mummy?' Grace calls from her room.

'I'm not cross, love. I'm *fine* . . .'

'You are. You've got a cross voice on.'

'Well, that's probably just because I'm a bit tired,' I call back, trying to sound light and perky and distinctly un-cross. I prick up my ears.

'Yeah, that'd be great, I'd love that,' Jed warbles downstairs. Anyone would think he'd called one of those pervo sex lines.

'Night, honey,' I murmur. Toby flicks his head away as I try to kiss him, as if I'm the one who's abandoned him in favour of a natter with Fancy Pants.

'Want Daddy,' he bleats as I click off his light.

'So do I,' I murmur, stomping downstairs.

Jed is standing in the kitchen, looking ridiculously pleased with himself. Almost *post-orgasmic,* in fact. 'What's up?' he asks brightly.

'It's just . . . Toby was upset that you didn't finish the story.'

'Oh, God, was he? I'll pop up right now.'

'I mean he was *really* upset.' I fix him with a fierce stare. 'Did you have to do that? Rush down like your life depended on it, to speak to . . . *her*?'

Jed stares at me. 'Laura . . .' He pauses. 'What is this about exactly?'

'*Dirty Bertie.* You were halfway through reading—'

'But it's not, is it? It's about me, taking a call from a friend, which you suddenly seem to have some kind of *issue* with . . .'

'I don't have an issue!' I protest. 'You seem obsessed, that's

53

all. Celeste this, Celeste that . . . oh, we had a picnic and a little craft session and look! Here she is in her lemon cardi at our kids' sports day for a supposed *meeting* . . .'

'A *supposed* meeting?' Jed repeats, blinking at me.

'Yes. Why did she have to be there?'

Jed shakes his head despairingly. 'Do you have a problem with Celeste?'

'Yes. No,' I bark, feeling my entire chest area glowing hotly.

'Are you saying I shouldn't have friends at work? Is that what you want?'

'No, of course not . . .'

'Or that they shouldn't phone me? Because that's the problem, isn't it?'

'All I'm saying is, one minute you were reading Dirty-bloody-Bertie . . .'

'Mummy,' comes Toby's voice behind me. 'It's *Dirty Bertie*. Not Dirty-*bloody*-Bertie.' I turn around to see our youngest standing there, with his pale curls sticking up in matted tufts, clutching the book to his chest.

'I'm sorry, Toby,' I mutter. 'It just sort of slipped out.'

'That's a swearing word, Mummy. Cara said it's naughty to say that bad word.'

'Yes, I know, and I shouldn't have said it. It was . . .' My mouth seems to shrivel. 'A . . . mistake.'

'Will you finish it now, Daddy?' Toby asks levelly.

'Yes, of course I will, Tobes,' Jed mutters.

'You got to the bit about bogies.'

'Yes, I remember.' He rakes a hand through his hair, as if trying to brush off the bad feelings that have been flying around our kitchen. Throwing me a stony look, he takes Toby by the hand and the two of them head upstairs.

My bottom lip trembles as I stand in the kitchen doorway. So he took a phonecall. Anyone would think I'd walked in and found him and Celeste having wild sex on the table. I perch on a chair, listening to Jed upstairs, chatting jovially in Toby's room. Our children love their dad. I do too, yet I'm making myself completely unlovable. The thought of losing him tears at my insides.

The house phone rings. I answer it; it's Kate, my sister, sounding distant and crackly even though she's only calling from Scotland. 'How's it going?' she asks.

'Good,' I say. 'Everyone's fine. How about you?'

'Oh, the usual chaos. Untrainable dog, terrorising sheep, lost a couple of chickens to a fox last night . . .'

'Oh, God.' Kate had her kids young – my two nephews are in their early twenties – and she and Will, her childhood sweetheart, have moved neatly from domestic mayhem to running a smallholding and B&B in the Scottish Borders. Which sounds like another kind of chaos entirely.

'When are you coming up?' she's asking me. 'The kids would love it. We've just got a couple of pigs. You'd better get yourselves up here soon if you want to see them before they're bacon and sausages.'

'You're right,' I say, smiling. 'Toby and Grace would love that. Finn would too – although these days, he reckons he's far too cool to like animals.'

'Oh, he's still your baby really,' Kate says. 'Anyway, stranger, I just thought I'd catch up. You never call me these days . . .'

'It's just hectic. You know what it's like . . .'

'What are you up to tonight?'

'Um, nothing much. Grace and I made some cookies and I'm kind of tempted to curl up with a plateful and a DVD.'

'Domestic goddess,' she laughs, before ringing off.

Feeling boosted – Kate's motherly tone always lifts me somehow – I eye our freshly-baked offerings. If you were being unkind you'd say they looked like chunks of moon rock but we decided they were 'rustic'. I nibble one, relishing its comforting sweetness. Another won't hurt. I nibble and nibble, soothed by Jed's distant murmurs as he reads not just *Dirty Bertie* but a whole bunch of other stories too, judging by the time he's been up there. He's probably putting off having to come downstairs.

I blink down at the plate. How did I manage to plough through so many cookies? I must stop doing this – cramming my face when I'm not even hungry. Emotional eating, I think you call it. All that's happening is that my clothes are getting tighter and I know that Jed must look at me and think . . . *ew*. Kate would say not to worry; she's always telling me I'm the 'gorgeous curvaceous one'.

But I don't *feel* gorgeous and I don't think Jed shares her view of me.

Desperate measures are called for, I decide, putting away the flour and eggs and wiping jammy smears from the worktop. I'll start a diet tomorrow and get into shape – make myself minxy again like in the old days. I'll show Jed that the woman he fell in love with – whom he could barely keep his hands off, if I remember rightly – is still here, right under his nose. I refuse to allow size-eight Fancy Pants to lure my beloved away from me.

In the meantime, though, there's one cookie left. Where diets are concerned, there's no time like tomorrow.

CHAPTER NINE

By Saturday afternoon I'm quivering with anticipation. This is combined with mild dizziness, due to substituting lunch with a glass of hot water with a dusting of cinnamon in it. I read somewhere that this combination helps to melt away wrinkles as well as being a miracle fat cure. I know it's ridiculous, but with my Big Surprise looming, these are desperate times.

'I've arranged a special treat,' I blurt out as Jed, the children and I head home from the park.

'What is it?' Grace demands, gripping her ice cream which I have been eyeing ravenously. 'What kind of treat?'

'I'm taking you, Toby and Finn to Granny Heather's. You're staying over tonight, and me and Daddy will come and collect you in the morning.'

'Yeah!' she cries, delighted.

'Today?' Toby asks eagerly.

'Yes, honey, a bit later today.' I glance at Finn. 'You okay with that, darling?'

He shrugs. 'Yeah. What are you and Dad going to do?'

'It's up to Dad,' I say, my stomach whirling with anticipation. 'What would you like to do, Jed?'

'Don't know,' he says, guiding Toby away from a ferocious-looking dog he wants to pat. 'It's all a bit sudden, Laura . . .'

'How much notice do you need?' I ask, teasing him.

'None, I just . . .'

'Did you have any other plans for tonight?'

He stops and frowns at me. Grace pauses mid-lick, her tongue thickly coated in strawberry ice. 'No, of course not. Are you sure it's all right, though? It's a lot to ask of your mum. And Finn has football in the morning, and I'm meant to be taking the junior team . . .' My heart slumps. *Oh no, he's thinking. A whole night alone with Laura and her hideous* au naturelle *do . . .*

'Actually,' I say, more subdued now, 'she was delighted. She hasn't seen the children for ages. And I've spoken to Calum's dad, and he's happy to stand in for you at football this week. You don't mind missing footie just this once, do you, Finn?'

'Nah,' he says with a shrug.

'Please, Dad,' Grace blurts out. 'Let us have a sleepover at Granny Heather's.'

'We'll be fine, Dad,' Finn says airily.

'Um . . . okay then,' Jed murmurs.

'So tonight,' I add cheerfully, 'we can do whatever we like.'

'Great,' Jed says flatly. I grin broadly at him. He grimaces back, looking for all the world as if he's about to have a bunion removed. Still, I won't let him dampen my mood. The problem is, Jed won't realise how much we needed this night by ourselves until we're actually having it. I don't mean having sex necessarily – although that would be pleasing – but time together without the children. Is it any wonder, I reflect later as I drive us all to Mum's, that our sex life has withered up? If I so much as try to cuddle Jed, Finn looks as if he might vomit and Toby starts shouting for a biscuit. They are allergic to adults showing each other affection. It's a miracle anyone manages to produce more than one child.

'Come here, my darlings,' Mum says, emerging from her red-brick cottage as we all tumble out of the car. She hugs me and the children in turn – even Finn, who reserves a soft spot for his granny, allows it – while I unload the kids' overnight bag. 'Hi, Heather,' Jed says, kissing her cheek. He hovers uncertainly as if about to deliver a particularly stressful public speech.

'We're so grateful for this,' I tell Mum, trying to blot him out of my vision.

'Yes, er, thanks, a lot,' Jed adds feebly.

'My pleasure,' she says as we follow her inside. 'You know I'm happy to have them any time.' Since Dad died nearly four years ago – just after Toby was born – Mum has lived here alone in the smart, touristy town of Kittering. I know she still misses Dad terribly, despite filling her days with art classes and volunteering for every community group in the area. There are no tears as we prepare to leave. 'Say bye to Mum and Dad,' she prompts the children, but all three – even Finn – are engrossed in Dad's old Hornby train set which still works, amazingly, and which Mum has painstakingly laid out on her living room floor.

'So what d'you want to do?' I ask Jed we drive away.

'I don't really mind,' he says vaguely, gazing out of the passenger window. I wonder now if he'd have preferred this not to have been a surprise, and to have had some input into the planning. Maybe *then* he'd be quivering with excitement.

'Well,' I say lightly, 'we could go to York, have dinner . . .' My mouth waters at the thought of tucking into a meal I haven't cooked. Stuff the calories. I'll even have dessert. Something chocolatey with a molten interior. Gooey cheese. Lashings of wine. Sod the water-and-cinnamon regime. It was starting to make me feel ill anyway and I don't even *like* cinnamon. 'We could even stay at a hotel,' I add, munching some Quavers from an open packet I found in the car. 'Fancy breakfast in bed? That would be lovely, wouldn't it, having it brought up to our room with the papers and . . .'

'A hotel?' Jed repeats. 'Why would we do that?'

'God, Jed! You don't have to sound so horrified. You'd think I'd suggested booking us into an abattoir.'

'It just seems, I don't know . . .' He shakes his head. 'Unnecessary.'

'Of course it's unnecessary,' I exclaim. 'That's the whole point, isn't it? To do something exciting and different and a little bit decadent. I thought it'd be fun, Jed. Anyway, I packed your overnight bag in case you fancied it.'

'Did you? You packed my pyjamas?'

'Yes, Jed. They're in the boot, travelling in this very car with us.' *And I stuffed in your cast-iron chastity pants too,* I want to add.

'It just seems extravagant,' Jed murmurs.

'It wouldn't have to be, would it? I don't care about posh. We could find a tawdry little place, somewhere nice and sleazy . . .' I grin at him, and try for a saucy eyebrow wiggle, but the joke falls flat.

'I'm not sure I'd fancy that, love.'

'Oh, come on,' I say, crunching a stale Quaver impatiently. 'It'll be a change, won't it?'

'A change from what?'

'From boring old domesticity. Putting the bin out and

60

wondering why there's a weird smell coming from the drain. Loading the dishwasher. All that stuff we never used to *think* about before we had the kids . . .' By now I'm feeling rather manic and driving a little too fast.

'I thought I'd fixed that drain,' he says tetchily. 'And could you slow down? You took that corner a bit too fast.'

I exhale loudly. It's a long time since I've read anything about reigniting passion, but I'm sure they never recommend talking about *drains*. 'Just an idea,' I say flatly. 'I was trying to think of something different to do, but if you don't fancy it, that's fine.'

Mustering a smile, Jed nicks a Quaver from the packet on my lap. 'Tell you what, love,' he says, patting my leg. 'Shall we just have a cosy night in?'

*

Despite my plummeting spirits, I'm determined to make this work out and for us to have an unforgettable evening. Jed and I hardly ever go out. He seems to have forgotten that emerging from our house after dark – just the two of us – is a real possibility. I see couples heading out at night, holding hands or with the girl kind of tucked under the guy's arm, being hugged as they walk. It squeezes my heart to see that. We used to walk that way, although doing that now would feel ridiculous. Jed would assume I felt faint and couldn't stand up properly. Yet sometimes it feels as if the whole world is out there, hugging and kissing in public, and that Jed and I have somehow slipped off its edge.

The first year we were together, I don't think we saw a single DVD right through to the end. We'd put one on, when he'd taken a minicab over to my tiny Archway flat, or we'd plan to watch one when I'd cycled over to see him in his maisonette in Bethnal Green. The credits would start, and we'd have a little kiss – and before we knew it we'd be tangled on the floor together, kissing and laughing that that was another movie we'd never know the end of.

And now, I can't imagine how Jed would react if I pounced on him while he was watching a movie. He'd probably think I'd lost my mind.

I unload our overnight bag from the boot – a gesture which seems particularly tragic – and let us into the house. It feels too still and quiet without the children. The carpet is littered with components from Toby's Lego fort, and I almost tread on a partially-constructed rocket which he and Grace had been making out of a plastic water bottle and a mangled toothpaste tube. 'One of my regulars told me that new Moroccan place is good,' I tell Jed, pacing the living room. It's a downside of being a hairdresser. You hear every detail of your clients' glittering social lives. You make them look gorgeous for nights out you'll never have.

Jed looks up from the armchair. 'I don't really fancy it tonight, love. I thought we'd agreed to stay home.'

'Oh, come on!' I snap. 'We can stay home any night we want. What's the point in arranging for the kids to stay over at Mum's if we're not going to do anything? It seems crazy. Such a waste. Let's, let's . . .' I flounder for words. 'Let's do something *spontaneous*.' Jed blinks at me and looks rather tired. He didn't used to be like this – a boring fart in an armchair who can't even muster the wherewithal to take his wife out for a drink. Back in the old days, before he lost the will to live, we'd go to bars and restaurants and parties all the time, and he'd tell me he was proud to be seen with me. We were perpetually skint, but he still managed to buy me sexy dresses, teetering shoes, beautiful lingerie in black silk and ivory lace. Things a man would only buy for a woman he wanted to have wild sex with.

'I've been working all week,' Jed protests. 'I'd just like to chill out, Laura, okay?'

'I've been working too,' I start, catching myself: of course I haven't been working like he has. While Jed's been mentoring disadvantaged kids, I've been . . . *cutting hair*. What does that matter in the great scheme of things? If there were no hair-dressers, what would people do? Hack it themselves with the kitchen scissors. It would be fine. No one *dies* from having badly-cut hair. Finn would probably enjoy that – chopping at it himself – as it's the effect he seems to be after at the piercing place.

'Why don't we watch a movie?' Jed suggests, his voice softening. 'I'll pop down to the Spar and choose something if you like.'

Well, whoop-di-doo. 'Okay,' I mutter. 'Let's do that. Let's stay in and watch TV.'

'Don't be like that, darling.' He throws me a wounded, big-eyed look.

'I'm not being like *anything*.' I snatch Grace's pens and scissors from the floor, unable to think of anything else to do. Once I've tidied the entire room, and rounded up a few stray dishes, I perch on our other armchair and peer at him.

'What's wrong?' he asks, looking up from his book.

'Nothing. I'm just thinking, maybe you're right. I can't remember the last time we were home alone together. Maybe it could be quite fun.'

Jed nods. 'It's nice, isn't it? Sort of . . . peaceful.'

'Well, it *could* be nice. Why don't I pop out for some shopping and cook us a special meal? Something the kids wouldn't like?'

'Sounds good,' Jed says, eyes fixed back on the book. I have to say, he doesn't appear to be primed for an evening of hot lust.

'And I'll get some wine,' I add.

'Yeah. Great.'

'And maybe we could, you know . . . go to bed early.' I move over to his chair, and try to nuzzle into him, but his gaze remains fixed on the page. What's he reading? Some American crime novel where people are bludgeoned to death every three pages. I can smell the testosterone radiating from its pages. God, it must be riveting. If he were any other straight man, in a child-free house with his wife dropping walloping hints, trying to drag him off to a *hotel*, for God's sake, he wouldn't be reading a goddamn book. What do I have to do – dress up as an air hostess? Trill 'doors to manual' while wearing an Ann Summers tunic emblazoned with a Lust-anza logo? A couple of years ago, Simone had a brief fling with a guy – one of her clients, in fact – who was into that kind of stuff. He even suggested buying a hostess trolley that she could wheel through her house to dispense drinks. Is *that* what turns men on these days?

'I'll go then,' I bark, causing Jed to flinch.

'Yeah. Um, what?'

'You relax and enjoy your book' – a mere smidgeon of bitterness there – 'and I'll nip out to Tesco.'

'Okay, darling.' His jaw twitches from the effort of glancing up from the page. 'That sounds great.'

*

Before leaving I quickly scan my cookery books. I used to love cooking fancy stuff – proper grown-up food involving coriander and limes – before my culinary gene shrivelled up. The children howled in protest whenever I presented anything with 'weirdy green bits' (i.e. herbs). So my confidence shrank, and my cooking acquired a distinctly retro vibe: pies, sausages, roasts. None of it terribly waistline-friendly. As I'm usually ravenous by the children's dinnertime, I tend to pick at their clammy leftovers, then often eat again later with Jed. Double-dinner Laura. No wonder I've gone up from a size twelve to a sixteen since we met.

I pore over recipes, uninspired by dishes involving grilled chicken and watercress. Can't imagine Jed getting revved up over that. He can eat like a horse, lucky sod, and not gain an ounce. My eyes land on a pasta dish with prawns, chillies and rocket. How delightfully non-fish-fingery. 'Won't be long,' I announce as I head out, feeling quite the hunter-gatherer. Okay, I'm not planning to grapple a wildebeest to drag home to my beloved – I'm only going to *Tesco* – but it's a step in the right direction.

I march along our neat, tree-lined street, full of purpose and bubbling excitement. What else should I buy? Something hormone-stirring to slip into Jed's drink? The only aphrodisiacs I can think of are oysters, which I don't know how to prepare, or essence of dried bull's penis or something, and I don't imagine Tesco stock it. Then, as I approach the store's entrance, an idea hits me.

Underwear. Nothing ridiculously porno – I have neither the nerve nor the body for that. Just a new bra and knickers that actually match, and are more alluring than the saggy articles I resort to these days. Maybe stockings, suspenders.

Corny, I know, but Jed would love that. It doesn't feel quite right, buying underwear in a supermarket, but he'll be far too excited to check labels.

I glide around the aisles, lulled by the bland music, ridiculously grateful to Mum for having the children overnight. After choosing supper ingredients, I browse the make-up section. While hardly vast, it's still overwhelming. Are the colours I used to wear hopelessly outdated, along with my *au naturelle* do? I'm supposed to know what looks good. It's my job, and I have enough regular clients to know that I'm reasonably good at it. Here, though, I'm lost in an ocean of lip plumpers and mineral face powders – make-up that didn't exist the last time I bought any. I grab a blusher, a smoky grey eye shadow and a sheer lipstick, making a mental note to hide them from Toby. Then, on a roll, I snatch some razors and passion-flower body lotion.

In the underwear aisle the knickers seem to fall into two categories – thongs or industrial old-lady pants – neither of which I had in mind. A man with generous chin-folds sidles up next to me and gives me a slimy, wet-lipped grin. This is the kind of male attention I attract these days. Middle-aged, sweating perverts who spend their Friday nights in the lingerie aisle. I realise with horror that that's how a stranger might describe *me*, lurking here, not quite knowing what to do with myself. Quickly, I grab a black lacy bra and knicker ensemble, then black stockings and any old random suspender belt and stuff them into my basket. Without checking the sizes, I hurtle towards the checkout.

My stomach rumbles as I join the queue, and I eye the king prawns in the clear plastic packet in my basket. Is it normal to lust over food the way I do? To feel constantly ravenous? The checkout boy, who looks all of twelve, is taking an age to barcode-bleep everything. Finally, it's my turn. I place my purchases on the conveyor belt, trying to conceal the underwear by laying the bag of rocket on top of it. The boy picks up the rocket and stares at the scraps of black lace. Only, they're not just black lace. Neatly stitched between the bra cups – and at the front of the knickers, I now realise – are tiny pink satin teddy bears stitched with the words 'Hugga Bubba'.

The boy smirks. I grimace back, willing him to bleep everything at breakneck speed so I can get out before my head bursts. 'No price on this,' he announces, dangling the suspender belt delicately between thumb and forefinger.

'I can get another one if you like,' I blurt out, blood swirling in my ears.

'No, it's okay . . . Cathy! Can you get another one of these? What size is it?' He turns to me.

'Um, medium, I think.' I wonder what might be the most efficient way of committing suicide in Tesco. Impaling myself on a cooking utensil? Or hiding until closing time, then shutting myself in a freezer? A woman with her lips pressed into a prim, scarlet line stands behind me in the queue. Her eyes meet mine. *Medium?* she's obviously thinking. *A little optimistic, aren't we, love?* I glance down at her basket. It contains soya milk, porridge oats and a punnet of raspberries. No pervo underwear. No desperate woman trying to perk up her disinterested husband on a Saturday night. Bitterly, I wonder if he's finished that book yet.

Somehow, though, by the time Cathy returns with another suspender belt, I'm beyond embarrassment and decide to just brazen it out. 'Thanks,' I say grandly, giving it a little twirl before dropping it into my shopping bag. 'Have a great evening.'

'You too,' the checkout boy says, grinning. As I leave, making a supreme effort to walk tall and proud – with a slight *sashay*, actually – I feel the scarlet-lipped woman's eyes boring into the back of my head. Who cares what she thinks? I am Laura Swan, a mother of three but also a woman, dammit, who is *reclaiming her sexuality*.

I march home, swinging my bag and breathing in the cool, soft air of a perfect April evening. Tonight will bring Jed back to me, I can feel it.

CHAPTER TEN

As I stride home, I figure that maybe Jed was right. Who needs a hotel room when there's a child-free house on offer? Lighting some candles and playing our music – without Finn thrashing his drum kit above our heads – will create a romantic ambience. I picture the two of us, snuggled up on the sofa, in a flattering candlelit glow. I won't bring up the Celeste stuff – not tonight. Anyway, I'm sure Simone's right. What's wrong with having a friend of the opposite sex? I should lighten up, learn to keep things in perspective.

I let myself in, pleased that I've cunningly concealed my saucy new lingerie at the bottom of the bag. However, I needn't have worried about Jed spotting it and the surprise being ruined. Clearly beside himself with lust at the prospect of my return, he's asleep in the armchair. His head has lolled to one side, and his bottom lip reverberates slightly with each soft snore. Hardly alluring, but at least he'll be nice and rested for later.

I creep through to the kitchen and unpack the shopping, plotting what to get up to later in bed. Will it be wild, like in the old days, or affectionate and gentle? I don't mind either way. Hell, I'll take whatever I can get. Just a kiss and a cuddle would be fine, if he's too *tired* for anything else. I do worry, though, that it's not normal to think about sex as often as I do, and that I'm having some kind of hormonal breakdown. Whenever the subject comes up among the playgroup mums, the others start cackling that they'd rather have a quiet lie down with no one pawing at them, or a DVD and a box of chocolates. 'Give me *Coronation Street* any day,' I heard Ruth groan last week. The difference is, their men actually *want* to do it. Yet these women talk about sex as something to be got over and done with, like having a wasps' nest removed from the loft.

Gathering up my saucy undies and beauty accoutrements, I tiptoe upstairs to the bathroom, ashamed at how surly I've been with Jed these past few months. He doesn't deserve it. He's a fantastic dad with endless time and patience for the children. It's not just sport, either: he thinks nothing of spending hours working on incredible Lego constructions, which Toby finds hilarious to smash up into pieces. He'll even set up foul-smelling science experiments in the kitchen. As for our lack of bedtime action, he's probably worn out, that's all. Aren't I knackered most of the time? Maybe we're just out of practice – plus, I'm hardly comfortable prancing around in the nude with my body looking so mournful and collapsed.

So what if he has a silly, schoolboy's crush? It's natural to fancy other people. It doesn't *mean* anything. Didn't I experience a distinct flickering of – well, not *desire* exactly, but something for Danny in Starbucks? It was the attention, that's all. I picture my male friends from college and wonder if it might be possible to ever have a man friend again. Would Jed mind? No, of course he wouldn't. He'd be glad to see me all cheered up and perky.

I undress in the bathroom and step into the shower's

steamy blast. As I run the cheap plastic razor over my legs and underarms, I start wondering if I should extend my endeavours elsewhere. What did that supplement say about *au naturelle*? I'm probably the last woman in Britain not to have a Brazilian. What *is* a Brazilian exactly? Is it as important to have one in Yorkshire as it is in Brazil?

I survey my soft, pale body as the water gushes down it. To be fair, it's not a total disaster. My boobs are quite enviable, I guess. My stomach and bum . . . no, let's gloss over those. As for my legs, they are reasonably shapely, even if things start to go horribly wrong around the thigh region.

I glare down at my pubes. They certainly need a little tidying, but I'm worried I'll mess this up. At least with head hair, if you're given a botched cut, you can derive faint pleasure at switching allegiance to a new salon. Thankfully, Simone always cuts mine, always praising its abundance and shine. That's one part of my anatomy I don't have to worry about. With this, I'd have no one to blame but myself. 'Laura, are you okay?' Jed calls from downstairs. Ah, the beast awakens.

'I'm in the shower,' I shout back.

'Shall I start cooking? I'm starving.'

'No, I'll do it, won't be long.' The razor hovers at the tops of my thighs. *Just do it. You're a grown woman at the helm of family life. How can you be scared of a little light pruning, for God's sake? Naomi probably has hers ripped off with hot wax.*

As the razor rasps across my skin, I wonder how far to take this. I tinker around gingerly until one side seems done. It certainly looks, whilst not better exactly, decidedly tidier. 'Laura!' Jed yells again. He's upstairs on the landing now. It feels weird, just the two of us here in our echoey house. I turn down the shower to a dribble so I can hear him properly.

71

'What is it?'

'Will you be much longer?' He raps loudly on the bathroom door. 'I need the loo.' He waggles the handle and will be wondering why on earth I've locked the door. We usually do all that bathroom stuff in front of each other, which might be another factor in the demise of our sex life.

'Hang on,' I call out, still gripping the razor, rapidly losing my nerve. The shaved bit doesn't look tidier. It looks scalped and chickeny, like something you'd see in the chill cabinet with a barcode slapped on it.

'Could you let me in?' he demands.

'I, um . . .' I glower down. One side still requires attention, and looks even more *au naturelle* when compared to the bald region. It's like when I wallpapered Grace's bedroom before Christmas. The fresh new spotty design made the rest of the house look condemned.

'Laura!' Jed thunders. 'I'm desperate.'

'Just a minute—'

'Let me in!' He raps on the door.

Jesus, it's like having a fourth child. Haven't I been saying, since we had Toby, that we urgently need a second loo? It drives me insane, this constant hammering every time I'm in here for more than a second. Is it any wonder I'm a little unkempt? Naomi has not one but *two* ensuites, like bloody royalty – one for her, one for buffed-up hubby. Switching off the shower, I wrap myself in a towel and unlock the door.

Although clearly on the point of combustion, Jed still manages to fling me a disdainful look as if I'm something he's narrowly avoided treading in on the pavement. He strides to the loo and starts to pee, emitting a groan of relief which

I find enormously off-putting. I glare at the back of him as he sploshes noisily, deciding that it doesn't matter if I'm poultry-like down there as I'll never be intimate with him again. I'll grow fatter and hairier with many cats.

For one brief moment, I wish I was playing with the children and the train set at Mum's.

In the sanctuary of our bedroom, I examine my handiwork as Jed pads downstairs. Although I look freakish, I don't have it in me to jump back into the shower and finish off the job. I pull on my new underwear and survey my reflection in our full-length mirror on which Toby has crayoned a person with stick legs and stick arms and a brick-shaped torso. I assume it's supposed to be me. My face is pink from the shower, my hair straggly and dripping down my chest. The new bra is a little baggy in the cups. The knickers are cut lower than my preferred style, and lack the reinforcements required to hold in my tummy. I don't look like a woman who's on the brink of making her husband faint with desire. I look like a clapped-out mother who buys her underwear two aisles along from the gherkins.

Gamely, I pull on the suspender belt – remembering too late that the knickers are supposed to go on top of it – then the stockings. The suspender belt's clips are a devil to snap on. Every time I manage to get one done up, another pings off. It's even more fiddly than Finn's old Meccano set. Why didn't I buy hold-up stockings? Because I planned to go for full-on foxery, haha.

I dart into Grace's room, rummage in her craft box for scissors and snip the Hugga Bubba teddies off my underwear. As a joke, I place them on her pillow. I'm overcome by a surge of longing, wishing she were here, wishing *all* the children were here, and that this was an ordinary family evening with bedtime stories and tucking in and Jed and I watching a movie together. Our normal life isn't so bad. I want too much, that's the problem. My expectations have shot off the scale, like would-be Angelina Jolie's at the salon. I should be content with the way things are. Look at Mum, with her art classes and volunteering, trying to fill the void where Dad used to be.

Why didn't he tell anyone he was ill? Because he didn't want to worry us, not even Mum. Then he had to tell her, of course, and then they told Kate because she's eight years older than me and far more sensible and capable. It was Kate who called, when I was trying to coax Toby onto the potty, and said, 'Laura, I'm sorry to tell you this, but I think you should know. Dad's really ill.'

I'd known he'd been for tests, and Mum had implied that it was something to do with cholesterol or blood pressure and that a change of diet would fix everything. She didn't mention the cancer that had spread to his spine. 'It's the shock,' I told Jed, tears pouring down my cheeks. 'If they'd warned me, I might have been ready. I might have been prepared.' He'd kissed and held me and, for a moment, he was my boyfriend again, who always managed, somehow, to make things better. Jed knew how close I'd been to Dad.

In our bedroom, I hold up my new emerald dress. I don't have the courage to carry it off – not with the shaving disaster lurking beneath. Instead, I pull on a more demure polka-dot sundress which used to be one of Jed's favourites but is faded and must be at least five years old. It's an improvement, though. I definitely look better clothed than

74

naked. I dab on my new make-up and try to adopt an expression of hope.

Downstairs, Jed is engrossed in his book. In the kitchen, I set the pasta to boil and follow the recipe with the prawns, rocket and chilli. The chillies look so pretty, flecking the prawns with deep red, that I sling in a few extra. Maybe my culinary gene is reawakening. I'm actually enjoying myself, creating a meal from scratch that doesn't involve sausages or the potato masher. I might not be able to make felt purses, or be half-French, but I can knock together a delicious supper and make myself look presentable (at least, *half*-presentable).

I carry our supper, cutlery and glasses of wine from the kitchen to the back garden. Our ancient iron table looks far too rusty and unhygienic to eat off, so I place everything on the garden wall while I hurry back in for a tablecloth. The only one I can find has an indelible orangey stain, but it'll do. Grabbing a bunch of tea lights, I set the table, placing my plate over the stain. 'Ready!' I call from the back door.

Jed appears, still clutching his book. 'We're eating outside?'

'Yes, why not? It's a lovely evening.' With a flourish, I light the tea lights and survey the scene.

'Oh . . . okay. I'll need a jacket though.'

'Get one then,' I say sweetly. It is a bit chilly, but I'm not going to spoil the effect of the dress with a jacket or even a cardi. I shall freeze my arse off instead.

Jed reappears in an Arctic-worthy jacket, thankfully devoid of book, and perches on a wobbly metal chair. I wait for him to register my new make-up and exclaim, 'Wow, Laura, you look gorgeous tonight. Let me kiss you, irresistible wife!'

Nothing is forthcoming. Next time Jed and I have a hot date, I may wear a boiler suit.

I glance around our garden. The bleak rectangle is bordered by brick walls all shedding their white paint skins. The borders are already sprouting weeds. 'You know,' I murmur, 'we really should do something with this place.'

'Like what?' Jed prods a pasta quill. He looks so good, so strong-jawed and handsome in the yellowy flicker of the tea lights, even with his big fat jacket on.

'Get some pots,' I suggest, 'or hanging baskets. Maybe even some turf to make a proper lawn.'

'Feel free,' he says with a chuckle, 'but I don't imagine it'd stay perfect for long. The kids would soon mess it up.'

'It wouldn't have to be perfect,' I insist. 'It could be wild, full of colour like, like—'

'Like . . . your dad's garden?' he says gently.

I nod. Dad lived for his garden. Finn would help him to plant things, when he was still eager to please. He even had a notebook in which he'd document what he'd planted and when the first shoots appeared. 'My cornflowers came up!' Finn wrote carefully, and Mum let us cut some to bring home. As Dad grew sicker, the borders ran wild. 'He'll knock it back into shape when he's better,' Mum would say as the exuberant colours blurred beneath a blanket of weeds. I could have helped, if I'd known. After Dad had gone, Mum had the whole garden turfed over.

'You okay, love?' Jed asks.

'I'm fine.' I muster a smile. 'I just think the kids would enjoy the garden more if we spruced it up.'

'There's the park, though, isn't there?' He forks in some pasta and splutters dramatically. 'God, Laura! How much chilli did you put in this?'

'Just what the recipe said,' I say curtly.

'Oh, wow . . . this is bloody hot.' He slugs his wine and starts blowing out air.

I take a tentative nibble. It tastes fine at first, if a little fiery. Then the heat builds up until an inferno tears at my throat. 'There's nothing wrong with it,' I croak, my eyes streaming as I fork in an enormous mouthful to prove just how bloody fine and delicious it is.

'I can't eat this,' Jed announces, lurching inside to the kitchen. I hear the tap being turned on full blast. My entire digestive system is combusting. No amount of chilled white wine can cool my throat. I slam down my fork and march into the kitchen where Jed is bent under the kitchen tap with cold water gushing directly into his mouth.

'It's not *that* bad,' I rasp, my mouth searing. 'You're acting like one of the kids.'

He straightens up and dabs his face with a tea towel. 'Oh, isn't it? So I suppose you don't want some water?'

'Um, yes please.' He hands me a glassful, which I gulp down. 'Sorry,' I murmur. 'I threw in a few extra chillies to make it look colourful.'

'Right,' he snorts. 'Like a little garden or something?'

'Something like that,' I say as he fills a second glass for me. The back door is open, and the tea lights flicker feebly on the table.

'Hey,' Jed says gently, sliding his arms around me. 'I'm sorry, love. I know you went to a lot of effort.'

'It's okay. It was my fault.'

'Look,' he adds hesitantly. 'I . . . I know I've been . . . wrapped up in other things lately . . .'

Like Celeste? 'I suppose we're just not used to being together anymore,' I cut in quickly. It feels so good, being held by him, that I don't want to spoil it by saying her name.

'Of course we are,' Jed says. 'We just don't have the chance very often.' He pulls back to study my face. 'You smell good,' he adds. '*And* you're wearing make-up. It suits you.'

'Oh, it's just some old stuff I found . . .'

'Well, you look lovely.'

'Thank you.' I smile, stretch up and kiss his soft lips. Then we're kissing and kissing, and it doesn't matter that I ruined our meal, or that Jed has spent the past four months in some parallel universe, because right now everything feels perfect. His hands, which were resting gently around my waist, slide down over my hips, pausing as he detects the suspender clips. He raises an eyebrow and smiles. 'You *have* gone to a lot of effort.'

'It's amazing what you can buy at Tesco these days.'

'Tesco?' He laughs softly. 'Classy.' Then he clutches my hand, as if it's something he'd lost and has just found and says, 'We, um . . . we could just go to bed.'

'Okay,' I say, grinning. 'If you insist.'

My heart is pounding as we climb the stairs together, the way it did the first time we kissed. We'd met at a party. Jed had just started out in teaching, and I'd vaguely known one of his housemates from college. *What if?* was our favourite game back then. *What if your date hadn't stood you up?* he'd ask me. *What if you hadn't gone home feeling totally fed up, and played that message from Helen who you hadn't heard from in years? What if you hadn't rung her straight back? What if she hadn't invited you to our party? What if my girlfriend hadn't dumped me, and I hadn't been sitting on the stairs, pissed off, nursing a warm bottle of Becks?*

He'd known instantly, he insisted, although he hadn't been remotely aware that I'd spied him too, the moment I'd walked in. Jed is oblivious to women's glances and flirtations. But he'd spotted me, breezing in and brimming with confidence, as if I had no expectations of the night ahead because so far it had been crapper than crapsville. 'And you thought I was just being friendly,' I used to tease him. 'You had no idea how cute you were. What did I have to do? Take you home to bed! The lengths I had to go to to make you realise I was crazy about you . . .'

'Even then, I thought I was just a sympathy lay,' he laughed.

Jed and I reach the landing. Hell, my unfinished chicken-shave job. 'I'm just going to the bathroom,' I murmur.

Disappointment flickers in his eyes. 'Don't be long this time.'

'I'll only be a minute. Honestly. There's just, um, something I need to do.'

It takes longer than a minute as I strip naked and stand at the sink, trying to make myself symmetrical as speedily as possible without causing myself irreversible damage. My libido is ebbing away rapidly. The stockings have formed a crimped ring around the top of each thigh. In my eagerness to escape from that perv in Tesco, I must have grabbed too small a size.

I'm covered in suds, and water dribbles in rivulets down my legs as I try to wash them away. The floor is soaked, and I mop up the water with a fraying bath towel and an old T-shirt of Jed's. By the time I'm back in my wretched under-wear and padding tentatively into our bedroom, he is tucked up in bed with one arm slung across my pillow. 'Hi,' I whisper, slipping in under the duvet. I slide a hand across his chest which prompts him to roll away from me.

I study his broad, lightly tanned back and shoulders, which rise with each inhalation. Soft snores fill the room. It would appear that my hot date for tonight has fallen asleep.

CHAPTER ELEVEN

Beth and I are unloading the toys from the playgroup cupboard. The children clamour around us, their voices echoing in the dusty hall. We lift the lid from the sandpit and fill it with mini trucks and diggers; we top up the water tray, drop in some little plastic boats and set out books in the reading area. I glance at her, my best mummy-friend looking lithe and faintly Boden-esque in her narrow jeans and snug-fitting raspberry T-shirt. 'Beth,' I say later, fixing us a coffee from the grumbling urn, 'how do you do it?'

'Do what?' she asks.

'Stay so slim and fit. I've been thinking, I really have to do something. I'm sick of being like this.' I glare down at my body in its loose jeans and even looser black top.

'But you're lovely as you are,' she insists. 'Men are always looking at you. You must realise that. You're sexy and voluptuous and—'

'Voluptuous? That means fat, Beth! The other day, I couldn't even do up the zip on my biggest jeans. They're a size sixteen!'

'Well, sizes vary from shop to shop,' she says firmly, nibbling a pink wafer biscuit. 'They're irrelevant really.'

'Not when you're going *up* in size. Then it's horribly relevant, I can assure you . . .'

'Oh, Laura. You look great, honestly. Anyway, no one's the same after having kids, are they?'

'I bet *you* are,' I say.

'You might think so, but I'm a disaster down here.' She pats her taut stomach. 'But after having two children, what can I expect?'

I set down my cup and tip out boxes of building blocks for the younger children. 'The thing is, I don't expect to be like I was before the children,' I add. 'I'd just like to not be expanding, to be able to resist all the snacks and biscuits . . .'

'What's brought this on, hon?' she murmurs.

'Oh, I don't know. That mums' race, I suppose. Me getting all dressed up for Jed the other night, even buying new underwear, even *stockings* . . .'

'Whoa,' she says with a grin. 'Lucky Jed.'

'Well, he wasn't. By the time I climbed into bed, he was already asleep.'

'You should've been quicker,' she sniggers. 'What took you so long?'

I smirk, deciding that playgroup isn't the place to tell Beth about my chicken-shave job. 'I was getting ready,' I murmur.

She rolls her eyes. 'Well, make sure you're quicker next time. He was probably just knackered. You should see Pete, falling asleep virtually every time he sits down. It's a man thing. They come home and switch off and, next thing, it's full-on REM sleep. Next time, give him a sharp prod and wake him up, especially if you've gone to all the bother of wearing stockings. I mean, what a bloody waste!'

I laugh, thinking, if only it was that simple. 'I can imagine how he'd react if I rudely interrupted his beauty sleep,' I murmur.

As the session progresses, the noise level increases to ear-splitting levels. Jack, Beth's three-year-old, grabs a scooter and hurtles recklessly across the gleaming wooden floor, bellowing out a shrill siren noise. Meanwhile, Toby proceeds to bang the metal xylophone furiously. 'Not so loud!' I call over.

'I'm playing music,' he yells back.

'Yes, I know, but—'

'No, it's mine!' he screams as a pig-tailed blonde tries to wrestle the hammer from his grasp.

'Toby, it's *not* yours.' I rush towards him, but not fast enough to stop him whacking the girl on the forehead with the hammer. Screaming, she tears across the hall to be scooped up by her furious, red-faced mother. It's their first time here. I doubt if they'll ever come back.

'I'm so sorry,' I witter, scuttling over to check on the damage, as if I'm responsible for the throbbing pink splodge on the weeping child's forehead. In a way, I guess I am. I'm Toby's mother, his prime carer who's supposedly in charge of teaching him how to behave nicely and kindly to others. Although he still demands to come to playgroup, and clearly enjoys it, he's one of the oldest kids here and has really outgrown it. Maybe these violent outbursts are due to the fact that I'm not stimulating him enough.

'It's okay,' the girl's mother says, her eyes steely. 'I don't think she's *concussed* or anything.'

'God, I hope not. I'm so, so sorry. I think he was just, er, overexcited.'

The woman pulls in her lips and turns away from me. 'Come on, Emily, darling. Let's find you someone else to play with.' Someone who's not intent on causing GBH, is what she means.

'You must never hit anyone like that,' I bark, marching back to the music corner where Toby looks totally unconcerned. 'That was very, very naughty and you've made a big pink mark on that little girl's head. I want you to go over and say sorry.'

'No!' he yells, haring off to play with the doll's house at the far end of the hall. He doesn't play gentle games with it. The miniature people don't sit around having quaint tea parties. If Toby's involved, there has to be a fire, a burglary or some dreadful natural disaster. 'It's *my* xylophone,' I hear him muttering.

Beth hands me another polystyrene cup of insipid coffee. 'I can't control him,' I murmur, trying to steady my breathing. 'God knows what he'll be like when he starts school.'

'Jack's just the same. He drives Kira crazy, always trying to barge in and trash her room. And this morning he pulled down one of the living room curtains to wear as a cape . . .'

I smile, feeling marginally reassured. Toby's behaviour probably is normal, at least for our family; Finn and Grace were a handful too, forever clambering all over the kitchen worktops and balancing perilously on the garden wall. However, I seemed to cope better when they were little, and fear that my reserves of tolerance have reached critically low levels.

Beth and I perch on the windowsill and sip our coffees. I was relieved to meet her, when we'd just moved to Yorkshire. Not only did she have big-age-gap children around Toby and Finn's ages; she also didn't assume I was some poncey, over-precious mother just because I'd come from London, as a few women seemed to. 'Are you still running these days?' I ask her.

She shakes her head. 'No, I've let it slide really. All that getting up at the crack of dawn, and going out before Pete went to work . . .'

'That takes dedication,' I murmur.

'Plus,' she adds, prodding a hip, 'I was starting to feel creaky. Age, I guess,' she says, smiling. 'It's not great for the joints.'

'Who cares about joints?' I snigger.

'You would, if you were an old crock like me . . .'

'You know what?' I say, filled with sudden enthusiasm. 'I think I might give it a try. Maybe that's what I need. Exercise I can just do, whenever Jed's home and I get the chance to go out. It'd be a lot simpler than going to the gym, and it might shift this . . .' I poke my belly.

'Good for you,' she says. 'It's brilliant actually. Great for stress levels too. I'd come with you, keep you company, but I don't think the old knees could take it.'

'Don't worry,' I say, laughing. 'I'd have to go in the middle of the night anyway. Couldn't risk being seen, could I?'

She shakes her head despairingly as I take my ringing mobile from my pocket. It's Jed, which is unusual. He rarely phones during the day. 'School boiler's broken,' he explains, 'so I'm coming home early. Just wondered where you were.'

'At playgroup,' I tell him, adding, as a joke, 'Why don't you come along?'

'I, um . . . where is it?' he asks, sounding alarmed.

'St Mary's Hall. Didn't you know that, Jed?' I tease him.

'Well, er . . .'

'It's on until three,' I add. 'Come on, you'll love it and you'll give all the mums here a treat.'

'Well, er, I was just, um . . .'

85

'Great. See you soon, love. Bye!' I finish the call and grin at Beth.

'What's happening?' she asks.

'I've just done something I've been trying to do for years. I've persuaded Jed to come to playgroup.'

'He actually agreed?'

'Well, not exactly,' I snigger.

'So we're going to meet him at last?' exclaims Ruth, who's dishing out bowls of chopped fruit for the children.

'Yep, it's your lucky day.' In fact, I'm slightly embarrassed that few of these women have met Jed. I suspect that most of them don't believe I have a man at all, and that the children were conceived by an anonymous donor.

'Hey, girls!' Ruth announces. 'Better get your lippy on. There's going to be a man in our midst.'

There's a burst of laughter, and Ruth is only half-joking. Despite claiming to prefer *Coronation Street* to sex, most of these women are tragically starved of male company. It's not about wanting to sleep with random blokes. We just want to revel in their maleness.

When Jed strolls in twenty minutes later, there's a palpable ripple of excitement, and I catch Ruth primping her sleek auburn hair and wiping an imaginary smear from her cheek. 'Daddy!' Toby charges towards him, still gripping that blasted xylophone hammer.

'Hey, little man.' Jed hugs him, then looks around for me.

'Everyone, this is Jed,' I announce, a little too loudly as I go over to greet him. 'He's new here. Please be gentle with him.'

'Like a tea or coffee?' Rush gushes, even though the etiquette here is that adults help themselves to drinks.

'Coffee would be nice,' Jed says meekly.

'How d'you take it?'

'Just milk please.' He sits gingerly on a too-small plastic chair and throws me an anxious glance. It's not that dads aren't welcome here; they simply don't come. I have no idea how full-time fathers fill their days.

'Biscuit?' Ruth trills, twirling a tendril of hair.

'Yes . . . er . . . great.'

'Penguin, Jaffa Cake or wafer?' *Or would you prefer oral sex?*

'Yes please,' Jed says. 'I, um, I mean anything. I don't mind.'

'I'll bring you a selection,' Ruth says, fanning an array of snacklets on a plate and slinking across the scuffed parquet floor towards him. As Keeper of Biscuits she must have a secret supply of chocolate varieties which she brings out once a decade when a handsome man happens to walk in. We mothers are lucky to get a stale fig roll.

'You're a brave man, Jed,' Beth laughs, 'joining us rowdy lot for the afternoon. Bet school's a walk in the park compared to this.'

He grins, taking his coffee and biscuit (chocolate Hobnob, damn him) from a drooling Ruth. 'Oh, it's not so bad,' he chuckles. 'I could probably get used to this.'

'Well, you're welcome any time,' Ruth simpers.

Jed smiles unsteadily. After downing his drink, he helps a bunch of children to construct a train track with a myriad of bridges and sidings. By the time we're ready to leave, I suspect that several of the women are on the verge of climaxing. 'You've never mentioned how gorgeous he is,' Ruth hisses. 'God, Laura. He's an absolute darling. You're *so* lucky.'

'Oh, he's all right,' I snigger. Even the vexed mother

– whose daughter is now sporting an impressive forehead egg – is regarding us more kindly now that Jed's in our midst.

The three of us leave playgroup and head towards school with Toby skipping ahead on the pavement. I'm startled when Jed takes my hand and curls his fingers around mine. 'Did I mention,' he says lightly, 'that Celeste's having a party on Saturday?'

'Is she? What for?'

'It's her thirtieth.'

'Thirty? She's only *thirty*?' I clamp my mouth shut. I'd realised she was younger than me, but hadn't realised there's almost a decade between us. Now I feel prehistoric.

'Uh-huh,' Jed says. 'Well, twenty-nine at the moment.'

'I . . . I'm not sure we'll be able to get a babysitter at such short notice,' I say quickly.

'We don't need one. It's an afternoon thing. A garden party.'

'What, like the Queen has?'

Jed lets my hand drop. 'It's just a *party*, Laura. You know – people chatting, having fun . . . it's really not a big deal.' He rolls his eyes at me.

'And Celeste's okay with children, is she?' What am I saying? She's a primary school teacher. Of course she's okay with children. It's like asking a surgeon if he's okay with blood.

'Of course she's fine. We're all invited and she said there'll be loads of kids there. Don't you want to go? You were complaining that we never go out.'

'Of course I want to go,' I say shrilly. 'It's just . . .'

'Can I come to Celeste's party?' Toby spins round delightedly.

'Yes, darling,' I say, keeping my voice perky. 'Of course you can. We'll all go.'

'Will there be cake?'

'I'm sure there will,' Jed chuckles as we approach school and join the cluster of parents all gathered around the gate. I spot several mothers checking Jed out – like an exotic bird, he's rarely spotted around these parts – and instinctively slip my hand into his. He squeezes mine back, triggering a surge of warmth in me. Hell, why shouldn't we all go to Celeste's party? It'll be a prime opportunity to show how *together* Jed and I are – how close and in love, despite his infatuation. It might even be a chance to get to know her properly. We hardly got off to a good start at the pub, when I made that terrible joke about being taken back to the institution. She's probably *a very nice person*, if only I'd give her a chance.

I should lighten up. The old Laura loved a party, and I could wow Jed by wearing my new emerald dress. I glance at my husband, proud that he stepped into my funny, daytime playgroup world and passed with flying colours. It's time I dipped my toe into his world too. But first, drastic action is required.

CHAPTER TWELVE

I walk quickly, head bent against the rain, wishing I'd considered wearing some kind of disguise. A balaclava, perhaps, or Santa's beard and moustache from the kids' dressing-up box, although that might look bizarre at the end of April. Only Jed knows where I'm going. When the children asked, I just said, 'I'm popping out to a meeting', as if that's something I'm prone to doing on a Thursday evening.

Outside St Mary's Hall, a cluster of women are laughing rowdily as they make their way in through the door. I bring Toby here for playgroup two afternoons a week, but tonight the place has a very different vibe. You'd think they were going to a party. No one looks remotely depressed, which must be a good sign. 'Hi, Laura,' exclaims Kirsty, a statuesque auburn beauty who's one of my regular clients at the salon. 'Are you joining us tonight?'

'Yes,' I say hesitantly. 'Thought I'd take the plunge. Not too scary, is it?'

'Oh, we're all friends here,' she laughs. 'It's great – I've lost a stone in six weeks. Couldn't have done it on my own. Come on, you can sit with me.'

I grin stoically and follow her inside, still worrying that, despite her reassurances, I'll have my weight boomed out through a megaphone and my fat bits measured with a sinister pincer device. Jed couldn't believe I was going tonight. 'Are you sure about this?' he'd asked, furrowing his brow. 'It sounds a bit . . . desperate.'

'I *am* desperate,' I'd replied.

'Well, I think you're fine as you are,' he'd added, although recent evidence suggests the contrary.

'Quite a scrum this week,' Kirsty observes as we squeeze into the hall's entrance area. Everyone seems to be clustering outside the loo. I'm surprised to see so many familiar faces: an elderly lady from down our street, a couple of girls who work at Scamps nursery, and the woman who sold me a highchair after Grace had somehow managed to dismantle hers at three years old. All greet me as if this were a perfectly ordinary evening out.

'That can't be the queue for the loo,' I whisper to Kirsty.

'Afraid so. Everyone goes before weigh-in,' she explains.

'Why? Are they nervous?'

'No,' she says, sniggering. 'So they're *lighter*.'

'You mean it really makes a difference? Surely a teeny amount of wee can't alter your weight . . .'

'Oh yes it does. Every ounce counts, our great leader says. Hope you're wearing something heavy tonight – that way, you're bound to lose for next week.'

I unbutton my trenchcoat and hold it open. 'Does this look heavy enough to you?'

Kirsty frowns, scrutinising my outfit. 'Your jeans are fine. Sweater's a bit on the light side, maybe you should've gone for a chunkier knit . . .'

'My boots are heavy, though . . .'

'Yes,' she snorts, 'but you take those *off* for weigh-in.' Damn. There was no mention of heavy clothing on the Super

Slimmers flier I saw in the newsagent's window. 'Embrace the new you!' was all it had said, plus a phone number and the promise of a 'fun, supportive atmosphere' and an idiot-proof eating plan. If I'd known, I'd have worn several outfits on top of each other.

My stomach churns nervously as Kirsty and I step into the main hall. Despite Ruth's stinginess with the biscuits, I'm yearning for the familiar turf of playgroup. A girl with a waist measurement of around twenty inches takes our money. 'First time?' she asks, flashing large, gleaming teeth.

'Yes.'

'Here you go. This is your Menu Masterplan' – she thrusts me a glossy booklet depicting a woman grasping a banana in a rather phallic manner – 'and your membership card. Fill in your name and address but *not* your weight, as we'll have to weigh you accurately.' She smiles encouragingly, and I smile back, wondering if she's implying that I might fib on the card, thus guaranteeing a gargantuan loss next week. *If* I come next week. I wasn't intending to carry on with this after Celeste's party. A quick fix – that's what I want. A short, sharp shock. Kirsty pounces on two vacant seats at the back of the hall, for which I am hugely grateful.

I glance around the room. It's filled with row upon row of chairs with a makeshift stage at the front. There's a table on the stage, laden with foil-covered plates, and the air is thick with excitable chatter. So where do I fit in in the fat stakes? Several woman are hugely, almost *heroically* fat, and are bantering jovially as if this is somewhere they come for fun rather than because they ought to. The majority, though, are around my size – women who might once have given their weight little thought until pregnancy and child-rearing made them rounder and softer and added a stone or two. I wonder if their husbands still find them attractive and go to bed without the protective armour of pyjama bottoms. There's no reason why not. They are all well dressed, with make-up and hair nicely done. They are perfectly presentable, and seem happy with life.

Further perusal reveals that several women are decidedly *thinner* than me. That doesn't seem right. 'Claire Holloway's lost three stone,' Kirsty whispers, as if reading my thoughts. 'She's hoping to reach her target this week.'

'What happens then?'

'Everyone claps,' Kirsty says.

'Is that all? God, I'd want more than that! I'd want cake and champagne at the very least.'

Kirsty giggles, and the woman in front spins round to throw us an irritated look. 'The thing is not to regard food as a reward,' Kirsty adds, lowering her voice. I nod, mulling this over. Do I do that? I don't think so. I eat to cheer myself up, sure, but mostly because I'm hungry, or because food is there and it tastes bloody fantastic. How am I supposed to think myself out of that?

A tall, slim-hipped woman in an elegant grey trouser suit strides onto the stage. 'Hello, ladies,' she says grandly, scanning the hall. 'And gentlemen of course . . . do we have our *male member* here?'

At this, everyone laughs. 'No?' she enquires. 'Well, let's get started anyway. Any newcomers, I'm Belinda, your group leader. As you came in, you'll have been given our Menu Masterplan. You'll see that there are no tricks here, no miracle solutions' – aren't there? Damn – 'as *slow and steady* is our motto at Super Slimmers. It's all about willpower, ladies, and making the right choices in life. It worked for me, and it can work for you too.' She grins expectantly. My heart slumps to my boots.

'Slow and steady?' I whisper to Kirsty. 'That's not what I want. I've got a party to go to in two days' time.'

'You'll have to be strict then,' she hisses back.

I waggle my Menu Masterplan at her. 'Maybe I'll stop eating altogether and just nibble the corner of this.' She snorts through her nose and directs her attentions to our Leader. God, I'm starving. Couldn't face dinner before I came out, and now my stomach is rumbling ominously. I wonder what's on those foil-covered plates on the table, and when Belinda will get around to sharing it out. On my other side, a woman in a shiny floral dress is texting urgently on her mobile. Bet it says WILL PICK UP FISH & CHIPS ON WAY HOME.

Hmmm, I can almost smell vinegary chips.

'Now,' Belinda announces, 'let me explain what we do here.' *We make you thin*, I will her to say. *You'll waltz into that garden party and be wondrous.* 'I start with a short talk every week,' she explains, 'which I hope you'll find inspiring. There's time for questions and answers, then we do weigh-in at the end.' She scans the room expectantly. 'So, if we're all ready, this week I'm going to talk about tuna.'

An aura of rapt interest descends. 'Tuna,' Belinda says gravely, 'is a slimmer's best friend – but it's vital that we choose the right type. Can anyone tell me which type that is?' Her dramatically arched eyebrows shoot up.

'It should be in water or brine,' someone pipes up. 'Never oil.'

'That's right!' Belinda exclaims as if a child of Toby's age has explained the theory of relativity. 'Now, let's look at the ways we can use it . . .'

I start to faze off, wondering why I'm here on a damp Thursday night, being told that my best friend is tuna. Maybe it's the club aspect that's the problem. I've never been good at belonging to things. I paid an astronomical amount to belong to Bodyworks gym and didn't shift an ounce. I felt obliged to leave the new mums' book group after Grace vomited over the hostess's glass coffee table, ruining a hand-crocheted doily. It was a relief, really, as it had become apparent that I was incapable of reading anything more taxing than *Dirty Bertie*.

'. . . Try to work out if you're really hungry or just thirsty,' Belinda chunders on. 'You can often quell hunger pangs with a refreshing glass of water . . .'

No, sorry. I have never confused hunger with thirst, although I could murder a drink right now – a proper one, I mean. A nice glass of chilled pinot and a packet of posh crisps or maybe some mixed nuts. 'You can make water more interesting with ice and a squeeze of lemon juice,' Belinda adds. Jesus, how difficult can her job be? She doesn't have to deal with clients with sparse, mousy hair expecting to walk out looking like Keira Knightley. Here, all people want is to be thinner. Maybe I should consider becoming a leader as a way of boosting my earnings. Surely I'd be capable of informing a hall full of women that they should opt for the rocket salad instead of the sausage roll seeping lard.

I eye the foil-covered plates greedily, wishing Belinda would hurry up and get to the eating part. The texting woman has snuck out. I *hope* she's gone to the chippie. 'We all know about mayonnaise, don't we?' Belinda continues. There's a ripple of knowing laughter. Oh yes, I know about mayonnaise. It's bloody delicious. Occasionally, I'll treat myself to a spoonful with cheese on toast. You could probably be shot for that in here. 'Try mixing your tuna with lemon juice instead,' she chirps, 'and save yourself a whole bunch of calories. And remember that we're all friends here, and our job is to support each other . . .' I check my watch. How long will this go on for? We've been here for a quarter of an hour. It feels like seventeen weeks.

'Oh God, not tuna again,' mutters a late-comer, slipping quietly onto the vacant seat beside me.

I turn to look at him. He looks at me, tilts his head and frowns quizzically, and there's a spark of recognition between us. 'Danny?' I whisper. 'From Starbucks in York?'

'The playsuit shoplifter!' he whispers back with a broad smile. 'Well, I'm glad I came tonight.'

I grin, feeling instantly better. 'Me too,' I whisper. Perhaps I'm going to like it here after all.

CHAPTER THIRTEEN

'What are you doing here?' I ask softly as Belinda rambles on about brine and calories, striding back and forth across the stage and waving her manicured hands about.

'Oh, I just come for fun when there's nothing on TV,' Danny replies. 'How about you? This your first time?'

'Yep. D'you think it actually works?'

He surveys his chunky body and frowns. 'I'm worried it's working too well actually. That I'll fade away to nothing.'

I snigger. He's perfectly fine, although a personal trainer would probably put him on some kind of 'programme' like the Bodyworks girl suggested for me. 'Okay, everyone,' Belinda's voice rings out, 'here are some meal ideas which you're welcome to come and look at. Then we'll do weigh-in.'

'*Look* at?' I splutter. 'Don't we get to try?'

'Sadly not,' Danny smirks. 'She just brings piles of food along to taunt us.'

'Do you two know each other?' Kirsty asks as everyone surges towards Belinda's display.

'Er, not really,' I say. 'We just ran into each other in York and got chatting over a coffee. Kirsty, this is Danny.' She pulls a quirky smile, and I feel a flush of pleasure at having a man friend to introduce her to. With a flourish, Belinda has removed the plates' foil coverings. A cluster of women are studying a wilted Niçoise salad as if it were a covetable handbag. There's a baked potato heaped with tuna, presumably in case we'd forgotten what a baked potato looks like, and some kind of fishy layer with a mushed vegetable topping, which Belinda explains is a 'bake'.

'It looks like something you'd see on the pavement outside the pub on a Saturday night,' Danny mutters into my ear.

'It's very tasty actually,' Belinda says defensively.

'Oh, I'm sure it is,' I enthuse. 'I, er, love bakes. They're so . . .'

'Versatile?' Danny chips in.

'And something like this is so easy,' Belinda adds, 'even if you can't cook at all. Even if you're not remotely domesticated.'

I smile tensely, edging towards a dish of low-fat tuna dip which I try to fix with an adoring gaze. The hall has taken on a decidedly fishy whiff, like Grace's lunchbox when it was returned from school after being left in her locker for two weeks. 'Danny's a cutie, isn't he?' murmurs Kirsty, sidling up to me.

'Think so?' I hiss back. 'I suppose he is. I hadn't really noticed.'

'Oh, come on.' She sniggers. 'Don't be so coy. Being happily married doesn't make you immune to other men. You're allowed to look, you know. He has lovely blue eyes, don't say you hadn't noticed? And a sweet, cheeky smile . . .'

'If you say so,' I laugh, wondering if I've been deprived of adult affection for so long that I really *am* immune to other men.

'Is he single?' she asks.

'I've no idea, Kirsty. Like I said, I hardly know . . .'

He reappears at my side. 'Come on,' he says. 'It's our big moment on the scales. Off with your boots.'

'Er, that might be a bit difficult . . .'

'Oh, no need to be shy around here.' He chuckles and glances at my feet.

'It's not that. I mean, I don't care who sees my feet. It's just, these boots are tight and I usually have to ask Jed, my husband, to help me get them off . . .'

Danny snorts with laughter.

'It's not funny! I can't get them off by myself. I bought them in a size too small.'

'Why did you do that?' He sounds mystified.

'They didn't have my size. And I really wanted them.'

'Well,' Danny says, smirking, 'I guess I'll just have to assist, if that doesn't sound too forward.'

'Um . . . would you mind?'

'I'd be delighted.' Jesus, what was I thinking, wearing these boots tonight? I can't see anyone else who needs help to remove their footwear. Women are gawping at us, giggling openly, as I grip the edge of my chair while Danny kneels before me and grapples with my foot.

'Take your time, you two,' Belinda trills with an amused twitch. 'There's no rush.' Clearly, there *is* a rush, as everyone else has been weighed except us. I'm overcome by an urge to forget the weighing part and bolt out of the hall.

'God, this is impossible,' Danny gasps.

'I'm sorry . . .' I grab at my other boot and tug ineffectually. As my feet are slightly swollen – it's far too hot and fishy in here – they're even tighter than usual.

'Isn't it great to have a man about the place?' Belinda snorts. 'What would we do without you, Danny?'

'Glad to be of assistance,' he mutters.

'Work at the heel, then it should loosen,' I urge him. He yanks off the boot with such force that he staggers backwards, narrowly missing Belinda's tuna display. Someone guffaws into their Menu Masterplan.

'Thanks,' I say as Danny – now *au fait* with the heel-tugging technique – removes the second boot.

'Nothing to it.' He grins at me, and we both explode with laughter.

'*Now* could you hop on the scales,' Belinda prompts me, 'before the caretaker arrives to lock up?' I step on obediently and peer down at the digital display. I am past caring that I'm wearing one red and one navy sock, both belonging to Finn. Belinda squints at the scales and bites her lip.

'Is it bad news?' I ask.

'Of course not,' she chuckles. 'I'd say you only have twenty pounds to lose. Remember not to lose it too quickly or it'll all just pile back on.'

'How long should it take?' I ask.

'Around ten weeks if you stick to the plan. That way, you're far more likely to keep it off.'

'No problem,' I say, hopping off the scales, feeling lighter already. Okay, I won't be a skinny minx in time for Celeste's party. Yet coming here week after week doesn't seem so bad, not with Danny for company.

'Slow and steady,' Belinda sing-songs as I struggle back into my boots. 'The key to success is to come every week. You can just drop by for weigh-in at the end, but I'd advise you to come for my talk. I think,' she eyeballs me sternly, 'you'll find it motivating.'

'I'll do that, Belinda,' I say.

Danny is weighed – 'Better luck next week,' she says, oozing sincerity – and we make our escape together. 'So, where to now?' he asks as we step outside.

'Well, home, I guess.'

'Where's home?'

'Bracken Lane, ten minutes' walk away. How about you?'

'I'm out in the wilds,' Danny says with a grimace.

'Which village?'

'Not even a village, unfortunately. It's three miles to the local shop and, even scarier, four to the nearest pub. Anyway, can I give you a lift home? I'm parked around the corner.'

'Oh, I'll walk, thanks,' I tell him. 'Could do with the exercise.'

'See you next week then?'

'Sure. You know, it wasn't half as bad as I expected.'

'It's not too painful, is it?' He pauses and smiles. 'Don't fancy swapping numbers, do you? So we can keep each other on track if, well . . . we run out of inspiration with tuna.'

I laugh and pull out my phone. 'Oh, I don't think we're likely to do that. Not with all those bakes and jacket potatoes and, um, what was the other thing . . .'

'The dip. Don't forget the dip.'

'Yeah, that's right. So what's your number?'

He tells me, and I text mine to him. Then I hurry home to Bracken Lane, feeling light and happy and desperately craving a steaming hot chocolate.

CHAPTER FOURTEEN

'Where have you been?' Grace yells from her room as the front door clicks shut.

'Had a meeting, love. It's really late – gone nine o'clock. You should be asleep by now.'

'Come up and see me!'

'Shush, you'll wake Toby . . .' I head upstairs, wondering what to tell her about my mysterious 'meeting'. I don't feel good about lying to the children, yet nor am I happy about them knowing that I now belong to a diet club. I want them to grow up feeling at one with their bodies, blissfully unaware of low-fat 'bakes'.

'What sort of meeting?' Finn asks, appearing on the landing in too-short PJ bottoms.

'A sort of . . . health meeting.'

'At night? In the dark?' Grace asks from her room.

'What kinda health meeting?' Finn wants to know. I pause, knowing I'm not going to get away with this. It's like being asked how babies are made and knowing that they'll no longer be palmed off with, 'By a special kiss with Daddy.'

'You've been to that diet club,' Finn adds, 'with all the fat people.'

'How did you know?' I frown at him.

'Your diary was on the kitchen table. I saw "Super Slimmers,

7.30 pm" written in it. Michael Tashford's mum goes. It's all fat people.'

'Diaries are private, Finn,' I mutter.

'It was *open*,' he says, the swirl of adolescent hormones almost audible. I notice that he's dotted minuscule chin pimples with white cream.

'Mum's right,' Jed says, chuckling as he emerges from the steamy bathroom. 'You shouldn't be reading her diary. God knows what dastardly secrets you might find in there.'

With a snort, I go to tuck up Grace in her room. 'You're not fat, Mummy,' she murmurs as I hug her. 'You're just right.'

'Thank you, darling.'

'Will you read to me?'

'Not tonight. It's really late. Toby's been asleep for ages.'

'Finn's stinky,' she growls.

'Don't say that. He's your big brother and he loves you.'

'No he doesn't. I made a hot air balloon while you were out and he stabbed it with scissors.'

'Did he? That's not very kind. I'll have a word with him.' I kiss her goodnight and wander into Finn's room where he's curled up under his duvet, reading. Although I can sense he doesn't want me there, I perch on the edge of his bed. He slams the book shut, and I see that it's not a novel but a red notebook. 'Everything okay?' I ask gently. I can smell his warm skin mingling with the faint biscuity scent from his duvet. It's emblazoned with a jaunty rocket print, which tugs at my heart a little. Finn is too old for rocket duvets.

'Yeah,' he murmurs. 'Sorry, Mum.'

'What for?'

'For saying that about the fat club.'

'Oh, that's okay. It does seem a bit sad I suppose, and anyway, my diary's not really private. It's just a boring mum-diary full of stuff I have to remember. I don't have any dastardly secrets in there.'

He smiles then murmurs, 'You don't need to go to that club. You're not like Michael Tashford's mum.'

'No, but it's all relative, isn't it? It's about how you feel about yourself, and I think I could feel a bit better, that's all. Come on, hon. Time for sleep.' He grunts and clicks off his lamp obediently, although I know he'll sneak out the torch from under his bed the instant I've left his room.

Later, while Jed marks Roman projects downstairs, I curl up on our bed with my Menu Masterplan and flick to the Rules for Success.

1. *Stick to the Super Slimmers face system. You'll notice that everyday foods are allotted 'faces' at the back of this planner. If a food has a smiley face, you can enjoy unlimited quantities. A 'so-so' face means proceed with caution. A 'no-no' face means danger – only for treats.* I flick to the back of the planner. A quick check confirms that all of my favourite things have been awarded scowling faces. Now there's a surprise.

2. *Make fresh vegetables the centrepiece of every meal and enjoy their colours and textures.* Here we go. The thing is, I know this stuff. A woman can't reach the grand old age of thirty-eight and be unaware that broccoli spears will do her more favours than a doughnut.

3. *Eating from a smaller plate fools the mind into thinking that you're having a larger portion.* My brain isn't that easily fooled. Although, as an experiment, I'm tempted

to eat off the dolly-sized plates from Grace's china tea set which Jed's parents gave her, and in which she has shown zero interest.

4. *If you're craving chocolate, try sniffing it. This often satisfies the sensory centre and helps to dispel the urge.* No. I do enough sniffing around here – damp towels, the kids' clothes to check if they're dirty or not. I'm not prepared to sniff food that I'm forbidden from eating.

5. *Keep a selection of crudités in the fridge to avoid naughty nibbling.* Leave them to shrivel up, then throw them away.

6. *Chew slowly, savouring every mouthful.* Considering the unrelaxing nature of our family mealtimes, this might be a tad challenging.

7. *In place of proper food, enjoy a refreshing bowl of ice cubes* (okay, I made that one up).

As I toss the Masterplan aside, my mobile bleeps on the bedside table. FUN MEETING TONIGHT, the text reads, HOPE U WEAR THOSE BOOTS NXT WK. Hearing Jed on the landing, I quickly place it back on the table. 'Coming to bed soon?' I ask lightly as he takes his work file from our bookcase.

'I'll be another half hour or so,' he says.

'Hope you get it all done.' I form what I hope is a normal expression.

'Thanks.' He kisses me lightly on the forehead. As I click off the light, I'm still glowing inside, even though Jed's 'half hour' will probably stretch to an hour, maybe two, and I'm unlikely to hear him when he finally sneaks into bed.

Tonight, I don't care. The difference is, I no longer feel

quite so alone. Danny and I will be friends, confidants, partners in crime – *and* we know twenty-seven ways with a can of tuna.

*

Saturday. Party day. Tragically, something seems to have happened to my gorgeous new dress. Instead of being a dazzling emerald, as it looked in the changing room, it now appears to be a less alluring pea soup green which has the effect of making my bare legs look paler than ever. As I rummage for tights, I spot the Body Reducer in my drawer. If any occasion requires it, it's Celeste's party – but when I open the box I find a sheet of instructions comprising nine steps to get the damn thing on. Who on earth has time for that?

'Why are you putting on tights?' Grace says, stalking in and plonking herself on the edge of the bed.

'They're not ordinary tights,' I explain, hoiking them up into position. 'They're kind of . . . special.'

'Why are they special?'

'Because, um . . . they make your legs smoother.'

'But they *are* smooth,' she observes. 'They're not lumpy at all.'

'Thanks, honey. It's nice of you to say so.'

'Except for up near your bottom,' she adds, 'where it's kind of . . . crinkly.'

I smirk. 'That's the point of these tights. To smooth out the lumps and crinkles.'

'But you've got your dress on! No one'll *see* your bare bottom.'

'No, thankfully . . .'

106

'So what's the point?' She purses her plump, pink lips.

'Oh, I know it's silly, love. But I'll feel better if I'm all smooth and, er, un-crinkly under my nice new dress.'

'In case it blows up?' she offers.

'Exactly.' I turn slowly in front of the mirror, figuring that I look okay – no, better than okay, as long as I hold my stomach in. 'See what a difference they make?' I ask.

Grace squints at my legs. 'Can't even *see* them.'

'That's the whole point. The colour's called Barely There.' I pick up the packet and read the blurb aloud: 'Impregnated with skin-soothing extracts . . .'

'What does impregnated mean?'

'Um, that there's stuff in there . . . actually *inside* the tights, that seeps through your skin and, er . . .'

'What kind of stuff?' Grace demands.

I scan the rest of the description. 'It doesn't say.'

She gives me a worried look. What kind of example am I setting, letting a seven-year-old think it's okay to be impregnated by some mysterious substance? Fast-forward to a sixteen-year-old Grace: 'Someone offered me a pill and I ate it.'

Me, horrified: 'What the hell was it?'

Grace, casually: 'They didn't say.'

'Are you ready, Laura?' Jed yells from the bottom of the stairs. 'We've been waiting for ages. Celeste did say it would kick off around two . . .'

'I don't think it'll matter if we're a few minutes late,' I call back pleasantly. 'It's a garden party, love, not the cinema.' Quickly smoothing my dress, I give my reflection one last fretful glance before heading downstairs with Grace bounding excitedly ahead.

Finn is lolling against the wall in the hallway, as if incapable of standing unaided. He smells freshly-showered, of pine with Lynx overtones, and his dark hair is mussed forward over his eyes. Toby, too, looks startlingly hygienic in his favourite custard yellow T-shirt and clashing purple shorts, with hair neatly combed (by Jed, obviously), as if he's off for a casting for Gap Kids. I decide not to comment on the weird side parting.

'New dress?' Jed asks, raising an eyebrow.

'Yeah, Mummy bought it for me,' Grace says, twirling in her red-and-black stripy T-shirt dress, a dead ringer for Minnie the Minx. She even allowed me to secure her hair in cheeky bunches to complete the Minx-like effect.

'I meant Mum actually,' Jed says quickly, 'though yours is lovely too.'

'Oh, I bought it in York,' I tell him. 'Like it?'

'It's lovely. Really suits you. You look great, Laura. Very sexy.' On hearing the 's' word, Finn shudders.

Grinning, I kiss Jed lightly on the lips. Finn turns away, as if the sight of his parents expressing the merest *smidge* of affection might cause him to hurl all over the floor. God knows how he'd react if Jed and I kissed properly – really snogged, I mean, with tongues. We should try it sometime, shock the hell out of him. 'You look good too,' I tell him, appraising the dark jeans and cream linen shirt. 'You're still handsome, you know. For an old duffer.' He laughs and playfully slaps my hip. 'Come on,' I add. 'Let's go. I'll drive if you like.'

'Seriously? You don't mind?'

'Not at all,' I reply truthfully. What I don't mention is that, in being designated driver, there's no chance of me drinking too much to quell my nerves and making a twit of myself. 'I bought some exciting sparkling grape juice,' I add.

'Great,' he says, clearly delighted as we usher the children out to the car. 'Stop at the florist's in the high street, would you? We should get Celeste some flowers.'

'Of course,' I say graciously, glancing at Jed. His dark eyes are gleaming, and he's flushed with excitement at the prospect of a proper adult party, in a garden, with alcohol. Pity my Tesco underwear didn't have the same effect.

CHAPTER FIFTEEN

The blurb on the packet didn't say, 'WARNING: driving whilst wearing anti-cellulite tights feels disgusting.' But it's horrible – clammy and sweaty. In fact, if it wouldn't freak out the children, I'd pull over right now, stagger out of the car and rip the things off at the roadside. Where does the cellulite go anyway? Will it bubble up over the waistband, or liquefy and ooze through the tights and onto the floor of the car? 'Are we nearly there yet?' Toby demands from the back seat.

'Yep, nearly,' Jed murmurs, studying the slip of paper bearing Celeste's directions. I peeked at it earlier, wincing at her curly-wurly writing with little circles for the dots on her i's.

'Are we nearly there *now*?' Toby pipes up three seconds later.

'It's round the next corner,' I mutter, wishing we were heading off on a family day out to somewhere like Whitby or Scarborough with a picnic in the boot. Even a trip to B&Q would be more enticing than this. The outlandish bouquet of red and yellow roses, plus salmon-coloured carnations (chosen and assembled, rather bossily, by Grace) lies across Jed's lap.

'Looks like this is it,' he announces, virtually *panting*, for God's sake.

'Hurrah!' Grace exclaims. 'Celeste's house!' I pull off the narrow country lane and into a gravelled parking area, wishing my family would dampen their enthusiasm a little. Everyone bounds eagerly out of the car.

'Wow,' Finn declares, gazing at the building. 'This is *so* posh.'

'Yeah,' agrees Grace. 'Why don't we live somewhere like this?'

'It's lovely,' I murmur, choosing to ignore her question and surveying the converted mill surrounded by beautifully landscaped gardens. The stout, creamy-toned building sits proudly on a vast, clipped lawn, and the row of cherry trees is heavily laden with pale pink blossom. Party guests have already gathered in clusters. My gaze skims the well-stocked borders bursting with lilac, lemon and blue. It's so similar to Dad's garden, exploding with colour in the soft early May sunshine, that for a moment it dampens my nervousness. Bunting has been strung between trees, and an oval-shaped table set out with a dazzling array of goodies. Grace and Toby scamper across the grass towards it. 'She must be loaded,' Finn murmurs.

'It's divided into flats,' Jed explains. 'Celeste doesn't live in the whole building.'

'A flat? Cool.' He grins, flips back his fringe and makes for the table.

'Hi, guys.' Celeste strides towards us, pecking first Jed, then me, on the cheek. I fix a determined smile on my face.

'Happy birthday,' Jed says, handing her the bouquet.

'Wow, thanks! These are gorgeous.'

'Grace chose them,' I explain. 'She has a very unusual colour sense.'

Celeste laughs. 'What a sweetie. But you needn't have bothered, you know . . .'

'Well, it is your birthday,' Jed says with a smirk.

'Yes. God. Don't remind me! I feel so old . . .'

'Can we have some cake?' Grace yells from the table.

'Of course you can,' Celeste calls back. 'Help yourselves to anything you like. That's what it's there for.' She fixes her blue-eyed gaze on me. 'You look fantastic, Laura. That green really suits you. Really brings out your, er . . .' She trails off and beams adoringly at Jed.

'Um, thanks,' I manage. 'You look great too.'

'Oh, I don't know. I've been running around, baking and getting everything ready all morning. Must be mad, right?' She throws back her head and guffaws.

'You made all that yourself?' I say, gesturing towards the table.

'Yeah. It was nothing really. Anyway, how rude am I? Come over and I'll get you some drinks.'

Jed and I trail after her across the lawn. Her short blue dress swishes fluidly around her slender thighs, and her wavy hair ripples in the light breeze. It's a sunny, golden shade, reminiscent of Sugar Puffs. No wonder my family is enchanted by her. I fear now that the greenness of my dress is making me look rather queasy around the gills, and realise that all of the female guests are lusciously tanned, as if moulded from toffee. A kernel of shyness fizzles in my stomach.

Still, at least she's being friendly and welcoming. I try to pitch myself back into my pre-mummy days, when our weekends in London would involve at least one gathering, and Jed and I would head out with our bottle of cheap wine, fizzling with anticipation.

112

'Did you bring the wine, Laura?' Jed asks.

'Of course, hon,' I say, whipping the tissue-wrapped bottle from my bag. Still nestling in there is my pretend wine.

At the table, Grace and Toby and Finn are already filling their faces with pastel-iced cupcakes and sugared cookies in a myriad of intricate shapes. 'Let me pour you kids some lemonade,' Celeste says, filling three polka-dot cups from a jug. 'It's home made,' she adds.

'Wow,' murmurs Jed.

'Oh, it's easy. Anyway, what would you like? Wine or champagne?'

'Champagne please,' Jed says eagerly.

'I'll have some of this, thanks,' I say, extracting my luke-warm bottle and pouring myself a glass of grape juice. I sip it with mock enthusiasm.

'That's such a fantastic project you started last week,' Celeste enthuses, turning to cut me from her line of vision.

'Well, let's see if we can pull it off,' Jed says.

'What is it?' I ask lightly. He hasn't mentioned a fantastic new project.

'Oh, it's amazing,' Celeste enthuses. 'Didn't Jed tell you about the lottery grant he managed to get for the school? It's enough to turn a whole wall of the playground into an amazing mosaic, *and* pay for a specialist art tutor to visit all the primaries in the region. It's going to be brilliant, isn't it, Jed?' He nods, and I detect a faint glow of pride.

'That's great,' I manage. 'Will all the kids be involved?'

'Of course,' Celeste explains. 'It's all about releasing their creative energy.'

'Oh,' I murmur. There's a pause, and they both glance at me as if I'm some irksome stranger who's burst into Celeste's garden to snaffle her cakes. Although I'm clutching one – chocolate with raspberry icing – I am no longer confident about eating it tidily in such a public setting. 'Come and meet the others,' Celeste announces, clearly addressing Jed and not his socially inept wife.

It's not that they hurry away from me exactly, but I feel so awkward – so out of place among these golden strangers – that I remain frozen at the table. My skin prickles uncomfortably, constricted by my tights. I wonder how much cellulite has melted away, and when I'll start to see a difference.

Chatting and laughing, Jed and Celeste glide towards a group which has formed a loose circle beneath a cherry tree. Elsewhere in the garden, people are locked in conversation and sprawled on blankets. They are relaxed. They are *normal*. Even my children, who are now investigating a hammock at the bottom of the garden, seem perfectly happy. What should I do now? Surely there's someone I know here. I glance around in mild panic, looking for any of Jed's teacher friends.

Three immaculate little girls in floral dresses wander over to sample Celeste's goodies as their mothers watch from a distance. 'Not too many now, Maisie,' one calls out.

'Okay, Mummy,' the child replies sweetly, selecting a heart-shaped cookie.

I'm awash with relief when Toby charges towards me and skids to a halt. The girls teeter back, clearly alarmed by this scruffy boy with his parting askew and grass poking out of his hair. 'Hi, love,' I say. 'Have you tried these cakes with hundreds and thousands on? They're delicious.'

He doesn't reply. Even my own child is blanking me, after I carried him in my womb for nine months and allowed him to gnash his baby teeth on my nipples. He extracts a white plastic horse from the pocket of his shorts and makes it canter between the plates. The table is littered with glasses of wine and champagne. The potential for spillage is immense.

'Careful with all these glasses, honey,' I murmur.

Toby slams his horse onto the cake stand's top tier and sends it skidding through a daub of lilac icing. 'He's skating,' he says. 'He's an ice skater. Look!'

'Toby, that's a cake stand, it's made of glass, be care . . .'

'What's a cake stand?'

'It's *this*, a thing to put cakes on and it's very delicate and breakable . . .' I try to snatch the horse from his grasp, but he spins away deftly and makes it perform a dramatic leap over a dish of strawberries. One of the girls' mothers flicks her ash-blonde bob and throws me a look of disapproval. How uncouth I sound, having to explain to my child what a cake stand is. In her house, they probably use one every day.

Toby has now slithered under the table, and I don't have it in me to coax him out. At least there's nothing to break down there. I catch Ash-blondie staring as he emerges with damp, filthy patches on his bare knees, and he laughs and rubs his nose on his forearm. *Good,* I think defiantly. *This is how children are supposed to be. Messy and at one with nature.*

At the bottom of the garden, Grace is swinging exuberantly in the hammock. Speedy risk assessment: the hammock could ping off the trees or – more likely – she could simply tumble out. There's grass beneath, so injury is unlikely, and it's probably not worth me haring down there and leaving Toby unattended by the cakes. 'Leave them alone, Toby,' I hiss as he picks off sugared violets.

'But Celeste said we could have everything.'

115

I glance round and meet Ash-blondie's infuriating smirk. 'He's just excited,' I explain. 'We don't go to many parties.'

Christ, what made me say that? I might as well add: *no one invites us because we're completely dysfunctional.* 'Don't you?' she asks with a small frown before swishing off to join the group under the trees. My legs are throbbing now, probably due to extracts of God-knows-what seeping into my skin. How can I relax and join in when I'm being impregnated?

Across the lawn, Jed and Celeste are laughing uproariously. He places a hand on her bare upper arm. Tears prickle my eyes as I realise that anyone would assume Jed and Celeste are a couple, and that I'm some weird stalker person who should be frogmarched out of the garden. Well, I can't have that. I will *not* allow that to happen. I shall reclaim my husband and show everyone that I have as much right to be here as they do. 'Come on, Tobes,' I announce, grabbing his sticky hand.

'Where are we going?'

'Over there by those trees.'

'Why?' He looks longingly at the cakes.

'Because it's a party, darling, and the whole point of parties is to have fun and be friendly and meet people. Come on. We're going to make some new friends.'

CHAPTER SIXTEEN

As we approach the group, I'm delighted to see Duncan and Mickey, friends of Jed's and the only other male teachers at his school. 'Hi,' I say brightly, positioning myself between him and Ash-blondie.

'Hi, Laura,' Duncan says, kissing my cheek. 'Wow, you look great. I saw your kids but didn't realise you were here too. Where've you been hiding?'

'By the cakes, for my sins,' I say, laughing. 'I was just trying to stop this fellow here' – I indicate Toby, who's freed his hand from mine – 'from being a bit rough with the cake stand.'

'Sounds dangerous,' Mickey chuckles. Jed, who's positioned next to Celeste, gives me an unsteady smile.

'Looked like you had your hands full over there,' Ash-blondie remarks, taking a dainty sip of champagne.

'Well, you know.' I shrug. 'Kids, parties, tons of cake . . . they're always a challenging combination.'

Celeste emits a tittery laugh. Toby is tugging my arm now, trying to pull me away towards the hammock where his brother and sister have set up camp. To top it all, I need the loo. Proper mothers can control their toileting functions, having performed those squeezy pelvic floor exercises several hundred times daily since the birth. 'Toby,' I murmur, 'I'm going to pop inside to the loo. Stay here with Daddy, would you?'

'No,' he says firmly.

'I won't be a minute, love. I really need to go.'

'Wanna come with you.'

'Not now, Toby. Jed?' I say hopefully.

'Umm . . . uh-huh?'

'Could you keep an eye on Toby for a minute? He's fascinated with that glass cake stand on the table and I'm worried he'll knock drinks over . . .'

Jed blinks at me. 'Okay.'

'And I'm concerned that Finn and Grace might wreck that hammock by swinging too hard . . .' God, how neurotic do I sound? Jed glances at the hammock. It contains two of our children and is tossing violently like a ship in a storm.

'They're just having fun.' He wrinkles his nose, as if I'm something he's found rotting in the salad crisper.

'Gosh, you're a worrier, aren't you?' Duncan says with a chuckle. 'They'll be fine, love. We'll keep an eye on them.'

'Thanks, Duncan.' I try for a relaxed smile, which is challenging as I am now desperate for a wee. Jed transmits a silent message: *begone, tedious wife, with your multitude of worries and beleaguered pelvic floor.*

'Oh, you're Jed's wife,' announces Ash-blondie. 'Sorry, I'm being really slow here. Louise, isn't it?'

'Laura actually . . .'

'Yes, of course . . . have you met everyone here?'

'Um, no, I er, really have to . . .'

'This is Felix,' she says, 'and Jason, Peter, Chloe, Maggie, Tamara, and I assume you already know Duncan . . .' The roll-call continues for a thousand years. They stop being

118

names and become random sounds with no meaning. 'Marcus, Mickey, Annabella, George . . .'

'Sorry,' I cut in. 'I really must nip to the loo. *Please* keep an eye on the kids, Jed . . .'

'They're fine, Laura. What d'you think they're going to do?' There's an exasperated edge to his voice.

'I need toilet!' Toby bellows.

'Come with me then,' I say, taking his hand and hurtling across the neatly-clipped lawn towards the mill's main entrance. It's easy to find our way to Celeste's flat, as jam jars of spring flowers have been placed on each stair. Imagine having the wherewithal to decorate your *stairs*. The door to her flat is open and festooned with brightly-coloured Tibetan prayer flags. Inside, it's pleasantly calm and airy after the hubbub of the garden. I lurch from room to room, gripping Toby's hand so he can't get any ideas about investigating Celeste's glass candle-holders or our bouquet, which has been arranged prettily in an elegant duck-egg blue porcelain vase on the table.

We find the bathroom: a perfect white cube of a room. I bolt the door and charge towards the loo. Tugging down his grubby lime shorts, Toby buffets past me and starts peeing into the loo. 'Me first,' he says unnecessarily.

This is awful. My whole body feels contorted, as if it's squeezing in on itself from the effort of not weeing on Celeste's immaculate rubberised floor. I fear that I'll collapse through the effort, and be found hours later slumped in a puddle of urine. That is, if Toby has the nous to unlock the bathroom door and fetch help. He might have to scream for assistance through the half-open frosted window until the fire brigade arrive and axe the door down. What would the party guests make of that?

Toby's tinkling seems to be going on forever. Just how much lemonade has he drunk? 'La-la-nee-nee . . .' he sings tunelessly, gazing around, clearly thrilled by our impromptu excursion. Who needs trips to Viking villages when there are other people's bathrooms to explore?

Ripples of laughter drift up from the garden. To distract myself from the very real possibility of bladder combustion, I examine every item in Celeste's bathroom. There's not much to look at: just a pristine bathmat of looped cream wool, one fluffy white towel neatly folded on a chrome rail, and a vase half-filled with blue glass nuggets perched on a shelf. Unfortunately, there's no bidet. Although I can honestly say I've never coveted one, I'd give anything now for one to pee in. Celeste would never know, unless Toby grassed me up, and I could tell him it was a funny-shaped toilet. Just as I'm seriously considering doing it in the bath, his peeing dwindles to a trickle, then finally stops. I drag down my tights and knickers and collapse onto the loo.

'Look, Mummy,' Toby says, indicating the vase of glass beads.

'Yes, lovely.'

He touches the vase. 'S' nice, isn't it?'

'Please don't touch, love.'

'There's marbles in it,' he observes.

'They look like marbles,' I explain, 'but they're not for playing with. They're really just for decoration.'

'Why?' He cocks his head.

'They just . . . look pretty.'

Toby looks baffled at this, perhaps comparing Celeste's bathroom to ours with slimy bath toys and rank flannels strewn everywhere. It takes me a moment to register that he's gripping the vase to his chest. 'Put it down!' I shriek.

'No,' he yells in delight.

'Toby, please. It's really heavy, you might drop—'

Cackling manically, he runs to the window. I spring up from the loo, assuming I'd finished my wee but – damn my malfunctioning pelvic floor – apparently not. Pee trickles down my legs and onto my bunched-up knickers and tights as I try to snatch the vase from his grasp. 'No, Mummy!' he squeals, laughing and twisting away from me. He's up at the window now, peering down at all those happy, champagne-sipping, toffee-coloured people.

'*Give-me-that-vase*,' I bark at him.

'Look!' he yelps. Then he leans forward and tips the vase, pouring glass beads through the half-open window so they rain down upon the heart-shaped cookies and the little girls in floral dresses, who were sitting happily on the lawn and are now screaming and running away.

Everyone stares up. I stagger back and lower myself onto the bath's cold, hard edge. 'God,' is all I can say.

'Sorr-*ee*,' Toby sing-songs. I stare blankly. My tights and knickers are still bunched at my knees.

His face wilts a little, and he places the empty vase on the floor. 'It looked like a waterfall,' he says.

A waterfall. Great. Isn't a child's imagination a wonderful thing? Perhaps I, too, could liquefy and dribble down the plughole and into the dark, stinking drains. Right now, it would be preferable to being here. My tights and knickers are damp. I hoik them up anyway, wondering which aspect of mothering I've got horribly wrong for things to have turned out this way.

Other people's children don't do things like this. When Jed told me he wanted us to have a baby, I'd hugged him, delighted; I'd never met anyone with whom I'd have remotely considered having a child, and he said he hadn't either. I'd never imagined that one of our offspring would run amok with xylophone hammers or pour glass nuggets from second-floor windows. Is it any wonder I forget to ask Jed what's happening at school, and didn't know about his mosaic enterprise?

Toby wipes his nose on his T-shirt sleeve. 'Wanna see Daddy in the garden,' he murmurs.

'Hmmm.'

'Wanna go on the 'ammock.'

Silence.

'Can I?'

'In. A. Minute.'

He twiddles the bathroom door handle impatiently. 'Wanna cake,' he growls.

Standing up, I realise that what felt like a few stray splashes have, in fact, entirely soaked the lower part of the back of my new emerald dress. I am drenched in wee. As I twist to survey the damage, I catch Toby scrutinising the wet patch.

Then his deep brown eyes, clear and unblinking, meet mine, and his mouth curls into a delighted grin. 'You peed yourself, Mummy,' he says.

CHAPTER SEVENTEEN

Whilst I hate to brag about Toby's capabilities, and I'm not about to start crowing that he can speak Mandarin or play the bassoon, I have to point out that he's pretty perceptive. 'Come *on*, Mummy,' he demands, trying in vain to unbolt the bathroom door.

'Hang on a minute, Toby.'

'Why?'

'Because . . . because I need a moment to think.'

'I want Daddy!' With a groan, he flops down and sets about trying to pick the circular bumps off the rubberised floor. Clicking into damage-limitation mode, I try to work out my options. One: rejoin the jolly gathering outside and spout some twaddle about Toby spraying me with the bathroom tap. Would that be convincing?

'Are you still thinking?' he asks solemnly.

'Yes, love, I am.'

He thumps the bathroom floor. 'This is boring. Wanna play in the 'ammock with Grace.'

'Okay, okay,' I mutter, figuring that he has a point: we can't stay locked up in Celeste's bathroom forever. For one thing, at some point, other guests will need the loo. Jed might even notice our absence a few hours down the line. He might even *worry*. Even if he doesn't, I have work on

Monday, and Toby has nursery. Life must continue as normal.

Option two: I could rush down to the garden, retrieve my cardi which I dropped onto a chair and tie it around my waist, thus camouflaging the worst of the damage. Option three: make a huge joke of the wet patch, as a kind of party ice-breaker with all the Felixes and Annabellas, and leave early with Ash-blondie murmuring, 'I'm not surprised they don't get invited to many parties.'

'I know,' I burst out. 'I'll *dry* my dress.'

'Yeah!' Toby leaps up from the floor and snatches the pristine white towel from the rail.

'No, I can't use that. I need a hand dryer or something.' Of course Celeste doesn't have one. This is a flat, not a public loo.

'A hair dryer,' Toby repeats mistakenly.

I grin at him. 'A hair dryer – yes, that'd be perfect.' Unbolting the door, I grab his hand and lead him into the first bedroom we come across. It's a small, narrow room, painted entirely in white, with a single bed covered with a jaunty crocheted blanket. Celeste's handiwork, no doubt. A shelf is neatly stacked with children's books: *The Ballet Shoes*, *Famous Five*, *The Water Babies*, all guarded by a plush rabbit wearing an oatmeal hand-knitted sweater. They must be Celeste's old books. Naturally, they appear to be in mint condition. I'd hoped to preserve our children's favourite picture books, but most are smeared with Nutella or scrawled with crayon. The other day, I discovered that *Room on the Broom* had a slice of salami wedged in it.

'Let's try the other bedroom,' I murmur.

'Wanna play with Grace,' Toby grumbles, already bored with our mission.

'Soon, honey. This won't take a minute, I promise.'

The second, larger bedroom is tastefully furnished in cream and taupe in the style of a boutique hotel room. Faint laughter drifts up from the garden. Everything must be okay down there. They wouldn't be laughing if someone had been maimed by a falling glass nugget and rushed to A&E. As I scan the room, taking in the floaty white curtains, and the artful array of appliquéd cushions arranged on the bed, my spirits start to rise. Surely there's a hair dryer in here.

'Don't sit on the bed, love,' I say, as Toby bounces lightly on its edge. He slips off without protest, deciding to rearrange the cushions instead.

'Please don't touch those,' I add, feeling fortunate now that our house is so unkempt that at least I don't have to constantly worry about the children fouling it up. Opening Celeste's wardrobe, I peer inside, with Toby hovering and breathing throatily beside me.

Her clothes are stored on padded hangers, all facing in the same direction. It's the wardrobe of a proper, sorted, grown-up woman, not one who wets herself at parties. My dress clings damply to the backs of my legs as I scan the cubby holes up the right-hand side. They are filled with neatly-folded T-shirts and sweaters – I spot the fine lemon cardi she modelled at sports day – but, it would appear, no hair dryer.

I kneel down on the creamy carpet. At the bottom of the wardrobe, her shoes are neatly paired up. All look immaculate. A pair of embroidered slippers in oyster satin look more like museum exhibits than something you'd jam your feet into. I feel as if I'm sullying them with my breath. Yet I can't help reaching out to touch them, and trace the intricate beading with a finger—

'Um . . . Laura? Can I help you with something?'

I whirl round and stagger to my feet. Celeste is standing in the doorway, clutching a glass of champagne and smiling quizzically. 'Oh, er, I was just . . .' I babble, aware of hotness surging up my chest.

'Mummy peed her pants,' Toby announces with a giggle.

'Sorry?' She frowns.

Sweat springs from my forehead. 'I . . . this is *so* embarrassing, and I don't know how to say this really, but I, um, had a bit of an accident in the bathroom . . .'

'Oh, that,' she says with a small laugh. 'Don't worry about that. We managed to collect most of them, and no one was hurt or anything.'

'Um, no,' I mutter, cheeks flaming now. 'There was another accident. I, um, needed the loo but didn't quite make . . .'

'You mean . . .' She winces, and her forehead crinkles.

'Yes, I'm afraid so.' I stare down at my feet.

'Oh, God, you poor thing . . .'

'And I was I looking for a hair dryer,' I add lamely, 'to dry my dress. I'm sorry, Celeste. I shouldn't have come in here and started prowling around without asking.'

She steps towards me, scrutinising the damage while taking care not to come too close. 'Ooh. You really *are* wet. Why don't we find you something to wear? You can have a shower if you like, get yourself freshened up . . .'

'I'll be fine, honestly. I'll soon dry off.' I no longer care about my unsavoury condition. I just want to get out of here, go home and be normal. I'll tell Jed what's happened and take the children home. He can stay on, quaffing champagne, unencumbered by wet-panted wife or offspring. Surely someone will give him a lift home.

'Oh, come on,' Celeste insists. 'You'll feel much better if you're all clean. Toby, want to help me pick out a nice dress for Mummy?'

He nods. Although he's not remotely interested in dresses, Celeste's collection clearly possesses a certain allure. 'That one,' he says, reaching up to tug at a scrap of flimsy pink cotton.

'Um . . . okay,' Celeste says warily. She takes the hanger from the rail and holds up the narrow, spaghetti-strapped dress. I picture myself crammed into it, looking like an over-stuffed sausage.

'I'm not sure if that would fit me,' I murmur.

'Don't worry. I'm sure we'll find something.' She flicks along the rail, causing the padded hangers to bounce together. 'I've got tons of stuff in here,' she adds. 'Things from years ago when I was much . . .' She tails off tactfully. My back teeth jam together. We both know what she was going to say: *bigger*. 'Er, what size are you, Laura?'

'Sixteen,' I say dully.

'Oh.' She bites her bottom lip, as if faced with a particularly tough exam paper. I'm primed for her announcement that nothing will fit me apart from a dressing gown or a sack.

'Celeste,' I add, 'if you really can't find anything I'll just stay as I am. I'm almost dry now actually . . .'

'Here!' she announces, brandishing a rather matronly dress in navy blue linen.

Toby scowls. 'It's 'orrible.'

'No it's not,' I correct him. 'It's, um . . . *elegant*.'

'It's much better on,' Celeste insists. 'Go on, try it. Take some underwear, too, if you need it – it's in that top drawer by my bed.'

'Thanks, Celeste.' I muster a faint smile and take the dress from her. 'And I will have a shower if that's okay.'

'Of course it is. Come on, Toby. Let's give Mummy some peace and see what the others are up to in the garden.'

*

Celeste's shower has an instantly healing effect, blasting steamy water from all angles and sluicing away my mortification, despite the prospect of wearing the matronly dress. Who cares what I look like anyway? Things can't get any worse today. My green dress lies in a damp heap in the washbasin. I glare down at my legs and twist round to examine my bottom. Those tights lied. My cellulite hasn't melted away at all. It's still there, now looking pink and angry – and who could blame it, after it's spent two hours being impregnated by tights?

An image of Jed, sipping champagne in the afternoon sunshine, makes me prickle with rage. Hasn't it occurred to him to investigate why I've been gone for forty-five minutes? Look at what happens when a man ventures into playgroup. He's bestowed with coffee and a dazzling array of biscuits. Yet I come to a party where I know virtually no one, and might as well be an insect, buzzing ineffectually around the garden.

I towel myself dry and pull on Celeste's knickers. They are turquoise, with a shimmery gold stripe and ribbon ties at the sides, and aren't from Tesco but Coco de Mer. They are ridiculously glamorous. My tummy bulges over them, even when I try to suck it in. I rummaged through Celeste's drawer for a less salubrious brand, but there weren't any. No saggy cotton articles, no greying whites. Must remember to launder them lovingly and not leave them mouldering in the basket with the kids' damp swimming things.

The dress surprises me by not only fitting perfectly but also being pleasingly flattering. Pulling on my sandals, I make for her bedroom where I dry my hair with the dryer she left out for me. As I glimpse my reflection in her bedroom mirror, I'm shocked by the transformation. The anxiety has melted from my face, and my whole demeanour is more relaxed. Who cares if I'm accessorising not with a dinky 'it' bag but a plastic carrier stuffed with my damp emerald dress? I feel light and happy as I skip downstairs to rejoin the party.

'Hi,' I say, striding across the lawn.

Jed steps away from the group and frowns at me. 'Why are you wearing that dress?' he hisses. 'What's been going on?'

'I'll tell you later,' I whisper.

'What the hell happened up there, Laura? I can't believe what Toby did, that you let him throw those—'

'I didn't *let* him!' I protest. 'He just did it, Jed, while I was on the loo. What makes you think I have the slightest control over anything he does? It's not easy, you know, trying to stop him from wrecking other people's houses. That's why I got pee all over my dress . . .'

'He peed on you?' Jed mouths.

'No, *I* peed on me. That's why Celeste lent me this dress.'

Shaking his head despairingly, he drains his champagne glass and calls out for the children.

'What are you doing?' I ask.

'I've had enough,' he mutters.

'We don't need to leave yet, Jed. I've had a shower, I'm all clean and fine now . . .'

129

'Well, *I'm* not fine,' Jed snaps. 'We're going home.'

We don't just leave the party. We make a *hasty exit*. 'Oh, are you going already?' Celeste asks, looking crestfallen as my family converges in the middle of the lawn.

'Yes, sorry,' Jed says. 'I think the kids have had enough.'

'*I* haven't,' Grace insists. 'We're fine, Dad. We don't wanna go home.'

'Come on, love,' I murmur, taking her hand. She snatches it away. 'Thanks for a great party, Celeste,' I add. 'And I'm really sorry about the, er, thing in the bathroom.'

'It's really not a problem,' she says, smiling down at a furious-looking Toby. Finn is glaring, pink-cheeked, into the middle distance as if trying to disassociate himself from the scene.

'I don't see why we have to go now,' I protest as we all bundle into the car. 'The kids were having a great time.' It's true. The girls in floral dresses were clearly delighted at being chased around the trees by Grace and Toby.

'I'd just had enough,' Jed insists.

'Are you drunk or something?' I start the engine.

'No, I'm not drunk,' he snaps. 'I had, like, two glasses . . .'

'Are you sure you don't mean two bottles?'

Jed snorts through his nose. 'Why's Daddy cross?' Toby asks bleakly.

'I'm not cross,' he says in an over-bright voice. 'I'm just a bit tired, that's all.' Of course he is. Flirting under the cherry trees must have been completely exhausting.

'It's not fair,' Grace mumbles. 'Nobody else is going already.'

'Well, that's up to them,' Jed remarks.

I bite my lip, trying to rein in my fury as we pull away from the parking area. There's no reason for this. I'd felt so good in Celeste's dress – a new-improved, buffed-up version of myself, despite the accident – that I'd wanted to yabber away to all those shiny, toffee-coloured people. 'I don't know what's wrong with you,' I mutter to Jed.

'I've told you – nothing's wrong. I thought you didn't want to come anyway.'

'Well, I didn't . . . but I didn't want to leave either. Not like that.' I rev far too aggressively as we turn into the road.

'You'll damage the clutch doing that,' Jed points out.

Do you want to drive, I want to yell, *and get breathalysed?* I inhale deeply, trying to calm my racing heart. A rivulet of sweat trickles down my cleavage, no doubt staining Celeste's dress indelibly. So much ill-feeling is flooding our car, every particle clearly directed at me, it's a wonder there's room for any oxygen in here.

Still, maybe it's just as well that we left when we did. I'd imagine that, as the party drifts into evening, Celeste will decorate the garden with flickering candles. I'm always nervous with Toby around naked flames. After the hammock, glass nuggets and cake stand, I don't think I could handle any more anxiety-making objects. I drive slowly and cautiously to avoid a further ticking off, hoping that, by the time we get home, all that grape juice sloshing about in my stomach will have fermented and turned into wine.

CHAPTER EIGHTEEN

Compared to Celeste's flat, our house looks even messier than usual when we get home. It's as if burglars have been but couldn't find anything worth taking. As Jed clatters about in the kitchen, I start to tackle the mess. The living room floor is littered with mangled cardboard tubes, and stray biscuits have been ground into the carpet. Normally I don't mind the chaos, or have at least accepted that moving from one room to another usually involves spearing my heel on a plastic knight. When we set off for the party, ours had seemed like a pretty chaotic but normal family home. Now, there's a distinct whiff of eau-de-not-coping.

After a mammoth cleaning session, and a tense dinner prepared by Jed, I launch into the bathtime ritual. We read stories, Grace and Toby and I, while Finn practises drum rolls despite it being past his cut-off time of 7.30 p.m. I put Toby to bed – exhausted, he falls asleep instantly – and, later, I find Grace pink-cheeked and sleepy, her story tape murmuring in the background. 'It was fun at Celeste's,' she murmurs. Despite having cleaned her teeth, her breath still carries a hint of lilac icing.

'Yes, it was lovely, wasn't it?' I manage.

'Wish we had a garden like Celeste's.'

'Me too, love.'

'Granddad's garden was like that.'

'Wow, I'm surprised you remember it.' My throat tightens as an image of Finn, picking the first runner beans, bursts into my mind.

'Yeah, 'course I do,' she retorts. I hug her, and am filled with warmth as she winds her slim arms around me. 'Come in for a cuddle,' she adds.

I climb in and lie beside her, lulled by her soft breath and not caring that I'm probably rumpling Celeste's dress. 'Night, love,' I whisper later, realising that it's already dark, and gone nine o'clock, and that I must have fallen asleep too.

From downstairs comes the low mumble from the TV. In our bedroom, I pull off my sandals, rub my sore, pink heels and step out of Celeste's dress. It was crisply pressed when she plucked it from its hanger; now it looks as if it's been used as pet bedding. Where should I put it? It doesn't feel right stuffing it into our laundry basket. I hang it up on my wardrobe door, ping the Coco de Mer knickers into the laundry and pull on my sensible checked pyjamas.

Jed doesn't look at me as I stride into the living room. 'Well, thanks a lot,' I murmur.

'Thanks for what?' His expression is uncomprehending.

'For making me feel so out of place at that party.'

He frowns and flips the TV to mute. 'What are you talking about? You knew people, didn't you? Mickey was there, and Duncan, and you were introduced to—'

'That's not the point. As soon as we got there, you were off, stuck to Celeste's side like a leech . . .'

'No I wasn't!'

'You were, Jed. Can't you see how it looks? It's like, like, you're *infatuated*. It's obvious from the way you talk to her, how you look at her, all your cosy little chats about school stuff and that mosaic thing . . .'

'We work together!' he barks, slamming the remote control onto the cluttered coffee table, causing its back to come off and a battery to ping out. 'When you and Simone go out, don't you talk about work too?'

'Probably, yes, among other things. But I can't remember the last time I went out . . .'

'Well, that's hardly my fault, is it?' he shoots back. 'It's not like you're trapped here, Laura. You can go out any time you like.'

I hover in the doorway, sensing our conversation heading down a completely different route from the one I intended. 'This isn't about Simone,' I say firmly. 'It's about Celeste.' My voice splinters, as if someone has knocked a nail through it.

Jed shakes his head. 'You're just being ridiculous.'

'Do you fancy her?'

'For God's sake, how old are you?' His dark eyes flash with anger. 'Look, I know we spent quite a bit of time together. She just needed to talk about something and . . .'

'What was it?'

'Just . . . stuff. Nothing important . . .'

'But why you? Why does she confide in you, Jed?'

He pauses, and the fury melts from his face as he fixes me with a cool, hard stare. 'I don't know, Laura. Maybe . . . maybe she just thinks I'm a nice person.'

I open my mouth to speak, to say that of course he's a nice person, and there's no need to imply that I don't think he is. But as I try to arrange the words in my brain, Toby screams out, 'Mummy! *Muuum!*' from upstairs. I turn and rush up towards him.

'What's wrong?' Jed asks, landing at his bedside behind me.

'Been sick,' Toby wails, indicating the spillage of vomit on his pillow and duvet.

'Oh love,' I say, pulling him up onto my knee. 'Maybe you had too many cupcakes.' There's a terrible smell, raw and fishy with a topnote of buttercream icing.

'Come on, darling,' Jed says, lifting Toby from my lap and carrying him through to the bathroom. 'We'll give you a wash and you can sleep in the big bed with us tonight. Would you like that?'

'Yeah,' he croaks. While Jed sorts out Toby, I strip off the sicky duvet cover and pillow case, fighting the urge to dump them in the laundry basket on top of the Coco de Mers. By the time I've stuffed them into the washing machine, and am back upstairs, Jed and Toby are curled up together in our bed.

'I was sick an' it was horrible,' Toby mumbles in the dark.

'It's okay, darling,' I whisper. 'Everything's all right now. You'll feel a lot better in the morning.'

Although Jed and Toby fall asleep within minutes, I can't doze off. My head whirls with unsettling images of Jed and Celeste laughing and touching beneath the cherry tree. Her: sexy, lithe and beautiful. Me: fat and incontinent. Clearly, something must be done.

Heart thumping, I slip silently out of bed and pad lightly downstairs. *I'll show Jed,* I think, with a surge of determination. I won't be fat, dumpy Laura any more. I won't need to wear vile, cellulite-melting hosiery because never again will I be the chubbiest woman at a party. I'll be like them – the slender, toffee-coloured people.

Jed is right; nothing is stopping me going out with Simone

or Beth or any of my friends around here, any time I like. He's not exactly holding me hostage. It's my weight, that's what it is – and spending so many years tending to the children's needs that I seem to have forgotten how to have fun. Is it any wonder that Jed likes hanging around with a slip of a girl in a teeny sundress? Groping in the hallway, I fish out my mobile from my bag, registering a half-eaten cupcake that someone must have planted in there.

Searching my contacts, I find Danny's number. Didn't we say we'd support each other after that Super Slimmers meeting? And didn't I experience a flurry of pleasure at the thought of having a new, handsome male friend? I tap out a text: THINK EXERCISE WILL DO ME MORE GOOD THAN TUNA BAKE. FANCY RUNNING WITH ME MON EVE? LX. Fingers trembling, I press 'send'. Almost immediately, a reply pings back.

LOVE 2, it reads. MEET U AT 8 IN LYEDALE PARK. DANNY X

CHAPTER NINETEEN

One advantage of sticking to grape juice is the complete absence of a hangover the next day. God, I feel virtuous and pure inside. Jed, on the other hand, is slumped at the breakfast table, waxy-skinned and a tad green around the gills, sipping meekly from a Superdad mug. 'Sure you're up to football today?' I ask.

'Yeah, I'll be fine.' Squinting in the glare of my smug glow, he nibbles an isosceles triangle of toast.

'Is Daddy sick?' Toby asks through a mouthful of Coco Pops.

'No, I'm not sick,' Jed replies. 'I'm just a bit tired, that's all.' Toby grins at him. 'Your face is funny. It's kinda . . .'

'Kinda what?'

'Sort of squidgy.' Choking back a snigger, I pop Grace's abandoned buttery toast crusts into my mouth.

'Is it?' Jed says flatly. 'Well, there's not much I can do about that.'

Toby spoons in cereal while continuing to study his ailing father with rapt interest. A snigger starts to form deep in my belly, and I gulp my coffee to keep it down. It's so tempting to wind up Jed, to offer to whiz him up a hangover cure involving raw eggs and anchovies or boiled tripe.

To further crank up Jed's unease, Finn is performing a

vigorous drum solo upstairs. It's causing our house to rattle alarmingly and seems to be going on for several weeks. That's the trouble with old buildings. Jed and I fell in love with this place when we came to view it, enthusing that it was 'quirky' and 'characterful' (i.e. a wreck that no one else wanted). We never suspected that bits would start pinging off it the minute it became ours.

'Finn's getting really good, isn't he?' I remark, refilling Jed's mug from the coffee pot. He nods and closes his eyes, as if wishing that his entire family, who inflict drum solos on him and make a big show of being perky and *sans* hangover, would melt away into the ether.

'Does he have to do it so early, though?' he groans.

'It's not that early, Jed. It's half-nine.'

Jed sighs heavily, glancing up as Grace stomps in from the garden in her wellies, tramping in flecks of mud. 'Can we make a volcano, Dad?' she asks.

'A what?' He looks aghast.

'A volcano. It's really easy. India made one with her dad and it spurted out real lava all over the kitchen.'

'Another time, maybe,' he says, wincing.

'Why not now?'

'Because . . .'

'Dad and Finn are off to footie in a minute,' I cut in. 'We can do it when they've gone, okay?'

'But I want to do it with Dad!'

'Grace, love, I am capable of mixing up a few chemicals,' I say brightly. Her brow furrows with concern, as if I might be planning to conduct an experiment involving mains gas.

'*I'll* make a volcano with you, Mummy,' Toby says loyally.

'Well, thank you, Toby.' I grin. 'We'll all do it together.'

As soon as Jed and Finn leave, Grace and I pore over her experiments book and assemble the required ingredients. I'm almost glad now that Celeste's party happened and turned out to be such a disaster. After texting Danny, I feel focused and purposeful; at last, I'm doing something positive.

In the back garden, Grace warms to our project as the three of us build a soil mountain and squish a plastic cup into its peak. I had in mind a volcano of dainty proportions – a volcano-ette, really – but Grace and Toby keep piling on more and more mud, clearly enjoying themselves. Fired with enthusiasm, I fetch the vinegar, baking soda and food colouring from the kitchen and we measure everything out on the garden table. 'This is so cool, Mum,' Grace enthuses.

'Well, let's hope it works.' I grin at her.

'Let me pour the stuff in,' Toby insists.

'No, let me!' Grace yells.

'Hey, stop squabbling, you two,' I say, glimpsing Celeste's blue linen dress flapping gently on the washing line. I hand-washed it first thing this morning, taking utmost care not to traumatise it. Speedy risk assessment: vinegar plus food colouring in the vicinity. Not good. 'Hang on a minute,' I add, snatching it from the line.

As I drape it over the radiator, the doorbell buzzes. It's Beth, with Jack and Kira, brandishing a carrier bag. 'Hi, come in,' I say, relieved to see her. 'We were just conducting a pretty messy experiment. You can help if you like.'

'Great,' she says, laughing as she steps into the hall. 'Here, I brought you this. Thought you might be able to use it, after what you were saying at playgroup about taking up running.'

I take the bag from her and pull out a navy blue tracksuit.

'Great, thanks. I've just arranged my first run, actually. I'm going tomorrow.'

'Oh, who with?' She follows me into the kitchen as Kira and Jack wander out to join Grace and Toby in the garden.

'Um, just someone I met at Super Slimmers.'

'Super Slimmers? You mean you've joined? God, you are reinventing yourself! What's brought this on?'

I laugh. 'Well, I've only been to one meeting and I'm not sure it's me, really, having to check what kind of face a food has before I can even think about eating it . . .'

'A face?' She frowns.

'Yeah. Like this . . .' I indicate our butter dish. 'That would have this kind of face. And that' – I jab a finger towards our fruit bowl of slightly wizened oranges – 'that's a happy face. You get the idea.'

'Sounds pretty simple.' She pauses. 'You seem pretty determined, anyway. Like . . . something's changed in you.'

'You're right. A few things have happened lately.'

'Like what?' she asks.

'Oh, Celeste's party, for a start – remember I told you we'd been invited?' Beth nods, and I fill her in on the horror of the glass nuggets, my peed-on dress and Jed spending most of the afternoon slurping all over our willowy hostess. 'I just felt so frumpy,' I add. 'And I met this man, Danny, at the slimming club . . .'

'Whoa, dark horse!' she exclaims.

'It's nothing,' I say quickly. 'But you know what's really weird? I first met him in York and nearly sent him flying in Starbucks' doorway. And I went to Super Slimmers and there he was . . .'

She grins mischievously. 'Sure he's not stalking you?'

'I wish,' I snigger.

'Is he cute?'

'Sort of. Well, yes. But it's not about that. We're just going to be running buddies,' I say firmly.

'Ah. Now I can see why you're so keen to start pounding those pavements . . .' I'm about to protest that Danny has absolutely *nothing* to do with my new health regime when mud spats against the kitchen window.

'Oops, getting a bit boisterous out there,' I say quickly. 'I think we'd better intervene.'

'It's working!' Toby yelps as Beth and I step outside to witness 'lava' bubbling up from the cup and fizzling down the craggy slopes. Beth gawps at Grace and Toby's red-splattered faces.

'It's okay,' I say, laughing. 'It's food colouring. It'll all wash off – eventually.' We're all giggling as we grab handfuls of earth to divert the lava flow. Even Kira joins in while Toby smears mud onto his face, war-paint style.

'*You* never let us do stuff like this,' Kira chides her mother.

'Yes, well, I'm a rotten old spoilsport,' Beth says.

'Laura? What are you . . .'

'Oh, Jed! I didn't realise you were back.' Laughing, I push back my dirt-splattered hair.

'Pitch was too muddy to play,' he says.

'Daddy, we made a volcano!' Grace exclaims. 'It's *way* better than India's.'

'That's brilliant.' Jed smirks at me. 'So Mum's good at this stuff after all.'

'Well, we managed,' I say, catching Finn stealing a glance at Kira, who's smiling winningly, and muddily, back. Catching me looking, he blushes scarlet and scuttles inside.

While Jed heads upstairs to change out of his tracksuit, Beth ushers her kids to the front door. 'Well, good luck with your run,' she says with a teasing grin.

'Thanks. Are you sure you don't want your running kit though? It looks practically new.'

'No, you can have it,' she says, 'as long as you tell me how you and your, um, *friend* get on . . .'

'Oh, stop it. He's just someone to run with, that's all, to keep me motivated.'

'Yeah, 'course he is.' Smirking, she calls for Kira and Jack who troop reluctantly towards her.

'Anyway,' I add, 'I'll phone you with a full, detailed report after the run – *if* I survive.'

'Look forward to it,' she laughs, taking Jack's hand as they head down the street.

*

All through Monday at work, I can't stop thinking about my maiden run. I should have gone out for a couple of jogs on my own, just to loosen up and make sure everything's working properly. I mean, you wouldn't take an old banger that's been stuck in the garage for months on a driving holiday around Europe. You'd give it a little runabout first. What if I fall over again, like at sports day, or throw up in public? I need to practise – but where, without being seen? I try jogging experimentally around the living room, which makes Toby clutch himself with laughter.

Another problem is feet. Having tried on Beth's tracksuit – it's a little tight but, mercifully, pretty stretchy – I round up all my footwear and set it all out in a line on our bedroom floor. The effect is of a tragic car boot sale. Witness: turquoise wedge sandals with mud/slug-like stain not entirely removed. Boots of Shame as removed by Danny at Tub Club. Collapsed loafers. Polka-dot wellies housing one large spider. Black strappy sandals as worn to Celeste's party which caused a particularly painful welt on my left ankle, which would have been bearable – almost *pleasurable* – if I'd had a fantastic time and acquired it through dancing. And that's it, my footwear collection in its entirety. Nothing screams athletic prowess.

How could I have overlooked this? I get forty minutes' break at lunchtime. I could have bought trainers *and* had the lard lipo-sucked out of my arse at that clinic next to the gym that carries out 'non-surgical cosmetic procedures'. I could have also practised jogging back and forth past the salon. That would have kept the clients entertained while they sat under the lamps, waiting for their highlights to take.

I know. Finn has spare trainers. We're roughly the same size and surely he won't mind if I borrow them. I creep into his room which, despite yesterday's operation clean-up, is an absolute cesspit with clothes and bedding strewn everywhere, as if a gigantic wind machine has whirled everything around. I open his window to let in a gasp of fresh air, in the hope of dispersing the fug. I peer into his chaotic wardrobe, spotting that red notebook he'd been clutching lying at the bottom, amidst a tangle of PJs and socks and discarded football kit. Gingerly, I pick it up. On the cover he's written FINN'S PRIVATE BOOK KEEP OUT ON PAIN OF DEATH. The effort required not to flick through its pages triggers a tic in my left eyelid. It would be so easy to have a little peek. I stare at it, then quickly put it back where I found it, snatch his glowing white trainers from beneath a mud-splattered football top and shut the wardrobe door firmly.

The trainers are a little tight around the toes but preferable to my other options. Now for the bra issue. None of mine are sturdy enough for running in, and I don't want a repeat of the mums' race. In Grace's room, I find an ancient Scooby Doo T-shirt and struggle into it, yanking it down with difficulty. It creates a terribly squashed effect but at least I'll be firmly reined in.

In front of my bedroom mirror, I bounce up and down experimentally. Whilst my bottom and stomach ripple disconcertingly, at least my chest remains firmly in place. I pull on a plain grey T-shirt over the top, tie back my hair in a tight ponytail and survey my new incarnation as a world-class athlete. I look apprehensive and slightly sweaty around the forehead, and I haven't even exerted myself yet.

From my bottom drawer, I unearth my make-up and apply a touch of powder, eye shadow and lipstick, just to feel a little more human. Can't risk mascara in case it slides down my face when I'm speeding along, gazelle-like. Plus, Jed will think I've completely lost it if I go out all caked up. He can't believe I'm actually going running. He, Finn and Grace are playing Monopoly downstairs – Toby is already in bed – and I still haven't mentioned that I'm actually meeting someone. Jed hasn't asked, so I'm not lying exactly. And springing it on him that I'm running with Danny would trigger too many questions, which would make me late, so what would be the point? Checking my watch – half an hour until I'm due to meet him – I head downstairs. 'Where are you going?' Toby yells from his room.

'Tobes, you should be asleep. You were exhausted tonight . . .'

'Are you going out?'

'Yes, love. Just for a run. Nothing exciting. Now go to sleep, darling.'

There's a scramble of limbs as he appears at the bottom of the stairs. 'Can I come too? I'm good at running.'

'No, love,' I laugh. 'It's bedtime and anyway, you'd be far too speedy for me. Back to bed, okay?' He sniffs and eyes my trackie bottoms. Even a four-year-old knows that, as a style statement, they're plain wrong. Taking his hand, I lead him back up to his room and tuck him in.

'Your boobies are hard,' he observes, prodding my compacted bosom.

'I know,' I chuckle. 'But they'll soon be squishy and normal again, I promise.'

In the living room, Finn looks up from the Monopoly board and glowers at me. 'Why are you wearing my trainers?'

'Just borrowing them for my run,' I explain. 'Hope you don't mind.'

Jed sniggers. 'Are you sure about this, love? What if you do yourself an injury?'

'Of course I'm sure,' I say quickly. 'I'm only running round the park, Jed. You make it sound as if I'm planning to climb the north face of the Eiger.'

'It's just . . .' His lips quiver with mirth as his gaze flickers over Beth's tracksuit and Finn's glowing trainers. 'It just doesn't seem very . . . you.'

'Well, it *is* me. It's the new me. I'm serious about this, Jed. I just want to feel fit, like my old self, before . . .'

'Before what?' Grace asks.

'Um, before I was old, darling. I'd just like to have more energy, that's all.'

'Well, you can't wear my trainers,' Finn growls.

'Oh, come on. Just this once. I don't have any others.'

'You'll make them stinky!'

'No she won't,' Grace cuts in. 'Mummy doesn't stink. *You* do. You stink of poo and wee and farts . . .'

'Shut up,' he mutters, flicking her house off Mayfair.

'I won't make them stinky,' I insist. 'I'll only be gone for half an hour. It's hardly a marathon and I won't even go fast enough to break into a sweat . . .'

'Wise move,' Jed guffaws.

'Why have you got lipstick on?' Grace asks, narrowing her eyes at me.

'Have you?' asks Jed, squinting.

'No. I don't know. It might be some old stuff I forgot to take off.'

'You *do* have trainers,' Finn announces. 'You don't need to wear mine.'

'I left them out in the garden,' I explain, desperate to escape now, 'and a cat must have peed on them or sprayed them or something because they smelt disgusting and I had to throw them away.'

'Why do cats spray?' Grace asks.

'To mark their territory,' I murmur. *Like, you know – women who pick stray threads off men's tops.*

Finn's nostrils flare, as if infiltrated by said cat odour. 'I wear those trainers for basketball. I have to carry them in my schoolbag with my books. And now my books'll stink of feet . . .'

'I'll make sure they're thoroughly fumigated,' I say sweetly. 'Bye, poppets.'

'Bye, mum,' Grace says, glaring at the spot on the board where her house used to be.

'Be careful out there!' Jed chortles after me. 'Or should I say, break a leg?'

'And don't stink my trainers,' Finn growls.

CHAPTER TWENTY

I step out into the crisp evening and scan the street. Wish I'd started this running lark in winter, not spring. It would be dark by now and there'd be less chance of being spotted. I walk briskly, head down, trying to make myself as small and inconspicuous as possible. I'm not planning to run along Bracken Lane. There are neighbours and passing cars with people inside them, looking out. At least the park should be nice and quiet.

I arrive ten minutes early so I can practise before Danny shows up. I know that running, like going to parties, doesn't sound like something you'd need to practise, but I don't want to risk any mishaps. Perching on a damp wooden bench, I try to rev myself up mentally. I'm sure that's a huge part of it: having a positive attitude. I try to visualise myself as a world-class athlete, streaking over the finishing line to rapturous applause. I picture myself adorned with gleaming medals, standing on one of those podium things.

An elderly lady is striding along the path and veers onto the grass when she sees me. Maybe I look threatening, sitting here in a slightly too-small tracksuit for no apparent reason. Should I limber up, or whatever athletes do, to minimise the chance of snapping something?

I get up and start to trot lightly along the path. It actually feels okay. I'm hardly going faster than walking pace, but that's fine. Don't want to peak too soon. I check my watch: I have been running for twenty-five seconds and nothing terrible has happened. Another runner – see, I already consider myself a runner – hurtles towards me and gives me a nod of acknowledgement as he passes. Perhaps this is a club I *can* belong to. I look forward to swishing into those department store changing rooms, and trying on a playsuit while some woman struggles into a vast, salmon-coloured pantie girdle and exclaims, 'Oh yes, that looks gorgeous. But then, you do have the figure to carry it off.'

I trot past the pond, its glassy surface rippled by a couple of meandering ducks. This is better than that poncey health club where the receptionist suggested I might like to attend a spin class, which made me feel giddy just thinking about it.

In the distance I spot a pink splodge. It's tall and skinny and cantering towards me at an impressive pace, and with a sinking heart I realise it's Naomi. 'My God, it's you, actually running!' she cries. 'I can't believe it. Well done, you!'

'Thanks,' I gasp, jogging towards her. I'm unsure whether to speed up to impress her, or to slow down even further to conserve energy for when Danny shows up.

'Didn't know you were the running type,' she exclaims, scanning my trackie-clad body and continuing to jog on the spot.

'Well, I'm not really. I mean, I've never done it before . . .'

'Well, good for you for trying. You'll soon start to look a lot more toned.'

I smile tightly, wondering how Naomi manages to make a seemingly innocent, even encouraging remark sound faintly insulting. As she bounds up and down, ponytail leaping, I wait for her to zoom off and leave me alone. 'I don't want to hold you up,' I add hopefully.

'Oh, don't worry about that. I've already done five miles at race pace so I don't mind taking it a bit easier. Why don't we run together? That'd be fun!'

'Um, another time maybe. I'd rather just have a little trot around on my own, to be honest, to see if I can, you know . . . *do* this . . .'

'Oh no, you don't want to run on your own,' she insists. 'It's much more motivating to have a running buddy. Come on. Let's do a few circuits together.'

'I er . . .' I check my watch. Seven minutes past eight. Maybe Danny's forgotten our little rendezvous or has developed cold feet. It's probably for the best. Running is horribly unphoto-genic, and I'd rather he didn't witness various bits of my body thrashing about in public view. I could do a few laps with Naomi. Just enough to acquire a healthy flush so Jed doesn't think I've been shirking.

'C'mon, let's go,' she says.

'Okay, but I'll have to take it fairly slowly,' I warn as she breaks into a jog.

'Don't worry. It's best to start slowly – you need to increase distance before pace. That way you'll build up your stamina.'

'Uh-huh . . .'

'And then, when you're fitter, you should add some hill training and fartleks.'

'Fartleks?' I repeat.

'Yes. Alternating sprinting with your normal pace. It's the best way to build up strength.'

Sprinting? Is this some kind of sick joke? And what 'normal' pace is she talking about? I don't have one. This is beginning

150

to feel anything but normal. We jog towards a teenage couple who are snogging enthusiastically on a bench. Alerted by the sound of my thudding feet, they spring apart and gawp at me. The boy snorts openly, and I see myself as he sees me: a tragic, middle-aged woman with a muffin top, staggering past in an ill-fitting tracksuit. He smirks and murmurs something into his girlfriend's ear. *Cop a load of that arse,* probably. The malnourished-looking creature sniggers into her hand.

I wonder now if I'm really cut out for running, or should just be put out to pasture in some kind of sanctuary for knackered old mums like they have for horses. I quite like the idea of ambling around a field, munching oats, being sponsored by a kind family who come to take photos of me in my twilight years. 'Hill's coming up!' Naomi announces with a freakish grin.

'There aren't any hills around here,' I gasp. I must have been to this park eight thousand times; I'm familiar with every flake of paint on the see-saw, every rusting chain link on the swings. There is categorically No Hill.

'Yes there is,' she says with a cackle. And she's right. It soon becomes apparent that there's a definite incline that goes on and on, like some cruel optical illusion that's only detectable when you're running up it. A fat winged creature dives into my mouth, causing me to choke. 'Lean into the hill,' Naomi instructs. 'Take small, bouncing steps and keep up a light, steady rhythm . . .'

Fuck off, I scream silently. 'I've swallowed something,' I bleat, trying unsuccessfully to cough the thing up.

'It'll just be a fly,' she says. Oh, that's fine then. A fly that's spent most of its life sitting on rotting food and poo. 'Try to breathe evenly instead of wheezing like that,' she adds. Now

I've really had enough. I'd like to see her breathing evenly with a filthy great bug in her throat.

'How long have we been running for?' I splutter.

She checks her lime green sports watch. 'Three minutes.'

Christ, is that all? It feels like *weeks*. Something weird has happened to make time virtually grind to a halt. Then a distant voice cries, 'Laura!'

I stagger to a halt and launch into a coughing fit which pings the insect out of my mouth and onto the path. 'Hi, Danny!' I call back, conscious of the vile insecty taste in my mouth.

'Who's that?' Naomi asks, stopping abruptly as he strides towards us.

'Oh, just a friend. We'd planned to run together actually. Danny,' I say as he approaches, 'this is Naomi. We were just, um . . . warming up.'

'Were we?' Naomi asks with a sparkly laugh.

'I'm impressed,' Danny says with a smile. 'The only warming up I've done is walk from the car.'

'You haven't stretched?' Naomi asks, frowning.

'Well, um, not recently, no . . .' He chuckles.

She shakes her head, then demonstrates a sort of forward lunge with her back leg jutting out strangely behind her. 'Do this,' she says.

Danny flicks me a baffled look, then forms a rough approximation of her stance. He, too, is wearing tracksuit bottoms, plus a rather ageing black T-shirt. His dark hair is ruffled, his eyes even bluer than I'd remembered. I watch incredulously as Naomi repositions his leg, prodding at the thigh region and explaining, 'You need to maximise the stretch to work your Achilles tendon, Danny. Don't want to pull anything, do you?'

'Er, no,' he mutters. Oh to be a man. Not that I'd want Naomi to reposition anything of mine – but the fuss and attention they attract, like Jed and the playgroup biscuit scenario.

'You could do with more supportive shoes,' Naomi scolds, eyeing his scruffy trainers.

'I'm not sure about buying new kit right now,' Danny murmurs. 'I mean, I'm just starting out. Me and Laura thought we'd . . .'

'Shall we just get going?' I cut in impatiently.

'Sure,' Naomi says brightly. 'All set, Danny?'

'Um . . . guess so.' He casts me an unsteady grin as Naomi sets off, and we fall into step with her.

'This pace okay for you?' she trills.

'Er, yes,' he says, clearly assuming I invited Naomi to join us.

'Done much running before, Danny?' she asks.

'Er, no. None at all actually . . .'

'You're doing great,' she enthuses. 'If we build up gradually, you'll soon be running three or four miles.' Hang on, *we*? 'Where did you two meet?' she wants to know.

'At, er . . . in York,' I bluster.

'Really? Where?'

'In Starbucks,' he says.

'Oh!' She throws me a mildly shocked look, as if startled by my habit of picking up strangers in coffee shops. At least he didn't mention Super Slimmers. I glance at him, trying to figure out if he's enjoying this. Although a little breathless, he's showing no sign of fatigue. In contrast, my lungs are bursting and Finn's trainers have started to pinch my toes. Surely a blister can't be forming already. I'm lagging behind now, and Danny and Naomi – who are locked in jolly conversation – don't seem to have noticed.

'Are we nearly there yet?' I yell in a lame attempt at a joke.

'Come on, Laura,' Naomi retorts. 'You need to run for at least twenty minutes to gain full aerobic benefit.'

'You okay?' Danny calls back.

'No!' I yell, which they must assume is a joke, as they both chuckle whilst cantering ahead. Finn's trainers seem to be shrinking and are now excruciatingly tight. I don't *want* full aerobic benefit. I want to rip them off, plus Grace's Scooby Doo vest, as my boobs are throbbing in protest at being so fiercely compressed. I wonder if they'll ever revert to their natural shape. 'Where are we going?' I blurt out in alarm as, without warning, Naomi swerves out through the park gates and onto the pavement.

'Thought we'd go down by the river,' she says, 'seeing as Danny's doing so well.' He glances back briefly, but Naomi carries on yacking at him and I can't read his mood. From what I can gather, he doesn't seem fazed by leaving the park for public streets. In a particularly cruel gesture, Naomi leads us past Café Roma which seems so alluring with its glowing lights and ravishing cake smells.

The inside of my mouth has shrivelled up, as if hoovered by the dentist's suction device. For the first time in years, I could murder a cigarette, *and* a gin and tonic. Outside the Golden Lion, a group of elderly men clutch their drinks, watching us with interest. They are murmuring to each other, and I suspect they're taking bets on how long it'll be before I land in a sobbing heap on the pavement. Naomi is streaking ahead now, her glossy ponytail swinging merrily, her backside as taut and unmoving as a shop mannequin's. 'I'd never have believed this was your first time, Danny,' she gushes.

'Really?'

154

'Yes, most people end up walking after two minutes. Want to come out again sometime?'

'Er, sure, why not?'

Something snaps in me then. I stop dead, watching as they trot on, gassing away like old mates. 'Hurry up, love!' calls out one of the men from the pub. 'They're leaving you behind.'

'Want a lift in my car?' yells another.

'I'll give you a piggy-back,' someone guffaws.

I try to muster a smile but it slides off my face and lands somewhere close to my throbbing feet. 'Stop for a drink with us, darling,' the first man calls out. 'You look like you need some refreshment. What are you having?'

'A mid-life crisis,' I yell back, triggering much merriment. I stand and wait, catching my breath, expecting that either Danny or Naomi will realise I've stopped and come scampering back to rescue me. But nothing happens. They charge on, like that pack of gazelles in the mums' race, then whip around the corner, out of sight.

CHAPTER TWENTY-ONE

'Back already?' Jed calls out.

'Yep,' I say, pausing in the hall while I try to compose myself. Although I walked home – limped, actually – my breath is still coming in ragged gasps. Blotting my face with my sleeve, I venture into the living room where Jed is engrossed in the newspaper, and Finn is reading a fat paperback with a fire-breathing dragon on the cover.

'You weren't long,' Jed says, glancing up.

'Long enough,' I say. 'To be honest . . .' I plonk myself heavily on the sofa between them and pull out my ponytail band. 'I think you're right, Jed. I'm just not built for speed.'

Jed smiles and ruffles my damp hair affectionately. 'Well, at least you tried. Running's not for everyone, you know.'

Finn looks up from his book. 'Can I have my trainers back now?'

'Sure.' I almost weep with relief as I pull them off and free my poor, mangled toes. Finn picks them up and inspects them for damage, holding them at a distance by the fingertips. I hobble upstairs to check on Grace and Toby, who are both asleep, then pad gingerly into the bathroom. After perching on the edge of the bath, and contemplating my blistered toe for a few minutes, I peel off my clothes, yanking the Scooby T-shirt over my head with difficulty, and glance down at my body. Disappointingly, I look exactly the same as before, apart from having acquired some angry chafe marks around my waist from Beth's trackie bottoms, plus that pulsating blister. In fact my feet look pink and rather angry, so really, I'm in a worse condition than before I set out. You have to question the logic.

I shower for ages, hoping to soothe my traumatised flesh. Gradually, as I dry off and pull on roomy PJs and sheepskin slippers, I start to feel normal again. Let Naomi and Danny *fartlek* to their bloody heart's content. I hope they're very happy together. Finn drifts upstairs, still clutching his book, and I pull him in for a hug on the landing. He grudgingly allows it, now that I'm thoroughly de-stinked. Downstairs, I find Jed brewing tea in the kitchen. 'So, that's the end of that, is it?' he asks.

'The end of what?'

'Running. Tub Club. All that "new you" business.'

I laugh uneasily. 'I don't know. D'you think I should quit the club as well?'

'It's up to you,' he says with a small shrug. That's so Jed. As if it doesn't matter to him what size I am, because he doesn't notice anyway. I take the tea he offers me and gulp it greedily, knowing that I shouldn't have sugar, or be munching a restorative chocolate digestive. In fact I should really be sipping the pond water tea that Naomi so enjoys.

'I'm probably dehydrated,' I murmur. 'In marathons they have all these water stations every couple of miles or so.'

Jed sniggers. 'Don't tell me no one had arranged that for you?'

'Sadly, no.'

'How far did you go exactly?' he asks, taking a biscuit from the open packet on the table.

'Just round the park.'

'Whoa! Steady on.'

I'm about to protest that it's actually quite hilly – although not to the naked eye, admittedly – when my phone bleeps with an incoming text. I step away from Jed to read it. WHERE DID U GO? It reads. Danny. What a cheek. Where the hell did he think I went? I'm tempted to reply: AM BLIND DRUNK IN GOLDEN LION. Instead, I text a curt HOME and stuff my mobile back into my pocket.

Jed appears at my side and nuzzles my neck, triggering a small prickle of guilt. 'Never mind, love,' he murmurs. 'I'm sure even Paula Radcliffe has her off days.'

*

At breakfast the next morning a row erupts over who 'stole' the last of the orange juice. 'Actually,' I tease, '*I* bought the juice so technically, it was mine.' Grace glares at me. Toby tries to shake dregs from the empty carton. Finn has his iPod on, which he isn't supposed to do at the table because meals are meant to be family bonding time, haha. Even more irritatingly, he starts drumming with his fingertips on the table, keeping time with a song.

'Please stop that, Finn,' I say.

'Uh?' He looks bewildered.

'It's not very pleasant, trying to eat with you drumming—'

'Why not?' He pulls out his earphones.

'You're making the table vibrate and it's rattling my brain, love.'

He yawns loudly. 'I need to practise, yeah? For my next lesson . . .'

'Forgot to tell you,' Jed says, breezing in, seemingly oblivious to the squabble as he snatches a pile of work folders from the far end of the table. 'Mum was on the phone, wondering what you'd like for your birthday.'

'Oh, just something luxurious and decadent,' I say, smirking, 'like last year.'

Jed raises an eyebrow. 'She mentioned a bread maker.'

'Did she? What for?'

'For your birthday. To, er . . . make bread, I guess. Or, um, maybe they do rolls as well.'

'But you can buy bread in the shops,' I remind him. 'I don't need to make my own.'

'Well, home-made bread is pretty tasty, and she thought, in your copious spare time . . .' He sniggers, clearly enjoying winding me up.

'Yes, maybe you're right. In fact I don't even need a bread maker for that. I could get up at 5 a.m. and start kneading so we can have fresh bread for breakfast every morning. That'd make better sandwiches for your lunchbox, wouldn't it, Finn?'

Finn is still drumming on the table with his earphones back in. 'Uh,' he says in response. Something must have filtered through, though, because he gets up from the table, finally de-iPodding himself, and picks up his lunchbox from the worktop. Flipping it open, he peers inside, peeling foil from his sandwiches and wincing slightly. 'These ham?' he asks.

'Yes. Not wet ham, though. It was completely dry. I checked.'

He pauses, as if presented with a particularly unappetising restaurant meal, and shuts the lunchbox lid. 'Nah thanks.'

'What d'you mean, *nah thanks*?'

'I'll just have a school dinner in the canteen.'

'Why?' I ask. 'You said school dinners are all soggy pizza and weird, bouncy meat. You said you felt sick the time you had that stew with floaty bits in . . .' With a roll of his eyes, Jed dispenses kisses to each of us and heads off, with undisguised relief, to work.

'It's £1.20,' Finn says, holding out a hand. I snatch my purse, rummage for change and find all of 37p.

'Hang on a minute,' I say, nipping upstairs to Toby's room where I manage to prise off the rubber stopper from his piggy bank. Grabbing a handful of coins, I replace the stopper just as Toby stalks into the room.

'What you doing?' he asks.

'Um, just borrowing some money, love, for Finn's lunch.'

'That's my money!'

'I know, but I haven't been to the bank . . .'

'You're stealing it!'

'I'm borrowing it, okay? And when I pay it back, which I'll do later today, okay, I'll give you some interest.'

'What's interest?' he asks warily.

'It's extra money to say thank you.' At that, he brightens, trotting downstairs behind me, and observes me depositing the coins onto Finn's outstretched palm.

'Uh, thanks,' he says.

'So what am I meant to do with the packed lunch I *lovingly* made for you at eleven-thirty last night, when I could have been tucked up in bed?'

Finn stuffs the coins into his pocket and pulls on his jacket. 'Dunno.'

'Give it to a homeless person?' Grace suggests from the table.

'Great. Good idea,' I say tightly.

'Anyway, I'm off to school,' Finn mutters.

'Hey, aren't you walking with us?' I call after him. 'Hang on a minute. I just need to find Toby's shoes and . . .'

'Nah, s'all right.' The front door bangs shut, and he's gone. As Grace, Toby and I head out, I wonder what's triggered this urge to reject my lunches and leave before us. For once we're not running late but, even if we were, it's not like Finn to worry about missing the bell. Clearly, he wishes to disassociate himself from me. Perhaps I should cease to exist completely, apart from when he requires a cooked meal or money or to be driven to a football game.

I kiss Grace goodbye at the school gates and drop off Toby at nursery via the newsagents (emergency Chunky Kit Kat required). As I head for work, rain starts bucketing down. Within seconds I'm drenched, and I stumble into the salon, making a beeline for the loo to towel myself down. 'Morning, Laura,' Simone calls out as I pounce for the loo door. 'Your first client's here already.'

'Is she?' I turn back and glance down at the appointments book. 'I didn't think I had a booking till ten.'

'Not in the book,' she adds. 'He's here – look. Popped in on the off-chance you could fit him in.'

Rain trickles slowly down my cheeks. I peer over at the sofa which Danny is occupying all by himself whilst pretending to read a copy of *Vogue*. 'Who is he?' she whispers.

'Just . . . just a friend.'

'Cute friend.' She winks as I turn to greet him.

'Hi, Danny,' I say. 'What brings you here?'

He looks up and smiles in a slightly lost way, as if he's wandered in by mistake and really wanted the library.

'I was just in town and, um . . .' He pauses. 'Thought I'd pop in to see you. Think I owe you an apology after our run.'

I shrug. 'That's okay. It's not a problem. It was my fault really, for being so slow.' Jess, our junior, takes care of our seamless playlist but has chosen this precise moment to opt for silence.

He glances down at the *Elles* and *Vogues* on the table. 'Your friend . . . Naomi, was it? She was chatting so much, going on about fartleks or whatever, telling me how to breathe and use my arms to propel myself forward . . .' He mimics her arm-pumping motion, and we both laugh. 'With all that going on – God, all I wanted was a quick run, you know. Not a personal trainer . . .'

'I know what she's like. I mean, you can't possibly just put one foot in front of the other, can you? It has to be all technical . . .'

'And by the time I looked back,' he adds, 'you weren't there. We came back to find you but those men at the pub said you'd stomped off.'

'*Jogged* off,' I correct him. 'I jogged home. Anyway, I thought I'd probably gone far enough for my first time. Didn't want to overdo it.'

'Right. Good idea.' I sense Simone watching us with rapt interest from the manicure table.

'Anyway,' I say breezily, 'I've got twenty minutes till my first client's due. What can I do for you?'

'Huh?' Danny says.

'Just a trim or a total re-style?' I tilt my head, appraising his dark brown, endearingly scruffy and rather damp hair.

'Oh – *that*.' He chuckles.

'Well, we are a hair salon, Danny. It's our speciality.'

'Yes, um, of course . . .' He rakes a hand through his hair as if seeking inspiration. 'I don't know, Laura. I suppose I'll just put myself in your capable hands.' He grins mischievously.

'Okay. I'll ask Jess to shampoo you and we'll soon knock you into shape. You don't mind that it's my first time, do you?' I tease him.

'Is it?' He looks momentarily worried, then cracks a grin. 'Oh, I'm feeling pretty daring today. Happy to be your guinea pig.'

'Great. See you in a minute, okay?'

While Danny's at the basins, I dart into the loo to blot my wet hair with a towel and wipe away rogue mascara smudges from beneath my eyes. When I rejoin him, he's swathed in a pale grey cape in front of the mirror.

'No need to look so scared,' I tease him. 'We're quite gentle in here.'

'It's just . . . I don't usually come to places like this.'

'A bit posh for you, is it?'

'Well, y'know.' A pause.

'So where do you usually go? For haircuts, I mean?'

'My, um . . . my ex used to do it.' His blue eyes meet mine. 'Haven't got around to getting it cut since we broke up. That explains the state it's in,' he adds.

'Oh.' I comb out his hair, aware of him watching me. 'I wouldn't say it's a state, Danny. It suits you actually. So, is your girlfriend – your ex – a hairdresser?'

'Nope, we were just skint, trying to do up an old farmhouse, and she was pretty handy with the scissors.'

'Well,' I say, combing out his damp hair and beginning to cut, 'she obviously had natural talent. I'm just going to take away some of the weight, thin it out a little while leaving most of the length, that sound okay to you?'

'Sounds good to me.'

I smile, enjoying cutting the hair of someone so easy and pleasant, someone who wouldn't dream of thrusting photos of unfeasibly glamorous Hollywood actors at me. That, I decide as I snip away, is what I like about Danny. Sure, he's cute, with the dimply cheeks, and those startling blue, dark-lash-fringed eyes – but in a totally non-threatening way. His kind, friendly demeanour, and his soft, slightly chunky body in faded jeans and old sweatshirts all add to his appeal as a man I could happily hang out with and chat about whatever comes to mind. 'So,' I say, 'when did you break up? If you don't mind me asking . . .'

'It's fine. I don't mind at all. It happened a few months ago now, just before Christmas.'

'Bad timing,' I say. 'Not that it's ever good timing, unless you wanted it to happen of course . . .' I tail off, suspecting that I'm in danger of overstepping the mark.

'Well, no,' he says. 'I didn't want it at all. Didn't even want the farmhouse, if I'm honest – the whole creating-our-dream-property thing. We'd had a flat in Leeds and been quite happy for the two years we'd been together. But Sarah wanted a big project, something to get her teeth into, I guess . . .'

'And you went along with it?'

He smiles ruefully. 'I was so infatuated I'd have done practically anything she'd suggested. That's probably why it went wrong.'

'Well,' I say, 'that doesn't sound so terrible. Being willing to give it a try, I mean.' I check his reflection. With less hair around his face, his bone structure is more defined. Before, he looked cute; now he's startlingly handsome. I snip a few stray hairs from above his ears.

'It hardly sounds dynamic, though, does it? I'd have been perfectly content to stay in Leeds. I had a photography business which was doing pretty well, but when Sarah had this idea about setting up a spa, a kind of holistic therapy place . . .' I clamp my mouth shut to stop myself from firing more questions. 'And then,' Danny adds, 'she went off with our builder.'

I clutch the hair dryer in mid-air. 'You're joking.'

'Unfortunately not.' He shrugs.

I grip the dryer, unsure of what to say next. It doesn't seem right, switching it on after his shock announcement, but I can hardly send him out without finishing properly. I turn it on at the slowest setting. 'Would it be cheeky,' he says over its roar, 'to ask you to come running again?'

'Oh, I'm not sure I'm really cut out for it, Danny. I mean, look what happened last time.'

'Yes, but if we went out on our own, without Naomi, we could take it at our own pace and do without all that hamstrings and fartleks stuff. Don't need to kill ourselves, do we?'

'No,' I snigger, removing his cape, 'we don't. So, anyway, what d'you think?'

He checks his reflection and his face breaks into a smile. 'It's great. Thank you. It was long overdue.'

'Ooh, yes, very nice,' Simone declares, sweeping past us with a more pronounced sashay than usual.

Danny looks at me. 'Was I a complete disgrace before?'

'Of course you weren't. You just needed a little . . . sprucing.'

'Well, I'm glad you've spruced me.' He follows me to the till and pays. 'So,' he adds, 'see you Thursday night?'

'Yep, I'll be there.'

'Great.' He gives me a quick backwards glance and a grin as he leaves the salon.

I stand for a moment, watching the door, willing him to hurry back and say he's forgotten something. Clients leave things all the time: gloves, scarves, bags of shopping. This is crazy. He's just a friend, and not remotely my type. 'So, seeing him on Thursday night, are you?' Simone murmurs into my ear.

'Oh, it's nothing. We go to this club, that's all.'

'What kind of club?'

'Just a slimming club. A load of overweight women, plus Danny, in St Mary's Hall on a Thursday night. We learn twenty-seven ways with a can of tuna.'

'He goes to *that*?' she splutters.

I nod. 'All sorts of people go.'

'Well,' she says, arching an eyebrow, 'if he's the kind of person you hang out with there, I can totally see why you joined.'

I laugh off her remark but it stays with me all morning. Finn's face flashes into my mind: glowing red when I spotted him glancing at Kira in the garden. Clearly the symptom of a crush. The difference is, I'm too old and gnarled to have crushes. I'm a married mother of thirty-eight whose mother-in-law wants to buy her a bread maker.

CHAPTER TWENTY-TWO

Thursday, May 22nd. I am thirty-nine today, and beyond getting fired up about birthdays. I don't wake up expecting breakfast to materialise at my bedside, and I certainly haven't been rummaging in Jed's wardrobe, hoping to glimpse something beautifully wrapped with my name on it.

So far I have been given:

- An extremely sweet, wobbly clay dish with sequins stuck all over it, created by Toby at nursery.

- An exuberant bunch of buttercups from our back garden, tied with hairy brown string from Grace.

- One of those free postcards you get in cafés from Finn. It depicts a red phonebox looking stranded in a colourless landscape. On the reverse he has written: 'To Mum from Finn.' I need to have a little chat with him about his over-emotional tendencies.

As yet, there's been nothing from Jed. As I dish out the kids' breakfasts, he chomps his customary toast slathered thickly with peanut butter. Peanut butter, I might add, is deemed so naughty by Tub Club, it doesn't even *have* a face.

Throughout breakfast, I keep casting sly glances in his direction, amazed that my beloved has made no reference to the day's significance. My gifts are set out on the table so he must realise something's going on. Yet . . . nothing. Still, exciting times lie ahead. Tonight, Belinda might announce that my best friend is celery.

Jed grabs his wallet and keys from the table. 'Doing anything later?' he asks.

'Just Tub Club,' I say bleakly, caressing the peanut butter jar.

'What's Dub-Dub?' Toby asks.

'Just a place I go to,' I say vaguely. *On my birthday. Because I have nowhere better to go. Remember, when you're a grown-up, that when a woman says she doesn't care about celebrating her birthday, she doesn't actually mean it.*

'Oh.' Jed frowns. 'I'd forgotten about that. Would it be okay to skip it this week? Or do they fine you or something?'

'Of course they don't. Why d'you want me to skip it, though? Worried I'm getting too skinny?' I laugh hollowly.

'No, um, it's just, er . . . I thought I'd take you out for dinner.'

'Oh, I'm not really bothered about going out,' I say quickly. 'And I doubt if we'd manage to get a babysitter at such short notice.'

'It's all sorted,' he says, smiling. 'I've booked Joelle *and* a restaurant table.'

'Have you?' I'd be no less shocked if he told me he'd successfully performed a triple heart bypass.

'Don't look so surprised,' Jed chuckles. 'I am capable of organising a birthday night out, you know.'

'Yes, I know you are. It's just, you hadn't mentioned anything so I thought you'd forgotten.'

He smiles and kisses me lightly on the lips, and I inhale the faint smell of peanut butter. 'Of course I didn't forget, silly girl.'

'So where are we going?' I ask eagerly.

'Rawlton House.'

'Oh Jed, that's so posh! Are you sure?'

'Of course I'm sure.'

I grin at him. 'Thanks.' I'm so delighted, I don't have it in me to stop Toby from slurping milk from his cereal bowl.

'There is, um . . . a *small* catch,' Jed adds, nudging a small pile of toast crumbs along the table with a finger.

'What's that?'

'My, er . . . parents are coming too.' His mouth sets in a firm line.

'Tonight?' I exclaim. 'What – here? For God's sake, why didn't you warn me?'

'Are Granny and Grandpa coming?' Grace asks delightedly.

'Yes, love,' Jed murmurs.

'Great! Does that mean we can sleep in the caravan?'

Jed throws me a panicky look. 'I don't know, Grace,' I say quickly. 'When are they coming, Jed? Are they bringing that caravan with them this time?'

Jed nods. 'Of course they are. They're on a tour – only found out yesterday and I forgot to mention it last night. I'm sorry, but I'm sure it'll be okay. They said they didn't want to put us to any trouble, that they'll only stay for a night and drop off your birthday present . . .'

'Oh yes,' I bark. 'The famous bread maker.'

'Well, I don't know if they actually bought you one . . .'

'You know what'll happen,' I charge on. 'Grace and Toby will insist on sleeping in the caravan, and I'll have to sleep out there with them with that stinking chemical toilet.'

'It's not stinkin',' Toby shouts, stomping into the kitchen.

169

'It's not that bad,' Jed insists, 'so long as you keep the lid down.'

'Isn't it?' I bark. '*You* do it then. You have a lovely dinner at Rawlton House, then sleep outside on your birthday on that tiny narrow bed with the bobbly nylon cover.'

'Can't we have the beds?' Grace grumbles.

'Ok. Sure you can. I'll sleep on the floor like last time . . .'

'Mum, I'll sleep out there with them,' Finn says, wandering in with his schoolbag looped across his body.

'Thank you, love,' I murmur, 'but you're not old enough to be in sole charge of your brother and sister in a dangerous fibreglass structure.'

'Jesus,' Jed mutters under his breath. 'I thought it'd be a treat. I thought you'd *like* to go out to dinner.'

'I would,' I say, following him to the door, 'if it was just me and you on a night out, like *normal* couples have. But this is a bit different, isn't it?'

'I'm off to work,' he says huffily. 'We'll talk about it later.' With that, he steps out, slamming the front door behind him.

'Happy birthday,' I murmur into the tense air.

'Are we normal?' Toby pipes up from the kitchen.

'Yes, darling, of course we are,' I call back. 'I can't think of anyone more normal than us.'

'Mummy, don't you like Granny and Grandpa?' Grace asks as we head out to school and Finn, as is his habit these days, tears ahead of us.

'Of course I do,' I tell her. 'It's just . . . a bit of a surprise, that's all. But it'll be fine. And you like it when Joelle comes round, don't you?'

She nods enthusiastically as I take her hand in mine. Of course I've lied, but what else could I do? I couldn't tell her that I've had an aversion to Jed's parents ever since they came up from London a week after Toby was born, and his mother said, 'I never thought you'd go for a third baby. But I suppose, with your child-bearing hips . . .' As if to produce less than three children would have been a waste of my generous proportions.

All day at work, I try to raise my spirits by imagining the Rawlton House menu and how a mouthful of gooey chocolate dessert will dissolve on my tongue. I attempt to conjure up visions of lemon tart and oozing cheeses and glasses of lovely wine. Yet I can't shake off the gloom over their impending visit. I'm so tense that, by the time I leave the salon for Toby's nursery, I don't have any appetite at all.

Their car pulls up as I'm clearing up after the children's dinner. I spot the caravan too, which goes by the optimistic name of *Vitesse*. As I let them in, Pauline allows me her customary mechanical hug, then stands back and gives me a speedy up-and-down look as if trying to ascertain how much weight I've gained since we last saw each other. 'You're looking . . . well,' she manages, meaning, *at least five or six pounds at a guess. Even though she's trying to disguise it by wearing black. God, what made Jed ditch that slim Natasha girl he went out with at college?* Pauline, who's of wiry build, is wearing a floaty button-up dress in a pansy-patterned fabric. Her copper hair is set in tight, brittle curls, and her face is liberally dusted with bronzing powder. The effect is oddly metallic, like Hammerite paint. Hovering beside his wife, Brian regards me with a faint smirk, as if bemused that their darling Jed – sorry, *Jeremy* – has wound up with such a substandard wife. 'So, how are you both?' I ask. 'Journey up okay?'

'Fine, thanks,' Pauline says.

'Oh, yes,' Brian adds, lips wet and shiny beneath a neatly-trimmed silvery moustache. 'Smashing drive up. Awful impatient, though, drivers today.'

'What, on the roads around here?' I ask.

'No, on the motorway.'

'Right,' I say carefully, 'but I suppose that's the idea. To be able to get to places quickly.'

'Well, we like to take things at our own pace, don't we, Brian?' Pauline says, lowering her gaze. 'We like to enjoy the scenery.'

'Quite right. Otherwise, what's the point of it?' I force a smile. 'Jed should be home soon,' I add, 'and the kids are having a snack in the garden. I'll just let them know you're here.'

Pauline nods, and I see her eyeing the messy pile of newspapers and drawings and half a Lego galleon teetering on the coffee table. 'Granny and Grandpa are here!' I announce at the back door. Grace shrieks in delight and shoots indoors, closely followed by Toby and Finn. As is their custom, Pauline and Brian are armed with a gigantic plastic sack of unbranded, neon-bright sweets. If they were analysed, they probably wouldn't even be classified as food.

'Just one or two each,' I say ineffectually as Toby plunges a grubby hand into the sack and rams a fistful of sweets into his mouth. In order to pick out her favourites, Grace tries to gain control of the sack, while Finn's mouth is already sloshing with molten, chemical-smelling jelly.

'It's your birthday today, isn't it, Laura?' Pauline says.

'That's right. In fact, Jed's taking us all out for dinner tonight to a lovely country hotel.'

'Oh, isn't that Jeremy all over?' Pauline gushes, clasping her hands to her neat bosom. 'So generous, treating us all.'

'Yes, isn't he?' I force a smile, and am overcome with relief when the door opens and he saunters in, greeting his parents warmly. He's clutching a small, posh-looking carrier bag which he hands to me.

'Is that for me?' Grace demands, her teeth bouncing off a jelly snake.

'No, love,' Jed chuckles. 'It's for Mummy.' He turns to me. 'I knew you'd say you have nothing to wear tonight, so I thought . . .'

'Isn't that lovely, Brian?' Pauline swoons before I've even opened the bag. 'Isn't he so *thoughtful*?'

'She's a lucky woman,' Brian observes, as if I've melted into the ether. I turn away to pull out my present, conscious of all eyes boring into my back. It's a putty-coloured wrap dress in a fine, silky fabric. 'This is lovely,' I murmur truthfully. What I really mean is: this would look lovely on someone else.

'You'll wear it tonight, won't you?' Jed asks hopefully.

'Yes, darling. Of course I will.' I turn and smile at him, picturing myself in the restaurant, the silky material clinging to every ripple and bulge. I've driven past Rawlton House countless times, and the place reeks of refined elegance. They probably don't even let fat people in. Or, if they do, they are handed a 'special' menu with those darn Tub Club faces plastered all over it.

'Now that *is* a stunning dress,' Pauline goes on. 'Think it'll fit you, Laura?'

'Um, I hope so.'

'Why don't you try it on?' Jed suggests. 'We really should get ready anyway. I thought, if we set out early we can have a glass of champagne in the bar first.'

My stomach twists, and I smile at him. 'That's a lovely idea, Jed. And thanks for arranging all this.'

'Hey, go and get ready, birthday girl,' he says, planting a kiss on my lips.

'If it's too tight,' Pauline calls after me, 'I'm sure they'll take it back.'

'Mum, just leave it, okay?' I hear Jed mutter as I head upstairs.

'It's just, that sort of silky material can be very unforgiving, love . . .'

I clatter across the landing, trying to quell murderous urges and wondering how I might possibly get through the evening ahead with my dignity intact. In our bedroom, I strip and hold the dress up against myself. It *is* lovely, and the putty colour is surprisingly flattering against my pale skin. It's just the fabric that's the problem. Pauline was right: it *is* unforgiving. Some sturdy undergarment is required. Not Celeste's Coco de Mers. Not even my Tesco ensemble. Something unyielding to suck everything in, like the stomach reducer girdle thingie I bought in York. Surely it'll be more effective than those anti-cellulite tights.

I retrieve the packet from my bottom drawer. As I'm scanning the blurb, I hear Joelle, our babysitter, arriving and Grace chatting excitedly to her. Joelle is a nineteen-year-old student. She has a nipped-in waist and certainly doesn't require fierce undergarments. 'Drop a dress size,' it says on the packet. Ooh, yes please. There are 'before' and 'after' photos of a model on the packet, and the contrast is astounding. I check the instructions which comprise nine steps:

1. *Step carefully into each leg of the Reducer.*
2. *Gently ease up so each leg is positioned approximately
   5 cm above the knee.*
3. *Now slowly roll up the rest of the Reducer . . .*

'Laura!' Jed calls up. 'Are you ready? Joelle's here, we're
all waiting to go . . .'

'Just a minute,' I call back. Jesus. Hasn't he the faintest
idea what it's like to be a woman? How long it takes to
make ourselves alluring for the outside world?

4. *Smooth the Reducer over your bottom, ensuring back
   seam lies centrally.* How can I see if it's central or not? I
   crane round. My backside looks horribly misshapen.

'What are you doing, Mummy?' Toby saunters in and stares
at the Reducer which is still only half on. I try to tug it
upwards and snatch the sheet of instructions from the bed.
'What are you doing?' he asks again.

'I'm, um, trying to put these special pants on.' He regards
me with intense, dark eyes, taking this in – his first lesson
about the curious habits of femalekind. The fact that we need
an entire manual in order to put on an undergarment.
Glancing down, I note with dismay that wodges of flab have
squished out below the leg bits. I hadn't realised those parts
were fat. It's like suddenly realising you have podgy eyebrows.

Toby cocks his head to one side. 'What's that?' he asks,
pointing at the weird-looking gusset. It's actually a *double*
gusset which, apparently, enables the wearer to pee without
taking the whole thing off. But I can't tell him that. Don't
want him getting ideas about it being okay to go to the toilet

through his underwear. Besides, at his age, I don't want him even *knowing* the word gusset or he'll be shouting about it at Scamps and Cara will ask me to come in for a 'little chat'. After the water tray incident, I've been trying to keep a low profile at nursery. Toby stares as I yank the thing up.

'Er . . . what *are* you wearing?' Jed, too, has now appeared at our bedroom door. I am tempted to suggest he invites his parents up too, maybe hand out some popcorn while they all sit down, make themselves comfortable and stare at me.

'Holder-inner pants,' I mutter, glimpsing my disturbing reflection in the mirror.

'What on earth for?'

'For a smoother line.'

'But . . . how the hell will you get them off?'

'I don't care about getting them off,' I snap. 'It's taken me twenty-five minutes to get them *on*.'

'I know,' he says hotly. 'We're all waiting downstairs and if you don't hurry up they'll give our table to someone—'

'Does this thing make me look thinner?' I blurt out desperately.

'Um . . .' He scans my body, clearly trying to dredge up a positive comment. 'You look, um . . . *compressed*. Sort of boxy.'

'Boxy? What d'you mean, boxy?'

'I, er . . .' He is laughing now, his shoulders bobbing with mirth. 'Your, erm . . . your bum . . .'

'What about my bum?'

'It's gone kind of . . . shoebox shaped.'

'Shoebox shaped?' I wail as Toby splutters with laughter.

'Oh, come on,' Jed sniggers. 'Once you're dressed, I'm sure you'll look, um . . . almost normal.'

Almost normal. Perhaps that's the best I can hope for. While Jed ushers Toby downstairs, I pull on my new dress and sandals and clatter down after them. 'Wow, you look amazing,' Joelle announces.

'Thanks,' I say, kissing the children goodbye before our curious group tumbles out into the soft spring evening. Brian pulls out a car key and unlocks the doors. 'Aren't we going in our car?' I ask.

'No, love,' Brian says. 'Thought I'd drive, let Jed have a drink. Look like you could do with one, son, after all the time it took Laura to get ready . . .' Everyone chuckles, and I force an icy smile.

'I could drive,' I suggest. 'I really wouldn't mind.'

'Oh, no, love,' Brian says, clearly horrified by the concept of me being in control of a car. 'C'mon, ladies. Hop in.'

Obediently, Pauline and I clamber into the back. 'We're not taking the caravan, are we?' I ask faintly as Jed climbs in beside his father.

''Course we are, love,' Brian says.

'But couldn't you . . . unhook it and leave it behind?' I glance back. Vitesse, its creamy exterior smattered with mould, fills the entire rear window. A woman shrinks away as she walks by, as if it might have a contagious disease.

'Oh no,' Pauline says. 'We wouldn't want to leave it unattended around here.'

'What?' I splutter. 'But you live in Peckham . . .'

She throws me a baffled look. 'What's wrong with Peckham?'

'Nothing. Nothing at all. But there's hardly any crime around here, and I'm sure it'd be safe for a few hours . . .'

'Better safe than sorry,' Brian observes as we pull away from our house.

I like to pretend that we're normal. That we do civilised things like go to a grown-up restaurant to celebrate a birthday. It's a little hard to pull off with a rotting caravan wobbling precariously at our rear.

CHAPTER TWENTY-THREE

By the time we arrive at Rawlton House, the Reducer has slipped down several inches and rolled up on itself. The effect is of a thick electrical cable wrapped around my waist. My instinct is to pelt across the gravelled drive to the entrance and into the ladies' before anyone notices, but I force myself to loop an arm through Jed's and walk demurely. 'You look lovely,' he whispers.

'Thanks.' I muster a smile.

'Hope you don't mind about . . .' He flicks his eyes in the direction of his parents, who are strutting ahead.

'No, it's okay.'

'There wasn't anything I could do. I wanted to take you out, just the two of us, then they announced they were coming . . .'

'I know,' I say, squeezing his arm. 'I'm sure it'll be fine, Jed. Just relax.'

And it seems as if it will be fine, as we are greeted at the restaurant's entrance and shown to a window table offering a fabulous view of the gardens and lake. Vitesse glows in the distance like a decaying molar. I focus hard on my menu. 'What are you having, Laura?' Pauline asks.

'I'm not sure yet.' Actually, I sense that someone who requires such a sturdy undergarment should consume as little as possible. A solitary broad bean, perhaps, or a sliver of poached fish.

'What do they recommend at that diet club?' she asks, copper hair glistening beneath the orangey lights.

'They, um . . . have a kind of face system,' I murmur, throwing Jed a quick, vexed look. What possessed him to tell his mother about Tub Club?

'What kind of face system?' Pauline wants to know.

'It's a way of classifying food to work out if you're supposed to have it or not.' I pause, flicking my gaze around the table. Some birthday this is.

'And how do the faces work?' Pauline enquires.

I glance at Jed and he pulls a wry smile. *Just humour her*, his look seems to say. *Play along*. 'Well,' I explain, 'every food has a face rating, like this . . . or this, or . . .' I find myself pulling the actual faces. Mum off the leash for the night, who no longer knows how to conduct herself in a restaurant. I picture Danny in St Mary's Hall, listening to a lecture about the fat content of cheese, and almost wish I was there with him.

'Gosh,' exclaims Pauline. 'Rather you than me. All those rules! I can eat anything I want, can't I, Brian?' He nods obediently. 'Never gained an ounce, apart from when I was expecting of course . . .' She throws Jed a fond look. 'And even then, it all fell away in a matter of weeks.'

'That's what happened to my sister,' I say. 'In fact you'd hardly have known she was pregnant. I don't share the same trait, unfortunately.' I laugh self-deprecatingly, and Pauline makes a small grunting noise, probably in agreement. I turn my attention back to the menu, aware of a sense of disappointment creeping up from my toes and settling somewhere around the stomach region. I'd imagined that Rawlton House would serve light, modern food which tastes so amazingly zingy that you don't need a whole pile of it to feel satisfied, and which might possibly be awarded a smiley face. But no. Everything appears to come slathered in creamy sauces, as if we've been catapulted back to the seventies. I spot the waitress transporting a vast rack of lamb to another table.

'Waitress!' Brian calls, waving a hand as if hailing a cab. An olive-skinned beauty strides towards us.

'Yes?' she asks pleasantly.

'Which is the biggest?' Although he's prodding the menu's steak section, he is staring pointedly at the girl's breasts.

'That one,' she says, jabbing the menu. 'The sixteen-ounce T-bone.'

'What, like this big?' He holds flattened hands apart, indicating something roughly the size of a disposable nappy.

'Yes, something like that. It's pretty thick.' *Like you*, she adds silently. Brian nods, as if reassured, and the girl takes our orders. I catch him appraising her curvaceous rear as she heads for the kitchen.

'Oh, I must give you your present,' Pauline announces, snatching her bag from the floor and clicking open its outlandish gold clasp. This looks promising. It fits into her bag, so we're not talking a non-stick frying pan, like last year, or the pedal bin which they bought me the year before that, which I facetiously labelled, 'LAURA'S BIN' as soon as they'd left. And it looks like the bread maker's been forgotten.

'Thank you,' I say as she hands me a thin, squishy, pink tissue-wrapped parcel. I squeeze it tentatively.

'Open it then,' Pauline commands, dark eyes glittering. I peel off the tissue paper and place my gift on the table. We all stare at the oven glove, as if expecting it to perform a somersault. It's printed all over with a wheatsheaf design. 'Well, that's handy,' Jed blurts out.

'It really is,' I agree. 'You know, I'm always burning myself in the kitchen. I'm getting so clumsy in my old age . . .' I laugh through my nose.

'That's what I thought,' Pauline enthuses. 'I know you're not much of a cook, Laura, but we thought you probably needed one.'

'Yes, I did.' I blink at it, at a loss as to what to do next and feel surprisingly, desperately sad. There it is, lying before me, surrounded by gleaming silver cutlery: the one item my parents-in-law thought would make my life complete. I wonder what to do with it now. Stuffing it straight into my bag would seem rude, and I'm determined to be gracious and not allow my in-laws, Vitesse or a sodding oven glove to spoil my special night out. Yet I can't leave the thing sitting here like a bizarre table decoration. All I can think of is to pull it on and rest my gloved hand on the table.

'You don't have to wear it right now,' Jed hisses.

'It's okay,' I whisper back. 'It's very comfortable.'

'Laura, please,' he starts, trailing off as our waitress arrives.

'Be careful, your plates are very hot,' she warns us.

'No worries,' I say, waggling my glove. 'I've got this.'

She chuckles, but there's an undertone of horror as she surveys my gloved hand and the scraps of tissue paper on the table. *My God,* she's thinking. *This is what happens on birthdays when you're old.* Smiling brightly at Pauline, I remove the glove, tuck it into my bag and try to relish my steak in its oily sauce. But I can't. All I can see are Tub Club faces, glowering at me.

My mobile bleeps extra-loudly in the hushed room. 'Better check it's not our babysitter,' I say, unearthing it from beneath the oven glove. Text from Danny. Conscious of Pauline swivelling her eyes towards it, I ram it back into my bag.

'Everything okay?' Jed asks.

'Yes, fine,' I say lightly. 'Just someone from Tub Club.'

Brian eyes me levelly and I notice a small fleck of some kind of vegetation nestling in his neatly-trimmed moustache. His fleshy face is pink and shiny, and his stiff checked shirt collar is tight at the neck. 'Do they let you have that, love?' He jabs a porky finger in the direction of my steak.

'Well, yes,' I say, 'as long as I don't eat anything tomorrow, or for the rest my life actually . . .' I laugh feebly.

'Maybe you should skip pudding,' Pauline observes. 'Or at least just have the forest fruits sorbet. That's just ice, really, isn't it?'

'Yes, I suppose it is.' I glance at Jed, mentally signalling that we should hurry things along – that Joelle always has stacks of college work to do, and our children are probably *sobbing* for us at home (they won't be, as they'd far rather hang around with an easy-going teenager who brings them comics than their craggy, ill-tempered mother – but *still*). I study the dessert menu as our plates are cleared away. 'Baked lemon cheesecake sounds good,' Jed enthuses.

'And they've got chocolate pudding,' Brian adds.

'I might have the profiteroles,' muses Pauline. 'I love that chocolate sauce they pour over . . .' I can't stand this. It's some kind of sick joke. Swooping up from the table, I grab my bag, make my excuses and scurry towards the loo. 'What are you having, Laura?' Pauline calls out after me.

'I'll be back in a minute. I'll decide then, if you'll wait for me.'

'Laura!' Jed hisses after me.

'What?'

'Your sucker-inner pants,' he mouths. 'You can *see* them.'

Oh lord. Stranded in the middle of the restaurant, I glance down at my legs. My new dress, which is meant to be knee-length, has ridden up and is clinging defiantly to my thighs. I try to pull it down, but some mysterious force – static electricity perhaps – makes it ride up again. Beneath it, clearly visible, are the legs of my Reducer. Brian snorts. Pauline looks away pointedly, as if trying to offer me a shred of dignity. I lurch for the ladies', glimpsing Vitesse through the window, parked by the lake. May the ducks savage its tyres with their beaks.

The loos are so palatial, it's almost a pity I don't need to use them, especially as I've been looking forward to trying out my double gusset. Steadying my breath, I perch on an ornate gilt chair and survey my reflection in the huge, artfully tarnished mirror. If the leg area wasn't humiliating enough, the top of the Reducer has now bunched up even more and is causing an unsightly bulge around my stomach. I don't have it in me to undress in a cubicle and readjust it.

Instead I just sit on the gilt chair, revelling in the stillness of the ladies' loos, wondering how long I can feasibly stay in here without Jed dispatching a search party. Will I go for the choc pudding or the cheesecake? I can try a bit of Jed's cheesecake, so maybe . . . hang on, wasn't there a raspberry tart as well? And crème brûlée? My mouth waters, causing my irritation over the oven glove to melt away. Awash with warm, dessert-induced feelings, I retrieve my phone and re-read Danny's text.

MISSED U TONIGHT, it reads, & U MISSED EXCITING STIR FRY TALK. JEALOUS? CALL ME, DX. With a smile, I call sender. Perhaps the night is looking up after all.

CHAPTER TWENTY-FOUR

'So,' Danny says, 'you missed a great talk tonight. Mushrooms and bean sprouts discussed at great length, and six different stir fries to look at. Did you decide you couldn't stand the excitement?'

I laugh. 'Wish I'd been there actually, but I'm out for dinner with Jed and his parents. Sorry, I should have let you know.'

'Oh, I'm sure you're having a far better time than I had tonight. So, is it fun?'

'Um, I wouldn't say that exactly. Actually, it's a bit of a disaster.'

'Really? Why's that?'

'Well, for a start,' I snigger, 'his parents have just given me an oven glove . . .'

'Oh yes – it's your birthday, isn't it?'

'How did you know?' I ask, amazed.

'I'm sorry, it sounds really nosey, but I noticed your date of birth on your membership card . . .' There's a pause, and I'm overwhelmed by an urge to see him – just to be with someone who accepts me the way I am, and is interested enough to notice my date of birth *and* commit it to memory. 'Hope you don't mind,' he adds.

'No, of course I don't! I'm just amazed you remembered. So, what else did I miss at the meeting tonight?'

'Oh, thrilling stuff. Twenty-five ways with beetroot, including making a jelly – a *sweet* one, I mean . . .'

'Oh, here you are!' Pauline exclaims, marching into the ladies' and straight to the mirror where she tweaks her unyielding hair.

'Better go,' I say quickly. 'I'll call you and we'll fix up a run, would you be up for that?'

'Look forward to it,' Danny says.

'Everything all right, Laura?' Pauline takes a pot and a brush from her make-up bag and dusts on more shimmery powder.

'I'm fine,' I enthuse.

She glances at my waistline which looks far from svelte in the soft, drapey fabric. 'So, how long have you been going to that slimming place?'

'Oh, I've only just started. Just been to one meeting.'

She nods, extracting a peach frosted lipstick and slicking on a thick coat. 'Went to one myself once. Not that I really needed to. Friend asked me to go with her and I wanted to show some moral support . . .'

I nod, picturing Danny at home in his tumble-down farm, wondering how he's spending the rest of the evening.

'. . . It was all women of course,' Pauline continues, 'apart from one man, and we knew what *he* was there for.' She cackles loudly.

I look at her. 'What *was* he there for?'

'Oh, Laura, you are naïve . . .' She's still chuckling away whilst prodding at her hair as if testing to see if it's properly baked. 'He was there to pick up women, of course. Why else would a man go to a slimming club?'

'Really? You mean, he went to all the trouble of joining and paying and queuing up to be weighed . . .'

'Yes, can you imagine? Mind you, the odds were pretty high. About fifty women to one man . . .' As she pops into a cubicle, I wonder if this was Danny's motive too. No, surely not. It would seem so . . . *premeditated*. Pauline emerges from the cubicle and washes her hands. 'Come on, let's get back,' she says brusquely. 'Dessert should be here. I ordered you the forest fruit sorbet if that's okay.'

I follow her, wanting to say, 'No, it's *not* okay', but am stunned into silence. My cheeks must be burning with irritation, because Brian looks up and frowns at me from the table. 'You're all flushed, love,' he informs me as Pauline and I take our seats.

'I'm just hot,' I murmur, avoiding his beady gaze. 'It's awfully stuffy in here.'

'Yes, I got that too,' Pauline chips in.

'Got what?' I ask, frowning.

'Those awful hot flushes when I was going through the change, especially if I'd been drinking . . .'

I blink at her. First she's implying that I should have a gastric band fitted and now, on my thirty-ninth birthday, I'm menopausal. Our desserts arrive, and I glower down at my frankly *insultingly* tiny dish of purple ice. With an undisguised smirk, Pauline forks an entire profiterole into her mouth. 'This is amazing,' Jed enthuses, savouring his cheesecake. 'Er, want to try a bit, Laura?' He offers me a fragment on his fork.

'Better not,' I say tersely, jabbing my spoon into my dish. Everyone else's desserts ooze cream, sugar and naughtiness. I push the dish aside and take a huge gulp of wine.

'Don't you like it, Laura?' Pauline enquires.

'It's lovely,' I say, 'but honestly, I'm so full from my steak,

I couldn't eat another mouthful.' I smile brightly and drain my glass.

By the time we leave I'm quite tiddly. 'You know your dad and I would be happy in the caravan, love,' Pauline reminds Jed as we drive home. 'We don't want to put you and Laura to any trouble.'

'Don't be silly, Mum,' he says. 'You're having our room – Laura's got it all ready for you. We'll be fine on the sofa bed in the living room.'

'Well, if you're sure, love,' Pauline wheedles as we pull up at our house, and I rake through my purse to find money for Joelle. As I pay her, I catch her glancing down at my legs; my dress has ridden up again, exposing my bizarre undergarment. Past caring, I hand her three tenners. It's only when she's gone, and Pauline and Brian have headed upstairs, that I remember that the Reducer instructions are lying on our bed. Oh well. It'll confirm Pauline's suspicion that Tub Club really isn't working for me.

Jed pulls out the sofa bed and retrieves bedding from the linen cupboard under the stairs. 'Well, thanks a lot,' he mutters, shaking out the sheet.

'Thanks for what?' I peel off my dress slightly squiffily, hoping to give him a laugh with my support garment.

'For drinking so much. For being so grumpy and refusing to eat that sorbet, just to make some kind of point . . .'

'But she ordered my dessert for me!' I protest. 'It's so rude, Jed. What made her think she could do that?'

He exhales fiercely. 'Look, I know Mum can be difficult, but it was hardly the time, in the middle of a restaurant—'

'I am capable of choosing my own food, Jed. How would your mother have felt if I'd ordered hers?'

'She probably just thought you'd like . . .'

'That's what I'm sick of,' I snap back. 'I'm fed up with everyone thinking they know what I want, when I did not want a bloody dish of ice!'

Jed opens his mouth and glances fretfully towards the ceiling. I glare at him, no longer caring that I'm standing here in nothing but a girdle, and that his parents might have heard our tense exchange. He's repulsed by me anyway. It's obvious. 'What's wrong with you?' he thunders, throwing the sheet haphazardly over the mattress and flinging the duvet over it.

'Nothing's wrong with me! I'm perfectly fine.'

'Well, you're drunk for a start.'

'No I'm not! I only had . . .'

'I know how much you had. You were knocking it back as if you were terrified it might run out . . .'

'So what?' I cry. 'It's my birthday, isn't it? For God's sake, Jed – I had about three glasses.'

'And the rest . . .'

'Were you counting or something? And weren't *you* pissed out of your head at Celeste's party?'

He freezes, still gripping a corner of the duvet. From upstairs come his father's low snores. 'What the hell does Celeste have to do with this?' he demands.

'Nothing,' I growl. 'Nothing at all.'

Dropping the duvet, he stomps towards the front door. 'I've had enough,' he mutters. 'Can't take any more of you being so damn ridiculous . . .'

'What are you doing?'

'I'm going out.'

'Out where?' I cry. Oh God. He's leaving me. I'm going to

be a single mother of three, and all because I wasn't delighted with my oven glove or the forest fruits sorbet. He's right: I've drunk too much wine. It would have been fine if I'd been allowed a nice stodgy dessert to soak up the alcohol, but I wasn't and now my head's swimming, and I've lost any sense of who's right and wrong and it's all such a horrible, tangled mess . . . 'Jed!' I yell after him.

'I'm sleeping in the caravan.' He whirls round angrily.

'But you can't. It stinks of chemical toilet. Please stay here. Let's talk about it . . .'

'Why should I?' he shoots back.

'Because it'll freak out the kids if they come down in the morning and you're not here, *and* we'll have to explain to your parents . . .' I tail off, not wanting to admit the truth: that *I* want him here, with me. I want, more than anything, to fall asleep all wrapped up together, like we used to, before his crush on Celeste when we were happy and in love and I never suspected him of doing anything wrong. 'Please, Jed,' I add, my eyes filling with tears, 'at least sit down and talk to me.'

'What about?' he snaps.

'Uh . . .' I pause a beat too long. He snatches his mother's quilted handbag from the coffee table, pulls out a keyring with jingling charms attached to it and storms outside, banging the front door behind him.

CHAPTER TWENTY-FIVE

I wait for him to come back in and say he didn't really mean it. But he doesn't. The house is horribly still and quiet. A pale yellow glow spills into our living room as he turns on the caravan's light.

I grab the duvet from the sofa bed and shroud myself in it. It smells stuffy – of sleepovers and illicit midnight feasts. A few crisp crumbs are stuck to it. Shuffling to the window, I peer out at Vitesse. In our early days, Jed would amuse me with stories of bleak caravan holidays with his parents in Southend and Bournemouth. 'You were lucky, having Kate to hang out with,' he said, and I realised I was, despite our eight-year age gap. It couldn't have been much fun being an only child, trapped in Vitesse with his mum and dad.

You'd think the wretched thing would have fallen apart by now. One window is cracked and held together with thick silver tape. Mottled marks have spread up from its bottom, like a sinister rash. I feel hollow inside, staring out at it. The stark fact is that Jed would rather spend the night with mildewed curtains and a pongy chemical loo than in here, with me.

Maybe, I think, brightening slightly, Vitesse will be stolen during the night. Isn't Pauline always keen to point out how crime-infested small North Yorkshire market towns are, compared to the serenity of Peckham? Jed could wake up with a start, realising too late that it – and he – is being towed away by dastardly thieves on the motorway. Serves him right for trying to taunt me with his cheesecake. I gaze out, trying to cheer myself up by picturing him, flailing wildly at the window and clad only in his underpants. Then the caravan's light goes off. Great – so he really *is* sleeping out there. Brilliant end to a birthday. Pauline and Brian will come down in the morning – plus the kids, of course – and I'll have to concoct some elaborate lie about Jed wanting to spend the night in Vitesse just for fun, as a reminder of those fabulous child-hood holidays.

They'll all know, of course. And Pauline will probably mutter something about it all being my fault, 'because she's going through the change and her hormones are all over the place.' And Jed's out there, oblivious, while I'm worrying about how to explain all of this to the children.

Perching on the sofa bed's edge, I pull the duvet tightly around my body and try to calm my urgent breathing. Of even more pressing concern is the fact that I'm still trapped inside the Reducer. Still swaddled in duvet, I waddle upstairs to the bathroom and bolt the door firmly behind me. Despite some desperate pulling and tugging, I can't get the Reducer to budge. I glimpse my reflection in our mirrored cabinet. I look pale and fearful, like someone on the run from the police. In the hope of achieving maximum shrinkage, I bought the smallest Reducer in the shop. Now I'll need an operation to take it off. You hear about people going to A&E to have all kinds of household objects removed from various orifices. It can't be more embarrassing than this.

With all my frantic manoeuvring, I manage to knock over

Grace's open bottle of Matey which was sitting on the edge of the bath and has now flooded the checked lino floor with lurid pink fluid. 'Is someone in there?' Brian calls out, rattling the door handle.

Yes, Brian, That's why it's sodding locked. 'Won't be a minute,' I reply, mopping up the puddle with a bath towel.

'Sorry, love, but are you going to be much longer? Call of nature, you know . . .'

'When will they get a second bathroom?' Pauline cries from our bedroom. 'Honestly, I don't know how they manage . . .' Tell me about it. Once, only partly as a joke, I wrote a note entitled TEN REASONS WHY WE NEED ANOTHER BATHROOM and stuck it on the bathroom door. I was even prepared to do more hours at the salon to pay for it. 'Maybe one day,' Jed said. 'But there are so many other priorities right now . . .'

'Laura?' Brian barks again.

'I'm coming,' I trill, pulling the duvet around me and opening the door.

'Oh!' he says, startled. 'Sorry, Laura. Didn't realise you were in a state of, er . . .'

'All yours,' I mutter, briefly glimpsing his alarmingly short dressing gown before I bolt downstairs. Right now, I need Jed. We might not be speaking, and at this precise moment I despise him intensely, but I need him to help me get the Reducer off. Then, when that's done, we can get divorced. I also need my dressing gown but it's hanging up in our bedroom and I can't face going in there and explaining things to Pauline. Pulling the duvet even tighter, I open our front door a few inches and peer out, checking the street.

It's a cool, slightly misty night, and there appears to be

nobody around. Quickly, barefooted, I dart to Vitesse and rattle its door. It won't open. Must be locked from the inside. I see that Jed has inherited his mother's fear of crazed, lawless Northerners. 'Jed!' I hiss, pressing my mouth against it. 'Jed. Open the door. It's me.'

I wait, glancing wildly around the street. A woman with a small, wiry dog has appeared from around the corner and is strolling towards me. On spotting me, she tries to look away, but her gaze is dragged back to the woman who's wearing a duvet in the street and trying to break into a caravan. The dog emits a sinister growl. 'Noodle!' the woman says sharply.

'Open the fucking door,' I hiss with my lips pressed against the door.

'Now, Noodle,' the woman murmurs. I smile tightly, backing away as Noodle trots right up to me and starts sniffing around my duvet. 'Are you . . . all right?' its owner asks, pursing her lips.

'I'm fine,' I say. 'I, um, just need to get into our caravan for something.' Hell, now I'm having to pretend it's *mine*.

'Are you locked out of your house? I've got my mobile if you need to call someone . . .'

She's failing to register that Noodle is now snarling menacingly and tugging at the corner of my duvet with its mean, pointy teeth. 'No, honestly, I'm fine.' *Please take your dog and go away.*

'Well, if you're sure . . .'

'Absolutely.' I force another grin. Noodle cocks a leg against Vitesse's back tyre and urinates. Good Noodle.

'Naughty!' the woman snaps, tugging the dog away and muttering as she hurries down the road.

I wait until she's out of sight, then bang the door with my

fist. No response. I'm freezing now, despite my thick, seven-tog wrapping. Can't risk rearranging the duvet to cover my shoulders in case it drops to the ground and I'm exposed in Bracken Lane wearing nothing but the Reducer. 'Jed, *please* open this door!' I yell, no longer caring that someone might hear me. This is a national emergency. The Reducer is growing tighter by the second. Does my husband want me to drop dead right here, in front of our house, due to having my circulation cut off? Does he want our children to find me, in a pale, lifeless heap, when they set out for school in the morning?

I thump the caravan's side, then shove it so it wobbles dangerously. 'Jed!' I cry, as I lean against the caravan and set it rocking until a vase of sun-bleached plastic tulips tumbles off its windowsill and Mrs Hendry comes to her bedroom window a few doors down.

The caravan door flies open. 'For God's sake,' Jed barks, hair jutting up at odd angles. 'Are you out of your mind?'

'It's my Reducer,' I bleat.

'Your what?'

'Those weird pants. The sucker-inners. I need you to help me get them off.'

He blinks at me. He must have pulled on his sweater in haste because it's inside out *and* back to front with the label poking up at his chin. 'You're joking,' he says. 'Please tell me this is a bad dream and not bloody happening.'

'Unfortunately it is,' I hiss as Mrs Hendry's door opens and she starts to walk hesitantly towards us. 'I'm sorry, okay? But there's no other option. You'll have to cut me out of it.'

'For Christ's sake, Laura. What with?'

'Um . . . wallpaper scissors?' I suggest.

'Are you completely mad?'

'Probably,' I growl as he shuts Vitesse's door and follows me grudgingly into the house. 'But I'd never have bought it if they'd put a warning about this on the packet.'

CHAPTER TWENTY-SIX

Jed and I hunt for scissors. Our house has a talent for swallowing up ordinary things: plasters, Sellotape, working pens. It makes simple tasks, like wrapping a present, virtually insurmountable. 'Where did you put those wallpaper scissors?' he asks.

'I didn't put them anywhere,' I retort.

'Yes you did. You must have. You used them last when you papered Grace's bedroom.'

'That was before Christmas! Can you remember where you put things six months ago?' Jed mutters something unintelligible. I, meanwhile, am resigning myself to spending the rest of my life trapped in the Reducer.

'What about your hairdressing scissors?' Jed asks.

'We can't use those. It'll blunt them! They're expensive, Jed, professional equipment . . .'

He fixes me with a cool stare. 'D'you want to stay trapped in that thing forever?'

'No, of course I don't . . .'

'So where are they?'

I sigh, feeling my fighting spirit ebbing away. 'Top left in my chest of drawers,' I murmur. 'You'll have to get them, though. I'm not going in with your parents in there.'

He shakes his head, smirking. 'I'm not fetching them. You'll have to go.'

'Jed, I can't. What if they're . . . *you* know . . .' I shudder involuntarily.

'For God's sake,' he splutters. 'You've got such a dirty mind.'

'Well,' I bleat, 'you never know.' What a galling thought: that Brian and Pauline are seeing more action than we are, in *our bed.* Come to think of it, just about everyone's seeing more action than we are. I have the sex life of a nun without the benefit of being able to drift around a quiet building all day.

Jed and I stare at each other. I can virtually hear his brain whirring as he runs through numerous grounds for divorce: insistence on wearing appalling undergarment. Refusal to eat sorbet. Attempted vandalism of caravan. 'Oh, I'll get them,' he snaps, making for the stairs as a horrible image judders into my brain: of Jed opening my knicker drawer and his eyes lighting upon Celeste's fancy silk pants with the ribbon side-ties, and being overcome by desire.

'No, I'll go,' I say firmly. Taking a deep breath, I grip the duvet around me like the pastry layer of a sausage roll and waddle awkwardly upstairs. Opening our bedroom door quietly, I creep in. While Pauline is, thankfully, huddled under the duvet, Brian is lying flat on his back, exposed and resplendent in shiny satin pyjama bottoms. His arms are outstretched, his phlegmy snores rattling the room. Bile forms in my throat as I tiptoe towards my chest of drawers.

The top drawer creaks open, making me flinch. From beneath the jumble of undies I unearth my leather scissor pouch and dart for the door. 'Get them?' Jed hisses from the top of the stairs. I nod, pulling him into the bathroom and thrusting my scissors at him. As the duvet falls away, I sense his scathing gaze running up and down my body. 'Er . . . are you sure it won't just pull off?' he asks.

I nod. 'I've tried and tried. There's no way it'll budge.'

He pauses, gripping the scissors with grim determination, as if he's been asked to do something quease-making like gut a trout. 'Er, what shall I do?' he murmurs.

'Just cut it, Jed. Get on with it. Surely you're capable of slicing your wife out of a girdle . . .' I tail off, wondering how long it'll be before the divorce papers plop through the letterbox.

'But how?' Jed asks. 'I mean, it's so tight and I don't want to cut your skin or anything . . .'

'I don't care if you do. Just get it off me.' My heart is racing now, and I'm sure parts of my body are starting to rot due to my circulation being cut off. *Why can't I be like the other school mums?* I think as Jed carefully inserts a scissor blade between the Reducer and my mortified flesh. *Why can't I just be normal, like Beth?*

Snip. Snip. The Reducer starts to spring apart. I glance down at the small area of newly-exposed skin. 'Nearly there,' Jed says gruffly.

'Thanks,' I breathe, nearly crying with relief as the Reducer falls to the floor. He picks it up gingerly, wincing as he dangles it momentarily between thumb and forefinger, then drops it into the bin. Then he unlocks the bathroom door, snatches our sleepover duvet from the floor, and strides out as if he's just done something completely ordinary like floss his teeth.

I glare down at my pink, naked body. The area previously encased in sucker-inner is clammy and vaguely sick-looking, as if it's spent several decades trapped beneath waterproof plaster. Winding a bath towel around me, I slump downstairs, relieved to find Jed tucked up on the sofa bed. At least he appears to have forgotten about sleeping in the caravan. I slip into bed, curl myself around him and tentatively stroke the back of his neck. Even touching him feels awkward these days, and he flinches, moving towards the far edge of the sofa bed, so it feels as if there are acres of rumpled sheet between us.

I shouldn't be surprised that he's shunning me. I know people are into all sorts, but I can't imagine that cutting a woman out of a rubberised sucker-inner overwhelms many men with lust.

*

For the rest of my in-laws' visit, I'm on exemplary behaviour. I cook, I tidy up after everyone and I smile so much my jaw aches. I even invite Beth and her kids over for a relaxed, rowdy dinner – in truth, to dilute the chilling effect Jed's parents seem to have on our household. Tears stream down her face as I tell her about my Reducer trauma as we load the dishwasher together. 'Did he film you, trying to get it off?' she asks, choking back laughter.

'Film me? No, why would he do that?'

'To put on YouTube,' she splutters. 'It'd probably be an underground hit.'

'Can you imagine what Naomi would think, though, if she saw it? After the mums' race fiasco? She tagged along when Danny and I went running, you know. Fartleks this, Fartleks that. *Ooh, Danny, you need to stretch before a run – here, let me position your thigh correctly . . .*' I mime her grappling with various bits of Danny's anatomy and we peal with laughter. Even Pauline marching into the kitchen and insisting on being given a brush to sweep the floor (our *disgusting* floor, obviously) doesn't dampen my mood.

I meet Beth during my lunchbreak the next day. She texted to tell me about a half-price sale at the sports shop, and as Finn has banned me from borrowing his trainers again, I need a pair of my own. What Beth failed to mention is that, in order to choose the right pair, I'd first have to run on the shop's treadmill. 'What kind of brand d'you prefer?' the assistant asks, transfixed by my thudding feet.

'I'm just starting out,' I pant, 'so I don't really have a preference.' In truth, I just want to get this part over, select my trainers and enjoy my lunch with Beth. I have an irrational fear of treadmills, suspecting that they'll speed up unexpectedly and ping me off into a heap on the floor.

The young, athletic-looking man is peering at an image of my soles on the treadmill's screen. Thank God it's only my feet and not my stomach or arse. He turns off the machine, and I stumble back onto the floor as he selects an array of blisteringly expensive trainers.

All look roughly the same. There's a bit of blue piping here, a fluorescent lace there. Nothing to get over-excited about. 'With these,' the man enthuses, 'you're paying for added cushioning which protects your hips and groin.'

'Groin?' I repeat.

He nods. 'You can really twang yourself down there if you're not careful.'

I don't fancy any hideous twanging, not when I'm sprinting, gazelle-like, with Danny this evening. 'You should get the best pair you can afford,' Beth adds. 'Look what happened to me, with my creaky old knees. That was from wearing duff trainers.'

'Okay,' I say firmly. 'I'll take these.'

'Wise choice,' the man says. 'They'll really benefit your running.' I like that: *my* running, as if one day it might belong to me. Encouraged by Beth, I also buy a proper runner's bra which guarantees zero bounceage. Now all I have to worry about is not blinding Danny with my dazzling new trainers tonight.

'So,' Beth says, as we linger over our lunch beneath the beech tree in the park, 'you survived the outlaws' visit, *and* the Reducer trauma. I reckon you deserved that little spending spree.'

I nod, savouring the melting brie in my baguette, despite knowing that I should have gone for plain chicken salad on rye with the smiley Tub Club face. 'Well, if I'm going to stick with this running thing, I can hardly wear Grace's T-shirt.'

Beth wipes crumbs from her lips and pushes back glossy black hair from her face. The sky is searingly blue, and the park hums with office workers enjoying the sunshine. 'Have you told Jed about Danny?' she asks.

'No, not yet.'

'Why not?' she asks. 'I mean, he is just a friend, isn't he? It's not as if you have anything to hide.'

I pause, gathering up our paper wrappers from the grass. 'I know. But I should have mentioned it the first time, when we went running together. And because I didn't, it almost feels too late now, as if I'm hiding something and it's some kind of *thing . . .*'

'Is it a thing?' Beth asks gently. 'I mean . . . d'you want it to be? I know it hasn't been easy with Jed lately, and he's behaved pretty badly, but . . .'

'No,' I say quickly. 'I'm not looking for a fling or anything. Definitely not. Life's complicated enough as it is.'

She nods and lets the subject drop. But I have the distinct feeling that she doesn't believe me one bit.

CHAPTER TWENTY-SEVEN

Danny and I are choking with laughter, which is the last thing I imagined I'd be capable of doing while running. I've regaled him with tales of Vitesse and the hideous meal at Rawlton House. I've even shared my mortification at being trapped inside the Reducer. Outside Café Roma, which is glowing welcomingly, we come to an abrupt halt. 'Fancy a coffee?' he asks. 'I don't think I could run much further.'

'Oh, why not? Just a quick one to revive ourselves.'

'Maybe a cake too?' he suggests as we step into the warmth. 'Think you could be tempted?'

'Yes, I reckon we've earned it.' He smiles teasingly as we step inside, and I feel glowingly happy as I untie my tracksuit top from my waist and slip it on over my T-shirt. Does he really come to Tub Club to pick up women? It hardly seems possible, despite what Pauline said. Taking a seat at the smallest table, I pick up the menu and peruse the goodies on offer. Even though it's supposed to be more restaurant than café in the evenings, they never object if you pop in for coffee and cake. 'Marble cake, d'you reckon?' Danny murmurs.

'Oh yes. It's out of this world.' As we tuck in, feeling deliciously sinful, I glance at the window in case Belinda from Tub Club should happen to glance in. 'We need our carbs,' I murmur to Danny, 'after all that exercise. Professional runners eat nothing but pasta for weeks before a big race.'

'I'm sure you're right,' he murmurs. 'It's called carb-loading, I think. God, this cake's good, isn't it?'

'The best,' I agree, stealing a glance as he wipes chocolatey froth from his upper lip. Eating with Danny is so *pleasurable*. He obviously loves his food as much as I do, and it feels so relaxed, as eating should be, instead of all tangled up in rules and shouldn'ts and those darn Tub Club faces which have started to haunt my dreams. Compared to Rawlton House, and my 'romantic' dinner in the garden with Jed, this is heavenly. I spoon melting whipped cream from my hot chocolate straight into my mouth.

'You must think I'm so rude,' I tell him. 'I've hardly asked about your photography, the kind of work you do.' Actually, I'm intrigued by his ex-girlfriend, and am keen to know more, and I'm hoping we'll work round to it.

'I do anything that comes up,' he says. 'Newspapers, corporate, bit of advertising occasionally. It's what I studied at college, and although there have been a few rocky times over the years, I've managed to scrape a living out of it.'

'Well, that's something to be proud of,' I remark. 'Doing something you love, and sticking with it. I think you're lucky actually.'

He shrugs. 'At college I always imagined I'd do portraits. I had all these dreams of working on my own projects and having exhibitions of, you know, my *art* . . .' He sniggers self-deprecatingly. 'And of course, the reality's been nothing like that.'

'Does that bother you?'

'What, taking pictures of weddings and fêtes and dog

shows for local papers? Not really. I'm realistic, Laura. We all have to make a living, and you're right, I am lucky.' He pauses. 'How about you? Do you like what you do?'

'Sure, but . . .' I stir the remains of the cream into my hot chocolate. 'I've done it for so long, and things just become habitual, don't they? And you stop considering if it's really what you want.' I tail off, wondering if it's my job I'm talking about, or my marriage.

Danny looks at me. I catch my breath, and wonder what on earth I'll tell Jed when I get home. He'll be expecting me back. If I'm much longer he'll think I've tripped over and am lying, whimpering, in a hedge somewhere. 'How about you and Jed?' he asks gently.

I sense my cheeks flush. It's as if he knows what I'm thinking, and can tune right in, yet somehow, it doesn't feel intrusive. 'Well, you know,' I murmur. 'There are all the usual frustrations of living together, and we've been together for donkeys' years obviously, but we're generally fine . . .'

'Apart from when he storms out to that caravan . . .'

'Yes, well, that was a bit of a blip.' I laugh and pop a sugar cube into my mouth. 'But every couple has them, don't they? I suppose we're pretty normal really for a married couple with a bunch of kids.' I reach down to poke my fingers into my sock and extract a rather sweaty ten-pound note. 'This is my treat, by the way, before you start protesting.'

'Oh no, it was my idea, I'll get this . . .'

'You can treat me next time.' I flash a smile.

'Okay, that's a deal.' He grins at me. 'Um, do you have a habit of keeping money in your sock?'

'Oh, I just put that there in case I had some kind of accident and needed to get a taxi home . . .'

'D'you think Paula Radcliffe does that?'

'Definitely.' I snigger and place my tenner on the saucer. 'I'd better get back,' I add as the waitress tots up our bill, 'before my family sends out a search party. That run wasn't too terrible, was it?'

Danny smiles, and it feels as if my heart flips over. 'Terrible's the last word I'd use,' he says.

*

I'm so revved up and happy that I manage to run all the way home, even with marble cake and hot chocolate sloshing inside me. Letting myself into the house, I find Jed stretched out on the sofa in front of the TV. 'How did it go?' he asks, eyes fixed on the screen.

'Great,' I reply. 'Much better than last time.' *Mustn't feel guilty. I have done absolutely nothing to be ashamed of.*

His gaze flicks towards me. 'You've been a while, love. I was starting to worry.'

'Not that long,' I say with an exaggerated shrug. 'I just, um, took it slowly.'

He frowns, checking his watch. 'It's almost nine o'clock.'

'Uh-huh . . .' I try to arrange my features to look normal, but worry that my mouth looks weirdly tense.

'And you went out at, what . . . half-seven?'

'Jed, I don't think I have to justify . . .'

'So you've been running for an hour and a half?' he guffaws. 'God, Laura, people run half marathons in that time! Where did you go?'

'All over,' I insist. 'Around the park and, er, through town . . .'

'You don't look tired at all,' he observes. 'There's not a bead of sweat on you.'

'Would you be happier if I'd been brought home by ambulance?' I retort, feeling genuinely aggrieved now, as if my cosy cake-fest with Danny had never happened.

'Don't be crazy,' Jed says. 'I was just saying . . .'

'Mummy, you're back!' Grace announces, cavorting downstairs in her nightie.

'You should be asleep, lady,' Jed observes.

'Yeah, but I heard Mum coming in . . .' She winds her arms around me and presses her soft, warm cheek against mine. 'You smell kinda . . . chocolatey,' she adds.

'Do I?' I laugh, sensing Jed's curious look.

'Yeah.' She grins. 'I can really smell it. D'you have chocolate? Can I have some?'

'Well, I um . . . I had a quick hot chocolate,' I bluster, 'after my run . . .'

'Where?' she demands.

'In Café Roma. Come on, hon, it's getting late. Let's go up to—'

'Can *we* go to Café Roma? You never take me.'

'Yes, I do. We went a couple of weeks ago, remember? When you had that giant cookie that was as big as your face.'

'Hot chocolate, huh?' Jed chuckles. 'They recommend that at Tub Club, do they?'

I blink at him. What is it about joining a wretched slimming club that makes everyone think they can force sorbet on you and tick you off for having a milky drink? 'I was just thirsty,' I say defensively.

He nods. 'I see. You were probably dehydrated so, obviously, hot chocolate was the best thing to have.'

'What's dehydrated?' Grace enquires.

'It's when your body's crying out for liquid,' Jed explains, smirking, 'because you've over-exerted yourself.' I pull a bitter smile and kiss the top of Grace's head.

'Up to bed now,' I murmur. 'I'll come and tuck you up in a minute.'

She sighs dramatically, then skips upstairs obediently. Jed looks at me. 'So,' Jed says, 'what really happened is, you went running for about five minutes, thought, "Sod this" and snuck off to the café?'

I smile unsteadily. 'Uh-huh.'

He grins, putting an arm around me. 'You're stark raving mad, you know that?'

'Yep.'

'You're my crazy wife.'

'I know, darling.'

He steps away, giving me a lop-sided smile as relief floods over me. 'Sure you want to carry on with this running lark?' he asks.

I look at him. 'I know you think I'm not cut out for any of this . . .'

'It's not that, Laura. I mean, you're a mum, you're thirty-nine years old . . .'

'Hey, only just . . .'

'Yeah, okay, and you're . . . you're *fine*, you know that? Honestly. You've got nothing to worry about.'

'I'm overweight, Jed. Even the Tub Club woman said so.'

'Of course she did!' he exclaims. 'That's her job, to make you come back week after week and hand over your money and stick to their stupid diet system or whatever it is. So what if you're on the curvy side? Neither of us are twenty-two any more, are we? It just seems, I don't know, like it's stressing you out . . .'

I nod, thinking how unstressed I felt while Danny and I were tucking into marble cake. 'I'll just go and check on Grace, okay?'

'All right, love.'

'And then I think I'll have a bath and go straight to bed.'

He throws me a teasing grin. 'Stirring your hot chocolate's worn you out, has it?'

'Something like that,' I say.

*

'I'm not tired,' Grace protests, stretching her eyes saucer-wide. 'I'm *completely* awake.'

'Come on, sweetheart,' I say. 'If you don't go to sleep now, you'll be exhausted in the morning.'

'No I won't. It's not fair. How come you can go to bed whenever you like?'

'Because I'm a grown-up,' I say, laughing.

'Grown-ups get everything they want,' she grumbles as I click off her light.

How right she is, I think, as I sink into the bubble bath. Grown-ups are reminded that they're thirty-nine years old and a mother so there's no point in trying to fix anything. I'm like Vitesse – shabby and mottled and embarrassing to be seen with in public. I can't even shave my nether regions without making myself look like a plucked chicken. Maybe Jed's right, and there's no point in any of this. I could just stay fat and refuse to take part in any ritual sporting humili-ations at school. Gradually, though, the steamy lavender

211

fragrance begins to soothe and relax me and I start to feel more positive. I lie there for over an hour, occasionally topping up with more hot water and mentally working my way through Café Roma's dessert menu. Sweet, moreish and irresistible.

I realise, with a jolt to my heart, that it's not cakes I'm thinking about anymore. It's Danny.

CHAPTER TWENTY-EIGHT

Emergency weight-loss tactics before Tub Club:

1. Trim fingernails. Estimated weight loss (EWL): one gram.
2. Pluck eyebrows to rough approximation of elegant arch. EWL: negligible.
3. Exfoliate by rubbing face with flannel to slough off dead skin cells. EWL: nil.
4. Emergency wee. EWL: two, three grams?
5. Consider slipping on Celeste's ultra-light Coco de Mers, but decide they'd feel all wrong for such an unglamorous outing (it would also seem weird, wearing them for a second time, as if we are cosy, knicker-lending buddies). Opt for high-waisted fat knicks instead. EWL: nil.
6. Put on summery print dress which is the lightest thing I own. EWL: a couple of pounds, as I wore (heavier) jeans last week.
7. Banish all lustful thoughts of Danny from brain. No more light flirting in Café Roma, no more letting him grapple with my boots. EWL: nada – but hopefully, if I can purify my thoughts, that'll lighten me *emotionally*.

As I spritz on a little fragrance (does perfume actually weigh anything?), Grace sidles up and appraises my dress. 'You look pretty,' she says. 'Are you going to a party?'

'No, love,' I say, laughing. 'That's very sweet of you, though. I'm just going to another of those, um, health meeting things.' I kiss her, head downstairs and take my jacket from its hook in the hall. Jed is humming as he clears up in the kitchen. I'd rather leave quickly before he, too, registers my dress and starts firing difficult questions. 'See you later,' I call out, giving Grace a quick hug before scuttling out.

In St Mary's Hall, I scan the milling crowds. No Danny. Probably just as well. I'll be able to keep my mind on Belinda's talk and maybe even learn something this week. 'Where's your friend?' Kirsty asks as I take the seat beside her. I frown, as if unsure of which friend she's referring to. 'You know,' she chuckles. 'Danny. The cute one with the nice blue eyes and cheeky smile.' She looks me up and down. 'You've made an effort to dress up as well.'

I laugh awkwardly. 'I didn't mean to. Just grabbed the lightest thing I could find. And I don't know where he is this week . . .' I affect a casual shrug.

'Oh, of course – something light for weigh-in. Me too. Anyway, how have you done this week? Managed to stick to the Masterplan?'

'I've been a bit lax, to be honest. Had a few snacks, a bit of naughty nibbling . . .'

She smiles ruefully. 'Ah well. You look great, though. Kind of glowing. Been using a new cream on your face?'

Smiling, I shake my head. 'I'm strictly soap and water, or at least I have been since Toby squirted a whole tube of Lancôme moisturiser down the loo.'

'That's criminal,' she murmurs as Belinda strides onto the stage and the hall full of women falls into a respectful hush. Belinda's long, slim legs are encased in sheer nylon, and her lithe body moves elegantly in a snug, scoop-necked top and fitted skirt. Bet she's never wolfed her child's entire cookie production and hated herself for it.

'Tonight,' Belinda announces, 'I have a shocking announcement for you.' She pauses for effect, and the entire audience appears to be holding its breath. What is it this time? Our best friend is cucumber? 'It's nearly bikini time,' she announces with a terrifying grin. Kirsty grimaces at me. I check the door; still no sign of Danny. It's okay for him – he doesn't *have* a bikini time. In fact neither do I, as we haven't had a proper family holiday since before Toby was born.

'I know it's still only May,' Belinda trills on, 'but take it from me, your summer holiday will creep up on you before you know it and then, of course, it'll be too late.' Christ. She makes it sound like brittle bones or sprouting nasal hair. Not something you'd actually look forward to. 'If you're anything like me,' she trills, 'you start wishing your holiday was months away, and not lurking around the corner!'

There's a burst of knowing laughter but I can't join in. I'd give anything to be somewhere hot and sunny with the ocean lapping at my feet. I certainly wouldn't feel as if it were something to be dreaded. Belinda is now telling us how to eat on holiday, trying to sabotage any pleasure we might have had before we've even got there. 'What I do,' she confides, 'is ask for a small, child-sized portion whenever I eat out.'

'Would you ever do that?' I hiss at Kirsty.

'Only for a starter,' she says with a snigger.

'Stick to your plan religiously,' Belinda goes on, 'and

don't even consider cheating. Dine out less, drink less . . . and it's goodbye porky, hello saucy!'

My entire body wilts. Hello saucy? I'm too far gone for that. Even my cleavage, which I'd thought looked almost attractive before I came out, seems to have lost its allure. I have to stop coming here. It's not doing my psyche any good. I was happier, I realise now, before I entered this weird world of beetroot jellies and tuna bakes. Belinda holds up a picture of a woman posing in a white bikini. 'Gemma's got a bikini body,' she announces. 'She's the star slimmer from our Oxendale branch. With a few diet tweaks and a whole lot of willpower, you too can have a body like hers.'

I gaze at the picture. The woman is even skinnier than that girl who was trying on a playsuit in that changing room. A few diet tweaks? Apparently, I haven't even managed that, as I have actually *gained* two pounds since my last weigh-in.

Belinda smiles tightly and writes the figure on my yellow card. 'Never mind, Laura,' she murmurs. 'It sometimes happens that way, even if there doesn't seem to be any reason for it. You'll probably see a bigger loss to make up for it next week.'

I smile stoically. 'I hope so.'

She narrows her eyes at me. 'Been picking at the children's leftovers? I know you mums are prone to doing that, without even noticing. And it all adds up.'

'Um, I probably have. It just seems such a waste not to.'

'Top tip,' she says, grinning. 'Before your hand even *lands* on the plate, do yourself a favour and squirt washing-up liquid all over it. That'll stop you picking.'

'Good idea,' I say, making my way back to my seat, even though I have no intention of doing such a thing. Does she really expect me to ruin perfectly edible food? It would be tantamount to vandalism. I leave the hall, shivering in my thin sundress, and pull my jacket tightly around me as I step out into the drizzle.

That's it, I decide, striding away from the hall and all the women who are tumbling out, chatting and laughing and congratulating each other on fabulous weight losses. I *will* be good. Next week, I'll show Belinda that I'm capable of controlling my urges. But first, to prepare myself mentally, I think I deserve a little treat. Instead of heading straight home, I turn left along the damp high street and into the sweet, warm fug of Café Roma. I see the hot chocolates first – two of them steaming in tall white mugs on the small circular table. And two wedges of marble cake on white plates.

Seeing me, Danny looks up and smiles. 'Hey, Laura,' he says, his face lighting up as I make my way towards him. 'I really hoped you'd come.'

CHAPTER TWENTY-NINE

'Why didn't you come to the meeting?' I ask, my weigh-in anxieties melting away as I take the seat Danny saved for me.

He sips his hot chocolate. 'It's not really me, you know, going to something like that. I mean, I know it works, it's all common sense, and I've nothing against Belinda and her bakes, but . . .'

'Danny,' I cut in gently, 'what made you join up in the first place? I mean . . . it's unusual, isn't it, for a guy? Most men I know, they'd do the Atkins for a couple of weeks – Jed did that once, when he'd gained a bit of a tum, and the weight fell off in about five minutes.' I smile and nibble a corner of cake. 'Infuriating really.'

Danny looks up from his plate, and his gaze holds mine for a moment. 'Um, this will sound kind of pathetic . . .' He pauses. 'I only joined up because of, well, after Sarah left.'

'But why?' I ask.

'The builder, the guy she went off . . .' He pulls a tight smile. 'You know the type. Gym-obsessed fitness freak, muscles on muscles . . . and I suppose I thought, I could do with getting into better shape, because I'd let myself slide, really, being in a relationship for a long time. It happens, doesn't it? You get comfy. You stop noticing. The years roll on and you realise, suddenly, that maybe that

218

person doesn't see you in – you know. The same way they used to.' His cheeks colour slightly, and I'm seized by an urge to reach out and take hold of his hand. I don't, though. This is a small town. Chances are, Naomi or one of the playgroup mums would ping in and I'd be the subject of scurrilous gossip.

'That's what's happened to us,' I murmur. 'Me and Jed, I mean. Not that he's run off with a builder yet . . .' Danny smiles, and the mood lightens. 'But yes,' I add, 'he doesn't look at me like he used to, and I guess I don't look at him that way either. Maybe it's inevitable. Sometimes, though, I'm convinced that it could be so much better. Life, I mean. Like it was when I was young, and had just met Jed – even after we'd had Finn and were thrilled to have this baby to look after. And now we're too busy bickering over his parents coming to stay, and he's storming out to a rotting caravan and cutting me out of that thingie. So I guess we're hardly at the peak of romance, at this precise moment.'

Danny laughs, then he touches my hand, startling me. 'I love the way you do that,' he says.

'What, trap myself in my underwear?'

'No, the way you make everything – even sad things seem so . . .' His lips twitch. 'So funny.'

'Glad I amuse you,' I say, carefully removing my hand from his.

'You do, Laura. I don't mean I'm laughing *at* you. More that you . . . well, you lift my spirits, you know? It feels good, being with you. You're different to anyone else I've ever met.'

I smile, feeling warm all over. 'We won't see each other, though, will we? Not if you stop coming to Tub Club.'

'We could still run,' he says hopefully. 'I thought I'd forget

219

about the club and concentrate on that instead. I don't think I'm really cut out for that self-denial thing.'

'Me neither,' I say eagerly, biting into my cake.

'Would you do that? Would you run with me two or three times a week?'

'Yes, I'd love to.'

His face breaks into a grin. 'Tomorrow evening good for you?'

'Sorry, that's Grace's birthday. I could do Saturday though . . .'

'Saturday morning? About eleven?'

'Perfect,' I say. 'And I think I'll knock Tub Club on the head too. I haven't even looked at that Menu Masterplan properly. Just the sight of it makes me feel hungry.'

'Same here.' He pops the last crumb of cake into his mouth. I might have gained two pounds since last week, but I still float home feeling as light and breezy as dandelion fluff.

*

Friday, 4 p.m. Grace's birthday tea party. The house mills with her friends, no longer decked out in pink dresses and sparkly party shoes as at previous girlie gatherings but in jeans, leggings and T-shirts, and all screeching with delight as I unveil my masterpiece: the volcano cake.

I am extremely proud of my creation. While I'd like to report that I was up until 3 a.m., dutifully creaming butter and sifting flour, it's actually a bought cake which I had huge fun squishing into a mountain shape and daubing with thick red and orange icing to create a dramatic lava flow effect. Grace is suitably impressed. We also have an abundant array of crisps, chocolate fingers, individual jellies and other assorted delicacies which Belinda would award an utterly disgusted face.

The only thing missing is Jed.

'When's Dad coming home?' Grace asks, sitting cross-legged on the crumb-strewn living room carpet amidst a sea of torn wrapping paper.

'He should be here any minute,' I tell her. 'He must just have got held up at work or something.'

'It's just . . .' She frowns. 'Dad's better at doing . . . you know. Party stuff.'

'Well, *I* can do party stuff too,' I say brightly, having planned two hours' worth of activities on my specially-bought clipboard which I hoped would give me an air of authority and make me feel vaguely in control. Admittedly, I hadn't envisaged that I'd only have Beth to help me to keep thirteen children under control. In fact, I'd imagined that my beloved would be home from work by now, at 6.20 p.m. – *participating*. I've left voicemail messages, and a niggling thought keeps bothering me: that maybe something awful has happened. Otherwise, surely he'd be here?

Beth and Kira are doing a sterling job of dishing out food and drinks. Even Finn is hanging around, joining in in a half-hearted way, perhaps due to the Kira factor. I'm ridiculously grateful to Beth for helping out. Parents rarely hang around at kids' parties any more. They simply drop off their charges and scuttle away with barely-disguised glee.

'Muuum!' Toby screams from the kitchen.

'What is it?' I rush through to investigate.

'Someone punched the volcano!' I stare down at it. There's an almighty crater in the middle of my cake, and further

221

investigation reveals that Toby's hand is daubed with red and orange icing.

'Did you do this?' I gasp.

'Nah.'

'Toby,' I start, 'I really hope you're telling me . . .' Then I decide that now is the wrong time to challenge my youngest on behavioural issues. For one thing, it's not scheduled on my clipboard.

'I think I'd better supervise,' Beth says, deftly squeezing her way to the table and chopping the remainder of the cake into bite-sized chunks before the children can grab handfuls. I knew, when I met her at playgroup, that we were destined to be friends. Although she exuded capability, she also lacked that simmering smugness which can be so prevalent among groups of mothers. When she told me that Jack had been a late addition – a 'surprise' as she put it – it was all I could do not to kiss her. Jed and I hadn't planned Toby, either. I'd been four months pregnant when I realised that my swelling belly wasn't solely due to my fondness for cookies.

While I beat back the devastation in the kitchen, Beth herds everyone through to the living room for music and games. 'Maybe something's happened at school,' she whispers, catching me checking my watch again.

'Surely he'd have let me know. I'm getting really worried, Beth. I know he can be unreliable, but not like this – not when his own child's birthday party's going on.'

'I'm sure he's fine,' she says soothingly. 'Maybe he's got the time wrong and thinks it's starting at seven, or . . .'

'Where's Dad?' Finn asks, sidling past with a bowl of jelly.

'Working late,' I say quickly. 'He'll be here soon.' I *won't* show my irritation; I can't, not with so many children in the

222

house, and the distinct feeling that everything could topple into chaos at any moment. Toby and Jack scamper upstairs, chuckling. I can't go after them; I'm needed here, as Beth's musical bumps game is becoming rather boisterous. The doorbell rings, signalling the first parent's arrival which means that the party is nearly over and Jed still isn't here. Helena – an unnervingly neat mother who's permanently kitted out in a razor-sharp trouser suit – surveys the mess. 'Gosh, you've been busy,' she says. 'Has it gone well?'

'Yes, great, thanks.' I wipe an icing smear from my cheek.

'You *are* brave, having parties at home. I'd never dare. But then our house is, er . . .' She tails off, obviously not wanting to add, 'Nice. Unlike this hovel . . .' She steps gingerly over a crushed paper plate and looks around for her daughter.

Toby and Jack are screeching with laughter upstairs, and I try to shut my mind to the possibilities of what they might be up to. The doorbell rings again, and this time it's Naomi, whose daughter Phoebe was last seen drinking runny jelly from a bowl. Naomi will probably put her on a strict bread-stick regime after this. 'Hope Grace has had a lovely birth—' she begins, tailing off as Toby and Jack dance their way downstairs, wiggling their hips and trilling some unrecognisable tune. It's not the singing that bothers me. It's the fact that they are wearing my underwear.

'My God,' Naomi mutters.

'Boys,' I start, 'go upstairs, put your clothes back on . . .'

'No!' Toby guffaws. Whilst Jack is at least wearing my plain old fat knickers pulled up to his chest – plus a second pair, as a jaunty hat – my youngest is decked out in my supposedly slinky Tesco lacy pants, plus a vast, off-white and clearly over-laundered nursing bra.

'Nice fashion choice,' Beth giggles into my ear.

I choke out a laugh as the boys strut on the stairs. More parents are arriving, and congratulating me on managing such a boisterous affair in our own home – 'So brave! But then you do have a *comfortable* family house'. Some point and laugh at the boys, while others, perhaps trying to afford me a shred of dignity, pretend not to notice. Even as I'm dispensing goodbyes and party bags, all I can see, in the periphery of my vision, is that tragic mummy-bra, modelled by my four-year-old son.

Big, old and washed out. Like its owner. The party guests mill around me, grabbing coats and jackets from the vast pile in the hall, and clatter out into the cool, still evening.

'Isn't Jed here, Laura?' Naomi asks, raising an eyebrow.

'He's working late,' I say firmly.

'Oh, that's a pity. Casper always takes the day off. We make a big thing of birthdays in our family.'

'Well, Jed's got a lot on at the moment,' I murmur, wondering why I'm even bothering to lie for him. 'Something unexpected came up.'

'He's very dedicated,' she observes. 'I saw him in the paper, amazing what he's done for all those kids . . .' I try to appear in agreement whilst wondering if Toby is exhibiting early cross-dressing tendencies. Not that I'd be worried. Compared to Jed, ducking out of our daughter's birthday celebrations, I'm sure I'll cope with any quirks our children care to fling at me.

The house empties remarkably quickly, as if a herd of wildebeest have stampeded through leaving a flurry of streamers, spilt jelly and ripped wrapping paper in their wake. I realise I'm still gripping my clipboard. 'Aw, why did everyone have to go?' Grace complains, looking a little berserk around the eye region.

'They were here for two hours, love,' I explain. 'That's the usual time for a party.'

'India's mum took us to the Water Palace. We stayed there all *day*.' Yes, and India's dad was probably there too, throwing himself down flumes, being a seal and all that dad-type stuff.

'We'll stay and help clear up,' Beth says firmly, 'won't we, Kira?'

'Honestly, it's okay,' I tell her. 'It won't take me too long, and the kids will all help me.' I catch Finn's wilting expression as he lurks by the TV. Of course he wants Kira to stay a little longer. Perhaps, if I encourage their blossoming friendship, her pleasant, cooperative nature might rub off onto him.

'Oh, come on,' Beth insists. 'I'm not leaving you with all of this.' I catch her eye, and I know she's really offering to stay to keep me company, to buoy me up and to try and stop me worrying. The front door opens, and we both turn towards it as Jed strides in.

'Hi, Jed.' Beth smiles brightly and quickly retreats to the kitchen.

'Er, hi, Beth.' He looks around, taking in the devastation, his eyes lighting upon a daub of volcano cake on the living room door. 'Er . . . Grace's party,' he adds, slowly clasping a hand to his cheek. 'Jesus, Laura. I . . . I totally forgot.'

'I think maybe we should get back,' Beth murmurs, scuttling towards me and beckoning Kira and Jack. 'You've got tons of homework, haven't you, Kira?'

'Mum, it's *Friday*,' Kira says, rolling her eyes. 'I've got all weekend for that.'

'Still, it's getting late. Bye, Laura. Great party.' She bundles her children to the front door.

'Thanks for all your help,' I whisper. 'You've been a lifesaver today.' She smiles briefly and kisses my cheek, and they're gone. I look at Jed, who appears to be transfixed by the icing daub.

'Laura . . . I . . . I'm so sorry.' His gaze drops to the floor.

'It's all right, Daddy,' Grace chirps, biting a chocolate finger as she stalks into the hall. 'It was a great party, except Toby punched a hole in my cake.'

'Did he?' Jed says faintly. 'That was mean, wasn't it?' He turns to me as Grace snaps off a piece of chocolate finger, pops it into her mouth and skips happily upstairs.

'I . . . I thought we were having it tomorrow,' Jed murmurs. 'On Saturday, like we usually do.'

'Grace wanted a tea party on her actual birthday,' I say coolly.

'I know, I realise that now. Honestly, Laura. I know it's stupid. I . . . I can't believe I missed it.'

'I did tell you, Jed. We planned this ages ago.'

He nods. Toby and Finn hover in the kitchen as if unsure what to do next. 'Could you two do me a big favour and grab a bin bag,' I say quickly, 'and clear all the paper plates off the table?'

With a disgruntled sigh, Finn opens a drawer and rips a black bag off the roll. I turn back to Jed and beckon for him to follow me into the living room, out of earshot of the children. 'So you actually forgot?' I murmur.

'I do remember now, you saying something about it . . .'

'You forgot her party, Jed. How could you? We gave Grace her presents this morning, or have you forgotten that too?'

'I just made a mistake,' he mutters. 'I'm sorry, okay? I'll make it up to her . . .'

'Where were you anyway?'

'Just out for a drink after work. It was nothing. Just sort of impromptu.'

'What d'you mean,' I hiss, 'sort of impromptu?' I beam hatred at him. So while I was dishing up jelly, and having two little boys parade in my underwear in front of Naomi and all those perfect mums, he was laughing, chatting and tipping alcohol down his throat.

'I . . . I mean it wasn't planned.'

'I know what impromptu means,' I snap. 'Who was there? Celeste, I suppose?'

'Um, yeah. And some others. Just a group of us . . .'

'Great. How cosy . . .'

'Look, I've said I'm sorry. I'm going to help the boys clear up, okay?' And he marches away to the kitchen where I hear him encouraging Toby and Finn as they tidy up, trying to make everything all right. 'Great, guys,' he's saying, all light and jovial. 'We'll have this place sorted in no time. Toby, could you pass the dustpan and brush please? And Finn, you could start washing those dishes.' They're chatting now, the three of them: Dad and sons, all happy and relaxed and busying away together. Grace, too, will forgive and forget, if she even minds at all. We'll carry on with our lives and say no more about it. Right now, though, I can't *wait* to get out of this house, pull on my spanking new trainers and run around Lyedale Park tomorrow night. And I never thought I'd say that.

CHAPTER THIRTY

Jed's contrite act continues through breakfast the next morning. Unusually bright-eyed and bushy-tailed for 9.15 a.m. on a Saturday, he serves up eggs according to each of our children's individual preferences. I almost point out that it's a little unnecessary, producing one boiled, one poached and one fried egg, and that I'm concerned it might set a precedent. The kids might even think that our house has morphed into a café and start demanding menus. But I think better of it. I'm still simmering with annoyance over Grace's party, and don't think I can trust myself to discuss anything in a rational manner.

The icing smear, I notice, is still stuck to the living room door. In a senseless act of rebellion, I decide to leave it – perhaps forever, so it sets rock hard and has to be sanded off – and head out to the back garden. Here, I gather up stray paper plates and semi-deflated balloons. Someone has left a shiny red ballet slipper, I notice. A birthday card lies damp and floppy in the weed-infested border.

From here, through the kitchen window, I can see Jed's eager face as he swoops back and forth via toaster, table and fridge. Anyone watching – Ruth, say, or any of the other playgroup mums – would faint at such fabulous fathering skills and have to restrain themselves from festooning him with underwear. I know, though, that those are guilty eggs, guiltily boiled, poached and fried because he knows that this time, he's gone one almighty step too far.

I pull out my mobile from my pocket and dial my sister's number. 'Laura?' she says. 'I was going to phone you yesterday, wanted to wish Grace a happy birthday. But the day ran away with me, you know what it's like, we had some last-minute guests arriving . . .'

'Don't worry,' I say. 'She wouldn't have had much chance to talk anyway. Her party was straight after school. I just wanted to thank you for her present . . .' I realise now how bizarre this must seem, thanking Kate when Grace is quite capable of conducting a phone conversation with her auntie herself. 'Sorry,' I add, 'is it a bad time? You're probably in the middle of breakfast . . .'

'No, the guests we've got staying this week are early risers, keen to get up those hills. I've been up starting breakfast at half-six every morning so Will owes me big time.' She sniggers. 'Anyway, what about you? Did Grace like her present?'

'Loved it. She's been nagging for a science set like that for ages. Wanted to get it all out yesterday and start making foul smells and a big mess in the kitchen, but we haven't had a chance yet.'

'Oh,' Kate exclaims, 'I can't believe she's eight! Seems like no time since I was her first visitor in that ward.'

'I know. It's terrifying really.' Kate's own boys, Rory and Nat, were already in their teens by then; she'd left them in Scotland with Will, their dad, when my due date approached, so she could be on standby to look after Finn. Our friends, and even Jed's parents, had offered to step in and help, but Kate had felt it was her role and I agreed. However, Grace had her own ideas. She was fashionably late, by two weeks, choosing to greet the world on the very day I was due to be induced. As a result, Kate stayed with us in our tiny Hackney flat for three weeks. I still look back on it fondly, that time of living and waiting together, my kind, capable big sister and me.

'How was the party?' Kate is asking. 'Complete mayhem, I imagine, but you're still alive, obviously . . .'

I pause, tempted to gloss over Jed's misdemeanour. It would be so much easier to make her laugh by telling her about Toby punching my volcano cake. 'Kate,' I murmur, 'I need to talk to you. I don't know what to do.'

'Are you pregnant?' she blurts out.

'God, no. No! That would be highly unlikely.' I laugh mirthlessly. 'No, it's about Grace's party. Jed missed it. He didn't come home.'

'What? Was he away or something?'

'No, just at work, then he went out.' I glimpse him clearing the table in the kitchen and the children scattering obediently to retrieve schoolbags and gym kits.

'He went out?' she repeats. 'And missed the party?'

As I clear my throat, I spot a withered balloon poking out of the watering can spout. 'That's about it. He went for a drink after work. That's what he said anyway – an *impromptu* drink – and by the time he came home the party had finished.'

'But that's so unlike him!' Kate exclaims. 'He'd never do that. Deliberately miss one of the kids' . . .'

'I don't think it was deliberate,' I cut in. 'I honestly think he just forgot.'

'What, forgot his own daughter's birthday? Why would he do that?'

'It's . . .' I take a deep breath. 'It's complicated, Kate. You're right, he would never have done that. But things have changed. There's this woman at school, a teacher, joined the school last autumn. They became friends pretty quickly, and it was all "Celeste this, Celeste that", and the kids all think she's fantastic of course . . .'

'Was he out with her?' Kate asks.

'Yes, and some others, he reckons. But he's infatuated with her. Since Celeste's been around, he hasn't been like . . . like the old Jed at all.'

'Hang on,' Kate murmurs, and I sense the background tone changing as she takes her phone out of the house and into the garden. I picture her standing there, with her wild, crinkly hair pulled up on top of her head, surrounded by her hens and a huge, open sky. 'You don't think he's having an affair, do you?' she asks bluntly.

'I don't know what to think, Kate. It's so hard to be rational. I mean, something's going on, I'm sure of that. He's never affectionate, not really, and we haven't had sex since something like 1992 . . .'

'Oh, come on,' she murmurs.

'Okay, but it's been ages. Months, actually. I know that happens when there are young kids around and everyone's exhausted. And I'm not expecting it to be like the old, pre-kids days. But there's something else, I can tell.'

'Well, you have to find out,' she says firmly. 'Have you asked him outright?'

'Sort of. He denies it anyway. Gets really defensive if I even mention her name.'

'But you need to find out, don't you? Something must be happening to make him miss a birthday party. I'm not saying he's sleeping with her – I can hardly believe he'd do that, not Jed – but something's wrong, isn't it?'

'Yes,' I murmur as he appears at the back door and gives me a quizzical smile. 'I'd better go,' I add.

'Want me to come down, spend a few days with you? I'm sure Will could hold the fort here . . .'

'No, you don't have to do that.'

'Well,' she says, 'and call me anytime, okay? Come up and see me, soon as you can, and give them all a kiss from their auntie.'

'Thanks, Kate. I will do.'

It's a deft hand-over of duties as Jed heads upstairs for a shower, looking beleaguered now due to complex egg preparations. 'Mummy,' Grace says, 'I didn't mind that Daddy missed my party.'

Something catches in my throat. 'Didn't you, love? Well, that's good of you. You know he'd have loved to be there.'

She nods thoughtfully. 'Did he go out with his friends?'

'Er, yes, love. These things, um . . . come up sometimes.' Sweat prickles my forehead. Stress-induced sweat, as if I'm the one who was quaffing booze while our daughter's birthday cake was dished out. 'He's really sorry, you know,' I add.

'Yeah.' She brightens, popping the last forkful of lovingly poached egg into her mouth. 'And it's all right,' she adds, 'as long as he promises to come next year.'

*

Next year, I think as the breeze cools my face through the open driver's side window. Who knows where we'll be then, and what will have happened to us? It doesn't bode well that the only party we've attended together this year ended up

232

with me peeing myself and him flirting wildly then insisting, in a furious temper, that we left.

Jed and I used to be known for our parties, I reflect as I drive out of town. We'd fill our flat with our friends and assorted people we'd collected along the way, and the bath would be piled high with lagers and ice. Friends had paired off at our parties: old mates from college mingling with friends from Jed's school, and girls I'd met at the hair salons I'd worked in. So many friends and parties. It's not having children that's curtailed all that; Kate and Will have an enviable social life, which never seemed to falter during their child-rearing years, even though they live in a tiny village surrounded by hills and farmland.

My phone bleeps with an incoming text. Intrigued and, admittedly, hoping it's from Danny, I pull over at the roadside to read it. HOPE ALL OK AFTER GRACES PARTY, Beth has written. GD LUCK XX. I call her number. 'Where are you?' she asks. 'Just called your land line. Jed said you'd gone out for a drive, which seemed weird . . .'

'That's what I told him,' I say. 'I'm going to Celeste's, Beth. I need to know what's happening and if he won't tell me, then hopefully, she will . . .'

'Are you sure about this?' she says, sounding alarmed. 'I mean . . . what are you planning to do when you get there?'

'Don't worry. I'm not going to burst in and start accusing her of anything. I'm bringing her dress back, you see, the one she lent me at her party . . .'

'And then what?' she asks warily.

'Well . . . I don't know, Beth. I'll see how it goes.'

'If you're sure,' she says. 'Don't do anything silly, though. It's really not worth it.'

'It just feels better than doing nothing,' I add calmly. 'It'll be fine, whatever happens. And at least I'll know.'

We finish the call and I glance at the posh carrier bag – the one my putty-coloured birthday dress came in – which is perched on the passenger seat. Inside it is Celeste's dress, perfectly laundered and pressed. I turn on the ignition and pull away from the verge, following the narrow country lane. Undulating fields are punctuated by the occasional proud stone house. This is how I imagine Danny's house. Solid and welcoming, with no volcano cake smears, but still relaxed and comfortable.

I drive on, my bravado ebbing away rapidly as I approach the mill. My chest tightens as I pull up at the parking area. Picking up the bag, I climb out of the car, shutting the door as quietly as I can. I try to stride purposefully across the gravel, the way I attempted to make a confident entrance at her party, with Jed clutching that flamboyant bouquet.

As I approach the mill's entrance, I spot something on the grass. It's a blue glass nugget, glinting in the sun. Licking my parched lips, I pick it up and slip it into my pocket. Then I walk slowly towards the front door.

It's not locked and pushes open easily. By now, I'm hoping that Celeste is out so I can leave the dress at the door to her flat and forget this stupid plan to confront her. What if I'm wrong? Or if she hasn't even noticed that Jed's crazy about her? How stupid will I look then? I had it all worked out early this morning, having woken at 6.30 a.m. I lay there, while Jed snored softly, planning what I'd say: *What were you doing with Jed last night? Didn't he tell you it was Grace's eighth birthday party? How do you feel about that – him missing it because of you?* Now my script feels all wrong, and my heart

234

is hammering urgently as I climb the cool stone stairs. I reach her landing and pause, wondering what to do next.

A jam jar of shrivelled flowers sits on the floor in the corner. Must be left over from the party. And she's in, dammit, because faint music is filtering through the door to her flat. I rehearse my lines: *I need to talk to you. It's really important. I need you to tell me what's going on between you and Jed.*

And I raise my hand, ready to knock, poised for my life to change forever.

CHAPTER THIRTY-ONE

The door flies open and slams against the wall. I stagger back, kicking over the jam jar of flowers and taking a moment to realise it's not Celeste but a younger girl who's stormed out of the flat, her finely-sculpted face shiny with tears. 'I don't want to talk to you!' she screeches over her shoulder. 'I'm not your *friend*. I don't have to listen to anything you say . . .'

She stops momentarily, registering my presence. Fury blazes in her wide blue eyes. 'I'm sorry,' I blurt out, 'I just came by to—' I jiggle the carrier bag. 'I have something to give back . . .'

'Celeste!' she yells, pushing chaotic dark hair out of her face. 'Someone here to see you.' She wrinkles her freckled nose and glowers at me.

'Sorry,' I say quickly. 'If it's not a good time, it really isn't important . . .'

'It's okay.' She chokes back a sob. 'I'm leaving anyway . . .'

'Please, don't go because of—' I start as she storms away, clattering downstairs in her flip-flops, one of her vest top straps dangling from a pale, bony shoulder. I stare through the open door into Celeste's flat. No sign of life. Just faint music coming from a radio, and a fizz of tension in the air.

I don't know what to do next. Knocking on the open door seems wrong, and it's obviously not the best time to try and have a reasonable conversation with her about Jed. Yet if Celeste spots me creeping back downstairs, she'll assume I've been loitering about on her landing for no apparent reason, and how would I explain that? It would get all around school: *Poor Jed, his wife was hanging about on my landing, you know. She obviously has issues . . .*

I stand dead still, gripping the bag, trying to formulate an emergency exit plan. As quietly as possible, I shuffle across the landing. I could be outside in seconds and she'd never know I'd been there. At least I'm wearing trainers. I could *sprint*. My stomach growls ominously, echoing around the stark landing.

I edge a little closer to the stairs. *Just go for it. Run.* 'Wait!' comes her voice as my foot hits the step. 'Please don't go. Look, I'm sorry, I know I'm a terrible person, I really don't deserve . . .'

I freeze, swivelling my eyes towards the door. Celeste appears, looking even more distraught than the younger woman. Her eyes are swollen, and her nose and lips are red and sore-looking. She's wearing a blue fluffy dressing gown and is barefoot. 'Laura?' she says faintly. 'What are you doing here?'

'I . . . I was passing and thought I'd return your dress.' My arm springs out like a robot's as I hand it to her.

'Oh. Thanks.' She takes the bag from me.

'Your, erm, knickers aren't there,' I babble. 'I couldn't find them but I'm sure they'll turn up . . .'

She smiles tightly. 'Don't worry.'

We look at each other. 'Well, I'd better go,' I add quickly.

'No, it's okay. Come in, have a coffee with me.' Her voice wobbles again.

'Really, I'm in a bit of a hurry . . .' I'd actually rather drink one of the soil-and-puddle potions Toby concocts in the garden.

'Just a quick one then?'

I nod. 'Okay. I'm due to meet someone for a run later. Could probably do with the caffeine shot.'

She smiles and beckons me in. 'I'm sorry about that . . . that *scene* you saw there. Don't know what you must have thought . . .'

'It's fine. I'm sure it was just . . .'

'It blew up out of nothing,' she cuts in. 'You know how it is.'

I nod, not knowing how anything is as Celeste pours me a coffee from the percolator jug. It's disconcerting, seeing her red and raw-faced, with her bare feet and chipped toenails and her honey-coloured hair hanging in loose tangles around her face. If she were Beth, I'd hug her, try to find out what's wrong. I have no idea what to do with a distraught Celeste.

'D'you take sugar?' she asks.

'Yes, two please.' A tense silence descends as I glance around the kitchen. It's less pristine than it was on party day. No vase of tulips today. Clothes are strewn over chairs, and a scruffy make-up bag has spilled its contents all over the table. There's a mangled concealer stick with its lid off, an abandoned mascara wand and a small circular mirror with fingerprints all over it.

Celeste gestures for me to sit at the table, and takes the seat opposite. 'You're looking good, you know. All this running obviously suits you.'

'Well, I've only just started really . . .' She blows into her coffee and a small silence descends. This is ludicrous. We have nothing to say to each other. I don't feel I should ask about the girl who virtually knocked me over as she flew past, yet we can hardly pretend she wasn't there. The real reason for my visit burns urgently in my brain. I sip my coffee, hoping its sweetness will soothe me, but all I do is scald my tongue.

'She's . . . very emotional,' Celeste murmurs.

'Yes. I could see that.' I'm now conscious of the ticking wall clock, heightening the tension in the room. I slip a hand into the pocket of my tracksuit bottoms, running a fingertip over the cool glass nugget. 'Celeste,' I begin, 'you know, um, a bunch of you had a few drinks last night?'

'Er, Jed and I did, yes. Just a couple.' She meets my gaze and forms a bright smile.

'It's just . . . it was Grace's birthday party. It was happening, I mean, when you were in the pub.'

'Was it?' She looks aghast. 'Are you sure?'

I laugh dryly. 'Oh, it was happening all right. I've got the war wounds to prove it.'

'But why didn't Jed say? I'd never have asked him to come out if I'd known. Honestly, Laura, I had no idea . . .' She tails off and stands up to rinse out her mug under the tap. Two small plates sit side by side on the drainer. Nothing else. No mad tumble of beakers and paint jars or any of the clutter that threatens to explode out of our house.

'He says he forgot,' I murmur, sensing the lines I rehearsed earlier becoming blurry and impossible to read.

'Well, I . . .' She clears her throat. 'I don't know what to say. Jed's been a good friend to me – you know that. He's a lovely, generous guy. I've been through some tough times lately and, honestly, I don't know what I'd have done without him sometimes. Not everyone at school's as understanding, you know.'

I nod wordlessly.

'God, you must be furious with me,' she adds, 'stealing your husband on his daughter's birthday. I'm so sorry . . .' She rakes a hand through her hair, and I wonder why he lied, why he told me a bunch of them had been to the pub.

'No,' I say firmly. 'It's not your fault. It was *his* daughter's birthday, not yours. Anyway,' I add, 'I'd really better get going, Celeste, or I'll be standing up my friend for our run.'

'Okay,' she murmurs, smiling stoically as she sees me to the door. 'Oh, and thanks for returning the dress. You needn't have, though. To be honest, it doesn't fit me.'

*

My head swims as I drive back to town. Of course it wasn't her fault. That seems obvious now from the way she reacted, and how mortified she was. She might have suggested the drink, being such great buddies with Jed and him being so incredibly *understanding*, blah-blah, but she didn't deliberately set out to wreck Grace's birthday. And what about him, telling me that a group of them had gone out for some impromptu thing? It was a small lie, but a lie all the same.

Pulling in at the street beside the park, I climb out of the car and glance around for Danny, keen to expend some energy and hopefully straighten out my thoughts. Spotting him waiting at the gates, I wave and quicken my pace. 'You drove here?' he says. 'Trying to conserve your energy for the run, were you? Or – don't tell me. You've only just got out of bed.'

I laugh. 'Hardly. I just had somewhere else to go first.'

'None of your excuses,' he teases. 'So, are you ready?'

'Guess so,' I say. It all spills out so easily as we fall into a jog: my intention to confront Celeste, using the dress as an excuse, and it turning out to be just the two of them who'd been out together.

'Are you even madder at him?' Danny asks.

'Of course I am, but you know what? After this morning, seeing her sitting there all upset and, well, *ordinary* in her flat, obviously having just had some huge row with that girl, whoever she was . . . well, I don't know. It's grown to be such a big thing in my life and I'm sick of it all, to be honest.'

'You sound different,' he says. 'Stronger, more determined . . .'

I glance at him, realising how evenly-paced we are. It feels good, being in step with each other, in the soft sunshine with the ducks drifting lazily across the lake. I don't even care that those snogging teenagers are there on the bench again, watching us. 'Well, I feel it,' I say. 'I feel good doing this, don't you?'

'It's definitely getting easier,' he says as we swerve out of the park, following the narrow path which runs alongside the river. 'I never imagined I could enjoy running, to be honest.'

'Neither did I.' When I glimpse the church clock, I'm astounded to see that we've been running for twenty minutes without having to walk, or anything terrible happening at all.

'Want to take a rest?' he asks as we approach a bench.

'Shall we see if we can manage another five minutes?'

'God,' he laughs, 'you're a ruthless woman.' We run and run, taking the steps back up to the road and following the shortcut alleyway until we're back in the park where we started. We stop abruptly, both of us laughing and gasping for breath. 'You were challenging me, weren't you?' he pants. 'You wanted me to suggest stopping first.'

'No,' I fib, allowing myself to drop onto a bench. 'But I could sense you were struggling there so maybe we'd better have a rest. I mean, I don't want you keeling over or anything.'

He sits beside me and catches his breath. 'We must have run three miles, Laura. Three miles! A couple of lapsed old Tub Club members like us.'

I giggle and look at him.

'We're brilliant, aren't we? Belinda would be proud.'

A solitary duck catches my eye, and I watch it, enjoying the stillness.

'Can I ask you something?' Danny says.

'Sure. What is it?'

'Could I take some pictures of you sometime? I'd really like to. Remember I told you I really love to do portraits? Well, I've let it slip lately. Focused on commercial work instead of taking pictures just for myself, the kind of shots I really want to do. And I thought you'd be perfect. Would you mind, or am I being horribly cheeky?'

'Of course you're not,' I say. 'You really think I'd be perfect, though? Are you sure about this?'

'Oh yes. Don't tell me you hate having your photo taken . . .'

I laugh, trying to work out whether I do or not. 'You know, I don't know how I feel about it because no one ever takes any pictures of me.'

'Seriously?' he says, frowning. 'Like, never?'

'Well, Jed used to. Hundreds, actually, and we're talking years back – pre-digital – so, somewhere in our house, there are stacks of prints of me in various states of inebriation at parties.' I snigger.

'Then what happened?'

'Well, then we had the children and it stopped.'

'Did it? Why?'

I smile, realising that of course he doesn't understand. 'Danny,' I say patiently, 'something happens when you have kids. Suddenly, they're the ones everyone takes photos of. Which is understandable, given the sleep-deprived general knackeredness of the parents and the cuteness of the children. I mean, they're far more photogenic than we are.'

'Right, I get it. But what about holidays? Surely you're in family holiday shots?'

'We haven't had a family holiday for four years,' I explain. 'Last one was to a damp cottage in Northumberland which had other people's toenail clippings in the bath. We came home with about 300 photos of the children, and Jed was in a few, but there was only one of me. And I was bending over in the background with my bum in the air, picking something up off the floor.' Danny is choking with laughter. 'I could dig that out for you if you like,' I add, 'if you need creative inspiration.'

'Well, um, I was thinking of something a bit more . . . dignified actually. In fact, this could be your reintroduction into the dazzlingly glamorous world of photography. What d'you think?' He gives me such an open, hopeful look that I want to hug him.

'Where would you do the shots?' I ask.

'Just at my place. There's plenty of space there.'

'Oh. Um, I think . . .' I hesitate. 'I think I need to think about it, okay?'

'Okay,' he says. 'No pressure at all.'

I smile, and we sit in easy silence, watching the ducks paddle across the lake. Then his hand touches mine, and my heart turns over. I don't move or look at him. I just sit in the milky sunlight, with a handsome man's hand over mine, thinking that whatever happens I'll never forget this weird, but strangely perfect morning.

CHAPTER THIRTY-TWO

Danny and I meet up three times together the following week, and the week after that. The soft May air turns drier and hotter as we slip into June, which makes running a little more challenging. We start bringing water bottles, like proper runners do, and swig and chat as we follow our usual route through the park and alongside the river. He tells me more about Sarah, and the illicit meetings with her builder boyfriend while he was out working, and how betrayed he felt. 'I've never told anyone about all of this,' he says. Nothing has happened between us since the brief hand-holding incident, which doesn't count for anything really. I try to convince myself that I'm doing nothing wrong.

One morning, I notice Kirsty checking me out as I start to cut her freshly-washed hair. 'Haven't seen you at the last few meetings,' she remarks.

'I decided Super Slimmers wasn't for me,' I tell her. 'My problem is, once something's forbidden, I want it all the more. I was starting to dream about all those foods on the banned list.'

'You've lost weight, though, haven't you?' she adds. 'And you're looking so healthy these days. Kind of *glowing* in fact.'

'Oh,' I laugh, 'that's just the trick lighting we have in here to make our clients walk out feeling amazing.'

'Hey, don't tell Kirsty about that,' Simone sniggers, over-hearing our conversation.

'Isn't Laura looking great, though, don't you think?'

'She always does,' Simone replies. 'But yes, there's definitely a bit less of her these days.' Later, as I remove Kirsty's cape and sweep the brush across her shoulders, I glimpse my reflection. I do look better, if I say so myself: brighter and sparklier. Not the kind of woman you'd present with an oven glove on her birthday.

'Well, something's doing you good,' Kirsty declares, raising an eyebrow as she pulls out her wallet to pay. 'If that's what running does, I might think about taking it up too. You've got a real glow about you, Mrs Swan.'

Beth notices too, and brings up the subject when we're making the most of a scorching afternoon by having an impromptu after-school picnic tea in her garden. 'So, are you going to tell me?' she asks, popping a strawberry into her mouth while our kids hang out at the far end of her lawn.

'Tell you about what?' I ask.

'Come on, Laura. You look fantastic, but it's not just that, is it? Not just the weight loss, I mean. You're seeing a lot of Danny these days, aren't you?'

'Well, yes,' I murmur. 'Two or three times a week. But it's only running, you know. We're just well-matched and we keep each other motivated . . .'

'Are you sure it's just that?' She throws me a teasing look.

'Okay, we did sit and hold hands in the park, just the once, which sounds silly, doesn't it? Like something teenagers would do . . .' I realise I'm blushing furiously. 'It was nothing,' I add quickly.

'It doesn't sound like nothing,' she murmurs. 'I bet you still haven't told Jed you run with him . . .'

'No, but how could I tell him now? It would look as if we had something to hide.'

Beth glances at me, and I detect a flicker of concern in her eyes. 'Just be careful,' she adds. 'Things can get out of hand, can't they? And I don't want to see your life unravelling.'

'It won't,' I say firmly, draining my glass of sparkling, calorie-free water. 'Nothing's going to unravel, I promise.'

*

Finn returns from school the next day with a startling announcement. Apparently, despite him handing it to me personally *weeks* ago, I have lost the vital permission form for his class outing to the art gallery. 'I told you I needed you to sign it,' he huffs during dinner, 'or I won't be able to go.'

I cast an eye around the kitchen. Piles of rumpled papers clutter the top of the microwave and fridge. In several drawers, so much paperwork is crammed in that the odd vital document flutters down the back to the cupboards below. 'When are you going?' I ask.

'Tomorrow.'

'Tomorrow? Why didn't you say?'

'I *am* saying,' he mutters. 'I'm saying now.'

I thought you didn't even like art, I want to shoot back. *Last time we went to a gallery, you said it made you feel sick . . .*

Jed arrives home promptly from work. Since Grace's birthday incident, three weeks ago now, his behaviour has been exemplary. He has changed the kids' beds, cleaned out all the nasties from the back of the fridge *and* started to dig over our weedy border. It's a little unnerving, as if he's eagerly working towards his Being Helpful at Home badge. 'Are you sure you brought the form home?' he asks Finn. 'I don't remember seeing it.'

'Yeah, I gave it to her.' He jabs his fork at me, as if I'm some random domestic help.

'You gave it to *Mum*, you mean,' Jed corrects him. 'There's no need to be so rude, Finn.'

'Yeah, and she went and lost it.'

'Well, it must be here somewhere,' Jed declares, flicking impatiently through the pile on the fridge.

'What'll happen if we can't find it?' I ask. 'Will they come round and shoot me?'

Finn throws me an ominous look and sucks in a strand of spaghetti. I watch, transfixed, as it shoots into his mouth, like the cable disappearing back into the hoover. 'Then I won't be able to go,' he mumbles, 'and I'll have to sit in class all day all on my own with nothing to do.'

'Oh, Finn,' I say. 'I'm sure we'll find it.'

'But I don't care,' he adds defiantly, ''cause art galleries are the most boring places on earth.'

'How can you say art's boring?' I exclaim. 'I mean, *all* of it?'

'Try to be more open minded, Finn,' Jed offers.

'How can I when Mum's lost the form so I can't even go?'

Taking a deep breath, I blink at our kitchen wall cupboard. There's a bottle of white wine in there. It's horrible cheap stuff from the school fête tombola, and it's not even chilled, but who cares? Even rancid lukewarm vinegar would be fantastic right now. It would be no trouble to uncork it and glug the lot. What's so awful about art galleries anyway? They

248

are calming. You're not expected to do anything apart from stand or sit quietly and look at pictures. I can't imagine many places more pleasing than that, unless Naomi's nude pictures were on display. I did find those a little unsettling.

'Ta-*daaa*,' Jed announces, waving the crumpled A4 sheet like a prize. 'One permission form.'

'Holy shit,' Finn growls.

'What did you say?' I bark at him.

'Now I'll have to go and look at all those paintings of naked fat women.'

'Voluptuous,' I correct him. 'They're beautiful, curvy and voluptuous, Finn. Not fat.'

'Why did they do paintings of fat ladies?' Grace asks, wandering into the kitchen. She looks healthy and sunny-faced, and her lightly-tanned nose and cheeks are peppered with freckles.

'Well, in those days,' I explain, 'people thought bigger women were beautiful.'

'Why?'

'I suppose being bigger and rounder meant you were richer, with more money to buy good food. So that made those women seem attractive.'

Grace fixes me with wide, dark eyes. 'Did people like rich women in the olden days?' Jed sniggers in the background.

'Um, yes, I guess they did.'

'They still do, don't they?' Finn remarks, excavating a nostril with an index finger. 'Loads of people get married just for money.'

'Well, I suppose some do,' I agree. 'But most people marry for love.'

Finn peers through his dark fringe and throws me a

249

narrow-eyed look, as if the very concept is horribly outmoded. 'You still goin' to that fat club?' he asks.

'No, as a matter of fact.' I grin at him. 'I gave all that up and started running instead which means that, from now on, I can eat whatever I like.'

Chuckling, Jed comes over and kisses my cheek. 'Hallelujah,' he says. 'Good to see the old Laura's back.'

*

Later that night, as I'm tipping out the tumble of crumpled school books and half-eaten snacks from Finn's schoolbag, a leaflet about the art gallery lands on the floor. I flick through it; he was right, there are lots of paintings of naked fat women. And they look good. They look *normal.* One in particular, a woman reclining on a turquoise chaise longue, dark hair piled up on her head, even looks a little like me. A terrible realisation hits me: what if Danny wants me *naked* in those photos? Of course he does! Doesn't he want to put his energies into more artistic work? What does 'artistic' mean, if not nude? And didn't he say our little 'session' could be my reintroduction into the dazzlingly glamorous world of photography?

My heart lurches and I sense the blood draining from my face. Of course – it seems so obvious now. Danny wants me to strip off and pose like these languid ladies in the art gallery. He wants to loom over my quivering flesh with his massive zoom lens. And I can't do it. Apart from the fact that no one sees me naked these days – not even Jed, at least not properly, unless he's slicing me out of my girdle, of course – stripping off in that remote farmhouse would be the first step to my whole life unravelling, which is precisely what Beth was

250

warning me against. I have to stop it right now. Focus on things here – the kids, Jed, work – instead of being swept away by ridiculous fantasies.

Really, I have to *grow up*.

Quickly, I stuff the contents back into Finn's schoolbag, without sorting them out as I'd intended to. Pulling my mobile from my pocket, and wiping a smear of spaghetti sauce from my wrist, I text: VERY BUSY THIS WK CANT RUN WITH U SORRY. I wait for a reply, but nothing comes.

So that's that. Whatever 'it' was, it's not any more. Maybe it's better this way. Extracting a freshly-washed Ted from the laundry pile, I try to convince myself that, for once in my life, I've done the right thing.

CHAPTER THIRTY-THREE

All week, I throw myself into motherly duties, culminating with getting up at 7.20 a.m. on Sunday to make extensive preparations for the annual Playgroup Picnic. This is only marginally less competitive than the mums' race. Every edible offering is scrutinised; whilst home-made onion tartlets imply that one is coping marvellously on the parental scale, plain old ham sandwiches, made from white plastic bread, hint that you're veering towards mental collapse.

The first time I attended the picnic, when Toby had just turned two, Ruth had brought an intricately iced three-layer chocolate cake which she'd apparently been decorating until 2 a.m. It baffled me why she was boasting about this. 'I'd never manage to do that!' one of the other mums kept shrieking. Manage to do what, I wondered? Make the cake, or be unhinged enough to stay up half the night smoothing chocolate frosting all over it?

I wondered, too, when *my* baking gene would kick in, and I'd morph into being a proper mother. Just stopping Toby from having terrible accidents – he was obsessed with climbing at that point – was virtually a full-time job. Everyone cooed over Ruth's outlandish cake, whilst glancing disparagingly at my family packet of Monster Munch as if it were crack cocaine. That's why Grace and I are preparing something spectacular. It's actually rather enjoyable, creating something together before the menfolk of our household have emerged from their beds. Plus, it's not anything as ordinary as cake. We are making a gingerbread house: a gingerbread *stately home*, in fact, with formal gardens and an annexe. Ruth will choke on her home-made taramasalata when she sees it.

'How will it all fit together?' Grace asks, surveying our freshly-baked sections. I glance at our library cookbook. The house in the photo is a thing of wonder, its roof tiled with neatly-overlapping white chocolate buttons, its windows edged with piped icing and sugar pearls. My confidence begins to waver.

'We'll stick it together with icing,' I say firmly.

'Are you sure? Have you made a gingerbread house before?'

'Oh yeah. Loads of times.'

'When?' Her voice is laced with disbelief.

'When . . . when you were much younger. You wouldn't remember.'

'You always buy my birthday cakes,' she mutters, 'except the volcano one and that broke.'

'You mean someone broke it,' I murmur, 'and anyway, this isn't a cake. This is going to be completely amazing.' While I mix up the icing, and Grace figures out where the various sections should go, I start to remember how bad I am at constructing things, and how Jed shouted at me for not 'holding the wood properly' when we were trying to build a flat-pack shelf unit for our CDs. Why does everything have to be flatpack anyway? I once ordered Toby a special singing toothbrush in the hope that it would help him to focus on dental hygiene for more than a cursory three seconds. Even

253

that was self-assembly, and its head fell off four days later and emitted nothing more than a pitiful squeak. Luckily, though, having appointed herself as chief builder, Grace is soon constructing the thing and decorating it with the vast array of sweets I bought for the purpose.

'Wow, that's impressive.' Jed appears at my side in his dressing gown, smelling pleasantly of warm sheets and soap.

'It's gonna be the best thing at the picnic,' Grace declares.

'Bet it will be,' Jed says. He's in a buoyant mood, as is often the case on Sunday mornings. While Finn has begun to regard football with the kind of gloom normally associated with a trip to buy a school uniform, Jed still loves coaching the team. Or perhaps it's the getting out of the house part that he enjoys. 'Clever you,' he adds, kissing me lightly on the forehead.

'Thanks. It's been fun, actually, if a little challenging.'

'I did it!' Grace protests. 'Mum just did the boring cooking part.'

'Ah. Right.' He winks at me. 'More of a team effort then.'

I watch as he retrieves his and Finn's football kit from the tumble dryer. Mum and daughter baking, boys off to play footie – we're almost a cardboard cut-out family. I'm starting to wonder if this is how Jed and I will be: living and running the family together, being nice and polite and careful not to tread on each other's toes.

Once Jed and Finn have left for football, Grace, Toby and I put the finishing touches to our gingerbread palace. Even Toby dislodging some white chocolate roof tiles does nothing to dampen our spirits as we step out into the bright, blue-skied day.

Toby skips ahead along the pavement, swiping at

overhanging bushes with a stick. Grace walks alongside me, casting nervous glances at the large tin I'm carrying, as if fearful that I might drop it. By the time we arrive at the park, Ruth and a gaggle of women have commandeered the grassy area by the lake. Some have brought older children, and Grace hurries off to join them. Toby prowls around the picnic area, studying the food, wanting the eating part to start immediately. 'You go running around here, don't you?' Ruth asks.

'Yes,' I say with a start. 'How did you know?'

'I've seen you out and about. You're looking great, Laura. Saw you out one evening with some man . . .'

'Yes, I often do an evening run,' I say quickly, relieved that both Toby and Grace are out of earshot. To distract her from further probing, I whip the lid off our tin, waiting for her to reel back in admiration.

'What on earth's that?' she guffaws.

'Er, it's a gingerbread house.' As I glance down at it, my heart sinks. Our painstakingly-decorated walls have all collapsed in on each other, and the roof is askew. It looks as if it was assembled by a drunk person.

'Oh dear,' Ruth says.

'Yes, well,' I say briskly, spirits plummeting further as Grace scampers towards me. 'I'm sure it'll all fit back together.'

Grace's face crumples as she peers into the tin. 'Oh, Mummy! Why did it break?'

'I don't know, darling. Something faulty with the design, maybe?'

'We should complain,' she says fiercely. But who to? The cookbook author? The library? It was clearly my fault for thinking it'd be okay to transport the house before its icing cement had set properly.

I catch Ruth smirking at Pippa, a supermum who's brought an extensive selection of crudités for everyone to nibble on. They are neatly laid out in rows on a rectangular tray, like a brand new set of coloured pencils. At least Grace and I tried to do something *creative* together. Is it my fault that the damn thing collapsed? I'm a hairdresser, not a construction worker . . .

As news of our derelict gingerbread shack spreads, virus-like, around the assembled mothers, the more brazen of the group come over for a proper look. 'God, you're so funny, Laura,' one of them witters. 'You always give us a laugh.'

'Yes,' Pippa sniggers. 'Whenever I worry that my life's out of control, I think of you, and then I don't feel so bad.' There's a hoot of laughter that startles the ducks.

I try to laugh too, but am capable only of chomping bitterly on a celery crudité. I'm ridiculously grateful to see Beth striding towards us across the grass, with Jack tearing ahead with a skateboard jammed under his arm. She sees me and waves. I march towards her, away from our derelict ginger-bread house and the gaggle of mothers who are discussing the fact that, these days, everyone buys their gingerbread houses in flatpack form at IKEA. 'It's much easier,' Ruth chirps. 'That way, you just get to do the fun, decorating part.'

'I'd started to think you weren't coming,' I tell Beth as we meet on the grass.

'I wasn't going to. Just didn't feel like it, but Jack nagged and . . .' She musters a smile. 'Here we are.'

This is disappointing. I'd been counting on Beth to raise my spirits, but she's obviously not in a picnic mood. 'What did you bring?' I ask her.

'Oh, nothing much.' Beth's nothing-much is usually a

delectable home-made Victoria sponge. She rummages in her bag and pulls out a packet of shop-bought oatmeal cookies. They look like something a budgie would sharpen its beak on.

'Yeuch,' Jack growls, scowling at the packet, then hares off to the water's edge.

The rest of the picnic is just plain weird. Beth is oddly quiet, and when I return from taking Toby to the loo, I find her sitting alone and looking doleful, flicking pebbles into the lake. 'Is something wrong?' I ask, crouching down beside her.

'No, not really.' She looks pale and stressed. We fall into silence while a bunch of children throw bread to the ducks. Then I realise it's not bread, but broken-up pieces of gingerbread house. 'Have you and Pete had a row?' I ask.

Beth shakes her head. 'No, it's not that.' Into the lake, amidst the children's raucous laughter, plops our gingerbread roof. 'It floats!' Grace announces.

'Let's sink it!' yells someone else, lobbing a rock into the water.

Beth turns to look at me. 'You know your running friend?' I nod, confused. 'What, Danny?'

Her eyes meet mine. 'Does it . . . mean anything, Laura?'

I look down at the grass. 'I'm not sure. I don't think so . . .' There's a splash as Toby scores a direct hit, shattering our roof. 'I do think about him a lot,' I add. 'I know it's nuts and I'm married and shouldn't . . .' Her hand touches mine. 'Nothing's ever going to happen,' I go on, 'but, you know, Jed would go crazy if he found out, and I can't believe I've kept it secret, really. I suppose I just wanted something just for me, something that lifted me and made me feel good . . .'

'Would he go crazy? Are you sure?'

'Of course! I mean, we're not exactly close these days, and I can't remember the last time he touched or kissed me and I'm sure he's still obsessed with that bloody Celeste, but still . . .' I break off. 'Why d'you say that?'

I look at Beth, and suddenly I know. Know for sure, I mean. All those hunches, those snags of unease, seem to bunch up inside me, swelling until I can hardly breathe. 'What is it?' I whisper.

'I . . . I saw them.' Her eyes are lowered to the grass. 'You're my friend, Laura, and I care about you. I just thought you should know.'

CHAPTER THIRTY-FOUR

'You saw Jed and Celeste?' I murmur.

'Yes. Well, I assume it was her, from how you've described her . . .'

'Where?' There are shrieks of laughter as a child charges into the lake.

'You know the stables near Barnswick? I'd gone to pick up Kira from horse riding. I was early, sitting waiting in the car, and I saw someone in the rearview mirror at a table outside the pub. And I realised it was Jed. I was about to jump out of the car and join him, assuming he'd be with you.'

'And he was with her? Just the two of them, at a pub miles from anywhere?'

'Yes.' Her voice drops to a whisper. 'I'm sorry. I didn't know what to do, whether to tell you, but I haven't been able to think about anything else since . . .'

'What . . . what were they doing?'

'Nothing. I mean, they were sitting and talking. It could be quite innocent, Laura. Maybe she needed to talk to him about something that had happened at work . . .'

'But why there?' I ask. 'They could have just gone to the Green Dragon by school where the teachers usually hang out. They obviously didn't want anyone to see them.'

259

'Well,' she says, 'it kind of looks that way. But don't jump to any conclusions.'

I nod. My eyes are blurring but, mercifully, they don't spill over in front of all the crudité-chomping mums. They just fill with hot tears as the picnic goes on all around us: women chatting, kids skimming pebbles, someone praising Ruth's extensive cupcake selection. 'Look out!' Toby yells as a long, flat object flies over my head, colliding with the oak tree behind us and collapsing damply onto the grass.

I survey the small brown pile. Pippa, who's gripping a carrot baton between two fingers, bursts into high-pitched laughter. 'What the hell was that?' Beth exclaims.

'That,' I say, 'was our gingerbread house.'

*

It's a relief to get home, despite the fact that Jed will be back from football by now, so I'll be confronted by his lying, cheating, country-pub-frequenting face. I haven't yet figured out when, or how, to confront him. He asks me about the picnic; clicking into autopilot, I tell him about our wrecked house, Pippa's crudités, and kids having to be coaxed out of the lake, stripped down to their pants and swaddled in their mums' jackets and jumpers. I tell him everything, apart from the part about Beth seeing him at a country pub.

And I try to keep calm, reminding myself that there might be a perfectly reasonable explanation. I do calming things like drink chamomile tea and open a packet of hazelnut and chocolate chip cookies, surprised that I can only manage one.

Having had his fill of news from the picnic frontline, Jed takes Toby and Grace out for a kick-around in the park. Finn is called for by his mate James, and they both head round to Calum's, probably for a completely unsuitable movie-fest. Instead of brooding, I tackle the really foul jobs, like sluicing out the kitchen bin, and investigating unidentifiable spillages under the cooker. I should be running with Danny tonight, but can't face it. I text: SORRY CANT MAKE IT THS EVE, WILL EXPLAIN, LX

'Okay love?' Jed is standing at the kitchen door.

'Oh,' I say, startled. 'I thought you'd gone out.' I slip my phone into my jeans pocket.

'Just started raining,' he says, and there's a distinct hint of sadness in his dark brown eyes. For a moment, I want to throw my arms around him and hold him close, to convince myself that it wasn't actually him at that pub. After all, while undeniably handsome, Jed's dark-eyed, strong-jawed look is hardly uncommon. It could have been another man, taking his girlfriend for a drink in the country. What nicer way to spend a lazy afternoon?

'Laura . . .' he begins hesitantly.

'Uh-huh?' The children's voices filter through from the living room, and there's a ripple of laughter. They are happy, most of the time. Surely, that means we're not doing too bad a job. Can I risk destroying all of this by confronting Jed?

'Is . . . is everything all right?' he asks.

'Yes, I'm fine,' I say briskly. I can't say anything now; it's impossible, with the kids around, especially as their laughter has morphed into furious shouts, with Grace yelling, 'You never let me watch anything, stinkhead!'

'Puck off!' Toby cries.

'It's not *puck off*, idiot. You don't even know how to swear, baby!'

'Yeah I do. PUCK OFF!'

'Jesus,' I growl, marching through to the living room to deal with the fracas. Once I've sorted that out, I might start to think how to fix the rest of my life.

*

All evening, the image of Jed and Celeste at that pub table bubbles and ferments in my brain. Finn returns from Calum's house, boasting, 'We had proper Chinese from the takeaway. Duck and pancakes and everything, all rolled up with this black sauce. How come we never have that?'

'Because you're a deprived child,' I tell him, 'although I do seem to remember us having a Chinese, what, about a week ago?'

'Yeah,' he says airily, 'but not the duck.'

'We *never* have duck,' Grace agrees, looking up from her drawing at the coffee table.

'Yes, could you rectify that, please?' Jed teases, giving me a wink.

'Oh, Mum,' Grace adds, 'did I tell you about my project?'

'No,' I say, my eyes feeling suddenly, scratchily tired. 'What project's that?'

'For school. Family history.'

'What, like a family tree?'

'Yeah, kinda. But it's gotta be a book and we have to describe the people and what it was like when they were little. I've got to have photos and stuff.'

'Gosh,' I say. 'It sounds like quite a lot to do. I'll need to dig out that big box of old family photos. I think they're in the attic.'

Grace smiles. 'Thanks. I need 'em tomorrow.'

'Tomorrow? Grace, we can't find family photos tonight! They could be anywhere and it'll take me hours to rake about up there . . .'

'You said they're in the attic,' she mumbles.

'Yes, but . . . have you ever seen what it's like? All the boxes and rubbish and . . . stuff?'

'I've got to take them in tomorrow!' she bleats. 'We start by picking one person and standing up in front of the class and doing a talk about them! And I wanted to do Granddad!' Her eyes fill with tears, her drawing forgotten and her pens scattered all over the floor.

'Oh, Grace. Don't cry, love. I think it's a great idea to talk about Granddad. I wish you'd given me a bit more warning, that's all.' *Then I'd have spent the best part of this morning in the attic, finding those photos, instead of constructing that damn gingerbread house. I might even have skipped the picnic so Beth wouldn't have told me about seeing your dad and Celeste and this would just be an ordinary Sunday evening . . .*

'I told you,' she murmurs. 'I told you last week.'

I sigh, knowing there's no point in arguing. Perhaps my kids do tell me these things: that forms need signing for art gallery trips, and family photos located in horrible spidery attics. Maybe I've just stopped hearing properly.

'Don't worry,' I say, bobbing down to kiss her forehead. 'I'll see what I can do, okay?'

She musters a weak smile. 'Thanks, Mum.'

*

By 9.30 p.m., I still haven't spoken properly to Jed, because he is getting ahead with some marking at the kitchen table and I am up in the attic. In fact, locating the box of photos isn't the ordeal I imagined, once I've negotiated the Ramsay ladder and remembered where the light switch is. I spot the box, on top of more boxes containing old books, videos and records and the children's outgrown clothes which I have never got around to taking to the charity shop. Jed's usually the one who lugs our surplus possessions up here. It must be years since I've been in the attic.

I lift down the wooden box and take off its lid. Proper mothers spend hours creating beautiful albums, chronicling every age and stage of their offspring. Our photos are all loose, and sorting through them up here, in the dim, yellowy light, would take forever. I must have sat here for longer than I've realised, as I hear Jed coming upstairs and calling good-night. 'Will you be much longer up there?' he asks.

'No, I think I've got what I need.' Waiting until I hear him pottering about in our bedroom, then clicking off the light, I grip the box and step carefully back down the ladder. Then I tip out my family's life onto the living room floor.

It's a bizarre, glossy patchwork, a mixture of babies in our arms and, further back, me and Jed on our wedding day looking ridiculously young and delighted with ourselves (and each other) as we gathered with our parents and friends in a cluster outside Hackney Town Hall. It was a dazzling, brilliantly sunny day with red buses trundling by in the background. I looked tanned and slim in a cream slip of a dress, with dark hair piled up, and Jed was dashingly hand-some in a navy blue suit which remains the most – actually, the only – expensive item of clothing he's ever bought. I pick out our old friends' faces, which are tiny in the group photos: mates from college, the various salons I worked at, and even

264

school. And I realise with a jolt that, apart from occasional phonecalls, which are invariably interrupted by children – plus dashed-off emails and Christmas cards – it's been years since I've had proper, meaningful contact with any of them.

And I wonder if any of these old friends' husbands have secret trysts in pubs.

Quickly pushing the thought away, I scan the rest of the photos. Naturally, as I explained to Danny, most are of the kids. Apart from our wedding and the odd indistinguishable party aside, it was as if we had only properly discovered the medium of photography when Finn emerged into the world. There I am, grinning from ear to ear, breastfeeding him in Homerton hospital. A dainty six-pound baby who grew into a fiercely strong-minded toddler who'd cling to my leg, wailing, if I so much as tried to go to the loo without him. And Grace, bald until after her first birthday and perpetually laughing, and Toby with his generous, girlish pink lips and angelic blond curls.

Finally, I spot Dad, standing proudly with his arms crossed over a Fair Isle sweater, his herbaceous borders in full bloom behind him. From then on, I find more and more: Dad on various beaches, Dad with a toddler Grace on his shoulders, and Dad and me sitting together at a restaurant table at my 21st birthday party. I was a slim girl, I realise now, although of course I complained about wobbly bits and non-existent cellulite, as everyone did back then. There are even older pictures of Dad, when his hair was dark brown and a little unruly, rather than the light grey of his later years. In one, he's waist-deep in a river with a fishing rod, laughing. I pick them all out and set them out in a row, starting with a young Dad with a Christmas cracker crown on his head and me in a vest and nappy on his lap, and ending with the last picture I took of him, in the hospice on his sixty-seventh birthday. I sit and look, my gaze running along the row from left to right and back again, until I can't see clearly anymore because tears are pouring down my cheeks.

I don't know how long Jed has been standing there. He steps towards me and sits on the carpet, surveying my makeshift gallery of Dad. He puts his arms around me and murmurs, 'You okay, darling?'

I shake my head vehemently. 'Jed,' I blurt out, 'I know you met Celeste at that pub, somewhere out by the stables in Barnswick. Someone saw you.' I look up from the photos of Dad to my husband, whose dark eyes shine out from a pale, startled face. 'Please Jed,' I add, 'I need you to tell me what's going on.'

He blinks and moves away from me, and I see his gaze flicker over the hundreds of photos spread out on our carpet, as if one of them might help him to find the right thing to say. Apart from our coffee table, which forms a kind of island, the entire floor is covered in pictures. Anyone glancing in through our window might think we're up at 1.30 a.m. to arrange them into some kind of art project.

'Jed?' I prompt him. 'What's happening?'

'We . . . we did go there,' he says quietly. 'Whoever saw us, they were right.' His tone is flat and neutral, as if there's no reason on earth why it might seem strange or even vaguely suspicious to take a woman to a pub four miles out of town.

'Why?' I ask. 'If you wanted to go out after work, why didn't you just go to the Green Dragon?'

'Because it's full of teachers.' I turn to him, amazed that I am managing to hold it together and not get angry. It's as if all these photos – the hundreds of faces of our friends, parents and children, all the people we've loved who have populated our lives – are watching me, making me feel eerily calm.

'Would that have been a problem?' I ask. 'Being with other people, I mean? Or did you and Celeste want to be alone?'

He meets my gaze. 'She wanted to talk,' he says, 'and I suggested that place. We've passed it loads of times, haven't we, on our way to the coast? And we've always said how nice it looks.'

'Yes, nice for us to go to, maybe . . .' My voice rises a little.

'Laura, stuff had happened, stuff she wanted to talk about. She drove us out there and we sat and had one drink.'

I blink at him. 'Just one drink?'

'Well,' he mumbles, 'maybe two. Does it matter?'

'It does matter,' I snap, 'when I've put up with you not turning up for your own daughter's birthday, and on top of all that . . .' I pause, taking a breath. 'On top of all that, there are the texts and calls and . . .'

'Laura,' he cuts in, stopping me dead. 'For God's sake. I've never done anything to jeopardise this family. I never would . . .'

'But you are!' I insist. 'It's always there, simmering away – this worry about what's really going on with you two, and it affects the way I am with the kids, and at work, everything. So it *is* jeopardising our family. For one thing, you lied and said a whole group of you were out while the party was going on. And I know it wasn't a group. It was just you and her. D'you know how I know that? Because I went round to her flat to try and find out the truth . . .'

'When?' He looks aghast.

'A couple of weeks ago. I took her dress back, the one I borrowed at her party . . .'

'But I could have just given it back to her at school, couldn't I? What was the point of . . .'

'I know, but that was just an excuse, don't you see? And you know what else? There was this weird scene there. This young woman – well, a girl, really – came rushing out of Celeste's flat, crying, and Celeste was so upset about it . . .'

'God,' he whispers.

'Any idea what that was all about?'

He shakes his head. 'No. Not at all.'

'So you see, Jed,' I say, starting to gather up the photos from the carpet, 'it is jeopardising our family, whatever you might like to think.'

I'm aware of him watching as I pile up our pictures and place them back in the box, apart from the ones of Dad which I set out on the coffee table for Grace to pick from in the morning. 'I don't know what else to say,' Jed mutters. 'If you won't believe me, then I can't make you.'

Picking up the wooden box, I turn towards him. The carpet seems bare now, without its layer of photos, and Jed looks stranded upon it. 'I need time to think,' I tell him firmly, heading for the stairs with the box. 'And I think, Jed, that I really need some time away from you.'

CHAPTER THIRTY-FIVE

The following evening, partly to avoid the tense atmosphere at home, I go for a run on my own. It feels good to be out, my feet slapping a steady rhythm on the damp pavement and the faint drizzle misting my face. I feel as if I could run and run, if not forever, for at least forty-five minutes or more. Beth's tracksuit fits me perfectly now. I can wear jeans which, until recently, hadn't emerged from the musty recesses of my wardrobe since before I had Toby. And, incredibly, I'm no longer appalled by the sight of my own body in the bath.

Across the street, near the centre of town, a man in overalls wolf-whistles. I glance around to see if some nubile teenager has caught his attention, but no – it seems to be me. And I wonder if Jed might notice a difference in me and perhaps even want to have sex with me again. I once read that, when you haven't done it for ages, you actually stop thinking about it and forget that the possibility of intimacy with another human being even exists.

I wonder when that will happen to me.

Heading along the riverside, I jog past neat red-brick cottages with pretty front gardens and bird houses. It's all so safe and ordinary, a world away from being photographed in Danny's farmhouse with my clothes off. Would he want me resplendent on a chaise longue, or what? I smile as I trot up the steps, picturing the ridiculous situation. *That* would make Naomi choke on her flapjack.

I speed up a little, enjoying the cool dampness of the evening as I follow the road with its bow-fronted suburban houses around the outskirts of town. My stomach rumbles, perhaps because by now I've run further than I have ever managed in my whole life. In fact I'm probably in a *negative* calorie zone by now. Six weeks ago I could barely jog to the end of our road.

I spot him then, another runner, heading steadily towards me with his iPod on. When he sees me, he slows down to a brisk walk and pulls out his earphones. 'So,' he says with a grin, 'too busy to run these days, are you?'

'Oh, you know . . .' I look at Danny. He's changed too, I realise now, and not just because I snipped his unruly curls into a slightly more manageable style. He looks like a fit, healthy man who, without tipping towards off-putting vanity, clearly takes care of himself. 'I've just needed some thinking time,' I add lamely. 'But it's good to see you. I've missed you, you know.'

'Well, I've missed you too, and I worried that I'd offended you or something.' He touches my arm, and I don't flinch or move away.

'It's just . . . I've never told Jed about us running together. And with things being complicated at home, I thought, maybe I'd better have a clear head so I can decide what to do.' Danny nods. 'I'm taking the kids to my sister's house in Scotland at the weekend,' I add. 'I think it'll do us good to be away for a couple of days.'

'Jed's not going?' he asks.

'No. In fact he doesn't even know we're going yet. I only just decided while I was running along by the river.'

'Well, if you want to call me when you get back . . . I mean,

'I'll understand if you don't,' he adds quickly. 'I don't want to make things difficult for you.'

'Danny,' I say firmly, 'I'm the one who's making things difficult around here.' And I hug him then, as any friend would, before turning back and running all the way home.

*

By some organisational miracle, we are ready to leave as soon as we come home from school and nursery on Friday afternoon. I made sure we were all packed, having said goodbye to a cheerily polite Jed this morning; didn't want him hovering around, not knowing where to put himself, as we all piled into the car. 'Can we get more photos for my project?' Grace asks excitedly as we pull away from the house. 'I need some of Granddad when he was a little boy and I need to interview Grandma about him.'

'I'm sure that'll be fine,' I say, grateful for the barrage of commands and questions to stop me thinking about Jed coming home to an empty house and an empty weekend, without us. Although he didn't try to persuade me not to go, he clearly wasn't happy about it. Still, it is only two days. We'll stop off briefly at Mum's to pick up said photos, then head on towards Scotland.

'But what if they're all lost?' Grace asks dramatically. 'What if Grandma's thrown them all away?'

'Of course she won't have thrown away pictures of Granddad,' I say quickly. 'Anyway, she knows all about your project and said she'll have the pictures ready for you. We won't be staying long, though, because I don't want to arrive too late at Auntie Kate's.'

Grace nods, as if finally satisfied. 'How long are we going for?' Finn mumbles suspiciously.

'Only two nights. We'll be back on Sunday evening.'

'Why are we going?'

'God, Finn! I want to spend a bit of time with my sister, okay? It's been months since I've seen her. Anyway, you've always loved it at her place, playing with the animals and everything . . .'

I tail off, realising that Finn has probably outgrown the playing-with-animals stage, which triggers a wave of sadness. These days, he'd rather lie on the sofa, doing nothing more taxing than deciding which bodily part to idly scratch next. I glimpse him in the rearview mirror, slack-jawed against the back of the seat.

'Why isn't Dad coming?' Grace pipes up.

'He just fancied a bit of peace and quiet at home, love.'

'Did you have an argument?' Finn asks.

'Of course not. When do you ever hear us argue, Finn?'

He sniffs in response. 'I want Daddy,' Toby murmurs.

'I told you, Toby, you'll see Daddy on Sunday night. That's only . . .'

'Are *you* staying at Auntie Kate's too?' Toby cuts in.

'Of course I am! We're all staying, and it'll be lovely . . .'

The four of us descend into a grim silence. In the rearview mirror I can see that the Peppermint Aero, which I had kindly allowed the children to share, now covers the entire lower half of Toby's face. This would never have happened if I'd brought a Tupperware container of crudités. 'Feel sick,' Toby mutters.

I lower all the windows and pray he'll hold it together until I can find a safe place to stop. 'Take deep breaths,' I instruct him. 'Look out of the window. Shall we play I spy?'

'I want Daddy,' he growls.

My jaw tightens. 'We'll-see-Daddy-on-Sunday.'

'I feel *siiiick* . . .'

'Oh Toby, please don't. Hang on for a second, take deep breaths and I'll stop . . .'

'*Muuuum* . . .' There's a loud burp, and the sound of liquid cascading from a small mouth.

'Ew!' Grace screams, pressing herself against the side window. 'Ugh, it stinks in here!'

'Stop the car,' Finn commands. 'Indicate, pull over . . .'

'I do know how to drive, thank you. But I can't stop now, there's a van right behind us . . .'

'Can I have my story CD on?' Grace asks.

'No, Grace. Not now. I'm just trying to find a place to stop.' I am breathing fast and shallow, and my thighs are gummed together with sweat. An acrid stench, laced with Peppermint Aero, fills the car.

'It would take my mind off this horrible smell,' she reasons.

'Grace, we've heard it already.'

'We've heard it twice,' Finn groans. 'The bloody BFG . . .'

'Finn, there's no need to speak like that . . .'

'I know it off by heart,' he crows. '"And the BFG got his little pipey-wipe and blew dreams in through ickle Sophie's window . . ."'

'Shut up,' snaps Grace. Toby is waggling the door handle irritably. Thank God for child locks. At least they actually work, unlike the so-called DVD lock which Grace ripped off within minutes, allowing her to seize up its workings by posting in dozens of toast crusts. No wonder the mice came. Jed even got on to the previous owners, from whom we'd just bought the house, asking if they had any tips on eradicating the problem. 'There were no mice in all of the fifteen years we lived there,' they told him, suggesting that we'd moved our rodent population in with us.

'I'll stop as soon as I can, Toby,' I explain, 'then we'll get you cleaned up and everything will be fine.' That *everything-will-be-fine* line, trotted out by mothers every second of the darn day. Do children actually believe it? Mine don't. At least there are plenty of clean clothes packed in the boot. There must be a public loo on the way, where I can wash and change him. We can't show up at Mum's reeking of vomit. For some reason, she seems to think I'm some kind of Supremely Coping Mother, and today's not the day to shatter that illusion. Spotting a sign I've never noticed before, to a place called Gulley Bottom, I indicate left and follow the lane into the village.

I pull up on a grassy verge and open both back doors. Toby flops out, and I mop him down as best as I can with a J-cloth I found in the boot. 'This is *so* embarrassing,' mutters Finn, fiddling with his phone as if it might somehow transport him away from his deranged mother and little brother covered in puke. Toby glares down at his T-shirt and shorts while I search the boot for his bag. 'Finn,' I say, 'you did put that black zip-up bag in the boot, didn't you? Like I asked you to?'

'Uh?' he asks, mouth ajar.

'That bag. The one with mine and Toby's clothes in it.'

He shrugs and pokes at his phone.

'You didn't, did you?' I swing round to face him. 'It's all I asked you to do, to put it in the boot while I ran around like a nut, getting everything else ready . . .'

'I dunno.' He glances around the village, clearly unconcerned that neither I – nor, more crucially, his little brother – have any clean clothes.

'What were you doing,' I demand, 'when I asked you to help me?'

'Uh, looking for my hair wax.'

'Oh, right! Well, as long as we've got that, we're all okay. It doesn't matter that me and Toby don't have any spare clothes at all for the weekend.'

He nods, apparently taking this literally. Toby whimpers and slides a slimey hand into mine. 'Where's my clothes, Mummy?'

'At home,' I snap.

'What'll I do then?' he cries.

'Never mind, love. We'll just have a look around this village and buy you a lovely new outfit, okay?' I check my watch. 'It's almost five. With any luck, if we hurry up, there'll still be a shop open.'

He throws me a sour look. 'I want Daddy.'

'Yes, I know you do, love.' Hell, so do I, the philandering swine – if only because bad things don't happen when he's in charge. If he were here, no bag would have been forgotten, and no one would be covered in vomit.

'Where are we?' Grace asks.

'In Gulley Bottom.'

'Is it near Gran's?'

'It's not far at all,' I say, beaming optimism. 'Oh, cheer up, you lot. I'm sure we'll find something here.'

We set off, and at the end of a row of huddled cottages, we find a general store-cum post office. I worry about going inside, in case we're ejected for smelling awful, but decide to go for it anyway. After all, this is the countryside where people are used to all kinds of bad smells. The post office stocks a small range of stationery, and for one crazy moment I wonder if it might be possible to fashion Toby a padded top and trousers out of jiffy bags.

With the children growing impatient and whiny, we explore the rest of the village. There is, of course, no junior fashion emporium. Why did I think we might find one? Then I spot a tiny shop with a bow-fronted window, filled with children's knitwear. I march towards it with Finn sniffing and groaning as we go in. It's bizarre. He never acquires sudden flu-like symptoms if we're on a trip to York to buy drum kit accessories.

The elderly shop lady nods a greeting from behind the counter, unable to conceal her look of distaste at the sight of Toby's stained clothes. I smile brazenly at her and scan the rails. Every garment is hand-knitted in chunky wool. This is fine for a sweater, or even bed socks, but is less fine for trousers. I examine a pair of chocolate brown knitted flares which are unravelling at the hems. 'Don't like them,' Toby declares.

'They're hand knitted,' the shop lady remarks.

'They're lovely,' I say, 'but I think they might be a bit, um . . . hot.'

'They're fine,' she insists. 'They breathe, you see. They're loosely knitted so there's plenty of air circulation.' Just what we need. Living, breathing trousers.

'I wanna go home,' Toby announces, causing the shop lady's lips to pucker. Grace starts giggling, while Finn stands, gaunt-faced, as if trying to spirit himself away.

'Toby, I think we're going to have to try them,' I say gently. 'There's nothing else in your size.'

'No!' he screams. 'Don't want jumper trousers . . .'

'But *everything's* knitted,' I hiss at him. 'It's either the jumper trousers, or you'll have to go to Gran's, then all the way up to Auntie Kate's, in your pants.'

'I'll wear pants,' he bleats as the shop lady fixes me with a glare. What kind of mother transports her young son to see relatives in his *pants*?

'I'm closing in a minute,' she mutters, drumming her fingernails on the wooden counter.

'We'll just take this sweater,' I say quickly, plucking a random one from a shelf. For all the quaint, homespun ambience, it costs an eye-watering amount. As I start the car, the jumper is declared itchy and pulled off in disgust.

The bright afternoon has now slumped into fine rain. At least Finn has stopped complaining, Grace is soothed by another playing of *The BFG*, and Toby has dozed off in his vest and pants. Mum emerges to greet us, all smiles and hugs, as we pull up in front of her gate. 'How are you, love?' she asks.

'I'm great, Mum,' I tell her, following her into the house. 'But I'm afraid Toby was sick and I wondered . . .'

'Poor love. I'll run him a bath right now. Come up with me, Toby – a quick soak and you'll be good as new.'

'And we forgot his spare clothes,' I add, managing not to look at Finn.

'Could he wear something of Grace's?'

'I'm sure he could.' Why didn't I think of that? Mum takes his hand, and even though he's muttering about not wanting to wear girls' clothes, by the time he's been coaxed into Grace's shark T-shirt, and a perfectly acceptable pair of her khaki shorts, normal service has resumed.

We all kiss and hug Mum goodbye, with Grace being unable

to decide which pictures of her Granddad to borrow, and therefore deciding to take all of them. My spirits rise, and even our car starts to smell more fragrant as we head north into the darkening sky.

CHAPTER THIRTY-SIX

The moment we step into Kate's house, I remember how much I love being here, and wonder why we don't come up to see her more often. 'Yeah,' she laughs, looking fresh-faced and outdoorsy in her pale blue sweater and faded jeans. 'Aren't I always nagging you to come up more often? We're practically neighbours these days.'

'I know,' I say, smiling, gratefully taking the tea which Will, my gangly and amiable brother-in-law, hands to me. 'I think I still have my London head on, after all this time. Or my baby head maybe.'

'Your *baby* head?' Finn asks.

'Yes. I mean, when we lived in London, Scotland seemed so far away, and the prospect of such a long drive with you as a baby, then with you as a toddler and Grace as a baby . . . well, it just seemed quite . . .'

'Challenging?' Kate asks.

'Yes, that's a good way of putting it.'

'Why was it challenging?' Finn asks.

'Oh, nothing really,' I snigger. 'Just the feeding stops and then, when you were older, the stuff you used to get up to, like spraying juice on each other or even on the back of my head, while I was driving up the M1 . . .'

Finn breaks into a smile. 'C'mon, Mum. We never did that.'

'Oh, you did, hon. Then one time, for some mad reason, I decided it would be a genius idea to keep you both occupied with a full-sized box of cereal to munch on in the back, and of course we ended up with this hailstorm of Shreddies . . .'

We're all laughing now in Kate's homely living room with its rough stone walls painted white, and faded sofas and armchairs all worn into comfortable softness. Toby is already in bed; I decanted him, still sleeping soundly from the car journey, into Kate's box room. Finn and Grace, looking a little pale and sleepy now, sip from mugs of hot chocolate. When the time comes, they're too tired to protest about going to bed, or even having to share Kate's small twin-bedded room in the attic.

'Why don't *we* have an attic?' Grace murmurs as I tuck her in.

'We do,' I remind her, 'but it's not a proper room like this one and anyway, it's stuffed with junk.'

She blinks in the dark. Finn has already dozed off and is muttering softly in his sleep. 'I like it here, Mummy,' she whispers.

'Yes, me too. Auntie Kate's right – we should come more often. Right now, though, it's half-ten and you really should go to sleep if you're going to have a fun day tomorrow.' She nods, and her warm, slender arms emerge from the duvet and slide around my neck. 'We didn't show Auntie Kate the Granddad pictures.'

'We can do that tomorrow, darling. Night-night.'

I'd planned for an early night too, after the drive, but it's so warm and comfortable downstairs that Kate, Will and I catch up on how their B&B business is going, and how Will's job as a plumber, and Kate's bread which she supplies to local

280

shops, all work together to keep everything afloat. 'The two of you seem to manage everything so well,' I remark with a hint of envy.

'Oh,' Will teases, his glasses glinting in the candlelight, 'I do all the real work around here. Kate just gets to do the fun stuff like making her famous plaited loaves and driving around all over the countryside. I mean, who's got the grey hairs?'

'Yeah, the fun stuff like stripping beds and getting up at six to do breakfast,' she quips, slapping his thigh good-naturedly. I glance at Will, who's just turned fifty; still a handsome man, his cropped, silvery curls thinning just a little, his eyes piercingly blue behind steel-rimmed spectacles. It seems incredible that they met twenty-five years ago, when Kate was just twenty-one, yet still inhabit a sofa all curled up and sort of *moulded* together, so natural and at ease.

'Anyway, it's easier, in some ways,' Will adds, turning serious now, 'with the boys away and doing their own thing. I mean, it was full-on back then, when we had *our* baby-heads on . . .'

Kate smiles and gives Will a fond look. 'Was it sad when they left?' I ask.

'Well, I had to stop Kate enrolling on Rory's archaeology course at uni,' Will sniggers.

'Oh, right,' she shoots back, uncorking a second bottle of red, 'and you only insisted on driving all the way up to Aberdeen to check that Nat's washing machine had been plumbed in properly . . .'

'Well, I just wanted to make sure.'

'They do have plumbers in Aberdeen, Will . . .' We chat on and sip wine, and by the time I slip into bed between the crisp, cool sheets, I've decided it doesn't matter if Finn's offish with me, as one day pretty soon he'll be a huge man-person too, and I'll give anything to have him still hanging around, grumbling about wet ham in his sandwiches.

Yes, that's what'll happen, I think, lulled by the red wine and the soft, rhythmic swaying of the beech trees outside. They'll all grow up and we'll let them go. No one will want to read *Dirty Bertie* any more. I'll look back at this Celeste episode and realise that, in the grand scheme of things, it didn't mean anything at all.

*

The next morning, as Will and the kids lounge over breakfast, Kate and I run in the hills. Real hills, I mean – not like the tiddly incline in Lyedale Park. 'So what's with the new Laura?' Kate asks.

'What d'you mean?'

'Well, you've brought your running gear, for a start. Didn't even know you'd got into this.'

'I started a couple of months ago,' I tell her, 'and it feels such a part of my life now, I can't remember why I fell into it. I do feel better, though. More in control, I suppose, and it's a great stress reliever, just being out in the fresh air.'

'And you've lost so much weight,' she adds. 'Not that you were huge or anything. You were lovely. But you seem . . .'

'It's a great fat reliever too,' I add, laughing.

'Well, Jed must be impressed. Bet he can't keep his hands off you.' She throws me a quick glance as we veer off the narrow lane and down a rocky path towards the bottom of the valley.

'Um, I wouldn't say that exactly.' I picture Kate and Will

snuggled up on the sofa last night, sipping wine, teasing each other in their familiar, affectionate way, and feel a pang of longing.

'Are you and Jed okay now?' Kate asks. 'Or are you still mad about him missing Grace's party?'

'I, er . . . it hasn't been great lately,' I explain, deciding not to spoil our run by mentioning Beth spotting him and Celeste at the pub. 'He's still infatuated with that woman from school and we're both being a bit . . .'

'Distant?' she suggests.

'Oh, yeah. Definitely.'

'You know that's completely normal, don't you? Both me and Will had our cases packed loads of times when the boys were little . . .'

'Not you two!' I exclaim. 'I can't believe it.'

'Well,' she adds, 'we never felt strongly enough to actually go through with it, to walk out. I guess, when it came down to it, even when we were stomping around, grabbing tooth-brushes and throwing things into the car, neither of us could actually ever imagine being without the other. Not really.'

I fall silent, taking this in as we run side by side, surrounded by sculpted lilac hills and a huge, open sky. And later, as I cut Kate's hair, and help to cook and clear up after dinner, I find that I'm keenly aware of the easy closeness between her and Will. 'Hey,' I say as Jed calls on my mobile. 'Are you missing us madly?'

'Absolutely,' he says. 'It's so quiet around here. It's *weird*. I lay in the bath for nearly an hour and couldn't work out why it didn't feel right, then I realised no one was hammering to get in and Toby wasn't poking his sword under the door.' I laugh, picturing Jed drifting from room to room in his dressing gown, not quite sure what to do with himself. 'So, what have you been up to?' he asks.

'We took the kids for a huge walk this afternoon,' I tell him, 'and you know what was amazing? No one moaned! Even though there was nowhere to stop for sweets or ice creams or anything . . .'

'Oh, come on. You must have bribed them.'

'Nope, not even that.' There's a beat of silence. 'Oh, and I went running with Kate, up in the hills. That was lovely. And, just in case you're worrying that I'm fading away, she's been plying us with so much home cooking I can hardly move.'

Jed chuckles. 'Sounds like you're having a great time.'

'We are, love. Want to speak to the kids?'

'Sure, put them on.' While Finn merely confirms that, yes, he's having a perfectly nice time, Grace and Toby are, thankfully, a little more communicative.

'I was sick in the car,' Toby enthuses, ''cause Mummy drove too fast. And then she made me wear 'orrible jumper trousers.' Laughing, I take the phone from him.

'Jumper trousers?' Jed enquires. 'Are they some kind of new hybrid garment or what?'

'Well, they're the height of fashion in Gulley Bottom, apparently.' As I describe them in detail, it occurs to me that Jed and I used to talk like this all the time – about silly, everyday things that would make us crease up with laughter. Perhaps, I think later as I head up to bed, some of Kate and Will's cosy normality will rub off on us. Yet the thought of going home tomorrow makes me feel tense all over, and I can't drift off to sleep. Clicking on the light, I sit against propped-up pillows with a pen and paper from my bag, poised to write a list. Lists are good. They make you feel like you're in control, like my clipboard at Grace's party. 'If you're wavering over having a cookie,' Belinda told us at Tub Club, 'grab a pen and list all the reasons why you shouldn't have it.' I was no good at that. In fact, the effort of thinking about what to write about cookies made me crave the real thing even more.

Anyway, this list's not about cookies. I write:

REASONS TO STAY WITH JED

Not wanting children to have broken home

What would we do? Sell house, get lawyers etc? Court and hideous amounts of paperwork. Easier to stay married??

His mother would be delighted if we split up ('See? I told you so . . .')

Who apart from Jed would cut me out of a stomach holder-inner?

Racking my brains, I add:

Because we are married.

On the right-hand side of the paper I write:

REASONS TO SPLIT

His obsession with fancy-pants

He wouldn't go to a hotel with me

He hates my cooking

No sex since Jurassic era

I study my list, and the reasons seem to float away like party balloons as I drift off to sleep with the bedside light still on. In what seems like a heartbeat, it's Sunday morning and my tiny bedroom is filled with sunshine.

*

The drive home is, thankfully, devoid of vomit or emergency detours for scratchy knitwear. At a pleasingly old-fashioned tea shop, I treat us all to huge slabs of chocolate cake. By the time we set off again, the afternoon sun has broken through thin, gauzy clouds. There are no arguments about in-car listening. Our brief stay at Kate's, or perhaps the cake, seems to have had an anaesthetising effect.

In fact, I feel quite renewed as we head down the motorway. I have eaten well without denying myself anything, and been buffeted by the sharp, Scottish air. Apart from the grumbling at Gulley Bottom, the children haven't even bickered once. Pulling in at a service station, I usher them loo-wards and glimpse myself in the ladies' mirror. My cheeks are glowing healthily and I look brighter somehow, like that day I ran into Danny in York.

In the service station shop, while the children browse the comics, I pull out my phone. I've missed Danny, and it's not just our runs. It's that easiness we have together. Not like Kate and Will, obviously, but a sense that I can just be myself, and don't have to be on guard or worried about a secret agenda. Stepping towards the shop's exit, and positioning myself so I can still see the kids, I call his number.

'Hey,' he says. 'Missing you, stranger. Where are you?'

'Halfway home,' I tell him.

'How was Scotland?'

'Great. I took my running gear and I even *used* it. Me and Kate did some fell running and, you know, it made me think that maybe I'm fit enough now to do a 10k. What d'you think? Would you run the Scarborough race with me?'

'Listen to you, all fired up,' he chuckles. 'Yes, I'm in if you are, as long as you promise not to leave me in a dying heap at the roadside.'

I smile, watching the children select their in-car reading matter: a music magazine for Finn and Simpsons comics for Grace and Toby to share. The three of them drift towards the sweet display. 'You know what?' I add, fuelled by a sudden burst of bravery. 'I've also been thinking about those photos you mentioned. I'm happy to do it, if you still want to.'

'Really? You didn't seem sure at all . . .'

'Well, I've just started to feel better about myself. I think I've been far too cowardly lately.'

'That's fantastic,' he enthuses. 'It'll be painless, I promise. One evening next week okay for you?'

'Can we have sweets, Mum?' Grace yells over, and I nod, striding towards them.

'Tomorrow night would be fine,' I add.

'Great. You know how to get here?' My heart quickens as he gives me directions, and I am uncharacteristically generous as the children choose their sweets.

'Do I need to bring anything?' I ask.

'Nothing at all,' Danny says. 'Just you.'

*

We come home to a beaming Jed, a shiny house and our beleaguered window boxes freshly planted with geraniums. 'These look lovely,' I enthuse, kissing him as we tumble into the house in a flurry of sweet wrappers and chocolate-smeared faces.

'Well, I had to fill my time somehow,' he laughs. I catch his eye, and he adds, 'You look great, Laura. The country air obviously suits you.'

'Thanks. I *feel* good. It was great to be away.'

'Was it? Well, that's nice to hear,' he says, pulling a mock-hurt expression.

'I don't mean away from you,' I add quickly. 'It was just lovely to be around Kate. You know.' I think he does know, because the atmosphere is easier around us. Later, when the kids are in bed, he doesn't even laugh, or make comments about me 'not being built for speed' when he catches me on the laptop at the kitchen table, perusing the Scarborough 10k website.

'You could do it, you know,' he says, peering over my shoulder. 'Duncan managed it last year, and two months before it he couldn't have run for a bus.'

'I think I'll manage it,' I murmur, filling in my details on the online form. 'What d'you think I should put for my predicted finishing time?'

Jed shrugs. 'An hour ten?'

'Naomi said she'd managed it in forty-five minutes . . .'

'Girl racer,' Jed groans.

'I'll put an hour,' I say, excitement fluttering in my stomach.

'Sounds reasonable. And that reminds me,' he adds. 'Naomi phoned while you were away. Something about the school athletics club you're getting involved in?'

He crooks an eyebrow and we burst out laughing. 'Who'd have thought,' I say, logging off from the website, 'that your old carthorse of a wife would be entering a race and helping the young people of Britain to get fit.'

Jed smiles and plants a soft kiss on my lips. 'You're full of surprises, Laura Swan,' he says.

CHAPTER THIRTY-SEVEN

Phoebe is poking morosely at some kind of unidentifiable bake at the table when I arrive at Naomi's the following evening. 'Remember that athletics club we were talking about?' she asks her daughter. 'Well, Laura's going to help to raise funds for it. Make some cookies or something.'

'Actually,' I say, 'I was thinking I'd rather be involved in the more, um . . . active side. I've just entered that 10k you were talking about . . .'

'Really?' Her eyebrows shoot up. 'Well, if you think . . .'

'And I wondered, maybe I could help to plot courses, if we're thinking of including some cross-country running . . .'

'Cross-country?' she splutters. 'D'you know anything about that?'

'Well,' I say airily, 'I've just been to stay with my sister in Scotland and we did a bit of fell and mountain running.'

'You ran up a mountain?' Naomi blinks as she hands me a mug of puddle-tea.

'Well, just a small mountain really . . .' I don't mention that, technically, it was a hill. It *felt* like a mountain, and that's what matters.

'God, that's impressive. And yes, I think some cross-country would be great for the kids. We should get Beth and the others together, form a sort of committee.'

'That's a great idea,' I enthuse, mulling this over as Naomi chastises Phoebe for rejecting her bake, and whisks her upstairs for a bath. I glance at a picture of Naomi, Phoebe and the motivational trainer husband Jasper or Casper or whatever he's called, stuck to the fridge with a frog magnet. They're in some sun-drenched location and are all wearing summery shades like mint and pistachio. How will I keep our kids entertained all summer long, if we don't go away? There's no getting away from the fact that the summer break is looming in just a few weeks. Belinda spoke of summer holidays as something to be feared and prepared for, like a military attack. This year I could, feasibly, wear a bikini in public without the police being alerted. I make a mental note to have a look online for any last-minute deals.

'Sorry about that,' Naomi says, striding back into the kitchen. 'Phoebe makes such a fuss about bathtime these days. Keeps insisting that she doesn't need one every day.'

'Well, maybe she doesn't at her age,' I offer.

'Oh, I couldn't have her all smelly and dirty,' Naomi says with a shudder. As she tips the remains of Phoebe's dinner into the bin, my gaze rests upon another picture stuck to the fridge door. It's so small, it takes me a moment to pull it into focus and realise it's a tiny, shrunken miniature of one of the nude paintings of Naomi from the gallery. 'That's you, isn't it?' I ask, indicating the image.

'Yes.' She laughs ruefully. 'At least, it's my younger, springier, less haggard self.'

I smile and wander over for a closer look. 'D'you think you'll ever do some life modelling again?'

'Oh, no,' she exclaims. 'Why d'you ask?'

'I just thought, you know, with you doing all this training for the 10k, and being in such good shape . . .'

'Life modelling's not about having a good body, Laura. It doesn't matter what you look like. I just did it because I was asked, and I thought, well . . . why not benefit the artistic community?'

I nod, chewing this over, and glance at the kitchen clock.

'Why, are *you* thinking of doing it?'

'God, no,' I say quickly.

'Is money a bit tight for you and Jed at the moment?' She pulls a sympathetic face. 'If it is, I'm sure one of the colleges could use you . . .'

'No, no, we're fine, really.'

'It pays well,' she adds. '£15 an hour in some colleges and you soon get over your shyness.' I laugh, draining the remains of my puddle-tea.

'No, honestly. I'm just curious. Anyway, I'd really better be going. I'm due to meet a friend at eight.'

*

I'm hardly ever alone in the car. It feels rather strange, driving with no bickering or vomit smells. No one is poking anyone else in the back, and all I have with me is a small bag containing my make-up, a hairbrush and my father-in-law's silken robe. I discovered the robe crumpled up in our bed after the Vitesse visit. I'd have preferred to bring my own dressing gown, but thought Danny would spot the burnt sleeve and assume I have a habit of setting fire to myself.

As I drive out of town, I start to wish the kids were here with me. In fact I'd give anything for some in-car squabbling to take my mind off my modelling session. I'm doing this for *me*, I remind myself. It's empowering. I will merely be *benefiting the artistic community*, and who could possibly object to that?

Unfortunately, though, I'm not entirely clear about the etiquette of posing naked. I would have pressed Naomi for details, but couldn't think how to without arousing suspicion. I've just managed to glean a few tips from the internet. *There's nothing sexual about it,* one life model wrote. *You are just an object to be drawn. You could be an apple.* 'I am an apple,' I murmur to myself. I also learnt that the model should be offered a screened changing area where she can disrobe as, apparently, the act of undressing *is* deemed potentially erotic. Model then emerges from behind screen, wearing robe (hence Brian's silken dressing gown, the very thought of which is now making my skin prickle uneasily), and assumes pose as directed by tutor/students. Only then does she slip off the robe to reveal nude bod.

The 'assumes pose' part is particularly unsettling. Surely he'll want me demure, with knees pressed firmly together, and not in some kind of splayed porno pose. A sickening thought hits me: what if Danny's planning to cash in by putting my pictures on the internet? My heart is thumping as I turn off the main road and up the narrow lane which leads to Danny's place. The road curves steeply up a hill, then down towards a cluster of trees where I spot, as Danny described, an old farmhouse in pale biscuit-coloured stone. The windows are small and square with darkness behind. I wonder what made me think that this would be empowering for me.

By the time I pull up at the house, Danny has come out to greet me. 'Hey,' he says, all smiles. 'You're really here.'

I grip the bag containing Brian's dressing gown. 'Yep,' I say, feigning enthusiasm.

'Well, are you coming in?'

'Yes, of course.' My smile sets as I follow him in. While the house looks crumbly from the outside, inside it's all stripped wooden floors and chalky white walls, giving an airy, spacious feel. 'Like a drink or anything?' he asks.

'Tea would be great, thanks.' In fact I'd kill for a huge, sedative glass of wine right now, but as I'm driving home it's not an option. I glance around the open-plan living space. Neat, shiny red kitchen at one end; chocolate-coloured sofa, a couple of armchairs and a simple fireplace at the other. No tawdry sheepskin rug that he'll expect me to lie on. No obvious porno accoutrements, as far as I can see. I swallow hard, trying to dredge up a smidgeon of courage. 'We should get a few runs in,' Danny is telling me, 'if we're not going to completely disgrace ourselves at the race. How are you fixed this week?'

'Um, I should be fine most evenings,' I murmur, wondering at what point he's going to produce the rubber catsuit or suggest I step into a cage.

'There's what, a month to go?'

'Yes, something like that.'

He turns away and busies himself by making a pot of tea. 'Are you hungry?' Danny wants to know.

'No, I've already eaten, thanks,' I fib. My gaze rests on three large black and white photos above the fireplace. 'Are these yours?'

'Yes, like them?'

'I really do. They're beautiful.' They are pictures of trees, each pin-sharp twig twisting elegantly against a colourless sky.

'Thanks,' Danny says. 'You wouldn't believe how many I took to end up with those three. I mean literally hundreds.' He chuckles. 'I guess I can be pretty obsessive.'

Will you be like that when you photograph me? I want to ask, nerves swirling in my stomach. *Will my pictures be in sharp focus like those trees, or a little more forgiving?* I was hoping for soft-focus. Dim lighting, stocking-over-the-lens kind of thing. 'Um . . . what kind of pictures were you thinking of taking?' I ask casually.

'Just as you are, really. Nice and natural. Nothing too posed.'

Right. Natural as in *naturist*, in the buff. 'Um, how long d'you think it'll take?'

'As long as you have,' he says, looking a little crestfallen. 'Do you have to rush back?'

'Er, no, not at all.'

He smiles. 'Great. Shall we get started then?'

'Um . . . is there somewhere I can get ready?' I blurt out.

Danny looks confused. 'Do you need to?'

Sweat prickles my brow and I'm conscious of my simmering cheeks. 'I'd prefer it, if you don't mind . . .'

'Sure. No problem. The bathroom's just down there, first right.' He indicates the far end of the living area.

Gripping my bag, I scuttle out of the room, grateful for a few moments' respite before getting down to the nitty-gritty. I feel terrible now, telling Jed I was popping over to Naomi's and omitting to mention this other, potentially more controversial part of the evening. Everything is bound to unravel, as Beth warned it would, like those jumper-trousers I forced Toby to wear.

I perch on the edge of Danny's bath, trying to reassure myself that at least there's no chaise longue for me to lie on.

So what will I do? Sit on the sofa or one of the armchairs, as if I'm watching TV and have simply forgotten to put on my clothes? Despite the fact that I've lost weight, being naked still feels alien to me these days. I try to picture Naomi in those paintings. She looked *neutral*, I remember, as if mentally compiling a shopping list. Maybe that's how I'll get through it. I could sit there and plan a menu of dinners for the week ahead, the way proper mums do to ensure variety and no wastage.

Slowly, I pull off my sandals and unzip my skirt, draping it neatly over the side of the bath. My upper lip is prickling with sweat and my heart seems to be rattling away at twice its normal speed. I mustn't freak out. There is nothing to fear – this is not a tenth as mortifying as my last sojourn into someone else's bathroom, which involved Toby, glass nuggets and an impromptu pee. Compared to that, this is *fine*.

I pull my T-shirt over my head and survey myself in the mirror over the wash basin. It's still a little shocking to see the new me – still Laura, but in a different body, with slimmer hips and thighs, smaller boobs and a flattish tummy. I pull off my bra, placing it over the skirt and T-shirt, then finally my industrial white knickers. Now I'm properly nude, about to benefit the artistic community. From my bag, I pull out Brian's dressing gown. I shrug it on, knotting it tightly at the waist. Glimpsing my reflection again, I see a scared-looking woman who looks as if she's about to undergo a particularly unpleasant operation.

'Laura?' comes Danny's voice in the hallway. 'Are you okay in there?'

'Yes, sorry, I was just er . . .'

'Are you putting on make-up?' he asks.

Damn. I've been so stressed about disrobing that I'd forgotten about that. 'Yes,' I call out.

'Don't put on too much, will you? You're fine just as you are.'

Right. Pale and corpse-like in my father-in-law's dressing gown. 'Won't be a minute,' I add unconvincingly, hearing his footsteps retreat to the living area. There are some clanking noises, which must be him setting up harsh, unforgiving lights. *Just do it*, I tell myself, unlocking the bathroom door and trying to exude confidence as I walk out. The corridor's only a few strides long but it feels like an eternity before I reach the living area where Danny is refilling his mug from the teapot.

He has his back to me as he pours. I take in two lights on silver stands and a black leather chair which I hadn't noticed before, placed in the middle of the room. His camera is perched on its sturdy tripod like a huge, unblinking eye.

Danny turns at the precise moment I pull off Brian's gown, letting it fall in a silken heap to the floor. 'Ready,' I announce, forcing a grin to show him I can *do* this, and that I'm at one with my nakedness.

He stops dead, then quickly turns away and places his mug on the worktop. 'D'you want me to sit in this chair?' I ask shakily.

Danny rakes a hand distractedly through his hair. 'I . . . I don't understand,' he murmurs. 'Why are you naked, Laura?'

CHAPTER THIRTY-EIGHT

'I just assumed, when you said you wanted to do pictures, you meant . . .' I snatch the dressing gown from the floor and struggle into it.

'You thought I meant . . . *nude* pictures?'

'Yes,' I reply coolly. 'I just thought, you know . . .'

'But . . . why? What on earth would make you think that?'

'I . . . I don't know. I just assumed, when you said natural pictures . . .'

'But that's all I meant,' he exclaims. 'Honestly, Laura. There was no hidden agenda or anything. I mean, I'm not prudish but . . . it's not what I had in mind at all.'

'Oh,' I murmur.

'I just wanted to shoot your portrait.' He smiles, and I grip the back of the leather chair.

'You mean . . . just my face?'

'Yes.' His cheeks flush, and the glossy blue teapot, which he's been clutching all of this time, hits the worktop with a solid thud. 'Unless you really want . . .'

'No, no, of course not.' I pull Brian's dressing gown tighter.

'We don't have to do the pictures at all,' he adds, 'if it's stressing you out.'

'It's not at all,' I say firmly. 'I'll, um, just go and get dressed then.' I turn and walk as calmly as I can to the bathroom.

Once there, I collapse onto the loo seat. Tears well in my eyes, even though they're shut tight as I try to block out the horror of what I've just done. Why did I think he wanted me naked? Was it Naomi's nude paintings? Or Finn going on about those naked fat women in the art gallery? Whatever the reason, no one else – no normal woman, I mean – would jump to such a ridiculous conclusion.

I wipe away the tears with my hands and wonder how I'll ever be able to walk out of here. Here I am again, trapped in a bathroom – just like at Celeste's, but in fact, this is far, far worse. Grabbing some loo paper to blot my eyes, I stand up and pluck my knickers from the neat pile on the side of the bath. I pull them on, followed by my bra, top and skirt and finally sandals, specifically chosen as they wouldn't leave crimpy imprints all over my bare-naked feet.

I inspect my face in Danny's mirror. It's the face of an idiot, a woman with a nice, normal husband and children who, for some unbeknown reason, decided to strip off in a man's house. A tear has left a silvery line down my cheek, like a snail's trail. Danny probably assumes I was trying to seduce him. He was appalled, too, judging by the shocked look on his face. And he'll be desperate for me to go so he can call a friend and tell him about this berserk woman who came round to his house for an innocent photo shoot and took all her clothes off.

'Laura?' he calls through the locked bathroom door.

'I'm coming,' I croak.

'Are you okay?'

'I'm fine, Danny.' His footsteps fade. Taking a deep breath,

I try to flatten my hair with my palms and stuff Brian's dressing gown into my bag. Slinging it over my shoulder, I open the bathroom door and stride down the corridor to the main living area where he's dismantling one of the lights. 'Well, I'd better be off now,' I announce coolly.

'Are you sure?' He turns around to face me, frowning. 'You don't need to. I mean, I hope you don't feel bad . . .'

'No, but I'd really better—'

'Why are you doing this?' he bursts out. 'I don't understand. It's like . . . I've done something to offend or upset you, and I'd really hate you to feel like that.' Hurt shines from his clear blue eyes.

'I . . . I'm not doing anything,' I say. 'I don't know what you mean.'

'I mean all the naked stuff, which was fine and everything, just not what I expected, then rushing off to the bathroom and coming back out and speaking to me as if, as if you're the *gas man* . . .'

'The gas man?' I repeat.

'Yeah! Saying, "I'd better be off then" as if we don't even know each other . . .'

'I'm sorry, I just meant . . .'

'It's . . . it's just a bit weird, Laura.'

'I know. I shouldn't have come . . .'

He comes closer, scrutinising my face. 'You're upset, aren't you? I know you are. Please don't be upset.'

'I'm not upset,' I insist, even though my vision is blurring again.

'Hey,' he says gently. 'It's okay.'

'I feel like such an idiot . . .'

'Well, you're not,' he says, and I'm aware of him holding my hand, and those kind eyes focusing on mine. 'You're just you,' he adds, 'and I've never met anyone like you.'

'What d'you mean?' I whisper.

'Well,' he smiles, 'the first time I met you, you literally knocked me off my feet.'

'Not quite,' I correct him.

'And you'd shoplifted a playsuit . . .'

My face breaks into a smile, and I'm about to remind him that I'd never even wanted the playsuit, but I can't because his lips are on mine and we're kissing, and every cell in my body is fizzing like the lava in my volcano experiment. My head fills with the touch and taste of him, and I'm vaguely aware of my shoulder bag dropping to the floor.

He pulls away and smiles. 'Are you okay now?' he asks gently.

'I am,' I say, taking in the clear blue eyes, and the smile that makes me feel so giddily alive. 'I really am okay.'

'Um . . .' He pauses and pushes back his hair distractedly. 'Can I be horribly cheeky and ask you something?'

'What is it?' I whisper.

'Um . . . would it be okay to take your picture now?'

I burst out laughing. 'Why, Danny?'

'Because . . . you look beautiful.'

'Oh, come on . . . with my pink nose and red, puffy eyes?'

'Believe me,' he says, 'you really are.' I fall silent and watch as he fetches his camera from the tripod.

'Okay, but what d'you want me to do?' I ask hesitantly.

'Nothing. Just look at me.' I swivel my eyes to the lens and he clicks the shutter. He clicks again and again, then I tell him I really have to go, as I'm only supposed to be at Naomi's. We kiss at the front door, the cool night air making my head spin as I tear myself away and say goodnight.

I start the car and drive away. My heart feels as if it's being walloped by Toby's xylophone hammer, and I wonder if it will ever function normally again.

CHAPTER THIRTY-NINE

I step into our house and glance around the living room where it looks like a Lego explosion has taken place. 'Jed?' I call out in a hushed voice, horribly conscious of a tingling sensation on my lips.

I hear footsteps on the stairs as I scoop up plastic bricks. Hiding under the coffee table is a complex Lego space missile which Jed must have made. My stomach turns over with guilt as I place it carefully on the table.

'You're back then.' Jed stands at the bottom of the stairs, observing me.

'Yes. Sorry I took so long.' I blink down at the carpet and retrieve a minuscule Lego sword. Wordlessly, Jed strides past me, lands heavily on the sofa and flicks on the TV.

I escape to the kitchen, heart hammering against my ribs. He knows. I *know* he knows. I fill the kettle, flick it on and try to check my reflection in the microwave's glass door. The only features I can make out are my eyes, which look large and dark and scared, and are definitely radiating guilt. I turn to our chrome toaster which looks posh, and which we bought in the hope that it would offer a touch of glamour to our home, but it functions erratically and is full of incinerated crumpets. My stomach growls, and I remember that I haven't had any dinner. Couldn't face anything before my debut photo shoot.

I feel light-headed as I peer at my haggard reflection in the toaster. It's partially obscured by a dollop of jam which Toby flicked onto it, and which has been there so long, I suspect it might have to be shot-blasted off. Do people ping jam about in Naomi's house? Of course not. I peer closer, tilting my head to avoid the smear. Just as I thought. A hint of recent snog activity around the mouth and jaw region. There are pink patches, which feel hot to the touch and are clearly punishment for my sin. I can't remember ever having snog burn before. Maybe I'm allergic to Danny?

I dampen a tea towel under the cold tap and dab at the pink bits, trying to soothe them before Jed notices anything. The TV burbles on. Maybe I'm being paranoid, and he's just tired from the bathtime-and-story routine. Or perhaps this is his normal response to me and I'm reading too much into everything.

'Hi,' he says lightly, appearing in the kitchen doorway.

'Hi.' I muster a smile and drop teabags into two mugs. 'I take it you'd like one?'

'Yes please.' He looks tired and sad, and a little older than when I left him earlier this evening. I take in the soft brown eyes, the thick wavy hair I used to love to bury myself in, as I breathed in his warm scent. He's still handsome, still the man I fell in love with. For a moment, I'm back at that party, aged twenty-three, spotting him nursing his bottle of Becks and plonking myself on the stair beside him.

'Um, is everything okay, Jed?' My voice sounds oddly detached.

He pauses and looks at me. It feels as if our house, which normally creaks and murmurs like a living thing, is standing deadly still. 'I've been thinking,' he says.

303

'What about?'

'What you wrote on that note.'

'What note?' I ask, frowning, then feeling sick as I remember the note I wrote late at night at Kate's. *Reasons to stay with Jed. Reasons to split.* Surely I didn't leave that lying about? I desperately try to think where I put it, and vaguely remember reaching down for my toilet bag on the floor by my bed, and dropping it in there. 'Oh, that was just silly!' I say with a ridiculous guffaw. 'I didn't mean it at all.' My kissing rash throbs urgently, or maybe I'm just imagining it. I can't believe he can't see it, doesn't *know*.

'Well, I've thought it over,' he says levelly, 'and I think it'll help all of us.'

'You . . . do?' It slips out in a whisper.

Jed nods. 'It's a mad situation and it's time we did something about it.'

'I really don't think we need to, Jed. I mean, we all write daft things when . . .'

'It'll be more practical,' he cuts in.

'Do you think so?' My lip is starting to wobble.

'It needn't cost a lot,' he adds.

Great! Unravel our lives, break up our family for a fancy French bit and what's he concerned about? Money. 'You're probably right,' I splutter. 'I'm sure you can do it cheaply online.'

'Sorry?' He frowns, causing furrows to appear on his forehead.

'I imagine it's easy if you want to go through with it . . .'

'Laura, why are you crying? I thought you'd be pleased. I assumed you wanted . . .'

'Of course I don't,' I wail. 'I only did it because I was trying

304

to decide what to do. That's why I took the kids up to Kate's. I had to get away, you see. I couldn't deal with being around you any more.'

'What on earth are you on about?'

'So I thought I'd write a list of all the reasons,' I charge on, 'then I'd know . . .' I fade off. Jed is staring at me uncomprehendingly.

'What list of reasons?'

'The, the . . . list of why we should, er, stay together. Or split up . . .'

'Split up?' He looks aghast.

I nod.

'Is that what you want? You want a divorce?'

'No. I really don't, Jed . . .' I swipe a sleeve across my face. Jed lowers himself onto a kitchen chair on which someone has left a solitary oven chip.

'But you thought about it, obviously.' He fishes the chip out from under his bottom and throws it angrily onto the floor.

'Well, yes, but only because of . . .'

'The thing I was talking about,' he adds in a resigned tone, 'is that note you wrote about us needing a new bathroom. Reasons why we had to have it. You stuck it on the door, remember? I know you haven't been happy and I decided, when I was doing bathtime with the kids tonight, that that's probably the reason. *That's* what I meant.'

I gawp at him. 'Oh.'

'And I spoke to Celeste about it – she popped in while you were away – and she said she could see your point.'

'Right,' I say tartly. 'So you've decided we need a new bathroom and then, when we've got that, everything will be all right.'

'Well, um . . . I hope so.' He smiles weakly. I wonder why I'm experiencing a distinct lack of excitement at the prospect of new bathroom fittings.

'Where would we put it?' I ask.

'Well, at first I thought we could carve a bit off our bedroom but then, Celeste said—'

'What is it with you and Celeste? Don't you see, Jed? We can't even talk about bathrooms, and God knows I don't even care about bathrooms, I'd be happy to pee in a *bucket* actually, if it meant her name didn't keep popping up . . .'

'Yes, but—'

'As if it's not enough,' I rant on, 'being subjected to you two pawing each other and sneaking off for cosy drinks in the country together, now I can't even go away to visit my sister without her dropping by!'

'Shouldn't I be the one worrying about what *you're* up to?' he snaps back. My heart thuds with alarm.

'What . . . d'you mean?'

'You know what I mean. Your cosy little runs with that . . . that man. That's if you even do go running, which I doubt . . .'

'Of course we do, Jed . . .'

'Didn't think I knew, did you? Sorry, Laura, but when you're a teacher, the kids take great delight in telling you all kinds of things.'

'What things?' I say faintly.

'Things like, "Saw your wife in the park, Mr Swan, with a man in a tracksuit. Got a personal trainer, has she?"' He emits a bitter laugh. Hell. Who spotted us? Those snogging teenagers on the bench, all those weeks ago? So Jed's known all along. Not that I have anything to be ashamed of, apart from a little

306

kiss, and stripping naked in front of Danny, and that was only to benefit the *artistic community* . . .

'And where were you tonight?' Jed thunders on. 'You weren't really at Naomi's were you, discussing the athletics club?' He spits out the words.

'Yes I was!'

'You don't even like her, yet you pop over to see her and you're gone for hours . . .' I take in the furious dark eyes and the bitter, downturned mouth.

'It's written all over your face,' he adds.

We fall into silence, and I pray that the children won't have heard us, they're all fast asleep, dreaming about Kate's chickens or drum patterns or Ted. 'You're right,' I murmur, studying a mysterious yellow splodge on the floor. 'I . . . I went to see him tonight.'

'Who?'

'Danny. The man I've been running with. You're right, Jed, and I'm sorry. I didn't tell you the truth.'

'What did you go there for? Or needn't I ask?'

'I, he . . . he wanted to take pictures of me. He's, erm . . . a photographer.'

'Oh. Right. And what kind of photos did he have in mind?' Jed narrows his eyes at me.

'Just a portrait,' I murmur. 'He, um, works for newspapers but likes doing portraits and he thought I'd be good for that.'

'Sure, bet he did.' Jed swings around and storms out of the kitchen. I want to follow him, to say I'm sorry and that, whatever he's been up to, it doesn't matter any more because I've hardly been the model wife. I've lied, I've sort of cheated, if kissing counts. Now I want to take it all back and do whatever I can to make things right again. But I can't, because when I find him in the hall, he's pulling on his jacket, and opening the front door, and leaving me. 'Is that why you've lost all that weight?' he snaps. 'Because you wanted to make yourself slim for . . . for *him*?'

I shake my head. 'There's no reason. It just sort of happened . . .'

'Because when we first met, you said being in love stopped you eating, that you were too excited for food . . .'

'That was different!'

'How was it different?'

'Because I was with *you*, Jed. And this is nothing, okay? I promise you . . .'

'Are you in love with him?' His face seems to crumple as he stands at the open door, and I want to put my arms around him and pull him close.

'Of course I'm not,' I cry. With a weird kind of snort, he turns away. 'Jed, please don't go. Listen to me . . .'

'You're a bloody nutter,' he barks, then steps out into the cool night and into our car which he revs *far* too aggressively and drives away.

I stand, watching it grow smaller as he drives away from me. Then he's gone, without a bag or anything. I stand on the pavement for a long time, waiting for our car to reappear and Jed to tumble out and hug me and say it's okay.

But he doesn't come back. Slowly, shivering now, I turn back to our house. Somehow, I decide, glancing up at our dangly gutter, I probably deserve this.

CHAPTER FORTY

I try calling Jed at 1.30 a.m., and 5.17 a.m., but he doesn't pick up. I wake up with a deep crevice running across my cheek from the rumpled sheet. 'Seen my trainers?' Finn asks as we meet on the landing. If he's noticed my haggard state, he's chosen not to comment upon it. Perhaps I always appear like this to him – pale and gnarled with bloodshot eyes, like a Halloween ghoul.

'I've seen them lying around,' I say distractedly. 'Maybe in the living or the kitchen. Or try the bottom of the stairs . . .'

He clucks loudly. 'Could you be more specific?'

'Finn, I'm sorry. I have other things on my mind right now . . .' That slipped out. I made a mental note early this morning not to tell the children anything about our little tiff. I'm trying to convince myself that that's all it was – otherwise I'll never get through the whole breakfast, cajoling-kids-into-uniforms routine. And I don't want them going to school and nursery and informing some concerned adult that Mum lied and Dad was furious and stormed off into the night.

'Well, I can't go to school in bare feet,' Finn says, crossing his arms confrontationally.

'No, love, I know you can't.'

'So . . . what . . .?' He shrugs dramatically.

'Keep looking,' I say in as sweet a voice as I can choke out, 'while I get breakfast together.'

'Can we have eggs?' Grace shouts from the bathroom where she's trying to construct a complicated up-do.

'Yes we can, if you hurry. Leave your hair, though. I'll do it for you. It's almost impossible to do it yourself at the back.'

'I can do it,' she snaps as I go in to help her.

'Grace, it'll only take a minute . . .'

'I said I can do it!'

'Fine.' I march out to the landing where Finn is still standing in stockinged feet, blinking into the middle distance as if expecting the elusive trainers to float towards him, perhaps on a flying flannel. I am unreasonably irked about Grace's hair. Surely, as a hairdresser, it would make sense for my children to request my hair-related services occasionally?

Finn tails me downstairs. 'Heard you and Dad shouting last night,' he growls.

My heart judders. 'Did you? It was nothing really. All couples have silly squabbles sometimes. I know it's not very nice, love, but it is completely normal.'

He squints at me. 'It was about shopping.'

I frown at him as we reach the kitchen. 'Was it? Yes, you're probably right. It was so silly and trivial, I can't actually remember *what* it was about . . .' I chuckle pathetically.

'It was about butter,' Finn says.

'Was it?' I busy myself by taking the milk from the fridge and sniffing it.

'Yeah. Dad said, "There's no butter".'

310

'Did he?' I say with a small laugh. What did he really say again? The words are etched into my brain. *You're a bloody nutter* . . .

'You should get some,' Finn adds, 'next time you're shopping.'

'Yes, I will. I'll make a note of it. In fact I'll do it now.' I feel pathetic, going through the charade of rummaging through our junk drawer, with its balls of string and crumpled Chinese takeaway menus in search of a pen and a scrap of paper.

'Here's a pen.' Finn hands me a Biro from the floor. It's cracked, I notice, like most things around here. Someone must have stood on it.

'Thank you, love,' I say pleasantly. *Shopping list*, I write, aware of his caustic gaze. *Butter*. Then, because I feel I should write something else, I add: *Salted and unsalted*.

'Where's Daddy?' Toby has appeared in the doorway wearing an old, faded Pokemon T-shirt that used to be Finn's, and nothing else. He scratches his blond curly hair and gives his willy an absent-minded tug.

'He's . . . out,' I say, scuttling towards the toaster where I attempt to scrub off the hardened jam with a pan scourer.

'Is he at work?' Toby asks.

'Um, yes, probably. I think he went in early, had loads to do. Er, now, d'you want toast or . . .'

'You said you'd do eggs,' Grace declares, marching into the kitchen with her hair pulled back into some kind of mangled bun that's not befitting the daughter of a hairdresser.

'Oh yes,' I murmur, fetching eggs from the fridge and wondering what Jed's doing right now. Is he wandering the streets, berating himself for wasting fifteen years of his life with a nut-job? I open the egg box. One egg.

'Can I have it?' Toby asks.

'I want it,' Grace protests. 'I asked first.'

'*He* should have it,' Finn breathes, proceeding to swing on the fridge door. 'He's the youngest and needs to grow more.'

'Thanks for your input, Finn. But I don't think swinging on the fridge door will help you find your trainers.'

'Unless they're in the fridge,' Grace adds.

'*You* borrowed them,' Finn declares, 'so you must know where you put them last.'

'Yes,' I say, 'but that was weeks ago when I'd just started running. You've worn them loads since then. You've even had new ones – they were forty-five quid, don't you remember?' I take the solitary egg from the box, momentarily enjoying its soothing coolness in my palm. I'm not sure who'll have it. Why are mothers expected to make seemingly minor but potentially life-shattering decisions about 500 times a day? I pull out a frying pan and heat the oil, deciding that the problem will sort itself out, in the way that Jed and I will sort ourselves out, and everything will come right in the end.

I crack the egg into the pan, wincing at its murky grey hue and distinctly off smell. 'Uh, it's farty,' Grace squeals.

I look at it, grey and flaccid in the pan, and check the box. The date's fine, and it should be okay, but inside its fragile shell things have clearly gone wrong. 'Sorry, the egg's off,' I say.

'Awww,' Grace groans.

'Hey, Mum!' I swing round to see Finn actually smiling, and for a moment it's as if my old, sunny-faced boy has reappeared. The boy who'd drink milk and loved Lego and would snuggle up to me in his pyjamas. 'Look,' he says, brandishing a silvery block of Lurpak. 'We do have butter, Mum. It was here all the time in the fridge.'

*

After dropping off the children I head straight to work, having only briefly considered throwing a sickie. What would I do at home all day anyway? Constantly phone Jed and worry like mad about his whereabouts? Or pace around our bedroom, burying my face in his slightly stale (gag) pyjamas? In fact work is *good*, because I'm rushed off my feet from the moment I walk in. Jess is off sick, so Simone and I are on shampooing as well as cutting duties. Head after head, without a break, right through until lunch. I switch to auto-pilot, making bland conversation about jobs and holidays whilst slathering soapy heads.

'Where's the girl who usually shampoos me?' asks the head from the basin.

'Jess? I'm afraid she's off sick today.'

'Oh. That's a shame. I like her. Don't you do a head massage?'

'We normally do,' I explain, 'but we're pretty pushed today. I'm sorry, I'm sure you'll be able to have one next time. In fact I'll make a note of it when you book.' I can sense vexation radiating from her scalp.

'Jess does a lovely head massage,' she adds. 'It's my favourite part of coming here. Most places, you get some bored teenager giving your head an idle little poke, but with Jessie it's so deep and relaxing . . .'

Oh, all-bloody-right. I start massaging, but can sense that service is still being regarded as substandard. This is what happens when you go upmarket. Clients expect massages,

313

lattes, seventeen varieties of herbal tea – even *food*, for God's sake, in the form of chocolate-drizzled macaroons which Simone picks up by the hundred at some bleak industrial unit outside York, pretending they're flown in specially from Paris. 'That's a bit too firm.' The woman squirms in her seat.

'Is it? I'm sorry. Is that better?' I work the pads of my fingers and thumbs rhythmically across her scalp, thinking it's hardly surprising that my massage technique is a little on the firm side today. Hers would be too, if her husband had walked out on her. My mind drifts to Jed, and whether he's shown up for work today, or is huddled on a damp bench somewhere, covered in newspaper, weeping for me.

And where did he sleep last night, anyway? At a friend's place? I haven't been able to face calling Duncan or Mickey and I can't think of anyone else he knows well enough around here to stay with. Unless – the thought makes bile rise in my throat – he went to Celeste's. Did they do it last night? If they did, it's a little hasty. I mean, we *are* still married. Hope he bruised himself on her bony arse.

'That was lovely,' the woman exclaims. 'Thank you.'

'Was it? I'm glad you enjoyed it.' I hadn't even realised I'd stopped massaging. My fingers had merely slowed down and stopped, as if their batteries had run out.

'Even better than Jess's massage,' she adds, baring small, rodenty teeth at me, 'though better not tell her that, eh?' She laughs loudly. I force a laugh too, which comes out as a kind of croak.

'You okay?' Simone mouths as I show my client to her seat.

I nod. 'Fine. Just a bit tired, that's all.'

'Want to take a break after this?'

'Honestly, I'm okay.' She frowns, clearly not convinced.

Yet I can't tell her about Jed leaving me – not here, at work, in the middle of a hectic day. Instead, I keep my head down. Eight clients down, seven to go. I might just make it through the afternoon.

'Not still going to that Tub Club, are you?' Simone asks just before I leave to collect the children.

'No. Decided life's too short to try out twenty-seven ways with a can of tuna.' I try for a smirk, but it wobbles.

'It's just, you're looking awfully pale . . . Not on some dumb crank diet, are you? Not doing that water-and-cinnamon thing again?'

I laugh, but only because the truth is, I couldn't feel less like eating. 'Just stuff going on at home,' I murmur. 'It's pretty complicated.'

'What, with Jed?'

'Um, yes. Sort of . . .'

'Nothing serious, is it?'

I could tell her, and she'd listen and sit me down with cups of tea. We could go to the kitchen and her next client could wait. But doing that would mean admitting what's happened; that it's not just a silly little thing that'll somehow sort itself out, like all our squabbles before. I shake my head. 'It was just a stupid argument.'

'What about?'

'You'll never guess,' I say lightly. 'It was about butter.'

Simone grins and squeezes my arm. 'Isn't it mad, the stuff that causes rows?'

'I know,' I say with a forced smile. 'It's completely ridiculous.'

*

315

'What are these sausages made of?' Grace asks at dinner.

'Pork or beef, I can't remember,' I say.

Finn flicks his gaze up at me. 'Don't you know?'

'No, love. Like I didn't know where your trainers were this morning. I don't know. Call myself a mother . . .' I grin, trying to make a joke of it. Anything to keep their minds off their father and why he isn't here, having dinner with us.

In fact I've had an idea. Each mealtime, I could present a detailed breakdown of the provenance of their food. *These sausages,* I'd write, *are 97% pork and 3% sinister non-animal protein. They were made in a factory in Warrington by a man called Bert.*

'There'll be other stuff in them,' Finn adds darkly.

'What kind of stuff?' Grace asks.

'Hair, eyeballs, that kind of thing . . .' He flares his nostrils.

'Ew.' Grace fishes a lump of chewed sausage from her mouth and deposits it on the table.

'Finn,' I sigh, 'do you really need to go on like this while we're trying to eat?'

'Pigs don't have hair,' Toby remarks.

'Yeah they do,' Finn says. 'You've never seen one up close.'

'I have! Auntie Kate's got pigs . . .'

'The thing is,' Grace announces, 'I'm thinking of going vegetarian for a week.'

'For a week?' Finn crows. 'What's the bloody point of that?'

'Finn!' I bark. 'There's no need to swear at the table . . .'

'What's not the point?' Grace shoots back.

'I mean,' he says loftily, 'if you have a serious issue with meat, like you object to eating animals or are concerned about how bad it is for the planet with all the farting cows and stuff . . .'

316

'Um, I . . .' Grace furrows her brow and rests her fork on her plate.

'I mean,' Finn continues, 'if it's not about either of *those*, and you just want to try it like a kind of experiment, then I can't see . . .'

'I just want to see what it's like!' Grace thunders. 'Why are you always horrible to me?'

'Listen, you two,' I say in an eerily patient voice, desperately trying not to take sides and incapable of deciding on an appropriate response. 'It's an interesting argument, whether it is actually better for the planet, and I suppose, if Grace wants to try it . . .'

'You mean you're going to let her?' Finn crows.

'Well, I'm not saying *that*. I mean, it would make things more complicated and we have enough of that, don't we, with the debates about lunchbox sandwiches and what kind of triangles they should be . . .' I smile, trying to lift the mood.

'Can I do it too?' Toby demands, rapping his knife on the table for emphasis.

'Can you do what?' Finn retorts.

'Er . . . that thing Grace is gonna do.'

'You don't even know what we're talking about!' Finn's voice ricochets around the kitchen, causing Grace to flinch and Toby's deep brown eyes to blink rapidly.

'That's enough, Finn,' I snap. 'We're having a discussion, all right? Just like normal families do. So I'd be grateful if you could *not* shout or pick on your brother and sister and not be so *unpleasant* . . .'

'Want Daddy,' Toby announces. 'Want Daddy now! Where's Daddy?' Fat tears roll slowly down his cheeks.

317

'Yeah. Where *is* Dad?' Grace asks, scowling, as if only just recalling that she has one.

'He's, erm, out,' I mutter, picking up Toby, plopping him on my knee and noticing that his soft, pale hair is flecked with poster paint.

'When's he coming home?' Toby wants to know.

'I . . . I don't know, love. Soon, I hope. He's really busy, has a lot on his plate right now . . .' Like me. Their dinners have congealed, barely touched. 'Now, d'you all want to watch something on TV while I clear up?' I kiss the top of Toby's head and lift him off my knee.

Grace nods and slithers off her chair. 'Mum and Dad had a fight,' I hear Finn informing them as they all troop through to the living room. 'That's why he wasn't here for dinner.'

'Where *did* he have dinner?' Grace asks.

'Somewhere better than this,' Finn replies.

*

Our bed feels enormous. Last night I was too distraught to even notice but it seems to have expanded to ridiculous proportions during the past twenty-four hours. Jed's pillows are plumped up, with no head indent, and look faintly accusing. I try to sleep with my limbs splayed out, occupying maximum space, and when that doesn't work I get up at 2.30 a.m. and decide to sort the laundry mountain. I tip it onto one side of the bed – *his* side – then, overcome by exhaustion, crawl back under the covers. At least sleeping beside a tumble of kids' T-shirts and pyjamas makes the bed feel marginally less lonely.

Still no Jed next morning, and he hasn't left a message,

begging for reconciliation during the night. Now worried sick, I even try calling my mobile from our house phone to check it's working. 'Your phone's ringing,' Grace informs me.

'I know, love. It's just me, calling myself.'

She scowls. 'Why?'

'To check it's working okay.' She throws me a despairing look.

All through breakfast, I keep praying that Jed will call and at least let me know he's all right, that he hasn't done something crazy or isn't driving and driving, with no destination in mind, simply to maximise the distance between us. I feel disgusted now that I kissed Danny. I don't actually fancy him, not really. Yes, he's cute, and he lifts me out of the domestic doldrums. When I'm with him, I no longer feel like an insignificant little satellite, orbiting the playgroup biscuit tin. It's been hugely flattering, too, acquiring a handsome male friend in my female-orientated world. But that's all it's been. Is Jed seriously leaving me over this?

Without properly noticing what I'm doing, I distribute packed lunches and lunch money and retrieve Grace's homework – a road safety poster – from the Lego box. I manage to wipe a milky smear from Toby's top lip, despite his protests, as I picture Jed having breakfast in Celeste's bed and her spooning some fancy granola-type cereal topped with blueberries into his gob. Maybe they'll get giddy on champagne and have more sex. They'll both call in sick, too lust-filled to care about rumours buzzing around the staff room.

There's a sharp rap on the front door, and I charge towards it, not caring that I'm still wearing my burnt-sleeved dressing gown. 'Morning, love.' It's the postman, handing me a package.

'Thanks,' I say distractedly.

'Good luck,' he says with a smirk.

'Sorry?'

'It's your race pack,' he adds, indicating the logo on a floppy plastic package. 'Been delivering tons of the things this morning. Half the town must be doing it. Keen runner, are you?'

'Not really. Just a beginner . . .' My anxious gaze flickers down the street. Still no sign of Jed.

The postman crooks an eyebrow. 'Looks like you're built for it anyway. The running type, I mean. *Athletic.* You'll have no trouble.' He grins flirtatiously.

Thanking him, I step inside, rip open the race pack and shake out my Superfit Challenge T-shirt. It's in 'Large' and is too big for me now. No doubt about it: I'm shrinking. But no longer in a good, healthy way. More in a dumped and abandoned way. I'd always assumed that thin = good, and that my life would blossom with opportunities if only I could shift my quivering muffin top. Now I'm discovering that there's another kind of thin, which Belinda never mentioned at Tub Club. This kind of thin means pale, hollow-looking and eaten up with worry. It's a long way from *besotted* thin – the kind Jed mentioned – when you're so full of love, there simply isn't any room for food.

I feel as if I'm drifting on a cloud as Finn heads off to school and I usher Toby and Grace to the front door. As we're heading towards school, my phone bleeps; I snatch it from my bag, crushed when I see Danny's name. I read it while walking. DID YR RACE PACK ARRIVE? it says.

YEP, I reply.

FANCY RESUMING TRAINING? he pings back. Doesn't he understand that I'm busy with three children to attend to, not to mention the wreck of my marriage? SORRY NOT AT MOMENT, I reply, plunging my phone into the depths of my bag.

Among the school gate throng, Grace kisses me and flashes a wide smile, which I take as a good sign. At least there are no outward signs of distress. 'Mum!' Finn has drifted towards the railings.

'Yes, love?' My stomach lurches as I hurry towards him. Not like him to acknowledge any connection with me whilst on school property.

'Did you make my hair appointment?' he asks.

'No, did you want one?'

'Yeah. Did you forget?'

'No, I . . .' I meet his challenging gaze. 'Actually, love, you don't need appointments at that . . . that *place*, remember? You just turn up. We can head over after school if you like.' He nods, turns away, and is gone. So my daughter insists on creating her own chaotic bun, and Finn will only allow his hair to be chopped by a malnourished teenager. Fine. Right now, I'm happy to take him wherever he wants. When he's thinking about hair, so my logic goes, at least he's not fretting madly about his father and me.

CHAPTER FORTY-ONE

Hi, sorry I can't take your call right now, please leave a message and I'll get back to you . . . 'Jed,' I say, striding towards work, 'it's me.' I pause. Will he know who 'me' is, or am I scrubbed from his memory already? 'It's Laura,' I add, trying to keep my voice steady. 'Look, love . . .' Wish I hadn't said love. Sounds too pleading. 'Jed,' I try again, 'I've left so many messages for you. Why can't you just call? I need to know you're okay, and if I don't hear from you, I'm going to have to call school and see if you've shown up . . .' I stop abruptly. Now it sounds like I'm threatening him. 'I don't mean that to sound like a threat,' I charge on, 'but you have to understand, I need to know you're all right and to be able to tell the children where you are, and what's happening . . .' I swallow hard. 'I'd be grateful if you could give me a call,' I add quickly, now sounding as I'm phoning an elusive delivery man. *Where's our fridge? I've been waiting in for it for days* . . . 'I just think we need to sort things out,' I finish, my voice threatening to crack, 'because I don't know what on earth to say to the kids.'

Still gripping my phone, I wonder whether to call Mickey or Duncan, and if I can't get them on their mobiles – which is likely, since they'll both be at school – whether I should at least leave them messages at home. They're the closest thing Jed has to confidants around here. Yet speaking to them will mean admitting that I don't know where the hell my husband is, and how seriously bad things have become. I haven't even told Beth yet. Rather inconveniently, she's spending a few child-free days with her sisters in Devon, having left a fifteen-page dossier on the care and feeding of Kira and Jack. Can't tell Mum either, as she'd be devastated, and without being judgemental, Kate would be bound to squirrel the truth out of me – that I'm partly, if not wholly, to blame. I think of her and Will, all cuddled up on their sofa and playfully jibing each other, and tears prickle my eyes as I tumble into the salon. 'Laura?' A woman leaps up from her seat.

'Hi,' I say vaguely.

'I don't have an appointment . . .' She smiles, exposing her small, pointy teeth.

'Oh, that should be okay . . . I'll be with you in just a minute.' I pull off my jacket, hang it up in the alcove and hope my eyes aren't still wet or scary-looking.

'I just dropped in on the off-chance,' she adds. 'Just a wash and blow dry if you can manage it. I've got a big work presentation this afternoon.'

'That should be fine, no problem.'

'Great. Do me one of those head massages, would you? Last one you gave me was out of this world.'

Even though Jess is back at work, and throws me a quizzical look, I wash the woman's hair dutifully, and she closes her eyes as I work my fingers across her scalp. Across the salon, a figure catches my eye. A man has walked in, and for a moment I think it's Jed, come to see me and say it's okay, we can fix this. But it's not. It's Danny, who acknowledges me with a hesitant smile, and takes a seat on the sofa. 'That's great,' my client mutters. 'You're so much better than that junior girl.'

'Well, I guess everyone has their own way of doing things,' I say, relieved that Jess has gone to tidy up the stock cupboard.

'Yeah,' she says, pausing before adding, 'Lost weight, haven't you?'

'Er, a bit,' I agree.

'Thought so. Been on a diet?'

'No, not really. I've never been very good at that. I've been doing a bit of running, though. And, to be honest, I've sort of stopped thinking about food.' I glance over at Danny. Despite the fact that he is undeniably cute, with his mussed-up dark hair and dimples, and even though Simone's smiling flirtily every time she strides past, I can't quite believe I kissed him, passionately, on the mouth.

And it feels as if every internal organ is shrivelling with shame.

'It works then?' the woman barks.

'Er, what does?'

'Running. Only, I'm thinking I might take it up. You're a good advert for it, love.'

I force a smile as I blot her hair in one of our pale lilac Shine Hair Design towels, then comb it out and take her to a seat. 'Thanks. To be honest, three months ago I couldn't even run the length of my kids' school sports field. So if I can do it, anyone can. Um, could you excuse me for a second? I just need to have a quick word with someone.' With a nod, the woman picks up a celebrity magazine and starts flicking through it.

Danny stands up as I approach, his face brightening. 'Hope you don't mind me popping in,' he says.

'No, it's fine,' I say, wondering if either of us will ever acknowledge that kiss.

He blushes. 'I . . . I just thought you might like to have a spot of lunch with me. Quick sandwich in the park or something.' Across the salon, my client shifts impatiently in her chair.

'Okay, just a quick one. Shall we meet at one by the lake?'

'Great. I'll bring lunch.'

Pale sunshine filters into the salon as I watch him leave. Then I go over to attend to my client whose fine hair clings to her scalp. 'Now,' she says, prodding a picture in the magazine. 'I was thinking of something like this. A big, glamorous Catherine Zeta-Jones kinda thing. That all right with you?'

*

Danny is waiting for me by the lake. I stride towards him, relieved to have escaped the heat of the salon, and hoping we'll manage to skirt around the delicate matter of my debut modelling session and our snog in his doorway and the fact that I am a despicable two-timing monster. He waves, and has brought not only a blanket for us to sit on, but an array of lunchtime treats. 'Wow,' I say. 'This is a cut above my normal lunch.'

'Well,' he says as I sit on the rug beside him, 'after I asked you, I realised I didn't know what you like.' He smiles, and those cheek dimples appear. 'Apart from marble cake, of course.'

'Haven't even felt like that lately,' I tell him.

He frowns. 'Look, I hope you're not embarrassed about, you know . . .'

'No, not at all,' I bluster, biting on a strawberry. 'It was my fault. I just misunderstood. I seem to do that a lot actually.' The strawberry is sweet, juicy and perfectly ripe, yet it tastes of nothing.

He looks at me. I glance away and pluck another strawberry from the punnet. 'I didn't mean the, er . . . naked bit,' he murmurs. 'I meant the other bit.'

'Oh. Right.' I gulp the strawberry down.

'And I hope it hasn't made you feel . . . you know. Weird or uncomfortable with me.'

I shake my head. None of it seems to matter now, not compared to what's happening with Jed and me. 'It was just . . . a thing,' I murmur.

'That's right. It was a thing that shouldn't have happened,' he says firmly. 'Not that it wasn't very nice, or that I didn't want to . . .'

'Danny,' I cut in. 'It's not important. You see . . . Jed's left me.'

He blinks at me, and the slight flush drains from his cheeks. 'Not because . . .'

'Oh, he doesn't know about that,' I say quickly. 'At least he doesn't know that anything, you know, *happened* between us. But he knows we've been running together for weeks, which would have been fine if I'd told him right at the start, but for some reason I didn't, maybe because I wanted to keep something for myself – something that wasn't about my family or work, which made me feel good and happy . . .'

'Did it?' He smiles.

'Yes. I've loved it actually. You've made me feel . . .' I search for the right words. 'Sort of human again. A real person. And it all started that day I ran into you in York.'

My heart is racing as Danny touches my hand. 'It's been like that for me too. When Sarah left, I didn't think I'd ever be happy again, or could care for someone. It was great, I thought. Having a friend like you . . .'

'We're talking past tense, aren't we?' I say gently.

Danny nods. 'I didn't mean to cause problems between . . .'

'Oh, it's not you,' I say quickly. 'It's about so much more than that. Maybe it needed to happen – to come to a head like that. I don't know. Haven't even heard from him since he left, which is disgusting, isn't it, whatever I might have done? There are the kids to consider, and we're all worried sick.' He squeezes my hand. 'Anyway,' I add firmly, 'I still want to run that race with you, okay?'

'Are you sure, with all of this going on?'

'Yes, I need to do something. I know it won't fix things with Jed, but it feels better than doing nothing, you know?'

Danny nods. 'You're on. We'll run it together.'

'Great.' I try to delve into more picnic offerings to show my appreciation, but give up after half a sandwich. 'Well, I'd better get back to work,' I say, checking my watch.

He indicates a slice of marble cake resting on a paper napkin. 'Why don't you take that? I got it specially for you. You might fancy it later.'

'Thanks.' Extracting my hand from his, I wrap the cake tightly in the napkin and slip it into my bag.

'Laura,' he adds, 'if any of this is my fault, then I'm really sorry.'

I stand up, brushing a few blades of grass from my skirt.

327

'Thanks Danny, but it's not your fault at all. It's completely, a hundred-per-cent mine.'

He smiles. 'See you soon then, I hope?'

'Yes, I hope so too.' I sense him watching me as I head for the park gates, and I wait until I've turned the corner before dropping my marble cake parcel into a bin.

CHAPTER FORTY-TWO

The children and I are heading for the Mecca of Hair-dressing Excellence that is Cut 'n' Pierce. The name is alarming, suggesting that you can't be sure which of the two the 'practitioner' (or whatever you call him) will subject you to. There's a long scuffed bench with random blobs of garish paint all over it, and the small room has a basementy smell, probably due to being located under a railway arch. 'Be with you in a minute, yeah?' the skinny boy says, casting our assembled group a quick glance. No herbal teas or macaroons here. The boy has sharp, jutting cheekbones and an angry boil on his cheek. A rumpled grey T-shirt hangs from his lanky frame. He looks about six months older than Finn.

The kids and I perch on the bench. 'What style are you going to have?' I ask Finn, to break the glum silence.

He gnaws at a fingernail. 'I thought I'd have this bit shorter and this bit longer and this bit left as it is.'

I look at him uncomprehendingly. 'You mean you want the top and sides cut short and the back left long?'

'Yuh.' He glances around nervously.

'That's a mullet,' I tell him.

'What's a mullet?'

'A terrible haircut, short and layered on top and long at

the back, like people had in the seventies. It's sort of like two different haircuts in one.'

'No, that's not what I meant . . .'

'That's what it sounds like, sweetheart. I'm just warning you.' I give his hand a quick squeeze and, surprisingly, he doesn't tug it away.

Toby has ambled off to investigate a trolley laden with scruffy bottles of product. 'Please sit down, love,' I tell him. He ignores me.

'It won't be like that,' Finn insists. '*He* knows what I like.' He nods in the direction of the whey-faced teenager.

'Right,' I whisper. 'Like that cut you had last time, that demented loo-brush scenario that I knew you hated but which you wouldn't let me fix because it would have meant admitting . . .'

'Shhh,' he hisses.

'It's up to you, though,' I add. 'It's your hair and you can have it however you like.'

Finn nods. 'Yeah. I know.' He pulls his hand away from mine.

Toby starts wheeling the trolley back and forth across the rough stone floor. 'Please leave that,' I murmur. He continues to wheel it.

'Leave that alone, mate,' the boy barks, zipping over an equally embryo-like person's head with clippers. Toby stops obediently, probably because this so-called barber is a male – a surrogate father figure, perhaps, in these desperate times. At least the piercing and tattooing are carried out in another room. We can hear the stop-start buzz of the tattooing machine. I pray that no one will start screaming.

'Can I have my ears pierced?' Grace asks, swinging her legs from the bench.

'No, love.'

'Why not?'

'Because you're too young.'

'When can I have it done? Everyone else has pierced earrings.'

'No they don't, Grace. What's got into you? You've never mentioned having your ears pierced before.'

'Yes I have. I've mentioned it hundreds of times and you never let me. India's had it done and it's not fair.' She kicks the bench in frustration.

'Can we talk about this at home?' I say under my breath.

'You never let me do anything!' Her anger shocks me, and causes the barber and his buzz-haired client to swing around in our direction.

'That's not true,' I protest. 'How many times do we have your friends over for tea? How often do we—'

'*And* you had a fight with Daddy and he went away!' Tears appear instantly, flooding down her furious pink cheeks.

'Oh, Grace!' My stomach lurches and the horrible basement smell makes me feel quite nauseous as I put my arms around her. 'That's not what happened, love. We'll sort it out, I promise.' She gulps into my chest as I hold her in my arms. How am I planning to sort it, exactly? I don't have the vaguest hint of a plan, apart from leaving dozens of increasingly desperate messages on Jed's voicemail and hoping he'll just walk right back into our house and our lives. Toby is sniffing too, and I'm willing him not to burst into tears. I should have known this would happen. That they'd figure that their dad's not just 'working'. What kind of schools are open twenty-four hours a day, for God's sake? I wish this barber would hurry up. Finn can have whatever haircut he likes, and I'll leave a huge tip and we'll get the hell out of here.

Grace pulls away from me and gulps quietly. She has never been interested in jewellery. She's spent the past eight years tumbling about happily in whatever mismatched outfit I've plucked out for her. Her pink phase lasted a mercifully brief three weeks. I was wrong to think she was sailing through this Dad-free period unscathed, and I can sense what's coming next: a phonecall from Miss Marshall at school, saying, 'Could you please pop in at your earliest convenience, i.e. today, in the next half hour, as we have serious concerns about your daughter . . .'

My insides crumple with shame. The barber finishes his cut, and his client grunts his approval. In the back room, the tattoo needle buzzes back into life. 'Who's next?' the boy asks with a disdainful glance. Finn stares, unmoving, at his shoes.

'It's you, love,' I say, nudging him. He stands up and makes for the chair.

'What d'you want?' the barber mutters.

'Er, I was kinda thinking . . .' He tweaks the top of his head with his fingers. 'I was kinda wondering, like, er . . .'

'You wanna number one, two or three?'

Finn throws me a confused glance in the mirror. He probably thinks the barber's asking if he needs the toilet. 'I, er, think he wants it longer here, and shorter here, and pretty much left as it is up here,' I babble, jabbing ineffectually at my own head.

The barber blinks at me. 'Yeah. All right.'

I can't watch as he starts to cut. Can't witness him fiddling with scissors in that haphazard way when he's used to clippering heads all day. Toby watches with rapt interest. Grace wipes her face on her sleeve and fixes her gaze on Finn. I focus on my pale knees poking out from my skirt. At least Finn will have the haircut he wants, which will be one less thing for him to be angry about. It seems to be taking ages.

'I need a number two,' Toby growls.

'What, you want your hair cut too?'

'No. I need the *toilet*.'

'Can you hold on, hon? We won't be long.'

'No,' he declares. 'It's gonna come out.'

'You can't go here,' I whisper. 'We'll be home soon, or we could stop at the public loos in town . . .'

'I need it now,' he wails.

'He can use ours,' the barber says gruffly.

'Oh, I'm sure he can hold on . . .'

'I can't,' Toby says, leaping up from the bench.

'Over there,' the barber says, indicating a narrow door with its paint peeling off at the far end of the room.

'Right. Thank you.' Taking Toby by the hand, I escort him to the loo. At my salon we have gleaming new stainless steel fittings and fragrant handwash in glass dispensers. Cut 'n' Pierce has a decrepit loo with a pull-down chain flusher and a grubby wooden seat. Toby plonks himself on it, and the whole business takes ages; I am beginning to doubt whether he was desperate at all, or just wanted to check out the facilities. Finally, business attended to, we emerge from the cubicle.

Typical. Some man has come in and taken my place on the bench. He is sitting there, head lowered, chatting to Grace. Her head is bobbing enthusiastically. I march over to explain that I was sitting there, and that's *my* daughter who's been warned not to talk to strangers. 'Um, excuse me,' I say. The man looks up and our eyes meet. I open my mouth and realise I have no idea what to say.

'Hi,' he says.

'Hello, Jed.' When he smiles, it's not an exasperated smile. It's not even a humouring-me smile. It's a hesitant, hopeful one which lifts my heart.

'You're here,' I say.

He nods and flicks his gaze towards Finn. 'Looks like our boy's getting a mullet.'

CHAPTER FORTY-THREE

Grace and Toby smother Jed with cuddles and chat as we leave. Even Finn cracks a broad smile. To my relief, none of them asks where he's been, or what's happened. 'I got a star for my picture at nursery,' Toby announces.

'That's fantastic,' Jed says. 'What was it of?'

'It had to be about families,' Toby explains, sending my heart into a spin. *Could you pop in when you have a moment, Mrs Swan? We're a little concerned. Toby drew a picture of the four of you, without his father, and explained, 'My daddy's gone.'* 'I painted us all at Auntie Kate's,' he says grinning.

'Great idea,' Jed enthuses.

'You weren't there,' Toby reminds him, 'but I put you in anyway.'

Jed's smile looks slightly strained. 'Thanks, Tobes. I wouldn't have wanted you to leave me out.'

'I've finished my project on Granddad!' Grace chips in.

'Have you?' Jed asks. 'How did it go?'

'Miss Forest said it was the best 'cause I'd got loads of old pictures and asked Gran questions about him.' Jed catches my eye as Grace skips ahead. No begging for ear piercings now. I realise how much they've missed Jed, how aware they were of a Dad-shaped hole.

The sky darkens, and we quicken our pace as it starts to

335

drizzle. The excitement subsides, and Grace looks back and sniggers, 'Your hair looks weird, Finn. Like a pineapple plant.'

'Shut up.' He flattens the top of his head self-consciously. Ah, business as normal. Jed and I lag a little behind the children.

'How did you know where we'd be?' I ask him.

'Finn told me.'

'Right. He called you, then.'

Jed nods.

'And you took his call . . . I mean, of *course* you would, I just . . .' I tail off.

'I'm sorry,' he murmurs. 'I should have returned your calls.'

'Of course you should,' I say softly. 'I've been worried sick about you. Two nights, Jed, and I've had no idea where you've been . . .'

'I know. I'm sorry, Laura. I just needed some time . . .' He looks at me, and I'm shocked to see his brown eyes glossy with tears. 'I need to explain a few things,' he adds, taking my hand in his.

I glance at him as we walk, taking in the strong jaw and handsome profile. He's wearing a slightly creased white T-shirt and his favourite soft, old jeans, the ones he was wearing when he left. *I need to explain a few things.* What does that mean? *I need to explain that I'm disgusted with you, sneaking off to your so-called running partner's place for a cosy photo shoot . . .* We walk home in silence, and I'm so desperate for him to tell me, I can hardly breathe.

*

I go through the motions of making and serving up dinner. No one quizzes me on the provenance of the pork chops, or

336

demands a detailed breakdown of the pigs' diet. Plates are cleared away without fuss. Finn even helps to carry them to the dishwasher. It's as if everyone's being terribly careful not to trigger another butter row. Later, after bath and bedtime, I find the kids' dirty clothes in the laundry basket instead of strewn all over the bathroom floor. Rather than being dumped in the washbasin, caked in toothpaste, their brushes have been replaced in the tooth mug on the shelf.

It's a little eerie. As there's no clearing up required upstairs, I spin out Grace and Toby's bedtime stories with Ted tucked in between us, wondering if the matted bear will accompany Toby to school when he starts in autumn. I can sense Grace reading ahead of me, fidgeting impatiently, and make a concerted effort not to over-do the characters' voices which she once complained about. 'Read it *normal*,' she'd instructed me.

'Mum,' she says now, stifling a yawn, 'are you and Dad friends again?' I look at her, wondering what a bona fide mother like Beth would say. But Beth would never find herself in a situation like this. Despite her extensive childcare instructions, she and Pete are rock solid. '*Are* you?' Grace asks again.

The house is so silent, I can hear the beat of my heart. 'Of course we are,' I say.

*

Jed and I are sitting side by side on the sofa. Anyone glancing in from the street might surmise that we don't know each other very well. There are at least two feet of brown upholstery between us, and a tiny yellow spear, which must have snapped off Toby's Lego warrior, sticks up between the cushions. 'You said you wanted to explain,' I say.

Jed nods.

'Where did you stay, when you left?' I hold my breath, almost wanting Toby to charge downstairs, demanding a drink or complaining that he can't find Ted.

'I stayed at a hotel,' Jed says.

'A hotel? Why?'

'Because . . . I needed to be away.'

'Were you . . . on your own?'

He turns to face me. 'Yes, of course I was.' I sense him closing up, like a clam.

Outside, a bunch of girls pass our house, giggling and in high spirits. 'I know you think I've slept with her,' he adds.

'Slept with who?' I whisper.

'Celeste, of course. I haven't, you know. But I can understand why you'd think . . .' He stops, looking tired and stressed. 'She needed someone to talk to,' he adds.

'Why, Jed?'

He pauses. 'She seemed to have the idea that me, you and the kids . . . we're some kind of perfect family. She thought I'd be able to help her out of the mess she found herself in.'

'I can't imagine Celeste being in any kind of mess,' I mutter.

Jed glances at me. There's still a cool distance between us, as if both of us know that he can't make everything right just by sauntering into Cut 'n' Pierce and making a mullet joke. And now, I don't know if it'll *ever* be right. At least, not how it used to be. I can't even load all the blame onto Jed. My kiss with Danny still happened, and there's no undoing that.

Jed clears his throat. 'Celeste likes you, you know. She

338

admires the way you look after our kids, hold down a job and keep the family together . . .' I laugh witheringly, which he chooses to ignore. 'It's what she wants,' he adds. 'She says it's all she's ever wanted.'

'What, a family?' Now I get it. She doesn't have her own so she plans to steal mine, as if it's as simple as waltzing out of a department store with a playsuit.

'Well, she does have a child,' Jed says quietly.

'Does she?' I frown, remembering the crying girl at her flat. 'Why didn't you mention . . .'

'Agnes lives in France,' he cuts in, 'apart from a brief trial period at Celeste's, of course, which ended up in disaster . . .'

'You mean . . . that girl who stormed out when I went round there? That's her daughter?'

'Well, it sounds like it. Their relationship was pretty fiery . . .'

'But I told you about that!' I cry. 'And you knew all along who it was. Why didn't you say?'

'I'd promised I wouldn't. No one knows at school. She didn't want to be the subject of gossip . . .'

'But I'm not someone at school, Jed! I'm your *wife*. Who the hell would I tell anyway? The women at playgroup? My clients at work? That's the problem with us, don't you see? Your loyalties are all messed up. She decides you're her new best friend, her confidant or whatever, and you put that before any of us . . .'

To my amazement, Jed doesn't disagree. He doesn't even fling my secret running trysts back at me. He just nods and twists his hands together and runs a thumb over his fingernails. 'You're right,' he whispers, shaking his head. 'I've been completely sucked in.'

'But why, Jed?' I say softly.

'I felt . . . sorry for her at first. There was something vulnerable about her . . .'

'And beautiful, of course,' I snap.

'Well, yes. But it wasn't that, not really. She started telling me things, finding excuses to be together and always making sure she was next to me if we were out in a group. Everyone noticed,' he adds, fixing me with dark eyes. 'Mickey, Duncan, the others from school – they all reckoned she had a thing for me.'

'Great,' I say witheringly.

'Honestly, Laura. I wasn't interested. But it was flattering, the way this young, kind of exotic woman chose me to confide in . . .' I nod, remembering how flattered I felt, every time Danny texted or confided in me. 'She told me all about having Agnes when she was still at school,' he adds, 'and how furious her parents were . . .'

'So what happened to Agnes?' I ask, the word *exotic* shimmering in the air between us.

'After they'd calmed down,' Jed continues, 'her parents decided to bring her up in France, where they live. And Celeste hopped from job to job, finally coming to England and doing her teacher training. Her parents bought the flat for her, probably to keep her out of the way, she thinks. They've always reckoned Agnes was happier and more settled when she wasn't around.' Despite everything, I sense a sharp prickle of sympathy.

'They were embarrassed by her,' Jed adds. 'Remember Finn and Grace's sports day?'

'Unfortunately, yes . . .'

'She was telling me all this while I was trying to watch the races. I mean, I could hardly just walk away from her . . .'

I picture the two of them, heads together at the fringes of the sports field, before my dramatic collapse into the mud. 'Then,' Jed adds, 'at her garden party, remember that . . .'

'I do have a working memory,' I exclaim. 'All these things, the Celeste incidents – every detail is burned into my brain, Jed.'

'Right,' he murmurs. 'Well . . . I know I was awful with you that day. She was telling me that Agnes had decided she wanted to live in England, and was due to move in . . .' When he looks at me, Jed's brown eyes are wide, imploring me to believe him. 'She was telling me how she'd redecorated the spare room for her. Then there was that, um . . . *incident* in the bathroom, and it was all so intense and embarrassing that, really cleverly, I decided the best thing to do would be to tip as much champagne as possible down my throat.' He laughs hollowly.

'I saw that room in her flat,' I tell him. 'It was perfect – the ideal girl's room. Though a little young for a teenager maybe . . .'

'That was the problem. Celeste didn't really know her. They'd had short times together when she went to visit, but living under one roof . . .'

'I can imagine. And what about that time you met at that pub?'

'It was a sort of crisis meeting. Celeste didn't want us to run into anyone from school. She wanted me to help her to figure out a way to get Agnes to come back.'

'But . . . why didn't you tell me any of this? I'd have under-stood, you know. I'd have listened . . .'

'Would you?' he asks. 'These past few months, with your running, all this weight loss, getting fit and becoming so

341

much stronger and more confident, a completely different person really . . .' He tails off and narrows his eyes at me. 'I wasn't sure you'd even *want* to know.'

I look at him, wondering how the two of us could possibly have thought we were doing the right thing. 'Oh, Jed,' I murmur. 'I'm still the same old Laura underneath.'

Jed shrugs. 'Anyway, she's leaving.'

'What, you mean leaving her job?'

'No, everything. She's selling the flat and moving back to be with Agnes in France. And I have to say, it's sort of a relief, really.'

'Really? She's giving up everything to be with her daughter?'

He nods. 'And what about you? What do you want?'

'I don't know,' I whisper, yearning to hold him in my arms, to know he's really back with me. But there is still an entire cushion, with a lone Sugar Puff stuck to it, between us.

He fishes a scrap of paper out of a pocket and uncrumples it. Startled, I recognise the late-night list I wrote at Kate's. *Reasons to stay with Jed. Reasons to split.* 'Where did you find that?' I gasp.

'It was lying on the bathroom floor.' He's studying it with a detached air, as if he's just discovered a rude note scribbled by one of his pupils.

'I . . . I didn't mean any of that,' I say quickly, plucking the Lego sword from between the cushions and digging its tip into my palm.

'"He wouldn't go to a hotel with me",' he reads. '"He hates my food". Actually, Laura, I've never hated anything you've made . . .'

I squirm uncomfortably. 'Well, apart from the chilli thing . . .'

'Okay, apart from that. What else? Um . . . no sex since Jurassic era.'

'Well, that's kind of true.'

'I know.' His fingers wrap around mine.

'It's made me feel so . . .'

'I'm sorry,' he cuts in. 'The longer it went on, the less I felt like . . .'

'Was that because of Celeste too?' I whisper. 'You can tell me, Jed, if you wanted to be with her . . .' My voice trembles.

'You're right,' he murmurs. 'I think I was a little obsessed. And then it all felt too much, sort of claustrophobic, by which point she was relying on me to talk to, to share every tiny development . . . and yes, I suppose that pushed me away from you.' He holds my hands tightly. 'I'm sorry, Laura.'

'Oh, Jed. I am too . . .' I don't finish because, suddenly, there's no cushion between us. He puts his arms around me and holds me so fiercely, I can feel the thud of his heart.

'I think we just lost each other,' he says, kissing me.

CHAPTER FORTY-FOUR

Jed wasn't working, those days he spent away from us. Couldn't face school, he told me, which is unheard of. I have never known Jed to throw a sickie. Even after that teacher's leaving do, when he woke up sweating and groaning, he hauled himself in and battled, heroically, through the day. I'm not sure if he chose The Railway Hotel (a few seconds' walk from Cut 'n' Pierce) because it was the cheapest on offer, or due to the fact that its grottiness matched the way he felt inside.

He's back at school now. Every day he comes home and has dinner with us, and supervises homework and bathtime and reads stories. It twists my heart to see him doing these dad-things. Then he says a quiet goodbye to me, and he walks into town where he's staying in Duncan's spare room above the Indian restaurant. Neither of us knows what will happen, or how long it will take to figure things out. But I do know that I'm not ready to have him back, and that I need time to think, by myself. In fact, I think we both need this space from each other. We can't just pretend nothing's happened.

One drizzly Tuesday at work, my new 'friend' pops in for yet another blow dry, this time in the style of a ragged photo of Cindy Crawford she's brought in. At lunchtime, I meet Beth in Café Roma. 'Why on earth didn't you call me about any of this?' she exclaims.

'Well, you've been away. I could hardly ring you on your holiday . . .'

'You should have,' she insists. 'I can't believe you've been through all of this on your own.'

'I didn't call anyone, Beth. I was . . . in a sort of fug.'

She squeezes my hand. 'And you believe everything he's told you?'

'Yes, I think so.'

'You're still not sure? Is that why he's staying at Duncan's?' She pushes away her half-finished marble cake. Beth always knows when to stop.

'I need to talk to Celeste,' I say.

'Not going to have some huge confrontation, are you? I mean, she's leaving the country, isn't she? What would be the point?'

'No, no,' I say quickly. 'It's nothing like that. I've just got something of hers that I need to give back.'

'What is it?' Beth asks, her eyes round with curiosity.

I grin at her and pop the last piece of cake into my mouth. My appetite's returning, and the cake tastes so sweet as it dissolves on my tongue. 'Her knickers,' I say.

*

First, though, I have to find them. I begin my search while the kids are lounging in the late afternoon sun in the garden. I plan to be logical and methodical. Qualities I hardly possess in great quantities, admittedly, but a new approach is what's needed here. First, I empty out my chest of drawers, checking through everything carefully in case the Coco de Mers have become devoured by an old greying nursing bra. While I'm

345

at it, I pile up all the clothes which are no longer 'me'. There are scruffy jeans in my old size which hang off me now, and vast pregnancy knickers which I'd hung on to 'just in case'. Just in case what? Jed and I decided to have another baby? Unlikely, at my age, and rumour has it you actually have to do it in order to make one. Anyway, they're all going. I also separate out my running gear, including my two sports bras which have the reassuringly sturdy names of 'Ultra Control' and 'Absorba-Bounce'.

Still no Cocos, though. I check Jed's drawers; nothing untoward there, apart from a stash of gardening catalogues hidden under his sweaters, like horticultural porn. I flip through the pages, casting my eyes over the brilliant pink lupins and sizzling red geraniums. Funny things to keep in a sweater drawer.

Moving on to my wardrobe, I find an old white cotton shirt of Dad's. Mum had passed a few on to us, thinking that the children could wear them for messy art projects, but I hadn't liked the thought of them being splattered with paint, and donated most of them to charity. This one I'd kept. Slipping it on over my top, I'm surprised to see how healthy my face looks against its soft whiteness.

My phone bleeps, making me jump. RUNNING THIS EVE? Danny's text reads. RACE IS LOOMING . . .

SORRY NOT TONITE, I reply. Don't feel like running with Danny right now. Our time together was entangled with Jed and me at our lowest ebb. Anyway, I need to do tonight's run alone.

CAN WE MEET? HAVE SOMETHING TO TELL YOU, he pings back. Without replying, I slip my phone back into my jeans pocket.

Still wearing Dad's shirt, I scour Grace's room, then investigate Finn's unsavoury sleeping quarters in the hope that the missing knickers have accidentally been put away with his clothes. His schoolbag lies in the middle of the room, disgorging its contents all over the floor. A sole Monster Munch has been crushed into the carpet, and a Rolo wrapper lies in a delicate curl. I spot the red notebook poking out from beneath a pair of football shorts. I pick it up, my fingers twitching, and I hold my breath, listening for footsteps on the stairs. Kneeling down on the carpet, I open it and focus on a random page. It's as if I've lost control of my hands and eyes.

Monday, it reads. *Mum and dad took us to granma and grandads we did the garden.* My eyes blur as I read the careful, blunt-pencilled writing of a seven-year-old Finn.

We planted beens and it grew! We ate them.

I feel light-headed as I read. I'd almost forgotten that this was once my Finn, a boy so young and excited that he forgot that the planting and eating part didn't happen in one day.

Grandad has loads of flowrs. I piked them with mum cos granddad sayd it was ok.

I remember that. The two of us gathering flowers, when such an activity wasn't deemed completely embarrassing for Finn.

We got conflowrs. Cornflowers, he means. My favourites. *Grandad gave us seeds so we can make our garden beter.*

The bedroom door creaks. I look up and Finn is staring at me. 'Uh . . . Mum?' he says. 'What are you doing?'

I drop the book on the floor. 'Oh, Finn. I was just . . .'

He thrusts his hands into his pockets and looks down. 'S'all right. S'just an old thing.'

'I'm sorry,' I murmur, cheeks burning as I retrieve the book, scramble up and place it on his bed. 'I should never have looked. It was just there and I . . .'

A flicker of tension crosses his lips, and I'm poised for him to spit out some cutting remark. 'It's okay. There's nothing that secret in it really.'

'I . . . I'm surprised you still have it.'

Finn shrugs and colours a little. 'I just like it.'

'Does it remind you of Granddad?'

He nods and sniffs, looking stranded in his own bedroom. Awkwardly, I put my arms around him and hug him, which he endures for several seconds. Then he pulls away, laughing self-consciously, and says, 'Mum, I'm not sure about this haircut to be honest. I saw this picture in a magazine and I thought . . .'

'Which magazine?'

'Dunno. A music magazine. *Kerrang!* or something.' He sniffs again.

I have to suck my lips together to stop myself from smiling. 'And you wanted to look like that?'

'Yeah.' He stares down at the crushed Monster Munch. 'It didn't work, did it? You were right. It's one of them . . . mallets. So I wondered, would you mind, er . . .' He mimes a scissor motion with his index and middle finger.

Grinning, I kiss the top of his roughly-chopped head. 'Of course I will, love,' I say. 'Come with me.'

*

I feel privileged, cutting Finn's hair in the bathroom. He sits patiently on the wobbly wooden chair, not fidgeting or grumbling the way the other two do. Thankfully, he still has plenty of hair to work with. 'Would it be embarrassing for you,' I say tentatively, 'if I was involved in organising an athletics thing at school at the end of term?'

'What athletics thing?' he asks.

'Something Naomi, Phoebe's mum, wants to set up. And she asked me to help . . .'

'She asked *you*?' he splutters.

'Yes, Finn! I can run, you know. I'm doing that Scarborough 10k. And we've been working out routes for cross-country. Would you be okay about that? Or would that be awful for you, having me running with the kids?'

He pauses, and my heart plummets as I steel myself for being dismissed as an embarrassment. 'Yeah,' he murmurs.

'Oh.' I stop cutting.

'Yeah,' he adds. 'I mean, yeah, that'd be cool. So long as you don't fall over this time.' He emits a gurgly laugh.

'I'll try not to,' I say, smiling as I finish the cut. 'Nearly done,' I add. 'I have to say, I wish your little brother sat still for me like you do.'

'Well, Toby's mad,' Finn chuckles.

'You're right there.' I snip a stray hair above his ear.

'He's perverted,' Finn adds, under his breath.

'Perverted? What d'you mean?'

'He's got this . . . this *knicker* thing, yeah? Like, women's knickers.' He makes a snorting sound deep in his throat.

'What, you mean when he and Jack pranced about in my underwear at Grace's party? Yes, that was pretty mortifying.'

'Yeah,' he agrees, clearly warming to his theme, 'and there's them ladies' pants in his bedroom as well.'

I hold my scissors mid-air. 'What ladies' pants?'

He laughs again. 'Fancy ones that tie up, like, here.' He jabs at his hips. 'They're kinda . . . shiny.'

'Right.' They don't sound like any knickers of mine. 'And they're in his room? Are you sure?'

'Yeah. Know what he did? He stuck them to his bookshelf to make a hammock for Ted. Said he wanted a hammock like that one in Celeste's garden.'

'Oh, I see. Well, that's very . . . inventive. What did he stick them up with?'

'Chewing gum, I think.'

'Really?' I manage to finish his cut, even though I'm desperate to retrieve the knickers and figure out how I might go about removing chewing gum from fine silk. I should read the kind of magazines that tell you these things. Placing my scissors on the side of the bath, I dart to Toby's room. There they are, ribbon ties stuck to the shelf, not with gum, thankfully, but liberal wodges of Blu-Tack. I peel them off, tucking Ted up in Toby's bed, and check them for damage. They appear to be unscathed.

'Told you he's mad,' Finn says, hovering at my side and running an exploratory hand through his hair.

I smile, taking in my newly-clipped handsome boy. 'You look good,' I tell him. 'It makes you seem older, actually. Not too short, is it?'

'No, it's cool. Thanks, Mum.' He smiles bashfully as we hear Jed arriving home for dad duties. The children haven't even cottoned on to the fact that he's still spending the nights at Duncan's rather than in bed with me. I'll have to tell them at some point, of course. But for now, in cowardly fashion, I am allowing them to believe that he has started going to work before they get up.

I follow Finn downstairs. 'Whoa, new man!' Jed exclaims, appraising Finn's cut. 'I like it. More grown-up. Not so . . . mullety.' He laughs.

'Everything okay at work?' I ask.

'Fine.' He smiles, going in to greet Toby and Grace in the living room, while I focus all my attention on making a family dinner that will be accepted and enjoyed by all. Except for me, that is. I have an important run tonight, before Jed heads off to his alternative sleeping quarters, and I can't do that on a full tum.

'It's okay, you know,' he murmurs as I lace up my trainers. 'I don't mind if you run with him.'

'I'm running on my own tonight,' I say truthfully.

'Okay, but if you still want to . . .' He tries for a smile. 'I mean, I imagine it's pretty boring, plodding along on your own.'

'Hey, less of the plodding,' I tease him. 'I've got a race coming up and I'm in serious training. We're talking fartleks these days.'

He chuckles, and I sense him appraising me, his slimmed-down sort-of runner of a wife. 'Well, whatever,' he adds with a small shrug. 'I bet it's good to have some company. I can understand that.'

'Thanks.' I pause, wondering if he's lonely without me at night, and if we'll ever be a proper couple again. Then I take a deep breath and step out into the cool evening.

*

Celeste's knickers are in the pocket of my trackie bottoms. I'm hoping their tissue paper wrapping will prevent them

351

from crumpling too much, or becoming tainted by sweat. I decide not to tell her about their temporary incarnation as a hammock for Ted. As I leave town, I realise how strong my legs feel now; running seems almost natural, in the way that I'm no longer conscious of my feet hitting the pavement. I've left town behind me now, hardly noticing the neat red-brick terraces petering out into rolling hills and the leafy lane which leads to the mill.

As it comes into view, I remember the first time I came here, annoyed by Jed's insistence on bringing flowers. Slowing down to a brisk walking pace, I stride across the lawn, trying to figure out why Celeste decided Jed was the one to confide in, to lean on. I pause at the front door, steadying my breath before pressing the buzzer.

'Hello?' Her voice sounds tinny through the intercom.

'Celeste? It's Laura,' I say briskly. 'Hope you don't mind me dropping by. I have something for you.'

'Oh, er . . . that's fine. Come up.' She buzzes me in.

Emboldened now, I push open the heavy wooden door and head up the cool stone stairs, planning to make this as speedy and businesslike as possible. 'Hi, Laura.' She greets me with a small smile at the door to her flat. 'Wow,' she adds, her gaze skimming my tracksuit. 'You haven't run all this way, have you?'

'Yes. It's not that far, is it?'

'It's four miles!' she exclaims.

'Is it? Well, I enjoyed it, actually.'

'You must be fit. I could never do that. Like a tea or a coffee? Or some water?' My heart quickens as she beckons me into the kitchen.

'Water would be great,' I say, fishing out the package from

my pocket. 'I brought these for you. Sorry I've had them so long.'

She frowns in puzzlement and peels off the tissue wrapper, laughing uncomfortably at the sight of the Coco de Mers. 'Oh! I'd forgotten all about them.'

Sipping from the glass she's given me, I watch as she folds them up into a tiny pile and places them on the table. They look outlandish now with their shimmery fabric and ribbon side ties. I clear my throat. 'Celeste, I'm not sure if you know, but Jed's sort of not living with me at the moment.'

She throws me a startled look. 'Isn't he? I . . . no, I didn't know that.'

I study her face, wondering if she really didn't know, and if she's secretly pleased or even feels a twinge of guilt. 'We've had some problems,' I add.

'Have you? Um . . . I'm sorry to hear that.' A tense silence fills the stark kitchen. It's the tiniest thing she does – a minute gesture – but as she bats a tendril of hair from her eyes, I see her as Jed did: a girl who needed someone, and decided that he was a good, kind person, the sort of man who could help her to be a proper mother and make everything all right. Just as I used to feel. And I realise with a start that, although I could probably manage without him, and that we could coexist as parents the way we are now, I still want him very much.

'Celeste,' I say gently, 'are you in love with Jed? Please tell me the truth.'

She lowers her eyes and turns away from me. 'He's been a good friend to me, Laura,' she says.

CHAPTER FORTY-FIVE

I leave, because I don't need to hear any more. She didn't choose him to confide in because he was kind, or understood about families, but because she's been in love with him, all along. I'm grateful for the gust of cool evening air as I step outside of the mill. The garden is in full bloom, exploding with colour, the herbaceous plants merging like watery inks. There is a strong, heady scent – stocks, maybe – and I'm propelled back to Dad's garden, with its wide borders bursting with pink and blue, and Finn eager to grow things and harvest his first runner beans. Something catches in my throat, and I bend down to re-tie a loose trainer lace. When I straighten up, Celeste is standing there, barefoot, looking pale and a little too thin in her navy vest and jeans. 'Please don't go yet,' she says. 'I need to talk to you.'

I frown. 'Celeste, I'd better get back. It's getting dark and . . .'

'Please. It's important. I . . . I owe you an apology. Would you come and sit with me?'

I nod, following her to the bottom of the garden where we sit side by side on the hammock. 'So, what is it?' I ask.

She turns to face me, making the hammock sway disturbingly. I press the toes of my trainers into the clipped grass. 'Nothing happened,' she blurts out. 'There was nothing between me and Jed. You have to believe that.'

I look at her, at this small, thin woman with goose-pimpled arms in the dusk. She wanted him, I realise now, despite me and our children.

'Do I?' I ask.

'I'd tell you. Honestly. I know how difficult I've made things for you. I didn't mean to, not at first . . .'

My breath catches, and the hammock rocks unsteadily. 'What do you mean, not at first?'

Her blue eyes hold mine. 'Jed's special to me. You know he's the only one at school who knows about Agnes?'

I nod.

'You know about my daughter?'

'Yes, of course.'

'It's not something I'm proud of,' she goes on, twisting her fingers together, 'living in a different country from her. I've tried to make it work. Jed helped me through all of that. He understood, Laura . . .'

'Yes, but it's always felt,' I cut in, 'like the two of you had secrets . . .'

'It wasn't Jed's fault,' she insists. 'Oh, he was there for me at first, always happy to talk after work, or go for a drink, then I sensed him pulling away and . . .' Her eyes glimmer with tears. 'You know what, Laura? He's so like Agnes's dad. We were only sixteen when she was born, and we split up even before I had her, and my parents insisted that we never had any more contact. So I've never known what my daughter's father is like as a man.'

'But Jed has a family of his own,' I say. 'He has us, Celeste. Three children who need him.'

'I know that. It's all I want too, you know. I thought I'd have that, when Agnes came over to live with me. I'd even managed to get her a place at school . . .' Her voice cracks, and she pokes her bare toes into the damp turf. 'I found it hard to be around you,' she adds. 'I felt kind of . . . inadequate, you being such a perfect mother . . .'

'You're joking,' I say with a mirthless laugh.

'Oh, but you are. And Jed adores you, you know?'

'*Do* you know that? How?' My voice is sharper than I intended.

'I do,' she says, 'because that first night he stayed at the hotel, under the railway arch, I went round to see him.'

It feels as if my heart has stopped.

'I know it was wrong,' she blurts out, 'and he's married to you, and the last thing I'd want to do is break up a couple . . .'

I breathe deeply, clenching my toes in my trainers.

'But I did it. I went to his room . . .'

Slipping off the hammock, I walk away slowly, eyes fixed on the gate.

'. . . Nothing happened,' she insists, hurrying along beside me as I stride across the lawn. 'He just talked about you. Kept asking me how I thought he could make things right again, and if I thought you'd be happier if he made the garden nicer for you, or had a new bathroom fitted . . .'

I laugh bitterly. 'A *bathroom*?'

'. . . and that's what we did,' she concludes, throwing me an imploring look.

I stop and stare at her. 'You went to Jed's hotel room and talked about gardens and bathrooms?'

She nods. 'And I realised what he has with you, and that he loves you so much and always will. And . . .' She swallows hard. 'That sort of decided it for me.'

'Decided what?' I ask curtly.

'That I should leave and go back to Agnes in France.'

'Well,' I say, 'I hope it works out for you.'

'Thanks.'

'I'd better head back now before it's completely dark.'

'But it's dark already. You can't run all that way. Please let me drive you . . .'

'I'm fine,' I say firmly, taking a deep breath. 'I really need to get home.'

I wait until I reach the main road before stopping and fishing out my mobile from my tracksuit. 'Laura?' Jed says. 'Where are you?'

'On my way home. I've been longer than I expected. I'm sorry.'

'I was starting to worry . . .'

'I'll be home in half an hour, love. I went to see Celeste . . .'

'Why? I thought—'

'It's fine, Jed. It really is. We just talked and I'm coming home now, okay?'

'I could come and pick you up. Toby's in PJs but I could tuck him up in the car, we'd be with you in five minutes . . .'

'Honestly, Jed. The run will do me good.' It does, too. I follow the grass verge back to town, running steadily with a new sense of strength, as if I could keep going forever. Perhaps it's the thought of the Scarborough race. Or maybe it's the fact that, even when faced by a beautiful woman in a tawdry hotel room, my husband chose to discuss bathroom fittings.

CHAPTER FORTY-SIX

I pull on my Absorba-Bounce bra and my race T-shirt. Shorts today, as it's too hot for tracksuit bottoms. My heart is thumping nervously, and I can't even choke down the advised pre-race snack.

Danny texted me, asking me to meet by the stage at the starting point. OK SEE YOU THERE, I texted back. I'll be glad of someone to run with today. Don't fancy doing this alone. 'Are you coming to watch?' I ask the children hope-fully as they toy with their poached eggs and Jed sips his coffee.

'Don't know,' Grace murmurs. Finn merely sniffs, and Toby is too intent on peeling off his toast crusts to answer.

'We might see you down there,' Jed says, 'but it'll be tricky spotting you in all those crowds.'

'Okay,' I say, grabbing my bottle of water and some newfangled chip thing which came with my race pack, and which I have to attach to my ankle. This will record my time accurately. I'm not really worried about that. I'm more concerned about the stage Danny mentioned, and what I might be expected to do on it.

I attach my race number to the front of my T-shirt with safety pins. *Now* I look like a real runner. 'Bye then,' I say hesitantly.

Jed flicks up his gaze. 'Bye, love. Good luck.' The children merely carry on eating.

They could show some interest, I think as I stride into town, noticing numerous people decked out in race T-shirts, all heading in the same direction. I know I'm not exactly setting out to traverse China on a yak, but still – it's a big deal to me. I think of all the times I've stood on the sidelines, cheering on Finn's football team, and yelling encouragement as Toby and Grace have staggered across the nursery garden or the school playing field with an egg and spoon. I'd have thought Jed might have been a little more supportive, too, if he wants to move back in with us properly instead of this indistinct half-at-Duncan's, half-at-home situation. It feels as if we are both poised, waiting for something to happen. In some ways, though, the breathing space is doing me good. Sleeping alone is okay. It's preferable, at least, to sharing a bed with someone who doesn't want me.

There are more and more runners, arriving from all directions, and crowds are gathering as I approach the starting point. Most are in pairs or groups, laughing and chatting excitedly. I start to feel quite alone in my T-shirt with Dad's face on, chosen from the selection of pictures we rounded up for Grace's school project. 'My Granddad Charlie', she called it, captioning each photo in careful handwriting and gathering memories from Mum and Finn and me. Finn was surprisingly helpful, especially with the gardening parts.

I glance around for Danny. As it turns out, the stage is for an exuberant trio of fitness instructors who are coaxing the assembled crowds through a warm-up routine. I pace around, queue for a portaloo and sip from my water bottle anxiously. *Still* no Danny. Not sure how we'll find each other in this crush.

'Hey, you're meant to be warming up,' Naomi cries, forcing her way towards me in a tight baby blue shorts and top ensemble.

I grin at her. 'Well, I walked into town. I feel pretty warmed up already.'

'Yes, but you don't want to strain anything or take a tumble, do you?' She appraises my gym-kit-style shorts.

'It's okay,' I snigger. 'I'm sure I'll be fine, but if I'm not, there's a piece of paper in my pocket with contact details for my next of kin.'

She laughs, launching herself into a series of enthusiastic star jumps. I spot Beth too, who's not running but has come along to cheer me on. 'You'll manage it no problem,' she tells me.

'Yes, I seem to remember you saying that at the school sports day . . .'

'But look at you now! You're like a different person. You're . . . unrecognisable.'

'Thanks.' I swallow hard.

She pauses and gives me a concerned look. 'How are things?'

'They're okay,' I say truthfully. 'Jed comes over every day. It's almost beginning to feel . . . I don't know. Not normal exactly, but workable.'

'But you want more than that, don't you?' she asks.

I nod. 'Yes, of course I do. But I need to know that he wants that too. And, somehow, he has to show me.'

She glances around at the assembling crowds. 'Hasn't he brought the kids to cheer you on?'

I grimace. 'No, but it's probably better that way. They'd be standing around for hours and only get fed up.'

She nods. 'You're probably right. Anyway, good luck. Or should I say break a leg . . .' She hugs me, then disappears back into the crowd.

Still no Danny. The warm-up ends, and with all the anticipation and build-up I feel quite exhausted already. I glance down at my T-shirt, at Dad's face, smiling in his garden. A proud face. I have gleaned sponsorship for his hospice from my clients at work and the playgroup mums, and although it's so tempting to sneak off to Café Roma, I have to go through with this.

An exuberant man with a megaphone directs us all towards the starting area. Ten kilometres now feels like a horribly long way to run without stopping, and I have visions of being scooped off the road and shrouded in a silver blanket, like a roast chicken. I'm already too hot. The sun beats down as we shuffle and wait. 'Seven minutes to go,' the man bellows. 'Good luck, everyone. There's water at the two-mile mark.'

I swig from my bottle, making a mental note not to drink so little that I collapse in a dehydrated heap, but not so much that I'll be forced to take an emergency loo stop in a bush at the roadside. Everywhere I look, groups of friends are revving each other up for the race. I feel as if I'm at a party where everyone's great mates, and I don't know a soul. Even Naomi's disappeared into the crowd.

'Laura, over here!' I squint and spot Danny, waving to attract my attention. He's not wearing a race T-shirt but a plain black long-sleeved top, for goodness' sake. I squeeze my way through the crowds towards him.

'Hey,' I say, 'I've been looking everywhere for you. You'll roast alive wearing that. And where's your runner's number? I thought—'

'Um, I'm not running,' he says.

'Aren't you? Why not?' *Three minutes to go*, the announcer calls. *Everyone in their correct muster areas please . . .*

'Because . . . you don't need me.' He smiles, and I see his gaze flicker over the picture of Dad on my T-shirt.

'But Danny, I thought . . .'

'Sarah's been in touch,' he adds. 'She wants to come back. Give things another try . . .'

Two minutes, runners! Good luck everyone. It's a scorcher of a day so make sure you top up with plenty of water . . .

'Oh, Danny. Is that what you want?'

He raises his eyebrows and smiles, and his cheeks dimple as the sunlight catches his clear blue eyes. 'I think so. Who knows? Maybe it'll be a new start for us. We'll see. How about you?'

'Good,' I say firmly. 'We're getting along, you know? Just being Mum and Dad.'

He nods, then adds, 'Could I show you those pictures I took of you sometime? I was really pleased with them.'

'Were you?' I laugh. 'I'm glad. Sure, I'd like to see them.'

'It's . . .' Danny pauses. 'It's been great, Laura.'

'Yes, it has.' The announcer is saying one minute to go. Without thinking, I quickly kiss his cheek. 'Better go. Don't fancy being the last person to finish.' I scamper away, aware of him watching as I hurry towards the starting area.

'Five, four, three, two . . .' There's a blast of horns, and I'm off, no longer feeling alone but jammed in amongst too many runners, all trying to find their own space. Slow and steady, that's what Belinda said at Tub Club. Mustn't run out of steam by that first water station. People are running with pictures of loved ones on the back of their T-shirts: 'For Mum', one says. 'For Deena, 1955-2010.' *For Dad*, I think, as the crowd

362

thins out and we head along the main street and past the pub where those men commiserated with me after my debut run.

I turn the corner and Café Roma comes into view, the smell of freshly-baked goodies teasing my nostrils. It would be so easy to swerve in. No one would know. That ankle-strap chip thing has fallen off anyway, and I could pelt around Lyedale Park enough times to make Jed and the kids believe I'd made it to the finishing line. The absence of a medal might perplex Toby, but I'm sure I could pick up an acceptable replica in town.

As I pass the café, something catches my eye on the small hill opposite. It's a banner, made from a roll of paper, and it's being held up by a couple of adults and a cluster of children. GO LAURA! it reads. Even as I'm running past, I can make out a cheering Beth and Pete, plus Grace, Toby and Jack, who are yelling excitedly. Finn is there too, standing a little away from the banner, and he's affected his nonchalant expression as he talks to Kira. I've almost passed them when he looks my way and offers a small wave. Tears fill my eyes, and I'm so choked to see them all here for me that running suddenly feels effortless. I'm laughing and crying as I charge on, sloshing water onto my scorching face. Realising I'm going a little too fast, I try to settle into a steady pace. Don't want to peak too soon. Don't want that silver-blanket-roast-chicken scenario.

'Laura!' a man calls out some distance behind me. Maybe Danny's changed his mind and decided to run with me after all. I glance back but can't see him. 'Hey, Laura!' the voice comes again, closer now. I turn again, scanning the runners' faces while taking care not to lose my footing among the discarded water bottles.

Then I see him, darting between groups of runners to get close to me. 'Jed,' I breathe. 'What *are* you doing?'

'Running.' He flashes a grin.

'What, all of it?' I gasp.

'Looks like it,' he says, 'unless you know of a shortcut we could take.'

I laugh, taking in the sight of my husband in shorts, a T-shirt and race number. 'Did you actually enter for this?' I ask.

'Yep.'

'But you never said! And there wasn't a race pack for you . . .'

'Late entry,' he says. 'Picked one up when I arrived. Hope I'm not cramping your style.'

'No, of course you're not,' I laugh.

'Well, I thought maybe you could use the company . . .'

'I can,' I say, feeling my heart swell with each step. 'I really can.' By the time we reach the halfway mark, Jed is clearly amazed that I haven't been carted away on a stretcher.

'You're not bad,' he pants.

'Well, thank you. I have been training, you know.'

'Yes, but a few months ago, I'd never have imagined you, um . . .'

'Doing this?'

'Yeah.' We run on, past the crowds all yelling support, and a samba band bangs a rhythm which, as I'm flagging now, gives me an extra spurt of energy.

Jed is lagging behind, red-faced, his breath coming in gasps. 'You okay?' I yell back.

'Fine. Just a stitch. You go on – I'll meet you at the finish. You can share your banana with me.'

'But I want to run it with you . . .'

'I'll only hold you back,' Jed insists, clutching his side.

I slow down to a jog and run alongside him. 'Take it slowly,' I say. 'Deep breaths, nice and steady. Here, have a sip of my water.'

'Thanks, coach.' He swigs from my bottle, and we fall back into step. Just one kilometre to go. My chest is burning, and the balloon-strewn arch, with its giant digital clock, shimmers in the distance. 750 metres to go. 500 metres. 'Sorry, I'll have to stop,' Jed says.

'You can do it,' I say, grabbing his hand. We slow down further until we're half-walking, half-jogging towards the balloons. Then, somehow, the sight of them bobbing against a brilliant blue sky, as if we're at a kids' party, makes us speed up and tear over the line.

There's a swarm of runners grabbing their finishers' packs from a table, plus bananas and bottles of water. 'Can't believe I didn't manage sub-fifty minutes,' Naomi snaps at her husband, who's holding their doleful child's hand. 'The clock must be wrong. I'm going to complain.' Without spotting us filing past, she takes a furious bite out of her banana.

'Wonder what our time was?' Jed asks. 'I forgot to put that chip thing on.'

'And mine fell off . . .'

We look at each other, and he takes my hand as we head for a space on the grass. 'It doesn't really matter, does it?' Jed asks.

'No, it doesn't.' I break into a grin. 'It's the taking part that counts.'

We wait amidst the milling crowds, and finally Beth and Pete head towards us with the children and their bundled-up banner. Spotting us, Grace breaks away from the group and tears ahead. 'Mummy!' she cries, sending me flying backwards with a hug and a kiss. 'Did you win?'

CHAPTER FORTY-SEVEN

September

Toby stares down at his bright blue school sweatshirt and pressed grey trousers. The top is a little too big for him, and he wriggles his arms, trying to make it fit better. 'Nervous, love?' I ask.

'No,' he says with a tinge of outrage. He picks up his schoolbag and slings it onto his back. That, too, looks too big for his slight frame.

'Pencil case all packed?' Jed asks, having got up extra early to help to ensure a hitch-free morning.

Toby nods. He also has a drink, snack, elasticated-front plimsolls and, stuffed at the bottom of his bag so no one sees, a freshly-laundered Ted. Finn, too, is wearing a new school uniform: the black top and trousers of the secondary school. Only Grace seems relaxed, having polished off three of the pancakes she requested this morning. Toby and Finn's pancakes lie cold on their plates, barely touched and fraying a little around the edges. 'Well, we'd better go,' I say, affecting a businesslike tone. 'Can't be late on your first day, Toby. Finn, had you better set off now?'

'Um, yeah.' He sucks in his lips.

'I'm assuming you want to walk on your own.'

He nods.

'Are you calling for Calum and James?'

'Yuh. I might.' Yet, instead of getting up to leave, he twiddles with the edge of his pancake, pulling off tiny pieces and lining them up in an arc around the edge of his plate.

'Okay, guys.' Jed's waiting at the door. 'Let's go.' We head out, and I'm delighted that he's managed to wangle a later start this morning, so we can do this together. Toby might be ready for Big School, but that doesn't mean I am. I glance at Jed, who's enviably brown from our Cornish holiday. 'First day nerves?' he teases as we all head out.

'Just a bit,' I tell him, taking his hand. Instead of marching ahead, Finn mooches alongside us, and I can virtually hear his brain whirring with all that lies in store at big, scary secondary school. Separate subjects. Timetables. A vast, grey concrete slab of a building with confusing corridors filled with over a thousand kids.

We stop outside St Mary's Hall where he'll head in the opposite direction. 'Sure you've got everything, Finn?' Jed asks.

'Yeah, Dad.'

'Know where you're supposed to go?'

'Uh-huh.' Finn looks down at his adult-sized feet, and runs a hand through his soft, floppy haircut.

'Well, good luck,' Jed says. I can tell he wants to hug him, but we're in the street, where anyone could walk by, so he doesn't. I have to keep my hands jammed at my sides to stop myself from grabbing my boy and squeezing him tightly.

'Thanks, Dad,' Finn says.

'Better go then,' I add.

Finn nods, managing to raise a precarious smile, then drops

his schoolbag with a thud on the pavement and flings his arms around me. 'Oh, Finn, it'll be okay. You'll know loads of people . . .'

'I know.' He pulls away, and although his eyes are damp, his smile is firmer now. 'It'll be good,' he adds which, from Finn, counts as crazed enthusiasm.

'It really will,' I agree. 'It's a whole new thing for you, love. You're far too grown-up for primary school now.'

He nods, and I sense him mustering strength before he turns and walks away. Spotting James and Calum across the road, he hurries over to meet them. My heart skips a beat as they start laughing and jostling each other, trying to pretend that this is an ordinary day. I spot the tall and elegant Kira, walking ahead with a couple of friends. No jostling there. Finn quickly smooths down his hair and quickens his pace.

I take Grace's hand, and Jed grabs Toby's as we turn the corner towards primary school. As we reach the gate, Grace kisses both of us and rushes in, eager to see her friends. Toby's new teacher has asked parents to take their children into the classroom so the three of us make our way to the open door. Jed's fingers interlace with mine as we step inside. Instead of charging ahead, as he used to at Scamps, Toby lurks close to my side.

His classroom is filled with brightly-coloured furniture. Jigsaw puzzles have been set out on the tables, and Miss Forest beams a welcoming smile. Jed grips my arm, and my eyes fill up. *Willpower's the key,* Belinda said. I try to will my eyes to suck the moisture back in. 'You okay?' Jed whispers as Toby peels away from me.

'Yes, I'm okay. Just a tiny bit wobbly, that's all.' I clear my throat, running through a mental list of why children growing up is completely brilliant: they stop lobbing your prized cosmetics into the loo. Mother of growing-up children is devoid of stains and can wear mascara daily. 'Okay, mums and dads,' Miss Forest says, 'once your child is settled, could you please say goodbye and make your way out?'

I look down at Toby who is perched stiffly on a pea green seat. Is he settled? It's impossible to tell. His lips are scrunched tightly together and his eyes are fixed on the jungle scene jigsaw on the table. 'Bye, darling,' I croak. 'Enjoy your day.'

'Bye.' He doesn't look up.

Jed and I walk away from school together. 'Well,' I say lightly, 'that's that. I'm glad it's over, actually.'

The clouds part as he looks at me, and sunshine warms my face. 'It's a new start, isn't it?' he says.

'Yes, love. It really feels like that.' Taking his hand as we walk, I remember the postcard that came a week ago, addressed to Jed and me. There was no message, but it was a home-made card, obviously created by someone who's good at crafts. There was a photo on the front, framed by pieces of sparkly braid all hand-stitched on. The photo was of Celeste and Agnes, huddled together and smiling somewhere sunny, somewhere French. I don't know why she sent it. So Jed wouldn't forget her, perhaps, or to say, 'Here we are. Look at us. We're doing okay.' I placed it on the mantelpiece but the next time I looked, it had gone.

'Well,' Jed says as we reach the street corner, 'I'd better get off to school.'

'And I'm due at work.' I check my watch. 'My Zeta-Jones wannabe will be arriving for her blow dry in ten minutes.'

'Lucky you.'

'You know what?' I say, looking at him. 'I think I am, and

I've only just realised that.' Jed smiles, then he kisses me softly on the lips. It's like the kiss on the stairs at that long-ago party when we were young, and fell madly in love, and didn't have to think about how to construct erupting volcanos or pack acceptable lunchboxes. It was just us back then, and it feels like that now on this perfect September morning.

People are milling around us, heading to work, ready to start their day. We stand, with the warm sun beating down upon us. Then he kisses me again. I don't care that we'll be late, or that someone might see us kissing on a street corner, because today tastes as light and sweet as marble cake, and so does he.

15 Brilliant (And Even Life-Changing) Things About Running

By Fiona Gibson

1. **It gets you out of the house.** That may sound faintly tragic. However for people like me, who work from home and rarely speak to a living soul, pulling on my trainers and pounding the streets is a complete sanity saver. Without it I'd be pale and light-starved, like a mushroom, and end up talking to myself.

2. **It's not the gym.** What do gyms do for us anyway? Take our money in exchange for a shiny card – then precisely nothing happens. Oh, I know there are those horrendous fixed weights to grapple with and classes you can go to – but these have always left me cold – and dripping with guilt because I've spent all that money and never go.

3. **It's dead easy.** People can come over all technical and try to blind you with science but, basically, we all know how to run. I'd done no exercise whatsoever until I was about 39, and I still managed to run without toppling over.

4. **You can chat while you run.** Not at first, admittedly – when you're just starting out, you can barely stagger along without fear of vomiting. But it does get easier, very quickly. One friend of mine, who had barely run in her life, completed a 10k race with only ten weeks' training. When I started, I used to feel like my chest might burst open, and now I can run for an hour or so and actually enjoy it (honestly).

5. **If you don't want to chat, you can run alone and think.** Or even *not* think. Certain friends claim that they don't actually think when they run; they just get into the flow and pound along in a sort of Zen-like manner. Me, I prefer a chat and a gossip. Perhaps I'm just not very Zen.

6. **Running makes you look glowingly healthy.** I started running about six years ago after visiting my friend Fliss in Devon. She looked great – not just super-slim and toned but also kind of . . . *radiant*. She told me she'd started running and I thought, rather greedily, I'll have some of that.

7. **They say running is great for a flat tum.** Admittedly, this has yet to happen to me. But things are less jiggly in the bum and thigh departments.

8. **You don't need fancy gear.** Not even tight Lycra shorts, mercifully. A pair of ratty old trackie bottoms or shorts will do – although a running bra is essential (as Laura, my main character, found out). Sorry, but your flimsy little under-wired number is not up to the job.

9. **You can run races and flash your medal about.** When I say 'race', I don't mean like Paula Radcliffe. A leisurely jog will do nicely (and you still get a medal for that. Oh, and a free banana).

10. **These races are non-competitive** (unless you're one of the elite runners right at the front, in which case you probably won't be reading this). It's incredibly heartening to glance around and see that you're running alongside people of all shapes and ages, and realise that some are going to be worse than you.

11. **If you're pushed for time, you can just pull on your trainers whenever you get the opportunity and head out.** No planning or scheduling needed, unless you prefer to run with a mate. Even then, if a few of you run together, you can usually get hold of someone for a quickie, so to speak.

12. **It's also brilliant for tension.** I can be in the foulest mood, having been unable to find my kids' school uniforms, homework folders and lunch money. Then they'll head off to school and I'll go out running with my mate. Forty minutes later I'm almost human again and a lot less shouty.

13. **If you're a former couch potato like me, you can feel incredibly proud as you improve as a runner.** In fact, it's a good idea to look back and revel in your progress and even make a note of how far you've run.

14. **Runners are allowed to eat sweets.** In fact it's recommended. One Jelly Baby per mile, they say. You're not stuffing sweets – you are *refuelling*.

15. **I feel guilty saying this.** But running is also an incredibly handy excuse if you need a little break from the children. Somehow, it's more acceptable than saying, 'I'm just going for a little lie down.'

Win a Town & City Spa pampering session for you and four friends with 15% off selected treatments* for every reader at Town & City Spas with

CHAMPNEYS

THE PLACE TO BE

Avon are offering one lucky winner the chance to win a pampering session at a Town & City Spa for themselves and four friends. The prize will be a Champneys 55 minute personalised facial, followed by make-up application.

Terms and conditions apply. Cannot be used in conjunction with any other offer. Valid at a Champneys Town & City Spa, from Monday to Wednesday only.

Champneys are also offering 15% off selected treatments* at their Town & City Spas for all readers until 17th August 2011. Visit www.harpercollins.co.uk/avon for details of how to claim your discount.

* contact the Spa for a list of treatments

To enter the free prize draw to win a pampering session, go to www.harpercollins.co.uk/avon and simply answer the following question:

In *Mum on the Run* by *Fiona Gibson*, what sport does Laura take up in an effort to get fit?

a) Swimming
b) Tennis
c) Running

Competition Terms and Conditions

1. This competition is promoted by HarperCollins Publishers ('HarperCollins'), 77-85 Fulham Palace Road, London, W6 8JB.
2. This promotion is open to all UK residents except employees of HarperCollins or Champneys (or their parent, subsidiaries or any affiliated companies) and their immediate families, who are not allowed to enter the competition.
3. No purchase necessary. Only one entry per household. To enter please visit www.harpercollins.co.uk/avon or send postal entries to: Avon, Mum on the Run competition, HarperCollins Publishers, 77-85 Fulham Palace Road, London, W6 8JB. Responsibility cannot be taken for lost entries. Proof of sending is not a proof of receipt.
4. Closing date for entries is 23.59 on 31st May 2011. No entries received after this date will be valid.
5. The prize is a Champneys 55 minute personalised facial, followed by a make-up application for you and 4 friends.
6. The prize is non-refundable, non-transferable and subject to availability. No guarantee is given as to the quality of the prize.
7. No cash or prize alternatives are available.
8. HarperCollins reserve the righst in their reasonable discretion to substitute any prize with a prize of equal or greater value.
9. The winner of the competition will be drawn at random from all correct entries and notified by phone or post no later than the 15th June 2011.
10. The prize will be delivered to the winner by the 30th September 2011.
11. Any application containing incorrect, false or unreadable information will be rejected. Any applications made on behalf of or for another person or multiple entries will not be included in the competition.
12. HarperCollins' decision as to who has won the competition shall be final.
13. To obtain the name of the prize winner after the closing date, please write to Avon, Mum on the Run competition, HarperCollins Publishers, 77-85 Fulham Palace Road, Hammersmith, London, W6 8JB.
14. The entry instructions are part of the Terms and Conditions for this competition.
15. By entering the competition you are agreeing to accept these Terms and Conditions. Any breach of these Terms and Conditions by you will mean that your entry will not be valid, and you will not be allowed to enter this competition.
16. By entering this competition, you are agreeing that if you win your name and image may be used for the purpose of announcing the winner in any related publicity with HarperCollins, without additional payment or permission.
17. Any personal information you give us will be used solely for this competition and will not be passed on to any other parties without your agreement. HarperCollins' privacy policy can be found at: http://www.harpercollins.co.uk/legal/Pages/privacy-policy.aspx
18. Under no circumstances will HarperCollins be responsible for any loss, damages, costs or expenses arising from or in any way connected with any errors, defects, interruptions, malfunctions or delays in the promotion of the competition or prize.
19. HarperCollins will not be responsible unless required by law, for any loss, changes, costs or expenses, which may arise in connection with this competition and HarperCollins can cancel or alter the competition at any stage.
20. Any dispute relating to the competition shall be governed by the laws of England and Wales and will be subject to the exclusive jurisdiction of the English courts.